I0677955

Sacrificing Serenity

Book 1 of the Sanctuary City Trilogy

Holly Ash

Copyright © 2025 Holly Ash

Published in association with Cabin in the Woods

Editor: Lillian Boyd

Cover Design: Maja Kopunovic

All rights reserved.

ISBN-13: 979-8-9855715-7-8; 979-8-9855715-8-5

For all the moms fighting every day to give their kids the best possible life. You are a hero.

Chapter 1

Reggie cursed wildly under her breath as the traffic light turned yellow and the driver in front of her slammed on their brakes. They were lucky she hadn't rear ended them — they both could have made it through the light if they had just kept going. She tapped on the steering wheel as she glanced at the clock. School had let out fifteen minutes ago. If she wasn't there soon, they could call social services on her. Which they had been threatening to do for the last few months. Reggie knew it was only a matter of time before they followed through on the threat.

The light turned green. Reggie weaved into the turn lane to pass the car in front of her, praying there weren't any cops around. The other driver flipped her off as she passed. "Right back at you," she muttered as she pressed the accelerator.

Her tires squealed as she pulled into the empty school parking lot. She made sure to park in the designated parent parking spots even though there were plenty of free spots closer to the building. She was barely making tuition payments as it was; the last thing she needed was another parking fine from the overzealous crossing guard. Reggie swore that woman had it out for her, which she seemed to have in common with most of the staff at the overpriced private school. It was like they had all gotten together and decided to make her life as difficult as possible.

She brushed drywall dust off her clothes as she walked briskly to the entrance. Reggie was sure she was the only parent at the school that did any kind of manual labor. She slammed the button for the intercom the moment it was within reach.

"Elk Grove Academy," an uninterested voice said through the speaker. Reggie knew it belonged to the admin that worked in the office. She could just see the woman sitting behind her desk, thin lips pulled tight into a smirk.

After the day she'd had, Reggie really didn't have the patience to deal with a self-righteous elementary school secretary on a power trip. She took a deep breath and pushed her annoyance down. "Regina Stone, mother of Jace and Miles Stone."

"We told them to wait in the office once we realized you weren't here on time." Each word dripped with contempt.

Reggie rolled her eyes as she waited for the irritating

buzz that indicated the door had been unlocked. Through the glass wall, she saw the boys sitting in the corner of the office on stiff blue plastic chairs. Jace had his face in his book, like he always did these days. Miles, however, looked like he was in a haze. Reggie could feel her stress-level rise as she looked at her youngest. Something was wrong. She forced a smile onto her face as she entered the office.

Scott emerged from the principal's office before she made it to her kids. She braced herself for the lecture she knew was coming. "This can't keep happening, Reggie. This is the second time this week you've been late picking up the boys."

One would think he'd have a shred of compassion for her, or even offer to help out. How much of a hassle would it really have been for him to drive the boys home after school? They were the only living family Scott had. But Scott Stone couldn't be bothered. It was easier to lecture and threaten her. She had no problem questioning her abilities as a mother without his input.

"I know, I'm sorry," she said, knowing it was what he wanted to hear. "It won't happen again," she added, even though they all knew it wasn't true. Reggie owned a nonprofit construction company. They repaired everything from public schools to low-income housing complexes. They were usually the last resort before buildings were condemned, which meant simple jobs usually snowballed into massive repairs. Which was exactly what had happened today. Her team had been repairing a low-income housing complex on the other side of town, and had discovered a huge stretch of frayed wiring as they were wrapping up for the day. Reggie couldn't leave it, knowing it was only a matter of time before the whole complex caught fire. She knew it wouldn't be the last time something like that happened.

"We've tried to make allowances after what happened to Charlie, but it's been over a year since he died." The offhand way Scott talked about Charlie turned Reggie's insides to ice.

"I'm well-aware of that," she snapped. As if a day had gone by that she hadn't thought about Charlie. She wondered when the last time was that Scott had given his younger brother more than a passing thought. Reggie glanced back at Miles and Jace. "I'm doing the best I can."

Scott sighed. "I believe you are, but the next time you're late, I'm afraid I'm going to have to report it to child protective services," he said.

Prick. "Boys, tell your Uncle Scott goodbye. We're going home." Reggie shot her brother-in-law a look of disgust before turning to her kids with a smile on her face. Jace didn't look up from his book as he stood. Reggie pulled him into a one-armed hug and kissed the top of his head. She got no response. She tried to reassure herself that this was normal. Jace was nine now—wasn't that when boys started to pull away from their parents? Reggie wished she knew for sure. Jace's whole personality had changed since Charlie died, and she had yet to find a way to bring back her sweet, curious little boy.

"Come on, Miles." Reggie turned to her six-year-old son, who stood up but looked unsteady. She knelt in front of him. "Baby, what's wrong?"

"I don't feel good." Miles's voice was small, and he wasn't making eye contact. Reggie knew in that instant that something must have happened. He had been his normal energetic self when she'd dropped him off that morning.

"Did you drink your water today?" She kept her voice calm despite the anger building inside of her. Miles shook his head, his face scrunched up like he wanted to cry, but no tears formed. That wasn't a good sign. "Why not?"

"Colton Murphy took it from me and dumped it on the ground in front of the whole class," Miles said weakly.

"I'm so sorry, baby." Out of the corner of her eye, Reggie saw the admin move her own bottle of water out of sight. "What did your teacher do?"

"She made me miss recess to clean up the mess."

Reggie bit the insides of her cheeks to keep a new string of curse words from escaping her lips. She turned to Scott, who was still lingering nearby. "Are you going to do anything about this?"

"What would you like me to do? I can't punish a kid over some spilled water."

Reggie rose to her feet. "I thought this school had the best anti-bullying program in the state. Or does that only apply to the kids with parents that donate to the school?"

"As soon as I get an official report of bullying activity, I'll handle it. Until then, there's nothing I can do. Now, goodbye, Regina." Scott turned and headed back to his office, making sure to close the door behind him.

"I bet you will," Reggie muttered as she glared at the closed door. She hated all of them—from the spoiled Colton who hadn't realized that at ten dollars a gallon, that small bottle of water was all she could afford to give Miles for the day, to the teacher who never did anything to stop the bullying, to Scott, who looked the other way rather than protect his nephew. She knew everyone at the school saw them as a charity. They were different, and that made them easy targets. Charlie had told them over and over to let it roll off their backs. He knew the education the boys would get at Elk Grove would be leaps and bounds better than what the public schools in their area offered. Scott had pulled a few strings to get them in, but that was where his support stopped.

She gave Miles's hand a gentle squeeze. "Come on. I have some water in the car. That will make you feel better." It looked like it would be another week of contaminated tap water for her. She was fine with slowly poisoning herself if it meant her kids had clean water to drink.

~

Miles was more himself by the time they reached their apartment. Reggie noticed that he had almost finished the bottle of water she had given him during the fifteen-minute drive. He would probably need more to get him fully back to normal. Reggie did a quick calculation to see what she could afford to give him: She had a bottle set aside for her to drink tomorrow, and she would give Miles half of that later tonight. That plus the watermelon she had managed to score at the grocery store would bring back her energetic little boy.

She wondered what parenting would have been like without having to worry about securing clean water. It had been twenty years since the government had rolled back the environmental regulations ensuring clean water and air to the public. Things had gone downhill fast—the air became thick with smog, and there were so many contaminants in the water that the local municipalities couldn't afford to keep treating it. Eventually, they stopped trying. Water still flowed through the lines, but it was loaded with heavy metals and other toxins. The government put out a Boil Water advisory ten years ago that was technically still in effect. Everyone knew it was a joke—boiling water might have killed the bacteria, but it did nothing to remove the dirt and metals suspended in the water. The advisory was purely to alleviate the government's liability.

Bottled water had quickly become the hottest commodity on the planet, with the price skyrocketing overnight. Putting it out-of-reach of the majority of people and exponentially increasing the number of people living in poverty. When Charlie had been alive, they had managed to earn enough between the two of them to afford clean water so the boys never had to drink the contaminated tap water, but Reggie was having a hard time keeping that up on her own. It was amazing what she was willing to sacrifice in order to provide clean water for her kids.

Reggie parked in one of the two spots assigned to her unit. She always tried to avoid looking at the empty space where Charlie's car used to be. She'd sold it a month after he passed to help cover the funeral costs.

Jace jumped out of the car the moment it stopped. "Hey," Reggie called out her window. "There's groceries in the trunk that I need help with."

"Do I have to? My hands are full." Jace had his backpack slung over one shoulder and a book in his left hand. That was it.

"Yes." Reggie got out of the car and opened Miles's door. "Put your book in your backpack and grab one of the bags."

"Mom," Jace said with that whine in his voice that grated Reggie's nerves. She was convinced he did it just to drive her insane.

"Now." She gave him a stern look, then handed Miles his backpack as he got out of the car. At least he was steadier on his feet now.

"Is this all of it?" Jace was standing with one hand on the open trunk looking down at the case of water, two bags of groceries, and the small watermelon that was back there. Reggie felt his comment like a punch to her gut.

"I couldn't get anything that would go bad sitting in the trunk all afternoon." Reggie looked down at the meager groceries. How could she tell him this was all they could afford at the moment, since the price of bottled water had gone up again?

"It's not going to be enough," Jace said without looking at her. He grabbed the two bags and made his way towards the building.

"Can you please do what I ask without complaining just one time?" Reggie grabbed the case of water and the watermelon before shutting the trunk. "Miles, can you get the door, please?" Reggie shifted the watermelon under her arm and followed the boys to the door.

Reggie's whole body sagged as she reached their floor and saw Miles pulling a red piece of paper off the door. She had opted to pay down the electrical bill she'd been a few months behind on instead of the full rent. She'd have to call up the landlord and offer to do some repair work for him to make up for the late payment. With the amount of free work she did around the complex, she didn't think they'd really kick them out, but she didn't want to push her luck.

"Mommy, what's this?" Miles held the late notice above his head.

"It's nothing. Let me have it." She snatched paper from Miles's outstretched hand.

Their next-door neighbor's door opened, and Mrs. Elmenheimer stepped into the hall carrying a stack of Tupperware containers. "Reggie, I'm glad I caught you. Hi, boys." The older woman smiled at Jace and Miles. She had watched the boys since Jace was a baby, and had become the mother figure Reggie had longed for while growing up. She didn't know how she would have gotten through the last year without Mrs. Elmenheimer's help.

"Hi, Mrs. Elmenheimer." Reggie shifted the watermelon to her other arm as she tried to dig her keys out of her pocket without dropping anything.

"Miles, Jace, help your mother," Mrs. Elmenheimer said. Both boys quickly turned to Reggie as if seeing her for the first time. Jace handed his bags to Miles and took the apartment keys from Reggie to open the door.

"These are for you." Mrs. Elmenheimer followed them into the apartment. "I made homemade marinara sauce, and I'll never eat it all before it goes bad. There's lots of extra noodles too." She set the containers down on the counter. "It's still warm."

Reggie set her bag down next to the food. She knew Mrs. Elmenheimer had made this specifically for them. She had been bringing food over a couple times a week since Charlie had passed, always playing it off as if she had just made too much so she didn't hurt Reggie's pride. "You don't have to keep feeding us," Reggie said, knowing that it would fall on deaf ears.

Mrs. Elmenheimer waved her away. "My kids are all gone. I like having someone to take care of."

"Thank you." Reggie gave her a kiss on the cheek. She knew there was no point arguing. "It smells amazing. Boys, go put your stuff away and get ready for dinner." She turned to Mrs. Elmenheimer once the boys were gone. "Are you sure you can afford this?"

"Reggie, it's just me. I have more than enough money to get me through the rest of my life."

"You aren't that old." She rolled her eyes as she put the groceries away. To hear Mrs. Elmenheimer talk you'd think she had been on her deathbed for the last five years.

"It's alright to let others help you sometimes. You don't have to do this all on your own. You know that, right?"

"I know, I know," Reggie said. "You're going to join us for dinner, right? It might be the only way I'll get Jace to tell me how his day was."

"He's still not talking like he used to?" Mrs. Elmenheimer pulled out a bowl and dumped the pasta and sauce into it.

"Only when he's arguing with me." Reggie took out four plates and set them on the table.

Mrs. Elmenheimer put her arm around Reggie's shoulder and pulled her close. "It'll get easier. I promise."

Chapter 2

Reggie stepped carefully around an overflowing box of wires on her office floor as she made her way to her desk. She had managed to get the boys ready and out of the house on time with minimal fighting and arrived at work early for a change. She knew she had Mrs. Elmenheimer to thank for that; the boys were always better-behaved after seeing her. Reggie wondered if she had threatened them as she'd tucked them into their beds last night. Mrs. Elmenheimer had become the mother and grandmother Reggie had always dreamed about having.

"Shit," Reggie muttered as she knocked over a stack of papers while trying to find a place to put down her coffee, which was undoubtedly tainted with lead and mercury. She hadn't been able to afford enough bottled water to get all three of them through the week, so she'd opted for tap water. It was more important that Jace and Miles got the clean water.

Besides, dehydration would kill her faster than lead poisoning. Life was about choices, after all.

"You're here early."

Reggie looked up to see Jesse leaning on the doorframe. Jesse Clausen was the director of operations at Homes, Hearts, and Hammers. He had been with her since she first founded the nonprofit, and it was just the two of them fixing up public playgrounds between their paying jobs.

"A lot of good it's doing me." Reggie picked up the papers she had knocked on the floor. "You'd think in the last twelve years, I would have found an organizational system that works." She plopped back into her chair.

Jesse laughed. "This is organized. The new repair requests are in that mound of papers over there, and the grant applications are in here." He picked up the overstuffed box from one of the chairs in front of her desk and sat down. "And I'd bet those are today's work assignments in your hand."

Reggie cracked a smile. "They were." She crumpled the paper up and tossed it on her desk. "I need to change some things around today. We need to send a team back to that apartment complex over on Birch."

"The one with the rotting staircase?"

"Yeah, the staircase wasn't the only thing that needed to be fixed."

Jesse rubbed his hand over his forehead and sighed. This wasn't the first time Reggie had sprung a new job on him. She almost always found a whole list of additional repairs that needed to be completed at every job site she visited. "What is it this time?"

"Electrical." Reggie grabbed her bag from the floor and pulled out the repair list she had put together for the site after the boys were in bed. "The entire place is a fire hazard. We need to rewire the whole thing." She handed the report to Jesse.

His eyes darted over the page. "This is going to be expensive."

"We still have some money from the housing improvement grant. This should qualify."

Jesse set the report down. "It does, but what about the group home we're supposed to start work on next week? I did the walkthrough with Malcome yesterday, and that place isn't suitable for the mice in the walls, let alone the kids that live there. We have to make that a priority."

"I can't walk away from the apartment building either. It's a low-income government-run complex. Those people have nowhere else to go and no way to repair it themselves. It's only a matter of time before the electricity fails completely and the place goes up in flames."

"We need more money." Jesse's eyes slid over to the box of grant applications.

"I know." Reggie put her head in her hands. "Do you ever miss working commercial construction jobs where you just showed up, completed your job for the day, and went home?"

"You mean the construction jobs where you were

constantly harassed and belittled for being the only woman on the crew?"

"Yeah, that one, with its steady paychecks and lack of decision-making responsibilities."

"I seem to remember you having daily fights with the foreman for his self-serving decisions," Jesse said with a laugh.

"Well, they were bad decisions."

"And you hated that job."

Jesse wasn't wrong. Reggie and Jesse had first met when she was working on her electrical apprenticeship. He was one of the few people who'd given her the time of day. The rest of the team had felt that a woman didn't belong on their job sites, and they hadn't been afraid to tell her that several times a day. She would have been able to deal with that if she had actually been given real work to do. Most of the time, they'd had her fetching tools or taking lunch orders. It hadn't mattered that she was better than most of them.

"I'll find time to work on the grant applications," she finally said. "And you're right. The housing improvement grant money needs to go to the group home. I only need two guys to help me replace the bad wiring at the Birch apartments. We can cut my pay to cover the extra cost."

"Reggie, that would be the third time in six months you've cut your pay."

"I'm not going to cut the team's pay. They have families depending on that money."

Jesse cocked an eyebrow at her. "And you don't?"

"We'll be fine. At some point, the insurance company

will have to pay out Charlie's life insurance policy, and the city improvement grants are set to be awarded next week. That will get us through the next few months while I work on finding other sources of funding."

"Cut my pay instead."

"Jesse, I can't do that. I promised you when we started this that you'd make the same as you did at the construction company."

"That was twelve years ago. I never had any intention of holding you to that promise back then, and I certainly don't now. We're in this together. We always have been. It's not fair that you're the one who always shoulders the financial burden. I can afford it. At some point, you need to let other people help you." Jesse stood up, making it clear the discussion was closed.

"That's the second time I've heard that in the last twelve hours."

"Maybe you'll listen this time."

Reggie crossed her arms over her chest. "How do you know I didn't listen the first time?"

Jesse's laugh echoed off the walls in her cramped office. "I'll have Bearden and Hoteling help you at the apartment."

"I'd be lost without you," Reggie said.

"Don't you forget it." Jesse left to start the morning debriefing.

Reggie leaned back in her chair and put her hands on her head as she surveyed the mess that was her office. She needed to pull it together. People were counting on her, and she wouldn't let them down. She couldn't let them down.

What would Charlie have thought if he could see her now?

~

Reggie set several alarms on her phone to ensure she would make it to school in time for pick up. The rewiring job had gone smoothly, and she was comfortable leaving Bearding and Hoteling to finish it up. More comfortable than being late two days in a row and having to deal with Scott again. She tried to limit the number of encounters she had with him.

The parking lot was full when she pulled in, even though school wouldn't be letting out for another thirty minutes. She parked her car at the back of the lot and went to join the cluster of parents waiting outside of the school. *Don't any of these people have jobs?* Reggie stood off to the side—she wasn't friends with any of the other parents. Most of them went out of their way to avoid talking to her. She didn't mind. It wasn't like she wanted to talk to them either.

The bell finally rang, and a moment later students flooded out the front door. She saw Jace first, though he didn't appear to be in a hurry like the rest of his class. "You're actually here on-time," he said by way of greeting.

"Hi, Jace, how was your day? Yes, I missed you too," Reggie countered, fighting the urge to roll her eyes.

"Sorry, Mom," Jace muttered under his breath.

"Have you seen your brother?" Reggie craned her neck to survey the stream of students leaving the building.

Jace shrugged his shoulders. "Sometimes he hangs back until most of the kids have left before coming out."

As the number of students leaving the building dwindled, she saw Miles making his way down the front steps, only he wasn't alone. A group of four boys followed close-behind. They were far-enough away that she couldn't tell what they were saying to Miles but she knew by the sneers on their faces that it wasn't friendly.

"See you later, loser." One of the boys stuck out his foot, causing Miles to stumble down the last two steps.

Reggie watched the boy in anger. "Do you know who that was?" she asked Jace without taking her eyes off the boys.

"Colton Murphy. He's always giving Miles a hard time."

Reggie nodded. It was clear that no one at the school was going to protect her son. It was time she took matters into her own hands. "Take your brother and go wait in the car." She handed Jace the keys, her eyes still locked onto Colton.

"Mom, what are you going to do?"

"Just do what I tell you to do." She thrust the keys at Jace.

"Mom, don't do this. You'll only make it worse," Jace said as he took the keys, but Reggie wasn't listening.

The moment the keys were out of her hand, she started to march towards Colton. He was talking to his friends while a tired-looking woman stood nearby watching. She glanced in Reggie's direction as Reggie approached. "Hi, I'm Reggie Stone," she said before the woman could escape. "Are you Colton's mother?"

"No," the woman said while shaking her head, "I'm just his nanny."

"Oh," Reggie said as her anger deflated. She took a closer look at the woman as she glanced at Colton laughing with his friends nearby. It was clear she didn't particularly like him either.

"But his father is waiting in there." The nanny pointed at a black car with heavily tinted windows.

"Perfect." Reggie turned on her heel and made her way to the car. She walked straight to the back door and knocked on the window.

A large man in a black suit got out of the front seat. There was a clear plastic earpiece in his right ear. Colton's dad had a private security detail. "Ma'am, I'm going to need you to back away from the car."

Reggie knew she should walk away, but she refused to be intimidated. "I need to speak with Mr. Murphy about his son."

"*Governor* Murphy is a busy man. You'll need to call his office and set up an appointment."

Shit. How had she not known that Colton was the governor's son? No wonder the little punk got away with everything. "I don't care how busy he is," she said with a confidence she didn't feel. "He needs to address his son's behavior before I'm forced to escalate things."

The security guard stole a glance at Colton and rolled his eyes. "Ma'am, I'm sorry. It'll be best for everyone if you just let this go." His voice was less stern than it had been a moment ago.

"I can't do that. Tell your boss that we can handle

this now, or I can bring up my concerns about his son tormenting my son at the next televised school board meeting. Wasn't his strong anti-bullying platform critical to him winning the last election?"

The back door of the car opened, and the governor got out. He nodded to his security detail before turning his attention to Reggie. "Is there a problem here?" He locked eyes with her, his face emotionless, though she sensed his anger boiling just below the surface. She didn't back down.

"Yeah, there's a problem. Your son, Colton, has been bullying my son for a while now and I want to know what you're going to do to make sure it stops. Now."

"I'm not aware of any instances involving my son," Governor Murphys said evenly.

"That's because everyone is too afraid to tell you. I witnessed Colton intentionally trip my son while leaving the building today and was told of an instance yesterday where he stole my son's only clean water for the day and dumped it on the ground. Now, I'm sure the public wouldn't look kindly on that. Honestly, I don't know which would be worse for you: the bullying or wasting such a valuable resource." Reggie crossed her arms and cocked an eyebrow.

Murphy's gaze shifted to Colton for a moment before returning to Reggie. "Do you have any proof to back up those claims?"

Reggie smirked. "When has proof ever mattered when it comes to public opinion?"

Murphy took a small step closer to her. "So, you have nothing."

"I wouldn't say that. There are cameras all over this campus."

"It was my understanding that the security footage gets deleted at the end of every week to protect the children's privacy."

"I'm sure it is. However, I happen to know the owner of the company that installed the security system at this school. We've done some work together over the years. So, I also know that all security data is archived for five years on a remote server. I'm sure he'd be all too willing to help me out if I asked."

"I'd be careful, Mrs. Stone. Yes, I know who you are," he said with a twisted smile, reading her look of surprise. "And you're not the only one with connections. See, I happen to know several people on the grant approval team. I believe your company has applied for several this year, hasn't it? It would be a shame if funding for those grants fell through, wouldn't it?"

"You'd really jeopardize the safety of your constituents to protect your reputation instead of correcting your son's behavior?"

Murphy leaned closer and lowered his voice. "You'd be shocked at what I'm willing to do, Mrs. Stone."

"Then let me tell you what I'm willing to do, Mr. Murphy." Reggie didn't bother to keep her voice low. She didn't care if anyone overheard her. In fact, she hoped someone would hear. "If your son comes near mine again, I'll press charges."

The veins in Murphy's neck started to protrude. She could tell he was fighting to keep his voice even. "None of it will stick."

"Oh, I know, but you won't be able to keep it out of the press and words like 'theft,' 'assault,' and 'restraining order' make for really intriguing headlines, don't you think?"

"No lawyer in the state would take your case." His voice faltered slightly. She was starting to get to him. She knew exactly which buttons to push. He was no different than her parents.

Reggie smiled. "Are you sure about that? My husband worked legal aid before he died. They were loyal to him, to me. I just have to make one phone call and the whole office will be all-too-willing to help. The choice is yours. Have a good day, Governor." Reggie turned just in time to see Scott running down the stairs towards them. She made her way to the front of the school where Jace and Miles were still waiting for her.

"What do you think you're doing?" Scott snarled as he blocked her path. "Do you have any idea who that was?"

"I do," Reggie said, looking him dead in the eyes. "And if you weren't such a spineless coward and actually did your job, I wouldn't have to get involved to protect my son, but here we are."

Scott glanced over her shoulder at Governor Murphy's car. "You can't go around making idle threats to government officials." His jaw was clenched so tight, his back teeth might have cracked under the pressure.

"There wasn't anything idle about it." She put her hands on her hips. "I meant every word I said. So, if you don't want this school wrapped up in a bullying scandal, you better make sure Colton Murphy stays the hell away from Miles or Governor Murphy won't be the only one I go after. Don't underestimate me, Scott." Reggie patted his shoulder and stepped around him.

"To the car," she said to Miles and Jace, who were still standing in front of the school, watching her.

"I can't believe you just did that." Jace sounded annoyed.

Reggie leaned down so she was at eye-level with him. "I'll do anything to keep you and your brother safe."

"Whatever." Jace handed her back the keys. "Come on, Miles." He took his brother's hand and started across the parking lot.

Reggie sighed and followed after them. It didn't matter if she was on time or not. She just couldn't win with Jace these days.

Chapter 3

There was only one light on in the apartment—
anything she could do to cut back on the bills meant
more clean water for Jace and Miles.

The boys had been asleep for an hour by the time
Reggie finished cleaning up the apartment. Exhausted,
she plopped down at the kitchen table with her
computer. She set a small glass of murky water down
next to her. She knew she shouldn't be drinking it. The
water in this part of town was terrible. The outdated
infrastructure leached lead into the water at an alarming
rate, and the water filter for their apartment had reached
the end of its life almost a year ago. Reggie did what she
could to clean it, but she wasn't convinced it actually did
anything. She took a sip, trying to ignore the metallic
aftertaste. It was easier than allowing the dehydration-

induced headache she could feel taking hold.

At least she could afford enough bottled water so the boys wouldn't have to drink it. She knew a lot of people weren't that lucky.

She opened the video chat program and waited. A moment later, a pleasant chime came from the speaker. Right on time. Reggie took another small sip before answering the call. "Hey, Amber."

"Reggie! How are you? You look tired." It had been a week since they had been able to talk, which was much longer than they usually had to wait between calls. Reggie and Amber had been friends since they were in elementary school. Since Charlie's passing, Amber was the only person in the world she could depend on.

"I'm always tired." She forced a laugh. She didn't want Amber to worry about her any more than she normally did. "How's life in the capital?" Amber had just secured her second term as a U.S. Senator. Her campaign had focused on reinstating the environmental regulations that had been rolled back twenty years ago, leading them to their current situation. It was a lofty plan that several others had tried and failed to do over the years, but that hadn't deterred Amber. She had a knack for getting what she wanted.

"Don't try that diversion shit on me, Regina." The fact that Amber used her full name let Reggie know she was serious. "I can tell something's wrong. Tell me what's going on. Is it work?"

"Work is fine. We're busier than ever." Reggie tried to put a positive spin on it, even though they both knew Reggie's company was so busy because the price of bottled water had increased again, and people had even less money to spend on home repairs.

Amber cocked an eyebrow. "And are you getting paid for any of that work?"

Reggie shrugged. "Some of it." It wasn't completely a lie. The owner of the Birch Apartments had been able to pay for half of the material costs for the stairwell replacement. "People need a safe place to live, and most people around here can't afford it. They pay what they can."

"That's a terrible business model. You know that, right?"

"I run a nonprofit," Reggie said with a chuckle. "We're not in this to make money."

"That may be the case, but you still need money. Are you going to be able to get by without all the grant money Charlie used to help you get?"

"We're managing. I haven't had to cut my guys' pay." Her own pay was another story, but she wasn't about to tell Amber that. "We're in the running for the state's safe housing grant. If we get that, we'll be set for the rest of the year." Though after her run-in with Governor Murphy, she doubted that would happen now.

"And if you don't get it?"

"I'll figure something out. I always do."

"Do you want me to see if there's anything I can do on my end?"

Reggie shook her head. "No. That wouldn't be right."

"At least let me send you some money. Enough to

get some clean water for you and the boys for a few weeks. Don't think I don't see what you're drinking."

Reggie picked up the glass and held it in front of her. "Miles is being picked on at school." She set the glass down out of view of the camera. "Some little punk has been stealing his water and dumping it out. This is just to hold me over until I can get to the store." Though she wouldn't be able to get to the store until she got some money to actually spend there.

"What did Scott do when he found out?"

Reggie scoffed. "Scott doesn't give a shit. I'm pretty sure the only reason he hasn't kicked the boys out of the school is because it would make him look bad. I'm pretty sure Jace's test scores are bringing up the average of the whole school. Did you know he asked me if I had thought about changing our last name back to Torres?"

"He's such an asshole."

"I actually confronted the kid's dad after school today." Reggie wasn't sure if she should tell Amber or not—it was likely to make her worry more, but she had never been able to keep anything from Amber.

"And?"

Reggie let out a breath. "And it turns out the little punk's dad is Governor Murphy."

Amber's hand covered her mouth. "What did you do?"

"I threatened to go public with the fact that his kid is a bully." Reggie shrugged.

"I'm sure he loved that." Amber shifted in her seat so she was closer to the screen.

"He countered by suggesting that Homes, Hearts,

and Hammers could lose all of our government funding."

"So, you backed down, right?" Amber tucked a loose strand of blond hair behind her ear. It was a nervous habit she'd had since childhood.

Reggie laughed. "It's like you don't know me at all."

"Oh, god, Reggie," Amber groaned.

"Instead of backing down, I made it clear I'd bring legal action against a six-year-old if he couldn't keep his brat away from Miles."

"Can you even get a restraining order against a kid for bullying?"

"I have no idea."

Amber rolled her eyes. "How's Jace doing?"

Reggie sighed and slumped down in her chair. "I wish I knew. He's withdrawn so much over the last few months. I can barely get a word out of him, and whenever he does talk, it's usually to yell at me."

"Have you thought about taking him to see a therapist?"

She rolled her eyes. "Like I can afford that."

"I thought you were getting somewhere with the insurance company," Amber said.

"My last appeal was denied. They don't pay benefits to rioters."

Amber scoffed. "Charlie wasn't a rioter."

"You and I know that, but as far as the insurance company sees it, he was killed during the water riots, and since he wasn't there on government orders, he was a rioter." Reggie massaged her forehead gently. She had been fighting the insurance company over Charlie's life insurance since he had died. He had gone to what was supposed to be a peaceful rally to get water treatment standards on the ballot. His law firm was there to take on new clients. Reggie had been planning on attending as well to promote Homes, Hearts, and Hammers, but Miles got sick, so she stayed home. When the rally turned violent, Charlie stayed to help get people to safety and ended up getting himself killed in the process.

"That's not right."

"That's the way it is." Reggie had been fighting this battle for a year with the help of the other lawyers at Charlie's firm. They had tried everything they could to force the insurance company to pay and had still come up empty. There was nothing else they could do. "But don't worry. We'll be fine."

"You could be better than fine." Amber raised an eyebrow.

"No," Reggie said. "It's not worth it." She should have expected that this was where the conversation was heading.

"People would kill for a chance to go to one of the Sanctuary Cities, yet you have a spot whenever you want it and refuse to take it."

"I'm not doing it, Amber. I can't. Besides, what's with that name? It just screams that the whole thing is bullshit. I can't live in a place like that."

Amber chuckled. She had heard the same rationale from Reggie countless times before. "Think about your boys and the life they could have there."

Reggie rolled her eyes again. She got this talk from Amber every few months, though something about it felt different this time. Or maybe it was that Reggie was different this time without Charlie there to reassure her that not going was the right thing to do.

"Call your brother, Reggie. You know it's time."

"I'll think about it." It was the closest to a 'yes' she had gotten in the five years the Sanctuary Cities had been accepting residents.

"Good. Now, go to bed. You look like shit," Amber said with a huge smile.

"Love you too, Ambs." Reggie ended the call and closed the laptop. Deep-down, she knew Amber was right. She had to set her own feelings aside and do what was right for the kids.

~

It had been over an hour since the call with Amber had ended, and Reggie hadn't moved. She had always been able to brush off Amber's suggestions about claiming her spot at one of the Sanctuary Cities, but something was different this time. Who was she kidding? Everything was different this time.

The Sanctuary Cities had been the brainchild of her parents. Her entire life, they talked about how their research would one day save the human race from destroying itself. It was a purpose that had been forced onto her and her brother their entire lives. Reggie had pushed back, but Isaac had been all-in. It cemented her place as the black sheep among a family of brilliant scientists.

She remembered how excited Isaac had been when

he'd called to tell her that he had finally cracked the code that would make the smart laser grid he had been developing for years a reality. She'd been living on her own at the time, working on her electrical apprenticeship. Charlie had been over for a movie night. They had only been dating a few months at that point, but he was spending most nights at her place.

They'd been ten minutes into the movie when her phone had started to ring. She'd tried to ignore it, but after the third call she'd picked up.

"I did it, Reggie," Isaac had said the moment the call connected. She hadn't thought she had ever heard him that excited.

"Did what?" She'd gotten up and walked over to the kitchen so Charlie could keep watching the movie.

"The laser barrier I've been working on."

"The one that's supposed to filter pollution from the air?"

"Yeah, it works. This is the key. This is what we need to make our family's dream a reality."

She'd wanted to correct him. To tell him the whole 'preserving humanity' thing had never been her dream. She'd had no interest in winning a Nobel Peace Prize, and frankly she was suspicious of anyone who set that as their goal. Which included their parents. Reggie hadn't said it, though—she hadn't wanted to ruin this moment for him. "That's great, Isaac. I bet Mom and Dad are thrilled." All emotion had left her voice the moment she'd mentioned their parents.

"I haven't told them yet. I wanted you to be the first to know."

"I'm really happy for you. Truly, I am." She'd forced herself to smile in hopes it would make her sound more excited.

"We're going to be able to help so many people with this."

Reggie had glanced at the couch, and Charlie had paused the movie and was watching her closely. She had told him a little bit about her family, and she could see the concern building in his eyes as she'd listened to Isaac talk. "Isaac, I hate to cut you off, but I have company. I'll call you later in the week and you can tell me all the details."

"You be safe." She could have almost seen the smirk on his face.

"Congratulations, Isaac." She'd hung up and rejoined Charlie on the couch.

"What was all that about?"

"My brother just had some big breakthrough on his research." Reggie had snuggled closer to Charlie's side. "He's been working on this pollution filtering barrier technology for years, and I guess he figured out how to make it work."

Charlie had wrapped his arm around her. "That's huge. If he's right, it could change everything."

And change everything it had. It wasn't long after that her parents had started to make their plans for the first Sanctuary City public. They'd framed it as a massive social experiment to preserve the very best of humanity. They'd theorized that they could make a utopian society by removing all the stresses of ordinary life—an idea that became all the more appealing as the government had rolled back environmental regulations in favor of corporate profits.

Things had snowballed pretty quickly from there. Her parents were able to secure government funding to build the first city. An extensive list of criteria had been developed to determine who would get to live there and construction began. As pollution had increased rapidly, so had the list of applicants for the city until it had become the most coveted ticket in the world.

There were four Sanctuary Cities now spread across the country in undisclosed locations. People would do almost anything to get a spot at one of them.

Except for Reggie. Given her family connection, she had been awarded a spot with the first batch of residents—a spot she and Charlie had immediately refused to take. Now, five years since the first residents had moved into Serenity, she was finally thinking about claiming that spot.

Reggie got up and walked over to the bookshelf. She ran her finger over the spines until she got to an old, tattered copy of Black's Law Dictionary. She pulled it out and let it fall open in her hands. The pages in the middle had been cut away to hold a flask. "Thank you, Charlie," she whispered as she took the flask. She would need something stronger than contaminated water to make this call.

Reggie took a swig from the flask before forcing herself to sit back down at her computer. Cell service wasn't great inside the Sanctuary Cities, though she had always been able to get a call to go through over the internet. Not that she tried to contact her family very often.

She looked at her watch. It was late, and there was a good chance Isaac would be asleep. She should probably wait until tomorrow to call.

"Screw it." She took another sip and opened the laptop. If she didn't do this now, she knew she never would. She moved the cursor over Isaac's name and hesitated. "You can do this, you can do this," she muttered to herself as she forced her finger to click the button. Her anxiety skyrocketed as it started to ring. There was no turning back now. She took another swig from the flask.

A few seconds later, the screen filled with the confused face of her older brother. "Reggie, is that you? What's wrong? Did something happen?" There was a large red patch on his cheek and his hair was flat on one side. It looked like he had fallen asleep at his desk—something he had done often when they were growing up.

"Hi, Isaac," she said slowly. "How's it going?"

"Seriously, Reggie! Why are you calling me in the middle of the night?"

Reggie diverted her eyes from the screen as her resolve wavered. Maybe she could play this off as a social call; it had been months since she last spoke to Isaac. "It's only 11:30. I'd hardly call it the middle of the night."

Isaac rubbed his eyes. "Are the boys alright?"

"Yes," Reggie said without thinking. Of course, nothing was really alright. If it were, she wouldn't have been making this call. But how could she tell Isaac that?

She was the stubborn, independent one. She was the rebel, the outcast forging her own way in the world. How could she admit that it was all a lie? That she had failed? That she needed help?

"Okay," Isaac said slowly. "Then why are you calling?"

Tears formed behind her eyes. This was her brother. She didn't have to hide this from him. If anyone was going to understand, it was him. Reggie let out a breath. "Everything's such a mess. I don't have any idea what I'm doing." Tears flowed down her cheeks.

Isaac sat up straighter. She had his full attention now. "Hey, it can't be that bad. Tell me what I can do to help. Do you need money?"

Reggie shook her head and wiped the tears from her cheeks with the palm of her hands. "I think it's time." The words slipped out of her mouth before she could second-guess herself.

"Time for what?"

"That we move to one of the Cities. That is, if we still have a space there." Reggie swallowed. "If not, that's okay. I'll figure things out here. We'll be fine. I shouldn't have called you. I'm sorry," she said quickly. "Just forget it. I should let you get back to sleep."

"Reggie, wait," Isaac said before she could end the call. "Of course, there's still a spot for you and boys, but are you sure you're serious?"

Reggie closed her eyes for a moment. She could do this. She opened her eyes and nodded. "It's what's best for the boys. I need to give them their best chance at life, and I can't do that here. I thought I could, but..." Her voice trailed off. She couldn't admit that she was a failure as a mother, especially not when her own family already thought so little of her. She knew she would never live this down, but she would take all the shame and guilt they wanted to throw at her if it meant keeping her kids safe. They were the only thing that mattered.

"Have you talked to mom and dad about this?" Isaac asked.

"Are you kidding?" Reggie scoffed. "I haven't spoken to them since they were too busy to come home for Charlie's funeral." Not that she talked to them all that much before Charlie either—maybe twice a year at most, and it never lasted longer than a few minutes before they started on the list of ways Reggie had been a disappointment, and she would be forced to quickly end the call before they could drag her back to the guilt-ridden, depressed teenager she had been when she'd lived under their roof.

Isaac nodded. "I'll let them know tomorrow."

"Does it have to be Serenity? Couldn't you get us a spot at Harmony City or something?"

Isaac shot her a look. "Do you really think that's going to fly?"

"I thought you had control over choosing the residents."

"We do, to a certain extent. We still have to follow the agreed-upon criteria of the experiment. I can get you into Serenity because we're family and I have more pull here."

"Fine," she said with a sigh. At least she had tried.

"So how does this work?" She needed to steer the

conversation back to slightly friendlier territory. There wasn't enough whiskey left in the flask for them to discuss their parents.

Isaac ran his hand through his hair, picked his glasses up from the desk, and started to type. "Normally, you'd have to go through a screening process, but you guys are already approved, so we can skip that. Then there's some orientation classes you're supposed to take."

"When's the next set of classes?" She hoped they would be soon. If she had too much time to think about this, she would back out.

"Don't worry about that. I'll put in a waiver for you and the boys." Isaac moved closer to the screen as if he were reading something. "There's a group of new citizens scheduled to arrive next Wednesday." He leaned back in his chair. "Can you be ready by then?"

Six days. "I'll figure it out."

"Good. I'll get the details to you when I get into the office tomorrow."

"Sounds good." She tipped her head back and drained the flask. She was really doing this.

"Reggie, I promise you're making the right call. You'll see once you get here. It's going to be good for everyone. Even you."

"As long as the boys are taken care of. That's all that matters. I'll handle the fallout."

"I developed the smart grid in order to keep the people I care about safe. You and the boys have always been at the top of the list. I won't let you down. I promise. It won't be like when we were kids—Mom and

Dad are different now."

"Of course you think that. You've always fit their image of success. You didn't have to deal with all the shit I did growing up. No perfect little town can change that."

"Just give it a chance. Have I ever let you down?"

"No."

"This time won't be any different."

"Thank you, Isaac." She gave her brother a warm smile and ended the call, then raised the flask to her lips, forgetting that it was empty. She tossed it on the table and put her head in her hands. This was really happening. She said a prayer to whatever god was listening that she wasn't making the biggest mistake of her life.

Chapter 4

Reggie was anxious to get to work. She knew the paperwork from Isaac would be waiting in her box. It would be the first real indication of what she had gotten them into. She had expected to regret her decision when she woke up that morning, but she didn't. As much as it pained her, she knew this was the right thing to do for Jace and Miles. That didn't do anything to calm the anxiety growing inside of her.

Reggie set her stuff down and opened her laptop. Sure enough, an email from Isaac was sitting at the top of her inbox. Her mouse hovered over it. If she didn't open the email, maybe she could pretend she'd never gotten it, and the whole thing would just blow over without another thought.

"Don't be a coward," she muttered to herself, then

opened the email.

Hey Reggie,

I'm so excited that you've finally decided to come to Serenity. Sorry if I didn't show it last night, but your call caught me completely off-guard. I haven't told Mom and Dad yet, but I will today. I will also make sure they don't try to contact you before you get her. I know how hard this decision was for you, and the last thing I want is for Mom and Dad to get in your head and make you start seconding guessing things.

Anyway, take a look through the paperwork and let me know if you have any questions.

Can't wait to see you and the boys next week.

All my love,
Isaac

There were several files attached to the email, including medical evaluation forms, nondisclosure agreements, and a massive .pdf file called *Welcome to Serenity*. Reggie rolled her eyes and opened the file.

Welcome to Serenity, the original Sanctuary City! We are an experimental town functioning on the hypothesis that by providing a safe and stress-free society, humans can achieve a Utopian society where everyone benefits.

"Well, that's bullshit," Reggie said as she read.

The residents of Serenity play a vital role in the

success of the experiment. As such, residents must agree to live by the parameters of the experiment, which can be adjusted as the experiment develops over time.

Reggie paused. That was a pretty big condition to put into the welcome packet. What kind of adjustments were they talking about? Reggie did a quick document search for *adjustments* to see if it was defined anywhere, but couldn't find anything relevant. An undefined clause like that meant her parents could do just about anything under the guise of advancing the experiment. She made a mental note to ask Isaac about it later.

"Good morning, boss." Jesse popped his head through the opened doorway. "I don't like that look. Don't tell me we lost another grant." He sat down in the seat across from her.

"No, it's nothing like that." She glanced down at her screen. "I was actually reading through the welcome packet for the Sanctuary Cities." There was no reason not to tell him It wasn't like she could really back out now. Isaac had made sure she didn't have time for overthinking.

Jesse laughed. "Why on Earth would you be reading that?"

"Because we're moving there," Reggie said slowly.

"Oh," Jesse said in shock.

"In a week," she finished. "Did you know the residents have to agree to limit their contact with the rest of the world in order to uphold the integrity of the experiment? No coming home for holidays or vacations to the beach. Hell, the kids there probably don't even know what Disney World is." She knew Jesse was in shock, so she kept rambling while he took in the information to avoid any awkward silences. Telling him this was hard enough as it was.

"Don't fuck with me, Reggie. Everyone knows that's not how it works," Jesse said. She couldn't blame him, people normally had months to prepare for the move to a Sanctuary City. There were orientation classes, examinations, medical screens, and training sessions to get through before you were allowed to set foot inside one of the cities. All steps they were getting to skip.

"We got a special waiver, so we don't have to go through the normal onboarding process."

Jesse raked his hand through his hair. "How the hell did you manage that?"

Reggie shot him a look. "You know who my parents are."

Jesse leaned back in his chair. "I always forget that you're related to the saviors of humanity." His voice was dripping with sarcasm, which Reggie appreciated. The term had been coined by the press shortly after the plans for the Sanctuary Cities went public. *Family of genius scientists announce technological breakthrough that will save humanity*, the first headline read. It only got worse from there. A few of the reporters had even tried to interview her about what it was like growing up the only normal one among such a remarkable family. Needless to say, Reggie had declined the interview by slamming the door in the reporter's face.

"I wish it was something I could forget," Reggie mumbled under her breath.

"So, your parents can just let anyone they want into the cities? So much for the rigorous and impartial screening process they told the public was in place."

"I don't think they have free reign over the selection process, but they were allotted a certain number of slots to use as they wished. I'm honestly surprised they saved one of those slots for my family."

"This is really happening, then?"

Reggie nodded. "I don't really see any other options. I have to do this for Jacc and Miles."

"I get it, really I do, but that doesn't mean I want to see you go. You're the heart and soul of this place. None of this would be here without you."

Reggie glanced at the computer screen. "I actually wanted to talk to you about that."

"About what?" Jesse asked cautiously.

"About Homes, Hearts, and Hammers. One of the conditions for getting into Serenity is forfeiting ownership to all property, businesses—basically all assets."

"That seems a little extreme. What happens if you decide to leave? You'll have nothing left to fall back on."

"I kind of think that's the point. They don't really want people to leave. That would defeat the whole purpose of the experiment."

"What does that mean for us?" Jesse gestured around the office.

"You know the last thing I want is to see this place fall into the government's hands. Which was why I was hoping you'd take over ownership."

Jesse let out a breath and ran his hand through his

hair again.

"I know it's a lot to ask," she said before he could respond. "But you've been with me from the start. This is as much your company as it is mine. I know you believe in the work we do here just as much as I do. I would feel a lot better about leaving if I knew the company was in good hands."

"Enough." Jess held up his hands. "I forgot how much you ramble when you're nervous."

"So, you'll do it?"

"Yes," he said with a resigned sigh. "Of course I'll take over the company."

"Thank you, Jesse," Reggie said while fighting back the tears forming in her eyes.

"Don't go crying on me now, Stone. You owe me and one day I'm going to cash in on that," he said with a smirk.

"You'll have to get into Serenity to collect. Maybe you should apply. It would be nice having an alley on the inside."

Jesse laughed. "And leave all this behind? Besides, once they realize how good you are, they'll realize they don't need anyone else on the maintenance team."

"If they even let me on the maintenance team." She hadn't confirmed with Isaac what she'd be doing once she got there. Part of her feared that they would try to push her back towards a more academic field. She'd have to make sure that wasn't the case before moving forward. She knew she would have to make a lot of sacrifices once they got to Serenity, but she couldn't give up her work.

"If they don't, then you demand it." Jesse got to his feet and pointed at her. "Remember, you aren't Regia Torres any more. You're Reggie Fucking Stone and no one messes with her."

"Thank you, Jesse."

Jesse nodded and left the office. There was nothing else to say.

~

Reggie pulled into the parking lot at Elk Grove Elementary an hour before the end of the day. Of all the things she needed to do to get them ready for the move, this was the only one she was looking forward to. She knew everyone at the school thought she had set the meeting to beg for a handout. It would have felt so good to prove them wrong. She wondered how many members of the staff had applied to the Sanctuary City program.

She walked into the office feeling more confident than she had ever felt in that building. "I'm here for a meeting with Scott," she said as she entered the main office.

"*Principal Stone* will be with you shortly," the admin said, not even trying to hide her annoyance. "If you'll have a seat." She pointed toward the plastic chairs in the corner that were clearly meant for children, never once looking up from her computer.

Reggie tried to maintain her confidence as she sat in the chair Miles had been in when she picked them up the other day. The image of her dehydrated six-year-old son flashed in her mind. The wave of anger that washed over her confirmed once and for all that moving to Serenity was the right thing to do. She needed to protect the boys no matter what. That's what a good mother would do and she desperately wanted to believe that she was a good mother.

Scott strolled out of his office ten minutes after their meeting was scheduled to start with an arrogance Reggie didn't think was possible. She had no idea how Charlie and Scott could have been raised in the same household and turned out so completely different. Then again, look at where she had ended up compared to Isaac, the golden child. At least she got along with Isaac.

"Hello, Regina," Scott said with a smile so fake she wondered if he had practiced it at home in the mirror. "It's nice to see you here early for a change."

Reggie rose to her feet. "Scott."

"Let's go back to my office where we can talk in private."

Reggie followed him, her anger simmering just below the surface. The office was sparsely decorated, but everything in the room looked expensive. He could have provided everyone in the school with clean water for a week if he had bought cheaper furniture. He settled into the leather chair behind his desk and folded his hands carefully on his desk. "If this is about the boys' tuition. I'm afraid there's nothing I can do to help."

Reggie leaned against the back of the chair on the other side of the desk. Her pent-up anger prevented her from sitting down. "I'm pulling the boys from your school effectively immediately. I'm going to need copies of all of their records." She was impressed that she had managed to keep her voice calm.

Scott shifted in his chair. "Are you sure that's for the best?"

Reggie knew that the school needed Jace to keep their test average up. A sudden drop in the average would reflect poorly on Scott. Frankly, Reggie thought it was deserved, given the way he favored the rich brats over his own flesh and blood.

"I am." Reggie slowly walked around the chair and sat down. "The environment you've created in this school isn't conducive to learning. How are students supposed to focus on their education when they are being bullied and deprived of their basic needs? How can they trust the adults charged with their care when they see them constantly ignoring these things?"

"This isn't what Charlie would want," Scott said through gritted teeth.

Reggie clenched her hand into a fist. How dare Scott use Charlie in an attempt to manipulate her? It wasn't like the two of them had any kind of relationship. Scott didn't know what Charlie's favorite color was, let alone what he'd want for the boys. "Charlie's not here, and I have to do what's best for my kids."

Scott pressed his palms on the desk. "Which would be keeping the boys at this school where they can get a decent education and maybe grow up to actually be able to provide for their own needs."

"Don't act like you care about them now. You barely acknowledge their existence."

"They're my nephews," Scott spat.

Reggie leaned forward so she was sitting on the very edge of the seat. "That didn't seem to matter when the Governor's son was bullying Miles. Did you offer him any clean water when that spoiled little punk dumped his on the ground?" Scott had the decency to look away. "Or how about when Jace started to struggle after Charlie died? Did you offer him any of that mental health support you flaunt on your website? Or is that only for kids whose parents donate to the school?" Reggie slammed her hand on the desk. "You never once looked out for my kids, so don't act like you have their best interests in mind now."

An evil smirk formed on Scott's lips. "I could go to the courts and fight you for custody."

Reggie laughed. She knew that was the last thing Scott wanted, but he would follow through on the threat if it meant saving his reputation. She casually leaned back in her chair. "You could try, but no judge in the country would find me an unfit parent after I've secured them a spot at Serenity City."

"There is no way you got into one of the Sanctuary Cities, let alone Serenity. The original city is the hardest to secure a placement at."

Reggie rolled her eyes. Scott was so self-absorbed he hadn't put together her connection to the cities, even with her maiden name in the kids' files. He had even met her parents at her wedding and spent at least an hour talking to them if she remembered correctly. Charlie had decided it would be best to place all their least favorite relatives at one table so they wouldn't ruin the whole party. While the Sanctuary Cities had still just been a theory at that point, she'd been positive her parents would have talked about them at the wedding. They had discussed it at every other family function. Hell, if Scott had been a little bit nicer to her over the years, she might have been able to get him a spot. She knew his name had been on the waiting list since they'd first started to accept residents.

"We leave in a week." The look of shock on his face made her smirk. This was going better than she could have imagined. "So how about you get my kids' records like I asked?"

"You're lying."

She shrugged. "I guess my skillset is more valuable than yours." Reggie pointed to the computer. "Do you need me to spell your nephews' names, or can you pull up their records all on your own?"

"Fine," he said through gritted teeth. He turned to the computer and typed aggressively at the keyboard. When he was done, he hit a button on the intercom on his desk. "Karen, please have Jace and Miles Stone pack up all of their belongings and report to the office. They have been pulled from the school."

Scott handed Reggie a flash drive with the boys' records on it. Reggie reached for it but he didn't let go. "I don't know how you managed to worm your way into one of the Sanctuary Cities but I can't wait to see your face when they realize their mistake and kick you out."

Reggie yanked the flash drive from his hand. "I'd say it was nice knowing you, Scott, but I'm not a liar. Good luck with all of this." She waved her hands around his office. "I'll wait for the boys out in the hall. Don't bother coming out to say goodbye."

She stood a little taller as she left the office. That was until she saw the look of anger and confusion on Jace's face as he made his way over to her with his backpack bursting at the seams. She hadn't told the boys about the move yet. She had been so focused on her showdown with Scott that she hadn't given much thought to how the boys would react to being pulled from the school with no warning. Maybe she wasn't as competent of a mother as she'd thought.

"Mom," Jace said as he walked over to her, "what's going on? Did something happen?"

"Jace, everything's fine."

"Then why are we being kicked out of school? Are we out of money?"

"It's nothing like that," Reggie reassured him, even though it had been money problems that had started all of this.

"Is this because you don't like Uncle Scott? Are we being punished because you can't mind your own business?"

"You aren't being kicked out. This is a good thing, I promise." She chose to ignore the insult. She could tell he was already close to the breaking point without the parental lecture. Doing it now would only make things worse.

Reggie took a breath and looked over his shoulder for Miles. The last thing she wanted was to cause a scene. "Let's talk about it over dinner."

"No! Tell me what's going on," Jace yelled. So much for not causing a scene. "This isn't what dad would have wanted."

"Hey," Reggie said, forcing her voice to stay calm. "You don't speak to me like that." Jace turned away. She reached out and gently turned him back towards her. "I wanted to tell you and brother together. I pulled you out of school because we're moving."

"What? Why? I don't want to move." Jace's voice echoed through the empty hall. Reggie could almost feel the admin's eyes on them through the office window.

"I didn't even think you liked it here," Reggie said, matching his tone. This was spiraling out of control. This decision had been hard enough without the added guilt Jace seemed to want to lay on her.

"That's because you only care about Miles. Dad wouldn't do this. He cared about me more than you do." The veins in Jace's neck popped out as he yelled at her. "I wish you'd died instead of him." He stormed past her and out of the building.

"So do I, buddy," she said softly as she watched him stomp to the car. She took a deep breath and closed her eyes to keep the tears at bay. It wasn't the first time he had said something like that, but every time, it hurt a little more.

"Mommy!" she heard Miles yell from the other end of the hall. The excitement was a jarring contrast to Jace.

Reggie quickly wiped her eyes and plastered a smile on her face before she turned to him. "Hi, baby." She scooped him up in her arms as he ran the last few feet to her. "Let's go home." She set him down, took his backpack, and headed to the car with his hand secured in hers.

~

Jace didn't say a word the whole way home. She thought the pizza and liter of pop she had splurged on for dinner would help to lift his mood, but he continued to glare at her while picking at his food. Reggie wasn't sure what to do. She'd never imagined he'd take the news of them moving this hard. She watched him closely for some sign that his anger was easing while listening to Miles talk nonstop about his day. To be six and not feel the tension of those around you.

"Everyone was super-jealous when they found out I didn't have to go to school anymore," Miles said with his mouth full of pizza.

"We still have to go to school, idiot," Jace mumbled under his breath.

"Hey," Reggie said in her best mom voice, "I get that you're mad at me, but we don't speak to each other like that in this family. Do you understand me?"

"Sorry, Miles," Jace grumbled down at his plate.

"So, I still have to go to school?" Miles's voice deflated.

"Yes, but it'll be a week or so before you start at your new school." Reggie set her pizza down. It was time to tell them, even if she was dreading it. "We're moving to Serenity Sanctuary next week to be closer to Uncle Isaac," Reggie hesitated, "and Grandma and Grandpa."

Jace looked at her for the first time since leaving the school. "Wait, are you serious?"

Reggie nodded, trying to gauge his reaction, but she

couldn't tell if he was excited or she was about to experience a fresh wave of anger. Charlie was always so much better at reading him. He would know exactly how to handle this, while Reggie was grasping at straws and hoping for the best.

"What's Serenity Sanctuary?" Miles asked, stumbling over the words.

"It's an experimental town where they are testing a laser grid barrier that filters out all the pollutants in the air and water. Uncle Isaac invented it." Reggie had read all the research papers Isaac and her parents had published on the technology. It could save a lot of lives, but it was expensive to operate and required a massive amount of maintenance to keep running. They'd have to make a lot of improvements before it could be used on a bigger scale.

"Is it safe?" Jace rubbed his hands across the tablecloth.

"Of course it is," Reggie said. "And more importantly, we'll have all the fresh air and clean water we could ever want. No more having to stay inside on bad air days or rationing bottled water. I wouldn't be doing this if I didn't think it was the best place for you boys." It wasn't the best place for her, but they didn't need to know that. "I know change can be scary, and we've been through so much this last year, but I really think this will be good for us." Reggie reached her hands across the table. Miles took it immediately. Jace hesitated before placing his hand on top of hers. "This is going to be good. I promise." She squeezed their hands and gave them what she hoped was a reassuring smile.

"What are grandma and grandpa like? I don't remember them," Miles said as he went back to eating his pizza.

"I don't remember them very well," Jace said, "but they were nice, I think. Uncle Isaac is really cool, though, and we'll get to see him all the time instead of just once a year." There was a hint of excitement in his voice that Reggie had never heard.

The boys started talking about all the things they remembered from Isaac's visits over the years, but Reggie wasn't listening anymore. She was thinking about the last time she had seen her parents. It had been right before they'd officially opened Serenity to residents, though her parents had already been living there for over a year at that point to oversee the construction. They had come over for dinner, and to see Miles, who was nine months old at the time. It was only the second time they had met him. Homes, Hearts, and Hammers had just been awarded their first big government grant, and Reggie had naively thought they would be proud of what she had accomplished with her nonprofit, but they'd brushed aside the topic within minutes of arriving.

Instead, all conversation centered around the opening of Serenity and how good their lives were going to be there. Reggie and Charlie had told them several times before that they were not going, but her parents never seemed to hear it. She remembered seeing Charlie get more and more frustrated the longer they talked until her even-tempered husband exploded in the middle of dinner. Her father had started to inform them of his plans for Jace's education until they could get a proper school up and running. He had apparently already interviewed several tutors. Charlie nearly flipped the table. Without saying a word he picked up their half eaten dinners and dumped them in the trash. Reggie will never forget the look of shock on her parents' faces when Charlie threw them out. Neither of her parents had even bothered with Miles the entire time they were there.

And now, Reggie's parents were getting exactly what they wanted. She was crawling back to them begging to help. She had become the failure they'd constantly told her she would be. She almost called the whole thing off right there—was clean air and water really worth having to deal with the toxicity that came being around Lena and Oscar Torres? Was she strong enough to keep it from affecting the boys?

Laughter drew her eyes to the boys' smiling faces. They were actually getting along for once. She wanted to freeze the moment and bask in it for as long as possible. She had no other options. She had to keep them safe. She couldn't back out now. She would do whatever she could to shield Jace and Miles from her parents.

Even if meant taking all their criticism and negativity herself.

Chapter 5

"I'm not getting rid of any of them!" Jace slammed his bedroom door in Reggie's face. She was getting really tired of his attitude but had no idea how to address it. Nothing she had tried so far had made any difference. If she was honest with herself, she could see his point, even if she wasn't thrilled with how he was choosing to voice his frustration. The kid just wanted to keep his things. He had been through enough change in the last year; was it really that unreasonable to let him bring whatever he wanted to their new home?

Reggie put a hand on her forehead as she looked at the closed door. The moving boxes had arrived yesterday, and since then, it had been nonstop arguing as they tried to decide what to take and what to leave behind. Reggie leaned against the doorframe and sighed.

"I know this sucks," she said to the door, "but we're only allowed to take what we can fit in the boxes they sent."

"It's not fair," Jace yelled through the closed door.

Reggie knocked and opened the door without waiting for an answer. Jace was sitting on his bed with his arms wrapped around his knees. She sat down next to him and draped an arm around him. To her surprise, Jace didn't move away. "I know," she said softly while kissing the top of his head. "Let's start by dividing your books into piles: 'absolutely must go,' 'would like to go,' and 'can be left behind.' Once you do that, we'll see where we are with space. Okay?"

Jace nodded against her chest. It was huge progress.

Reggie's eyes scanned the room. Jace had books crammed into every available space. She had no idea where they had all come from, but there was no way they would fit into the four boxes she had set aside for his personal items. Maybe she could consolidate some of her things to make more room for him.

Reggie's pocket started to vibrate. She shifted her weight to get her phone out of her pocket without letting go of Jace. He rarely let her hold him like this, especially recently, so she was determined to savor every second of it.

She glanced at the phone. Isaac was calling.

"I have to take this. You get started and I'll be back in a few to help." She gave him one more squeeze and got off the bed.

She waited until she was in the hallway with the door closed before she answered. "Hey, Isaac." She wedged the phone between her ear and shoulder so she could pick up the overfilled laundry basket that had been abandoned in the hall halfway to the laundry room.

"Hi, Reggie," her brother said on the other end of the line. "I just got the results of the medical screenings and everything looks good. You and the boys are officially cleared to come." The excitement in his voice brought a smile to her face. At least someone was happy about this move.

"What would have happened if one of us hadn't passed the medical screening?" Reggie readjusted her grip on the laundry basket as she made her way to the stacked washer and dryer in the cubby at the end of the hall.

"I would have pulled some strings and made sure you were let in anyway. I'm not sure if you're aware of this or not, but I'm kind of a big deal here."

"I had no idea." Reggie laughed and dumped the laundry into the washer. Along with the moving boxes, Isaac had sent a temporary water filter for the line coming into their apartment. It had to have cost thousands of dollars and would only last a few weeks before it became plugged. There were instructions to wash everything they would bring with the filtered water to reduce the pollutants coming into the city.

"All three of you will still need chelation therapy due to the heavy metals in your blood, but that's normal."

Reggie's gut twisted. They had worked so hard to keep the pollutants out of the boys' systems. "How high are the numbers?" It had been years since any of them had gotten checked. The government was supposed to provide testing on a regular basis, but funding for the program had dried up a long time ago.

"Yours is really high, but Miles's and Jace's results are some of the lowest I've seen in a long time. You've done a good job keeping everything out of their systems."

A wave of relief washed over Reggie. It had been a long time since anyone had told her she was doing anything right as a mother. In fact, she was pretty sure Charlie had been the last person to compliment her parenting skills. She'd began to believe she wasn't capable of doing it without him.

"I wish you had done more to keep yourself safe," Isaac said.

Reggie shrugged even though Isaac couldn't see her. "Better me than them."

"Thankfully, you won't have to make those kinds of choices anymore. How is everything going there?"

"It's chaotic. Miles is so excited he asks me at least fifty times a day when we are leaving. Jace, on the other hand, has spent more time complaining than actually getting ready to move. Oh, and I'm pretty sure he hates me, though that's pretty par-for-the-course these days."

"I'm sure he doesn't hate you," Isaac said.

"I wouldn't bet on that." Reggie finished loading the washing machine and started it. She leaned against it focusing on the gentle vibrations it emitted. "Moving is ruining his life, and now I won't let him use all of our allotted space to bring his books. You'd think I had asked him to cut off his arm and leave it behind."

Isaac laughed. "Oh, to be nine again."

"Just wait 'til we get there and you get to experience

his attitude for yourself. I thought I had a few more years before he hit the oppositional defiance stage."

"Well, he's always been advanced for his age."

"I didn't mind when it was potty training and learning to talk. I really didn't need the teenage attitude to hit this soon."

"I can tell you one thing: He didn't get it from Charlie."

Reggie knew Isaac was smirking. Even at a young age, she had fought constantly with her parents as they'd tried to force their priorities on her, but she didn't remember having the guts to talk back at Jace's age. That came later.

"Maybe I can make the transition a little easier for him," Isaac said.

"How?" Reggie walked back to the bedrooms. She peeked in at Miles, who had set up an elaborate battle scene with his action figures instead of packing them like he was supposed to be doing.

"Can you get me a list of all the books he has to leave behind?"

"Probably." She cracked open the door to Jace's bedroom. He had stacks of books in the middle of the floor—or rather, one large mountain of books and a few small piles around it.

"If you can, then I should be able to get them all loaded on an e-reader for him. I know it's not the same, but at least he'll still have them."

She let out a sigh. "He might go for it, though not if I'm the one that suggests it."

"Then let me talk to him."

Reggie cocked an eyebrow. "You sure you're up for it?"

"Just put the kid on the phone."

"You asked for it." Reggie pulled the phone away from her ear and knocked on Jace's door. "Uncle Isaac wants to talk to you." She held the phone out to him. Reggie took a few steps away to give them some privacy. Every now and then, she would feel Jace's gaze on her through the opened door as he listened to Isaac. They only saw Isaac once or twice a year; leaving the city too often could jeopardize the integrity of the experiment, but he had made it a point to maintain a relationship with her kids.

After a few minutes, Jace handed her the phone back without saying a word. He turned towards the large stack of books in the middle of his room and started to go through them again. Reggie took it as a good sign. "Isaac?" she said putting the phone back to her ear.

"I think I helped," Isaac said. "He didn't really say much, though."

Reggie turned away from Jace's room and headed towards the kitchen. "He never does these days. Unless he's yelling at me." Until a year and half ago, Jace would talk incessantly, to the point that Charlie would get so annoyed he'd challenge Jace to see who could stay quiet the longest. Jace would always lose after a few minutes, which was when Charlie started to read with him. They would spend an hour every evening sitting quietly on the couch, each reading their own books, and then spend another half-hour discussing what they were reading. The nonstop talking didn't seem to bother Charlie as much when there was a purpose to it. Jace read a lot more now that Charlie was gone, but he no longer wanted to discuss what he was reading.

"It'll get better once you're here. I promise."

"I hope so, though I don't really see how." Reggie heard a beep on the line and pulled the phone away from her ear. Amber was trying to video chat with her. "Look, Isaac, I need to go. Amber is calling."

"I didn't realize that the two of you were still in touch," Isaac said offhandedly.

Reggie had no idea why Isaac would think that. Amber was her family. She had lived with Amber's family when she moved out of her parents' house a few weeks after she turned eighteen. The two of them had been planning for it for weeks.

"Today," Reggie said while shaking out her hands. "I promise." A few months ago, she had received a full scholarship to Princeton. Reggie hadn't even applied to the school, but wasn't surprised when the letter showed up. She had no doubt her parents had submitted the application on her behalf. Given how much grant money her parents' research had won the university over the years, the whole thing felt like a formality. No one had ever asked Reggie if she wanted to go to Princeton, or even to college at all. It was just expected. She was a Torres, and a Torres went to Princeton.

"Do you have everything ready?" Amber asked. They had reached Reggie's house. "Hey," Amber said gently when Reggie didn't respond. She took Reggie's hand. "It's going to be okay. You got this."

Reggie nodded, took a deep breath, and headed

towards the house. "Mom. Dad," she called the moment she was inside. She needed to do this before she lost her nerve. Maybe the fourth attempt would be successful.

"We're down here," her father's voice came from the basement laboratory.

Reggie had managed to avoid the lab for over a year, but now she descended the steps with shaking legs. "Can I talk to you guys?" she said before she reached the bottom step.

"Certainly." Her mother came over to meet her while her dad watched her closely from behind his lab table. She might as well have been one of his samples under a microscope.

"There's no easy way to say this. I want you both to know that I won't be attending Princeton in the fall. I have a carpentry apprenticeship with Amber's dad, and I'll be starting that after graduation."

Oscar came over to join them. "What are you talking about? Of course you'll be attending Princeton in the fall. This isn't open for discussion."

"No, I won't," she said with a confidence she didn't feel. "I've already turned them down." The weight of her parents' disapproval hung heavy on her shoulders. It wasn't anything new, but this one carried a little extra weight.

"How could you do this to us, Regina?" Her mother looked close to tears.

"I didn't do this to hurt you. I just want a chance to live my life, to do what I love. I'm sorry that science doesn't make me happy like the rest of you. I really am. I wish I could be more like you guys and Isaac, but I'm not. I need to live my life for me. Not for you."

"Fine." Oscar's voice was tense. "You're an adult now, Regina. You think you're mature enough to make this decision for yourself, then fine."

"Thank you." Reggie's voice shook with relief. In all of the situations she had planned with Amber, it had never occurred to them that her parents would just accept her decision.

"But that also means you have to live with the consequences." There was a new sort of coldness in her father's voice that she hadn't heard before.

Reggie took a deep breath. This was what she had been waiting for. She knew there was no way they were just going to accept her decision. She had prepared for this. She was ready.

"Legally, you're an adult now. We won't tell you what to do. But if you want to continue living in this house, then you *will* go to Princeton. If not, you'll need to find a new place to live. Today," Oscar said while her mother stood by silently. Reggie knew better than to look for support there. Her parents were a unit, and she was the opposition.

Reggie nodded. She'd known this was the likely outcome. She'd had her bags packed for days. "Fine. I'll be gone in a few minutes." Reggie quickly gathered her things and left. Her parents did not come upstairs to say goodbye. It would be years before Reggie set foot in her childhood home again.

Amber was waiting outside for her. She took one of the bags from Reggie. "Let's go home."

Reggie had lived with Amber's family for almost a

year while she finished high school and saved up enough to put a deposit down on an apartment. The two had even shared an apartment for a few years while Amber had finished college. The fact that they no longer lived in the same city didn't matter.

Isaac just didn't get it. He had never had any close friends, as far as she knew. Growing up, he had devoted all of his free time to his research. "We talk a few times a week," Reggie said. "I wouldn't have made it through last year without her."

"Well, tell her I said hi, and I'll see you and the boys in a few days."

"Bye, Isaac." Reggie ended the call then quickly accepted the video call from Amber. "Hey," she said with a smile.

"I haven't heard from you in a few days," Amber said. "I was just calling to check in."

"Yeah, sorry. It's been a crazy few days."

"Wait, are those boxes I see?"

Reggie glanced behind her, where a pile of empty boxes had taken over the counter. "Yes."

Amber's eyes were wide. "So, you really did it?"

Reggie put her free hand on her forehead and glanced around the apartment. "We leave in three days."

Amber let out a small laugh. "No wonder I haven't heard from you."

"I'm sorry. I should have called to tell you sooner." She went and sat down on the couch, careful not to knock over the pile of folded laundry still sitting on the other side.

"You don't have to apologize. I'm just shocked you

actually did it."

"Maybe I'm getting less stubborn with age," Reggie said.

"Somehow I doubt that."

Reggie looked around the apartment, making sure the boys were still in their rooms. "I wanted to ask you something."

"Anything. You know that."

"We're only allowed to bring a limited number of boxes with us. It's barely enough to cover the essentials for the three of us."

"So, what's the problem? It's not like I can help you sneak more stuff in."

"It's not that. I won't have room to take Charlie's things with us. I don't think I can get rid of them, though. Can I send some of it to you? It would be easier if I knew his things were stored somewhere safe."

"Of course," Amber said, her features softening.

"Thank you." Reggie felt like a huge weight had been lifted—she had been focusing so hard on packing the boys' items because she wasn't ready to purge Charlie's belongings. "I don't know how long I'll need you to keep them for me. I don't want to rock the boat too much when we first get there. We're already skirting most of the rules to get in."

"Reg, I'll hold onto it for as long as you need me to."

"What about Trina and her newfound minimalist lifestyle?" Reggie raised an eyebrow at Amber. She had only met Amber's girlfriend a handful of times. She seemed nice enough, even if she was a little too peppy for Reggie's taste. She loved Amber, and they were a good couple. That was really all that mattered to Reggie.

"She'll just have to deal with it. I love Trina, but you're family, and family comes first. Besides, her minimalist lifestyle doesn't really work when she's taken over one of the spare bedrooms to store all her party supplies. Have you ever heard of a minimalist event planner?" Amber rolled her eyes. Trina was always jumping from one fad to the next, much to Amber's annoyance and Reggie's general amusement.

"Whoa, love? Sounds like Miss Independent is finally letting someone in."

"Don't go sending out wedding invites yet," Amber said with a smile. "It's still new."

Reggie laughed. "The two of you have been dating off and on ever since you got to D.C. four years ago. And hasn't she been living with you for like a year now?"

"Ten months," Amber said defensively.

"Oh, in that case, you're right, it's a brand-new, meaningless relationship." Reggie laughed again. She missed Amber. She'd always had a way of making Reggie forget her stress. Even if it was only for a few minutes.

"Get your toys out of my room!" Jace's voice echoed through the apartment.

"But they need to climb the mountain to save the lost puppy," Miles said, matching his older brother's volume.

"Mom!" Jace yelled. "Tell Miles to get out of my room."

"Tell Jace he has to share," Miles said.

A loud crash followed, which Reggie assumed was

the mountain of books in Jace's room tumbling to the floor. She closed her eyes for a moment waiting to hear if anyone would start crying. Thankfully, the only sound that came was both of them yelling "Mom" at the top of their lungs.

"I should probably go deal with that," Reggie said.

"Just remember, they're cute," Amber said.

"They're not that cute," Reggie countered with a smirk. "I'll talk to you later."

"I'm proud of you, Reggie. I'll call you tomorrow."

The call ended as a new chorus of yells met her ears. She remembered sitting in this very spot negotiating with Charlie on whose turn it was to break up the boys. Now, it was always her turn.

Chapter 6

Reggie walked through the rows of gravestones alone. The sun beat down on her from high in the sky. She knew the path to Charlie's grave by heart. She had no idea if she would be able to visit again and it was killing her. Once residents entered one of the Sanctuary Cities they weren't supposed to leave except for emergencies or while on city business, which seemed to extend only to Isaac. She doubted wanting to visit her husband's grave would qualify.

She ran her hand gently over the top of the headstone. "Hey, Charlie," she said softly. She sat down under a large tree across from the grave, her back settling into the grooves of the trunk. It was a spot she had spent a fair amount of time in over the last year. "The boys and I are moving today."

She blew out a breath and fixed her gaze on the sky as tears started to form. "I didn't know what else to do. Things have been so hard lately. And I know you would say we just have to be strong, that things will get easier, but I don't know if that's true this time. I don't know how to be that strong without you by my side."

The branches above her creaked, and she looked up to see a squirrel running through the trees. Would there be any wildlife in their new home, or did the smart grid keep them out too? "Miles is being bullied at school, and your asshole brother won't do anything to stop it. I don't even know what's going on with Jace these days. He's so withdrawn, you wouldn't recognize him. He barely says a word to anyone. I really hope this is a good change for him," Reggie paused. "I hope it's a good change for all of us."

Even though Charlie had never said it to her, she knew that a big reason he was opposed to moving to Serenity when it had first opened was because of her parents. She had overheard a conversation he'd had with Isaac the last time he visited when Charlie was alive. Serenity had been open for three years and Isaac had still been trying to convince them to move there. Reggie was leaving Miles's room after tucking him in when she heard Isaac and Charlie fighting.

"I can keep the boys and Reggie healthy and safe. The world is a shitshow right now, and it's getting worse and worse every day," Isaac said.

"Don't you think I know that?" Charlie fired back. "We're the ones out here living with it every day. We're the ones trying to make it better instead of hiding inside your bubble, where you can pretend nothing bad is happening."

"I'm trying to find a way to save the human race before it has a chance to destroy itself. I know the work you and Reggie are doing is important, but it's a short-term fix. I'm thinking about the bigger picture. I'm thinking about what the world will be like when the boys are adults."

"Then work on improving your smart grid so it can be applied more broadly instead of just protecting the people you select to live in your towns."

"I'm working on it, but that takes time. Time you guys might not have if you don't move there."

"I'm willing to take my chances," Charlie said.

"I don't understand you, Charlie. I'm offering you a way to protect your family, and you won't take it. Tell me why. Make me understand."

Charlie signed. "Because I can't do that to Reggie. I won't force her to be subjected to your parents' toxic behavior. The best way I can keep her safe and happy is to keep her away from your parents. She deserves to be happy, doesn't she?"

"Of course." Isaac voice lacked the conviction it'd had when Reggie had first started to listen. She stayed in the hallway just out of sight.

"Then why would you want to put her through that again? I have a better chance at keeping my family happy outside of the Sanctuary Cities than I ever will inside one." Reggie didn't think she could have loved anyone more in that moment.

Reggie looked at the stone marker in front of her,

wishing she could go back to that moment with Charlie and Isaac. If she'd known what was going to happen, would she have stepped in and insisted they move sooner? Would Charlie have still been alive if they had relented? It certainly would have been easier to move there with Charlie by her side. "I hope you understand why I have to do this. I know you were always against the Sanctuary Cities, and how exclusive they are. Honestly, I agree with you. We should be looking into ways to use the technology to help everyone. It's just that at some point, our kids have to come before our advocacy work. You know I want to help as many people as I can, but not if it means my own kids have to suffer. There has to be a breaking point, and I've reached it. Maybe that means I've changed from the woman you fell in love with, but I don't know what else to do. If I don't protect Jace and Miles, no one will. I hope you don't think too poorly of me."

Reggie wiped a rogue tear from her cheek. "Why did you have to go to that rally? Why didn't you leave the moment things turned violent?" The tears flowed freely now, and Reggie didn't try to stop them. "I know you thought you could help people, and that's why you stayed. You were always looking out for people, and I love that about you, I really do, but why couldn't you have been a little bit selfish this one time? Why didn't you think about the boys and me before jumping into hero mode? We needed you too. I needed you." She wiped her nose on her jacket sleeve.

Reggie's phone started to vibrate in her pocket. She didn't need to pull it out to know what it was for. Her time was up. She blew out a breath, hoping it would help her get her tears under control. "I need to head back. We'll be leaving tonight, and I have to make sure the boys are ready. We're supposed to travel there under cover of darkness to help keep the location of the city secret. It's crazy to me that no one has been able to identify its exact location in the five years it's been open to residents. It's probably all just for show. You know Isaac—he's always loved to add a little flare of drama to everything." She let out a small laugh as she wiped away the last of her tears.

"I don't know why this is so hard. It's not like you're even really here." Reggie bit her lower lip, her eyes coming to rest on Charlie's headstone. With a sigh, she rose to her feet. "Goodbye, Charlie. I love you."

She kept her head held high as she walked away. She couldn't give into her pain now or she knew she would back out of the whole thing. She needed to find a way to be strong for Jace and Miles. She was giving them their best shot at a healthy life, and she would sacrifice everything for that. Even Charlie.

~

Mrs. Elmenheimer was waiting for Reggie at the kitchen table when she got home. Reggie had asked her to stay with the boys while she went to say goodbye to Charlie, and she'd happily agreed. Mrs. Elmenheimer had been helping her with the boys since they were born—they would have been lost without her. Reggie felt incredibly guilty taking the boys away from her. She had become their family, and Reggie wished there was a way she could take Mrs. Elmenheimer with them.

"How were the boys?" Reggie asked as she went into the kitchen and grabbed the water filter Isaac had sent her. She had removed it earlier that morning after filling up enough bottles of clean water to last them through their trip.

"They were angels, just like they always are."

Reggie laughed. "They're only like that for you."

"They're good kids." Mrs. Elmenheimer got up and put a hand on Reggie's shoulder. "You and Charlie have done an amazing job raising them. I'll miss them, and you."

Reggie bit the inside of her cheek to keep herself from crying again. "I know this hasn't been easy for anyone. I really wish I didn't have to do it, but it's what's best for the boys," she said, for what must have been the thousandth time that day. Maybe she would start to believe it at some point.

"It is," Mrs. Elmenheimer reassured her. "You're giving your kids an amazing gift by getting them into a Sanctuary City. They might be sad now, but they'll see that in time. Change is always hard."

Reggie nodded as she fought to hold back the sobs building in her throat.

"And you're stronger now. Remember that. You're allowed to stand up for yourself and your kids. You can set boundaries and hold people to them." Mrs. Elmenheimer was one of the few people who knew the truth about Reggie's parents. Reggie had vented to her more times than she could count over the years. She had shown Reggie what a mother's love was supposed to feel like.

"I want you to take this," Reggie said, taking a deep breath. She handed the water filter to Mrs. Elmenheimer.

The older woman held her hands up and shook her head. "I can't accept that. It's too much."

Reggie gently took her hands and placed the filter in it. "Yes, you can. They sent it as part of our moving prep. There's still about three-quarters of life left in it. Someone should use it."

"You and the boys need it more than I do." She tried to hand the filter back to Reggie.

"Not where we're going. I've already called Jesse, and he's going to send someone out tomorrow to install it for you."

With tears in her eyes, Mrs. Elmenheimer pulled Reggie into a hug. "This building won't be the same without you. I know you don't believe it, but you really are such an amazing mom, Reggie. Those boys are so lucky to have you."

Reggie wasn't sure she agreed, but she kept it to herself. "Thank you. For everything. You've been like a mother to me for years. I'll never forget what you've done for me and my family. I wish there was a way for you to come with us."

Mrs. Elmenheimer held Reggie at arm's length. "Go have an amazing life."

"I'll try. And you better take care of yourself. I'm going to have Jesse stop by every couple of weeks to check in on you."

Mrs. Elmenheimer waved her hand. "I've been on

my own for years. I'll be fine. You don't have to worry about me. Give the boys my love." With one last smile that Reggie would keep etched into her mind for the rest of her life, Mrs. Elmenheimer left.

Reggie stood frozen, looking at the closed apartment door. The urge to back out had never been stronger. Could she really leave this life behind and go back to her parents? She had sworn when she'd left that she would never live near them again. She had made it seventeen years before having to crawl back and admit she couldn't do it on her own.

She felt her phone buzzing in her pocket again. It was time to go.

Chapter 7

The hovertrain, another of Isaac's inventions, glided effortlessly over the uneven ground. The process of getting to the train had been overly complicated and taken hours. There were several transfers between cars and buses, where more and more new residents slowly joined them. Everything was a private charter to help keep the exact location of the city hidden. The first location her parents had chosen to start building had been discovered before they'd even started construction. The area was flooded with people within days. Everyone was desperate to gain access to clean drinking water and fresh air. Three people had been killed in the chaos that'd followed. They had been forced to pick a new location after that. Reggie knew that the secrecy was needed, but the whole process still felt excessive.

They hadn't been on the same mode of transportation for more than three hours, making it impossible for anyone to get any kind of rest. Which was a problem, since they were also required to travel at night—clearly, overly tired children hadn't factored into Isaac's arrival schedule. From what Reggie could tell, Jace and Miles were two of eight children making their way to the city. None of them were handling the journey well. The last bus leg was almost unbearable as the kids and parents reached their breaking point.

Reggie was beyond grateful when they finally arrived at the train station, and they were able to settle in for the six-hour ride to Serenity City. Most of the train was taken up with cargo, leaving two cars for passengers. She settled the boys into the back of the second passenger car. Miles laid his head on her lap and was fast-asleep before they finished loading the train. Jace sat down on her other side and pulled out one of the many books he had crammed into his backpack. Reggie honestly wasn't sure how he was managing to carry the thing.

After an hour, Jace fell asleep with his head leaning against her shoulder. The book lay open on his lap. Reggie soaked in the moment. He shifted closer to her and the book slid off his lap. Reggie bit her lip and stretched out her leg to try to get it before it slid under the seat across from them. She didn't want to risk waking either of them, but she knew Jace would never forgive her if the book was lost.

"Here, let me get it." A man sitting on the other side of the train got up and picked up the book. "In here?" He pointed to Jace's overstuffed backpack on the floor.

Reggie nodded. "If you can make it fit. Thanks."

The man took a seat on the bench across from her. Reggie guessed he was in his early forties, though his features were soft which always threw off her guesses. She spent most of her time with men who did the majority of their work out in the sun. It always made them look older than they were. She doubted the man sitting across from her had ever put in a hard day's work out in the elements.

"I don't remember seeing you in any of the orientation meetings. I'm Theo."

"Reggie. We skipped all the orientation stuff. Special circumstance," she said with a shrug. She wanted to keep her connection with the Sanctuary City founders to herself for as long as she could. Once they arrived, there would be no more hiding it, but for now, she could be just another new resident. She could hold onto the last shreds of Reggie Stone—mother, wife, business owner, a person she was proud to be—before she had to go back to being Oscar and Lena Torre's other child, or Isaac's sister, not even worthy of her name being mentioned.

"That's some pretty heavy reading for a kid his age." Theo nodded to the backpack. She guessed he wasn't going back to his seat. At least he was keeping his voice down so he didn't wake up the boys.

Reggie glanced down at the book Jace had been reading. It was a detailed look at social justice in America. "They were his dad's." She turned her head a little and kissed the top of Jace's head while she stroked Miles's hair.

"Is their dad here?" Theo strained his neck to see if anyone was coming up behind them.

Reggie bit the inside of her cheek and gently shook her head. "No. He passed away last year." She was proud that she had managed to keep her voice even as she said it.

"Oh." Theo settled back down into his seat. "I'm so sorry."

"Thanks," she said softly. "What is it that you do?" It was time to steer the conversation away from her.

"I'm a psychiatrist," he said carefully, "and a psychologist, for that matter. I couldn't settle on a discipline, so I did both."

"If you think you're going to turn this into a session, you can head right back over to the other side of the train."

Theo laughed. "I'll be on my best behavior, I promise. It's been years since I actively saw patients. I wouldn't know how to start. I'm just trying to pass the time."

Reggie smirked. "I guess you're in the clear." She didn't see the harm in chatting with him, though she would need to be careful about what she said. "Getting to Serenity has been quite the endeavor."

"You don't buy into the whole 'extreme secrecy' thing?"

"I mean, I understand why they do it, but there has to be a better way to go about it. It's clear whoever came up with the system didn't have kids in mind."

"Maybe you should take it up with those in charge when we finally get there."

"Maybe I will," she said with a sly smile. Though she doubted they would listen to her.

"Don't tell me you're on the city leadership team," Theo groaned.

Reggie struggled to keep from laughing. She didn't want to wake up Jace or Miles. "God, no."

Theo crossed his arms and slid down in his seat. "What is it that you do, then?" He said through a stifled yawn.

"I used to own a nonprofit construction company. We would repair group homes, public schools, government housing complexes. We made sure people had a safe place to live even if they couldn't afford it." Reggie couldn't keep the hint of pride out of her voice. She had worked hard to get where she was, and she had done it without her parents' help. Now that she was running back to them, she needed to hold onto whatever shreds of self-confidence she had left. "I assume they'll have me doing something like that here too. Maybe construction, maintenance, I don't know."

Theo cocked an eyebrow at her. "You don't know your job assignment?"

Reggie shook her head and shrugged. "Like I said, it was a special situation. We only found out we were coming here last week. It's been a bit of a whirlwind."

"I can imagine. The rest of us have been preparing for months, or even years. I actually secured my spot a few years ago but then my mom got sick, and I was the only one left to take care of her. I had to defer coming until she passed last year."

"So, you don't have any family at Serenity?"

"No, but a good friend of mine is there. It's been a while since we've seen each other and I'm looking forward to getting reacquainted with him." There was a longing in Theo's eyes that told Reggie that whoever this friend was, Theo wished they were more. It was sweet— it reminded her of when she'd first met Charlie while trying to fundraise at a community outreach day. He'd been there running the legal aid table, though he'd stopped by her booth several times throughout the day. Reggie and Jesse had been trying to get Homes, Hearts, and Hammers off the ground. It had felt like they were spending more time fundraising than they were actually fixing people's homes. Normally, Reggie despised it, but that day, it hadn't seemed so bad.

"I hope it works out for you." She smiled as she remembered how she'd felt when she and Charlie had first started dating. The butterflies she'd gotten every time he looked at her, the breathlessness she'd felt after he kissed her, how cherished he'd made her feel every day, like she was the center of the world. Everyone deserves to feel that kind of unconditional love at some point in their life. Reggie hadn't realized it was a real thing until Charlie. Growing up, her parents' love always had conditions attached to it. She'd had to behave a certain way, get perfect grades in the subjects they deemed worthy, show an interest only in the areas they thought were important. If she'd fallen short in any of these areas, so had their love.

"How about you? Do you know anyone in Serenity?" Theo asked.

Reggie hesitated. She never told people how closely

she was connected to the creators of the Sanctuary Cities; it always led to questions she didn't want to answer. Even though it would be public knowledge soon, she still wanted to hold onto that secret for as long as she could. "I do, actually," she started, unsure how to answer his question without giving away the details. "I have some family there, though I'm not sure how happy they'll be to see me."

Theo cocked an eyebrow at her. "Why would you say that?"

Reggie smirked. "Are you trying to get some work hours in before we arrive?" She was far too tired to talk about her family.

"Sorry," Theo said with a chuckle. "I can't help myself sometimes. It might help pass the time, though."

"Why don't you tell me about yourself, then?" Reggie said. She would rather listen to this stranger ramble than answer questions about herself, especially when the person asking the questions was an out of practice therapist.

"There's really not that much to say. I've dedicated all of my time to my work, putting me at the top of my chosen profession."

"Naturally." Reggie fought not to roll her eyes. Of course, she would meet someone like Theo on the train ride to Serenity. He was exactly the type of person her parents would want in their town—hell, he was exactly the kind of person her parents had pressured her to become. "Congratulations," Reggie said quickly when she realized Theo was watching her with the hint of a smile on his face. It seemed like the right thing to say in the moment.

"I'm not sure congratulations is the right sentiment, but thank you all the same. I'm proud of what I've been able to achieve, but it's come at a cost."

Reggie adjusted the boys' position slightly as she was starting to lose feeling in her arms. "What kind of cost?"

"Personal happiness." Theo's gaze drifted to Miles sleeping on her lap.

"Well, I hope you find it here."

"I wish the same for you. Being around family is a gift."

Reggie scoffed. "For some, maybe. It depends on the kind of people in your family."

"I take it your family is the wrong kind," Theo said.

"My brother's not, but my parents..." Reggie's voice trailed off. "Anyway, the boys are the only thing that matters to me now. I've had a good life. It's time to give them their best chance at having one too. It's just unfortunate that means we have to move here."

"You might be the only person on this train that's not excited to be moving to a Sanctuary City," Theo said with a smile.

Reggie mirrored his expression. "What can I say? I've always been one to go against the beaten path. It's worked out well for me so far. I'm really hoping that's not going to change now."

~

Reggie tried to rest during the last hour of the trip, but couldn't stop her mind from racing every time she closed her eyes. The train was quiet except for the soft snores coming from Theo. Her anxiety grew with every passing moment until her insides were nothing but a jumble of knots.

She woke up the boys when the ten-minute warning came over the speakers. Everyone on the train huddled around the windows as they approached the city. Reggie was looking forward to seeing the smart grid barrier system Isaac had invited—it might have been the only thing she was looking forward to, actually. She was sure the descriptions of it in the papers he had published didn't do it justice.

Up ahead, a soft red glow could be seen through the gaps in the trees. This was it. They were here.

The train emerged from the trees, and for a moment, they had a good view of the fifty-foot-tall laser grid before a gap appeared in the grid to let them pass through. Reggie strained her eyes to try to make out any details of how it was constructed, but they were moving too fast.

Inside the hover train, the air buzzed with excitement. Now that Reggie's curiosity about the barrier has been appeased, she was left with nothing but dread. Especially as she watched the smart grid reform behind them. There was no turning back now. The train started to slow before it stopped at a large platform on the edge of the city.

Beyond the picturesque train station, Reggie could just make out the skyline of the Serenity City bathed in morning light. 'City' wasn't the right word to describe it. It looked like they had pulled up to the set of a cheesy holiday movie complete with charmingly painted buildings with perfectly manicured landscaping. Everything looked too perfect to be real.

Reggie could see people waiting to greet them. She quickly scanned the crowd through the window as everyone else gathered their items and started to disembark. She couldn't see her parents yet, but she knew they had to be there. She had never asked, but she was sure Isaac had told them she and the boys were arriving today.

Reggie hung back for as long as she could, busying herself with their bags until they were the last ones on the train. "Alright, I guess we should go." Reggie looked down at Jace and Miles, who were getting antsy in their seats. "Are you guys ready?"

Miles nodded, jumped to his feet, and grabbed her hand. Jace simply picked up his backpack and walked off the train as if it were nothing. Reggie envied him. Her feet felt like lead as she forced herself to walk towards the open door.

The platform was full of people as they stepped off. It was like everyone in town had come out to welcome the new arrivals. There must not have been much to do here if watching people get off a train drew this kind of crowd. Jace was standing off to the side looking over the sea of people in front of them. He was clutching the straps of his backpack so tightly, his knuckles had turned white. Charlie had been killed when a peaceful protest had suddenly turned into a riot. They had been forced to have a closed casket at his funeral because the bruises on his face had made him almost unrecognizable. It hadn't been in the coroner's report, but at some point, he had been trampled. None of them were fans of crowds after that, but it had affected Jace the most.

Reggie pulled him close and kissed the top of his head. She knew what he was thinking. "Hey, it's fine. You're safe. I'm right here and I won't let anything happen to you," she whispered. She could feel the tension radiating off his body. "Stay by me and nothing will happen, I promise. We'll stick to the outside." Jace nodded and took a step closer to her, his eyes never leaving the crowd.

"Regina!" A voice called out above the noise of the crowd. It was her mother. "Oscar, I see her over there."

It was Reggie's turn to tense up. With one arm still around Jace, they slowly worked their way around the crowd to her parents.

"Regina, I can't believe you're actually here," Lena said as soon as she reached them. She pulled Reggie into an unexpected hug.

"Hi, Mom," Reggie said as she tried to keep her balance. She couldn't remember the last time her mother had hugged her. They had never been an affectionate family. Thankfully, it only lasted a few seconds.

"When Isaac told us that you and the boys were finally coming here, I thought he was playing some kind of joke on us." Her father beamed at her.

This was not the welcome she had been expecting, and to be honest, she wasn't sure how to handle it. She was prepared for the I told you sos and the if you had listened to us in the first place; she wasn't sure how to handle her parents being happy to see her.

"Jace, look at you. You've gotten so big," Lena said. "And this must be Miles." She bent down so she was at eye-level with him. "You were just a baby the last time I saw you. I'm your grandma."

Miles clung to Reggie's leg. She put a protective arm around him. These might be his grandparents, but they were still strangers.

"And I'm your grandpa," Oscar said as he leaned down next to his wife. "You look just like your uncle did at your age."

"Speaking of Isaac," Reggie said, "where is he?" She needed him here to help her make sense of her parents' behavior. These couldn't be the same people that raised her.

"Hey, little sis," Isaac called behind her.

Reggie turned to see him jogging over from the back of the train. He must have been overseeing the supply delivery. "Hi, Isaac," she said with a smile. She had always been close to her brother. Being able to see him regularly was the one good thing about here, aside from keeping the kids healthy.

He swooped her up into a hug the moment she was within reach. "I'm so glad you're here," Isaac said as he released her. She hadn't seen a smile on his face that big in a long time. His eye drifted from hers to someone behind her. "Teddy," he said softly with a twinkle in his eye.

Reggie turned to see Theo making his way over to them. She smirked. So, Isaac was the person Theo was hoping would turn into more than a good friend. And from the look on her brother's face, it seemed the feeling was mutual. Isaac had never really been serious about anyone, at least as far as she knew. He had dated a few people off and on in high school, but none of them could ever compete with his work. She hoped it would be different this time. Isaac deserved to find someone that made him feel the way Charlie made her feel.

"Dr. Nicholls, it's been too long since we last saw you," Lena said as she walked over to Isaac and Theo. "I'm so glad you're finally able to join us here." Lena held out her hand to him.

"Isaac has been keeping us updated on your work," Oscar said. "I found your paper on cognitive recall especially interesting. Maybe once you're settled in, we could discuss it further."

"I would be delighted, Dr. Torres," Theo said, a blush creeping onto his cheeks. Reggie knew this wasn't the reunion he had been looking forward to. Every few seconds, Theo's eyes darted to Isaac, who was now joking around with Jace and Miles.

"Please, call me Oscar."

Reggie fought not to roll her eyes. She shouldn't be surprised that her parents were much more interested in the arrival of another highly regarded academic than they were for her and the boys. Reggie turned back to Jace and Miles, who were quietly watching the crowd. She crouched down in front of them. "I know this is a lot, but you're handling it amazingly well. I'm so proud of both of you." She took their hands in hers. "How are you guys feeling?"

Jace shrugged, his eyes darting over the crowd. It was enough to let her know that he was still on-edge.

She needed to get him away from the crowd soon. She squeezed his hand and smiled, trying to ease some of the stress she knew he was feeling.

"I'm tired," Miles said through a yawn.

"I know, baby. I am too. I'm sure they will show us where we're going to be staying soon and then we can all rest for a bit, okay?"

Behind her, Reggie heard her mother say, "Dr. Nicholls, have you met our daughter, Regina?"

Reggie took a deep breath and stood back up. She turned back to her parents, Isaac, and Theo, who were all looking in her direction.

Theo beamed at her. "We met on the train, actually."

Reggie opened her mouth to say something, but her father cut her off before she could get a sound out.

"Isaac, Lena, we should go do the welcome address. If you'll excuse us." Oscar nodded to Theo and walked away without even looking in Reggie's direction, her mother following dutifully behind. Isaac gave her an apologetic smile before leaving.

"I should have suspected you were a Torres when you mentioned you didn't have to go through the orientation process," Theo said with a sly smile.

"Let's get one thing cleared up right away, Teddy," she said, cocking an eyebrow at him.

"Only your brother can get away with calling me that," Theo interrupted.

"And I haven't been Regina Torres for a very long time. I came here because it was the only way to keep my kids healthy. Believe me, I wouldn't be here if I had any other options."

Theo smirked at her again. "Message received. I look forward to getting to know you better, Reggie."

"Likewise, Theo. Especially where it involves my brother."

A light flush crept across Theo's cheeks. At that moment, Isaac and her parents appeared on a small raised platform in front of the crowd, saving him from having to respond. Reggie turned and picked up Miles so he would be able to see. She pulled Jace to her other side and held him against her. For once, he didn't pull away. The crowd grew silent as everyone focused their attention on the stage.

"Hello, everyone. I'm Oscar Torres, along with my wife Lena and son Isaac," Oscar nodded to each of them. "We are the creators of the technology that has allowed us to form the Sanctuary Cities, giving people the chance to live and work in a cooperative society free from the pollution and stressors of surviving in the outside world."

"Let me be the first to officially welcome you to Serenity City," Lena said with a smile that Reggie knew was fake. She had seen it a lot growing up, usually after telling her parents something she thought they would be proud of. "We are thrilled to have all of you join us here."

Isaac stepped forward. "During the orientation process, you were matched with a current resident to help you transition to life here. If you haven't found them yet, please let someone know and we'll get you connected. They have been working to prepare your new residences for you and will make sure you're taken care of tonight. If there's anything you need, please don't hesitate to ask. And once again, welcome!"

The crowd applauded as they left the stage. Slowly the crowd thinned as people started to leave with their hosts for their new homes. Reggie hadn't seen any information about resident hosts in the paperwork Isaac had sent her. As her parents walked back over to them, she had a sinking suspicion as to why.

"Now that that's out of the way, why don't we show you your new home?" Lena said, confirming Reggie's worst fear.

"We were able to get you a house just a couple of doors down from us," Oscar said. He picked up Jace's backpack. "What do you have in here?" he asked Jace as he slung it over his shoulder.

"Books," Jace mumbled.

"You are a Torres, after all," Oscar said. "Once we get to the house, you'll have to show me what you're currently reading." Oscar put a hand on Jace's shoulder and led him down the street.

"I hear you like superheroes," Lena said to Miles. "I think you'll like how I've set up your room." Lena held out her hand. Miles looked to Reggie, who nodded. Slowly Miles took her hand. "Come along, Regina," Lena called over her shoulder.

Reggie rolled her eyes, picked up Miles's backpack and slung it across her shoulder along with her backpack.

"I'm sorry," Isaac said. "They insisted."

"It's fine," Reggie said as she watched her parents chatting with the boys.

"I have to show Theo to his place, but I'll see you later tonight for dinner at mom and Dad's, okay?"

Reggie plastered a fake smile across her face. "I can't wait. First family dinner in twenty years. What could go wrong?" She gently squeezed Isaac's arm and followed her parents down the street.

Chapter 8

"This is too much," Reggie said as she looked up at the house that had been assigned to her. It was a cute two-story cottage with a large wraparound porch. It looked like something that belonged in a different decade. It was painted navy-blue with white trim, making it feel a little too much like the house she had grown up in. She wondered how much trouble she'd cause if she tried to paint it. She glanced up and down the street to see it was filled with similar-style houses, except for the house two down that was noticeably bigger than the others.

"That one is ours," Oscar said, pointing to the large house.

"Fantastic," Reggie said, failing to keep the sarcasm out of her voice. She wondered if Isaac lived in the house in the middle or if some other poor family was going to be stuck between them. Either way, it wasn't enough of a buffer for her liking.

"Is this really all for us?" Jace looked from Lena to Reggie. The boys had only ever lived in their apartment. They were fortunate enough to be able to afford the rent on a three-bedroom, even if it wasn't in the best part of town. Houses like this would cost a fortune in the real world. Reggie wondered if they were getting special treatment, which was the last thing she wanted. She knew there would be strings attached—there always were when it came to her parents.

"We would have been fine in an apartment, really." Reggie looked from her mom to her dad.

"Don't be silly," Lena said, waving her off. "All families get a house. Now come inside." She walked up the walk to the front door with Jace and Miles racing after her.

Reggie stood on the sidewalk long after the others had gone inside. Part of her felt like this was all some elaborate nightmare she would wake up from any moment. Charlie would be sleeping soundly next to her in their hand-me-down bed, completely oblivious to the sound of the boys fighting over the television in the other room. She'd get out of bed, exaggerating her movements in a vain attempt to wake him up—that man could sleep through anything—and head to the coffee pot. The cheap coffee grounds camouflaged the color of the contaminated water it was brewed with. It would be a perfect morning. But in her heart, she knew that life was the dream now.

"Mom, you have to see this place," Miles yelled from the open front door.

Reggie shook her head to clear her mind and forced herself to smile. She had become skilled at pushing her tears down over the last year. "I can't wait." She jogged up to the door where Miles was excitedly waiting for her. She took Miles's hand and let him pull her into the house. She wasn't sure what she expected, maybe a basic kitchen table and a secondhand couch, but the carefully decorated house took her breath away. Had they really done all of this for her? There had to be a catch.

"Do you like it?" Her mother had a hopeful look on her face. Reggie tried to remember the last time her mother had asked her opinion on something but was coming up blank.

"It's beautiful," Reggie said as she took in the overstuffed couch with a blanket carefully draped over the arm in the family room and the built-in kitchen table that looked like it had been set up to be on the cover of an interior design magazine.

"I'm so glad you like it," Lena said. Reggie couldn't remember the last time her mother had looked this happy when they weren't discussing Isaac's latest achievement.

"There are three bedrooms upstairs," Oscar said. "Why don't you boys go up and see if you can figure out which one is yours?"

"Okay!" Miles ran up the stairs. Jace turned to Reggie, who nodded for him to follow his brother.

"Oh, you haven't seen the backyard yet," Lena said as she moved to the back of the house.

"We have a backyard?" Reggie followed her parents through the kitchen to the back porch. The house backed up to what looked like the school's playground, with a large expanse of grass peppered with a handful of small trees separating the two.

"Everyone here is encouraged to have a garden to grow some of their own vegetables." Lena pointed to the four large, raised garden beds off to the right.

"It helps take some of the pressure off the community gardens and allows for greater biodiversity," Oscar said. Reggie bit the inside of her cheeks and nodded, much like she had as a child. She knew they didn't want or expect her input. "Once a week, everyone gathers their excess produce and takes it to the community center to share with the rest of town."

"Isaac reminded me how much you used to love fresh tomatoes, so I went ahead and planted one of the beds with a few different types to get you started. Later, I can take you to the nursery and you can choose what you would like for the others."

"Sure, Mom. That sounds great." Her parents were being overly nice to her, and she had no idea how to handle it. She wanted to believe they were genuine, but she couldn't help feeling like the other shoe was going to drop any second. She had gotten in trouble as a child for sneaking tomatoes from her mother's garden. They were part of an experiment on soil nutrition, and weren't meant for little girls with a taste for off-the-vine tomatoes. And now her mother had planted her some out of the goodness of her heart? It wasn't adding up.

"Come look at this room over here." Oscar walked to

the end of the porch where another door led back into the house. "I had this room put in special for the boys." He opened the door.

Reggie's heart sank when she saw it. The room had been converted into a science lab. There were lab tables set up with beakers and scales, a model skeleton was displayed in one corner, and several closets that she was sure were filled with scientific equipment covered the back wall. They'd had a room just like this at her house growing up, and Reggie had hated every moment she had been forced to spend in there. She and Isaac had been required to complete an additional five-to-ten hours of science work a week on top of any homework the school had sent home. She would not force Miles and Jace to do the same, no matter what her parents thought. The first chance she got, she would be gutting this room.

Reggie turned and went back to the kitchen. "You know, we had a long trip, and we're all pretty tired," she said as her parents followed her.

"Of course," Lena said. "We'll let you get settled in. Just don't forget dinner at our house at 6:00 sharp." Her mom came over and hugged her. Reggie's whole body tensed. "Try and get some rest before then. You're looking a little worn-down."

Reggie sighed as she watched them leave. She had spent less than an hour with her parents and she could already feel all her childhood insecurities fighting to come to the surface. She had to find a way to do this. This was where the boys needed to be. She would find a way to get through this for them.

~

Somehow, Reggie convinced both boys to take a nap while she unpacked. Dinner with her parents was going to be bad enough without having to deal with two overly tired kids. Reggie's nerves were too fried for her to get any rest herself.

She was in the middle of unpacking the kitchen when she heard someone knock on her door. Reggie glanced at the clock on the microwave—it was almost time for dinner. It was probably her parents coming to make sure she didn't forget. For a second, she wondered if she could ignore it. Maybe pretend they had all fallen asleep and miss dinner completely. There had to be something in the cupboards she could throw together for a passable meal for herself and the boys. She'd already had more than enough bonding time for one day. It was best to take her parents in small doses, ease them back into her life slowly.

Before she had a chance to decide how she wanted to handle things, Miles was opening the door. "Uncle Isaac!" Miles exclaimed as the front door banged off the wall.

Reggie rolled her eyes and placed the cast iron skillet she was unpacking on the counter. It had been a wedding gift from Charlie's mom, passed down for generations. It was one of Reggie's most prized possessions, though she rarely used it anymore. She wondered what Charlie's parents would think of this place. They had both died from cancer shortly after Jace was born. It was only a year after the government had rolled back the drinking water regulations.

"Don't tell me Mom and Dad sent you here to get us. We aren't even late yet," Reggie said as she made her way to the front door. She saw Theo standing behind Isaac on the porch. He must be joining them for dinner. The sucker.

"Not exactly," Isaac said.

Reggie waved them both inside and shut the door. Miles was already running back upstairs to his new room, the novelty of Isaac stopping by having worn off. She glanced at the wall where the doorknob had slammed into the wall. She made a mental note to see if she could get some wall shields. This place certainly wasn't Miles-proof.

"They asked that we swing by on our way to dinner so you wouldn't get lost," Isaac said.

"They live two doors down." Reggie waved her hand in the direction of her parent's house. "Thanks for that, by the way."

Isaac held up his hands in surrender. "You were eligible for a house because of the kids and there were only so many open. I'm not in charge of housing assignments."

"Likely excuse," Reggie said with a smirk. She glanced over her shoulder at her partially unpacked kitchen. "What do you think are the chances of me getting out of dinner so I can finish unpacking?"

"Oh, less than zero. If you don't show up, Mom will make us walk dinner down to you, and then she'll want to help you unpack," Isaac said. Reggie groaned in response. "Believe me, going to dinner is the better option."

"I take it you don't get along with your parents?" Theo asked. He was leaning on the wall next to the door. His gaze kept drifting to Isaac every few seconds.

"It's a little more complicated than that." She looked to Isaac before saying more. She didn't want to jeopardize whatever was happening between him and Theo. Isaac shrugged, giving her permission to continue. Reggie quickly scanned the room to make sure the boys weren't listening. She didn't want to burden them with this. "Our parents had a very specific vision for what our lives should look like. Isaac always fit; I didn't. It's caused a lot of tension over the years."

Isaac let out a huge laugh. "That might be the nicest way you've ever explained your relationship with Mom and Dad."

Reggie threw a dish towel she had just unpacked at Isaac. "You sure you don't want to bail on what is sure to be a stellar family dinner?" she asked to Theo.

"Are you kidding? I'm looking forward to it even more now. I spent some time doing family counseling early in my career. It'll be good practice." Theo winked at her.

"You always were a glutton for punishment." Isaac playfully nudged Teho with his shoulder.

"I guess we should be going, then," Reggie said with a resigned sigh. She walked over to the stairs and called up to the boys. "I wouldn't want to be assigned a ten-page research paper on the invention of the clock."

"She's kidding, right?" Theo asked Isaac.

"Oh, you'll see," Reggie said as she helped Miles

with his shoes, one of which had managed to find its way under the couch.

"I guess I never really told you much about growing up with my parents," Isaac said to Theo.

Reggie smirked as she grabbed their jackets off the back of the kitchen chair and passed them to the boys. She followed Isaac and Theo out the door. She wanted to believe that Theo joining them would make her parents easier to deal with, but she knew deep-down that wouldn't be the case. Having company had never saved her from her parents' scrutiny before. Why should it now?

Chapter 9

It was weird walking into her parents' house for the first time. It felt very similar to the house she had grown up in, with the same laboratory level of cleanliness, minimalist decorations, and sterile color palette. This was not a house that welcomed you inside and allowed you to relax; this was an extension of the classrooms and labs where her parents had always felt the most comfortable.

A few pieces of antique furniture were scattered around the house, most of which she recognized. The ornate trophy case was situated so that it would be one of the first things company would see upon entering the house. During her childhood, it had been filled with awards Isaac had won at various science fairs and expos. Nothing of Reggie's had ever been displayed there, not even when she'd won the master mechanic award from her shop class as a freshman—an award normally given to a senior. Seeing it sitting on top of the pile of junk mail on the counter had hurt, but she wasn't surprised by her father's behavior. That wasn't the type of award she should be winning. Deflated, she had left it there, knowing it would eventually end up in the trash. She was shocked to find it hiding under her blankets on her bed two days later. It was now framed. He'd never mentioned it, but she knew Isaac had saved it for her. She still had it, tucked away in a small box of keepsakes she had brought with them.

She moved closer to the cabinet as her parents fussed over the boys. Inside she saw the usual awards and certificates, plus a few new ones specific to the technology used to make the Sanctuary Cities a reality. She was surprised to see small, framed baby pictures of Jace and Miles on the top shelf—finally, something she had done was worthy of the display case. She looked over at her boys. Of all the things she had accomplished, Miles and Jace were what she was the proudest of.

"Thank you so much for having me over for dinner," Theo said to Lena. Reggie hadn't realized her parents had entered the room. She cursed herself for getting distracted. She'd need to keep her focus if she had any hope of protecting the boys and herself from their criticism. She really should have tried harder to get some sleep.

"Of course," her mom said as she waved a hand at Theo. "Isaac is your host, and trust me, you don't want to eat whatever he would have made."

"I didn't realize there was anything that Isaac wasn't good at," Theo said with a conspiratorial wink in Reggie's direction. She was glad she wasn't the only one to poke fun at Isaac's constant perfectionism. At least Isaac never made a habit of relishing his success.

"You still look tired, Regina," Oscar said. "Did you get any rest after we left?"

Reggie turned towards her dad with a smile they all knew was fake. "This is just how I look."

Oscar looked her up and down with his lips pursed. "Yes, well, you'll have to work a little harder to keep yourself presentable, now that you're here."

Reggie felt her hands clench. She went to take a step closer to her father, ready to tell him off, but felt a hand on her arm gently holding her back.

"It's not worth it," Isaac whispered in her ear. He stepped in front of her and started to talk to their dad about the work. Reggie was grateful for the break while she got her emotions under control.

"For what it's worth, I think you look great," Theo said. "Though you really aren't my type."

Reggie smiled despite herself.

"Dinner is just about ready. Everyone, come in and sit down." Lena ushered them all into a large dining room off the foyer. The table was set with the fancy dishes they only used for special occasions, complete with elaborate candelabras and intricately folded cloth napkins.

"This can't be because of me, can it?" Reggie whispered to Isaac as she looked over the elaborate table setting.

"Don't be ridiculous. This is for Theo. He does have two PhDs after all," Isaac said with a smirk.

Reggie bit the inside of her cheek to keep herself from laughing while she gently elbowed Isaac in the stomach. Growing up, they had hosted many highly acclaimed academics. Reggie and Isaac had made a game of trying to figure out how many doctorate degrees their guest had based on how over-the-top the decor was.

Reggie took a seat between Isaac and Miles. Jace was across from her sitting next to Theo who was trying to engage him in conversation. From what Reggie could hear, it wasn't going well. She had told him to leave his books at the house, saying it would be rude to read during dinner, but really, she didn't want to expose him to her parents' questioning. She was sure that whatever he was reading wouldn't be what her parents deemed appropriate. Jace typically read books on social issues, not the hard sciences her parents thought were the only things worth studying.

Lena walked out from the kitchen with a large bowl of salad. "I hope everyone's good with porkchops," she said as she set the bowl down. "I know they're Regina's favorite."

Reggie had picked the worst time to take a sip of water, and nearly choked on it at her mother's words. She had no idea how to respond. She actually hated porkchops and hadn't eaten them in years, but she didn't think pointing that out would do any good.

"Mom, if they're your favorite, why have you never made them before?" Jace asked. Next to her Isaac snickered, quickly taking a sip of his water to cover it up.

He might have been a brilliant scientist, but he clearly hadn't let go of that dorky teen who could always find the humor in every uncomfortable situation. As annoying as it was in this particular moment, Reggie loved that he hadn't lost that side of himself.

"Um," Reggie said as she glanced at her parents who were looking at her expectantly. "I guess my tastes must have changed over the years. Besides, they're expensive."

"Am I going to like them?" Miles asked.

"Of course you are," Reggie said to avoid the disapproving looks coming from her parents. "You've had pork before in Mrs. Elmenheimer's meatballs, and you love those."

"Let's get started on the salad." Oscar picked up the bowl and handed it to Theo. "Lena grew all the vegetables."

Theo put some into his bowl before passing it to Jace. Reggie shot him a look as he attempted to refuse. Thankfully, he understood what she was trying to tell him, and put a small portion of salad into his bowl before passing it across the table to her. Fresh vegetables were also outside of her normal budget. She wondered if there would be anything that her kids would actually want to eat.

"Mom, is this safe to drink?" Jace held up his glass of water and examined it closely.

"What a ridiculous thing to ask," Oscar said. "All the water here has been cleaned and purified. You don't have to worry about things like that anymore." He turned to Reggie. "Your children should have a better understanding of what the Sanctuary Cities are, and why we built them. This is basic stuff, Regina. I can't believe you chose to raise them in an environment where they have to question if their water is safe to drink and you can't afford to feed them decent food."

Reggie crumpled her napkin in her fist. "My children are perfectly fine. We've managed just fine without your input. So don't act like you have any idea what life is like out in the real world. You've been holed up here for so long, you can't even begin to comprehend what our lives were like." Reggie needed to get her anger under control fast. There was still a lot of dinner left to get through.

"Oscar, why don't you come help me get the rest of the food?" Lean tapped him on the shoulder and they both disappeared into the kitchen.

"Did I do something wrong?" Jace looked at the closed kitchen door.

"No," Reggie said. "Your grandparents just have a different way of communicating," she said carefully. She didn't know how to explain to him that this was about her and her failures, not him.

"I don't like this." Miles pushed the leaves of his salad around the bowl.

"Just eat what you can, okay?" Reggie said, rubbing a hand over her forehead. "We don't want to hurt your grandmother's feelings." That was, if she had any, but Reggie didn't say that part out loud.

"I made sure your house was stocked with stuff to make peanut butter and jelly sandwiches," Isaac said with a conspiratorial wink.

"Thank you," Reggie said, then turned to the boys.

"Let's just get through dinner and then I'll make you something else to eat when we get back to our house if you're still hungry. Deal?" She held out her hands to Miles and Jace.

"Deal," Miles said quickly, and made a show of shaking her hand.

"What about not wasting food?" Jace asked.

"Not an issue tonight." Reggie shot Isaac a look out of the corner of her eye to see if he would say anything. Most of the time he would side with her, but she had been burned by him more than once growing up, when he would unexpectedly side with their parents. "As long as you eat a few bites of whatever grandma brings out, I'll be happy."

A small smile crossed Jace's lips as he finally reached across the table and shook her hand. It was the first smile she had seen from him in months.

Lena and Oscar returned with arms loaded down with food. Reggie was happy to see the boys put a little of every dish on their plates. Reggie took a deep breath and prepared to force herself to eat the massive pork chop her father had put on her plate. She also wished it was a PB&J.

"Dr. Nicholls," Oscar said once he had reclaimed his seat, "tell us about your research."

Theo glanced at Isaac before answering. Reggie wondered if he was concerned about being the center of attention after watching her father interact with her. "I've been doing a lot of work regarding memory suppression and recall."

"Working towards a cure for Alzheimer's?" Lena

asked.

"Yes, among other things. At a high level, I'm trying to get a better understanding of how and why the brain stores and recalls data. I've had some luck with memory suppression in clinical trials," Theo said.

"Why would you want to suppress someone's memories?" Reggie coated the piece of porkchop on her fork with applesauce to try to mask the flavor of the meat.

"We're looking at it as a treatment method for patients who have experienced trauma. The thought is, if we can suppress the traumatic memory and then allow them to recall small pieces of it at a time, we can make the healing process easier."

Reggie nodded before fixing her attention on her food. She could understand the logic behind what Theo said, but she wasn't sure she agreed with it. The last thing she wanted to do was forget Charlie. She didn't think it would be easier to handle his death if she had to relive that day bit-by-bit. No. Grief was supposed to be painful. Losing Charlie had hurt so much because she had loved him so much. Suppressing her memories of him would have taken away what their relationship had meant. It would have been like erasing him from the world, and she could never do that.

"Do you plan to continue your work now that you're here?" Lena asked.

"I do," Theo said, and Reggie made a mental note not to sign up for any of his trails. "Though I already have a pretty full patient load as well, so I'm not sure how much time I'll have to devote to it. It's been years since I worked directly with patients. I'm looking forward to getting back into it."

"You know, I studied neurobiology. I only went as far as my Master's, but I'd be happy to lend my services should you ever need help," Oscar said.

"I'll keep that in mind. Thank you," Theo said as he shifted in his seat.

"Oh, Regina, that reminds me," Lena said. "There's this surgeon at the hospital I need to introduce you to."

"Mom, now might not be the best time," Isaac said, but Lena waved him off.

"His name is Aaron Standforth. He's been here about two years now. Very nice young man, hard worker, great with kids."

"What does any of that have to do with me?" Reggie looked around the table. Her parents were beaming but Isaac looked like he wanted to crawl under the table until the topic of conversation changed.

"I've told him all about you and he's looking forward to meeting you," Lena said noncommittally.

"Wait, are you trying to set me up?" This couldn't be happening. She had to have been reading the situation wrong. Her mother had never cared about her love life. She certainly hadn't cared when Reggie had first met Charlie, and had made it clear that they were only attending the wedding out of obligation. Where was this interest coming from now?

"There's no harm in having dinner with him and seeing if there's a connection," Lena said.

This couldn't be happening. "Charlie's only been gone a year. I'm not ready to start seeing anyone else."

Somehow, she managed to keep her voice even.

"Who's Charlie?" Lena asked.

"I'm sorry, what?" Hints of her building anger were starting to break through.

"Oh, wait," Oscar said, "isn't Charlie the young man you started your little company with? I don't see how your business partner dying would stop you from going on a date."

"This is a joke, right?" Reggie looked from Lena to Oscar. Out of the corner of her eye, she saw Isaac slump down in his chair. "Charlie Stone, my husband of eighteen years and father of your grandsons."

"Right, of course," Lena said. "Is he going to be joining us tonight? I can go get another plate."

Reggie was at a loss for words. She knew her parents didn't have much interest in her life, but to not even remember Charlie was unforgivable. Her eyes locked with Jace's across the table. She could see the hurt on his face, and her anger grew. Charlie was Jace's hero. "If you'll excuse me," she said, rising to her feet. "I need to get some air." If she stayed at the table, she knew she would lose it, and the last thing she wanted was for Jace and Miles to see that side of her. She wouldn't let her parents change the way her kids saw her.

~

Reggie leaned against the railing on the front porch of her parent's house. She desperately wanted to leave, but she wouldn't abandon her kids. She just needed to get her anger in check before she went back inside, which was turning out to be harder to do than she thought. It would help if she knew exactly what she was feeling. Part of her wanted to scream until her voice was gone, while the other part wanted to curl up into a ball and cry until she had no more tears left. Instead, she just stood there with her eyes closed and took deep, cleansing breaths.

She didn't know what to make of the fact that her parents seemed to have no memory of Charlie. Was that why they didn't call after he died? She knew Charlie and her parents had never gotten along, but she assumed that they cared about him on some level, even if it was only out of a sense of obligation to her. Now it was clear that wasn't the case.

"That was an interesting dinner," Theo said behind her.

Reggie turned to face him. "I tried to warn you."

"Is it always like that?"

"Honestly, that really wasn't that bad. I don't know why it bothered me so much. They've certainly said worse things to me before. It's just been such a long time since I saw them. I guess I wasn't as prepared for them as I thought." She wasn't sure why she was apologizing, especially to Theo. She barely knew him. She shouldn't have cared what he thought of her, but for some reason she did.

Theo leaned next to her. "Are you okay?" He didn't look at her; instead, his gaze was fixed across the street, just as hers had been.

Reggie looked at him closer. There were a few wrinkles around his brown eyes that paired nicely with the small, tranquil look on his face. She wondered if that was his default expression. It was a drastic difference from the look of exhaustion her face usually found itself in. "You don't have to pretend to care. I'm not one of your patients. I'm used to this. It's nothing I haven't dealt with before. I'll be fine in a few minutes."

Theo turned towards her. "Who says I'm pretending?"

Reggie scoffed. "You don't even know me. We just met a few hours ago. You clearly have a lot more in common with my parents than you do with me. I'm surprised my father hasn't already started to put together a work schedule for your research."

"Just because I'm also a scientist doesn't automatically make me friends with your parents. I've only met your parents one time—years ago, at Isaac's graduation. The conversation lasted maybe five minutes. So, if we go by time alone, I know you a lot better than I know them."

"An hour of small talk on the train doesn't mean you know me." Reggie rolled her eyes.

"It's enough for me to know I'd like to get to know you better."

"Tell me, Theo, how many of your close friends are mechanics, or plumbers, or electricians?"

Theo looked down at his hands.

"You have no idea what my life has been like. Maybe I am the irresponsible screw up that my parents think I am. Maybe I'm a terrible mother that has neglected my kids' needs their whole lives because I'm too stubborn to fall in line with my parents' plan. All the terrible things they said could be true."

"I can already tell that none of it is true. I might not have realized who you were on the train, but Isaac talks about you all the time."

Reggie turned away from Theo once again, fixing her gaze on the houses across the street.

"He's so proud of you," Theo continued. "You know that right? You're his hero."

Reggie scoffed. "Yeah, right. There's no way that's true."

"It is. He would do anything for you and your kids."

Reggie blushed as she felt the tears starting to build.

"And for the record, my dad owned an auto repair shop, so I'm not as high and mighty as you think. I have nothing but respect for your line of work."

"I'm sorry," Reggie said with a sigh.

"It's okay. You're not the first one to make that assumption. It's the whole 'pretentious professor' vibe, isn't it?" Theo stepped back and gestured to the off-white cable knit sweater and slacks he was wearing.

Reggie smiled. "It certainly doesn't help. If you pull out a pair of horn-rimmed glasses it's all over for you."

Theo made a show of patting down his pockets. "I must have left them outside the city."

Reggie laughed and shook her head.

"Hey, at least I got you to smile."

"You should come with a warning label. I was enjoying being angry," Reggie said. Her gaze shifted away from him. The sun was starting to go down. The soft lights of the sunset were interrupted by the red glow of the smart grid that surrounded the town.

"No, you weren't," Theo said gently. "My guess is that it felt familiar."

Reggie cocked an eyebrow at him. "Are you charging for this session, Doc?"

"This session is on the house," Theo said with a smirk. "Why don't you tell me about that anger?"

She knew it was a risk to trust Theo. Even if he was being honest and was more her friend than her parents. Whatever she told him could still get back to her parents. One wrong word to Isaac was all it would take. As well-intentioned as Isaac was, he had always been terrible about keeping secrets. Then again, she wasn't sure she really cared if her parents knew that they had upset her. Getting along with her parents would certainly make things easier, but it wasn't a necessity. She would need to find her own people inside Serenity. Build up a support system to balance out her parents' cruelty. She might as well see if Theo was up to the challenge.

Reggie pushed off the railing and ran her hands over her arms. "I don't even know where to start."

"There were a lot of passive-aggressive comments made towards you in there. Most of them didn't seem to bother you. Start with the ones that did."

"It's that easy, huh?" Reggie turned away from him for a moment. She wasn't sure how much she should tell him. He was interested in Isaac, and she would hate to do anything to jeopardize that. She was sure spilling the truth of their family dynamics would be enough to send anyone packing. But Theo was a trained professional—if anyone could handle it, it was him, right? "I was ready for the comments about how much of a failure I am. I knew they'd tell me I wasn't raising the boys right, that I was a disappointment to them and our family name. I thought the hardest part would be making sure they didn't make the same kind of comments to Jace or Miles. I was ready to jump in and protect my kids. It never occurred to me that they'd try to replace Charlie, like he was nothing. He was my life, and they're acting like they never even met him."

"When was the last time Charlie and your parents were together?"

Reggie sat down on the top step of the porch. "It was about five years ago. Miles was only a couple of months old, which was why we had invited them over. I figured they'd want to see their grandson."

Theo sat down next to her. "What happened?"

Reggie let out a breath. It was easier to recall memories of Charlie now. For months after he'd passed, she couldn't think of him without breaking down. Now the sting only lasted for a few moments. "We had just started dinner. I don't think my parents had even been there a half-hour yet, but the comments and criticisms were coming at a record pace. I was exhausted and still dealing with postpartum shit, and I started to have a panic attack. Which of course my parents took as me being overdramatic. Charlie flipped out. He snatched their plates away and told them to leave and never come back." A small smile formed on her lips as she pictured the shocked looks on her parents' faces as Charlie threw them out. "It might have been the best dinner we ever had with them."

"Mom?"

Reggie turned to see Jace standing in the doorway. "Hey, bud."

"Are you alright?" Jace asked.

Reggie got up and walked over to him. She wrapped an arm around him and pulled him close. The last shreds of anger lingering inside her evaporated. "Yeah, buddy, I'm fine. My nerves are just fried from the trip, you know? Sorry. I didn't mean to worry you."

Jace nodded and released a breath. "You should come back inside. Grandma gave Miles a piece of strawberry cheesecake."

Reggie felt all the color drain from her face. Miles was deathly allergic to strawberries. "Did he eat it?" She tried to look past Jace into the house.

"No, Uncle Isaac took it before he had any."

"Thank god." Reggie put her hand on her head as a wave of guilt crashed down on her. She had let her parents' comments get to her, and she had abandoned her kids so she could deal with her own emotions. She put Miles at risk because she wasn't strong enough to deal with her parents. "Why don't you go back in and get your brother so we can go home. Then I can make us a real dinner." She tousled Jace's hair and sent him back inside.

"You're a good mom, Reggie," Theo said.

"I don't know about that."

"Trust me, you are. It's even more impressive now that I've seen your parents in action. You're nothing like them."

"You have no idea how much I needed to hear that." She gently squeezed his arm and headed back inside.

Chapter 10

After the disastrous dinner at her parents' house, Reggie knew she had to do something to take all their minds off it. Especially with the way Jace kept shooting her looks of concern. The last thing she wanted was for him to worry about her. She had to fix this. She was thrilled to find their fridge stocked with simple kid-friendly foods, including premade pizza dough and ice cream. She quickly threw together a simple pepperoni pizza and got them all bowls of ice cream to eat while they waited for the pizza to cook.

Jace had queued up a movie and was sitting on the couch with Miles. The boys were actually getting along for once. She settled into one of the armchairs to watch the movie, though she probably spent more time watching Jace and Miles than she did the movie. The moment was almost perfect. They were just missing one thing: Reggie felt the lack of Charlie's presence more deeply than she had in months. She could almost feel his warmth as she snuggled against his side to watch the movie, his arm draped over her shoulders like a protective blanket.

Halfway through the movie, she realized both boys had fallen asleep on the couch. Reggie grabbed her blanket and snuck outside so she wouldn't wake them. She opened the video call app on her phone and called Amber.

"You're alive!" Amber said the moment her face appeared on Reggie's phone. "Tell me everything."

Reggie laughed. This was exactly what she needed to put the dinner with her parents behind her. "The trip was long and uneventful, but we made it."

"Do you have any idea where you are?"

"Actually, no," Reggie said. Isaac's security measure had worked. "We kept changing modes of transportation. It was impossible to know where we were at any given time."

"Well, that's disappointing," Amber said with a pout that did not look like it belonged on the face of a U.S. Senator. "Is it nice at least?"

"Why don't you ask me what you really want to know?" Reggie cocked an eyebrow at her, though she wasn't sure Amber would be able to see it with the dim lighting. She appreciated that Amber was trying to ease into it, but this was one of those situations where it was better to just rip off the bandage and get it over with.

Amber sighed. "How did you handle seeing your parents again?"

Reggie was ready for the question—she had been thinking about what she was going to tell Amber since leaving her parents' house. She didn't want Amber to worry, but she also knew Amber would see through any lie she tried to tell. "It was weird. At first, they were all happy and excited. My mom even hugged me. And not like an obligatory 'people are watching' kind of hug, it was a real hug with actual emotions tied to it."

Amber laughed. "Are you sure it was really her?"

"Believe me, I questioned it. Then they showed us to our new house, which is beautiful, even if it is only two doors down from them. They put a lab in, just like the one we had growing up. My dad was already talking about extra science lessons for the boys."

"Oh, man, what did you say?"

"I was too shocked to say anything. I'm going to put a stop to it the next time he mentions it. I'm not forcing Jace and Miles to take extra lessons to try to please their grandparents. The lab is coming out the first chance I get." Reggie pulled the blanket around her shoulder. The temperature was dropping fast, now that the sun had set. "Things got worse when we went to their place for dinner."

"What happened?" Reggie could hear the concern in Amber's voice. Amber knew everything her parents had put her through when they were kids. She was the only person who could really understand what Reggie was feeling at that moment.

"After getting a lecture about how terrible of a

mother I am, because Jace questioned if his glass of water was safe before drinking it, my mom tried to set me up with a doctor here."

"Oh, no, she didn't," Amber groaned.

"And when I kindly said I wasn't ready to start dating, they both acted like they didn't know who Charlie was. Like, I know they didn't respect him, but to act like he never existed was a new level of cruelty, even for them."

"Did you flip the table?"

"I'll have you know that I acted like a mature adult and excused myself. We left after my mom tried to kill Miles with a cheesecake."

"Strawberries?"

"Yep. Thankfully Isaac remembered his allergy. You'd think his grandparents would know something like that." Reggie rolled her eyes to drive home her point.

"I know it sucked, but I'm proud of you," Amber said.

"I'm proud of you too," said a voice in the dark. Reggie squinted and saw Isaac making his way onto her porch with a bottle in each hand. "Who are you talking to?"

"Amber." Reggie turned the phone around. "Say hi."

Isaac bent down so his face was now centered on the screen. "Hey, Amber. It's been awhile." Amber and Isaac had a casual friendship while they were growing up. She was sure Isaac hadn't given Amber much thought in years. Reggie was trying to remember the last time the two of them had been in the same place and she was pretty sure it had been at her and Charlie's wedding.

"Damn, Isaac, you got old," Amber said with a laugh.

"Hey, I'm only two years older than you," he said with a laugh of his own.

"Yes, but it looks so much better on me," Amber said.

"I don't know what you're talking about. I think I look damn good." Isaac stood up and gestured to himself.

"Hard to say. You're not really my type," Amber teased.

"Back at you," Isaac said with a wink.

"Well, I can see that you have big plans there, so I won't keep you," Amber said.

"It was good to see you," Isaac said.

"You take care of my girl," Amber said.

Reggie rolled her eyes, though neither was paying attention to her.

"Always," Isaac said.

Reggie turned the phone back to her. "I'll call you tomorrow. Love you."

"Love you too, Reggie."

The screen went black. Reggie slid her phone in her pocket and gave Isaac her full attention. "What are you doing here?" She pulled the blanket closer.

Isaac leaned on the porch railing in front of her. "I wanted to check on you after dinner."

"It sure took you long enough. Dinner ended over two hours ago."

"I had to make sure Theo made it back to his

apartment first." A slight blush was visible on Isaac's cheeks despite the lack of lighting.

"Sure, you did," she said with a smirk. "And how did you know that I'd still be awake?"

Isaac laughed. "When in your life have you gone to bed before eleven?"

Reggie scoffed but didn't answer. He was right, of course—she had always preferred the night where she could be herself without the pressure and constant disappointment from her parents hanging over her. These days, it was the only time she felt like she could slow down long enough to breathe.

"And I thought you could use these." Isaac held up the bottles in his hands.

"What is it?"

"Bourbon," he held up the bottle in his right hand, "and red wine." He held up the other bottle. "We have a distillery here. It's one of our more profitable exports. I wasn't sure what you drink these days."

Reggie stood up and grabbed the bottle of wine. "Let's get drunk, but you need to help me with something first."

"Okay," Isaac said cautiously as he followed her inside.

Reggie nodded to the couch where the boys were still fast asleep. "You get the big one and I'll take the little one."

"Deal," Isaac said with a chuckle.

Miles barely stirred as Reggie carefully picked him up. He was too big for her to carry easily, but she didn't care. After the ups and downs of the day, she needed to hold her baby close and feel his heartbeat against her chest. She tucked him into bed and kissed his forehead before heading back downstairs. She expected to find Isaac waiting for her, but he wasn't there. With a shrug, she headed to the kitchen to find some glasses.

"Did you make this?" she heard Isaac call from the family room.

She walked back into the room to find Isaac sprawled on the couch with a piece of cold pizza in his mouth.

"Yeah." She handed him a glass before pulling out her pocketknife and opening the bottle of wine. She was sure there was a corkscrew somewhere in the kitchen, but she didn't have the energy to look for it.

"I didn't know you could cook," Isaac said with the pizza still hanging out of his mouth. He sat up and poured himself a glass of bourbon.

"Of course I can cook." She poured a glass of red wine and took a small sip. It had been years since she could afford wine. "This is pretty good." She sat down on the armchair next to the couch. "I've been on my own since I was eighteen. I couldn't afford to eat out all the time, so I taught myself to cook. Honestly, it's really not all that different from those chemistry lessons dad forced on me."

"You were always full of hidden talents. You probably would have done really well if you had gone to Princeton."

Reggie shot him a look. "Don't start."

Isaac held his hands up in surrender. "I'm sorry. It just slipped out."

"Don't let it happen again." Reggie raised her glass

to him. "You were up there awhile. Did Jace give you a hard time?" It was best to steer the conversation back into friendlier territory. She knew Isaac shared her parents' admiration for academic endeavors, but he was usually good about keeping those thoughts to himself. It had allowed them to stay close while growing up, despite him clearly being their parents' favorite. He might not have understood or agreed with all of her life choices, but he never shamed her for them.

"No. He wanted to make sure you were okay."

Reggie sighed and slumped down farther into her chair. "I hate that he had to see that. He shouldn't have to worry about me." She took a long sip of her drink.

"He loves you."

"I know, but I'm the parent. It's my job to worry about him, not the other way around. I shouldn't have let Mom and Dad get to me like that. I should have sat there and ignored them, but I couldn't take it anymore. How could they act like Charlie never existed?"

Isaac sipped his drink, at a loss for words. "I'm sure they didn't mean anything by it," he finally said. "They're so wrapped up in everything here that they forget to think before they talk sometimes."

"That's a bullshit excuse and you know it." She pointed at him with her wine glass still in her hand. "One of these days, you're going to have to stop trying to play mediator and accept the fact that I will never have the relationship with them that you do. I made my peace with that years ago. It's time for you to do the same."

"Forgive me for wanting my sister and my parents to

actually like each other."

Reggie sat up and refilled her glass. "Let's talk about something more interesting."

Isaac got up to fill his glass with ice. "Like what?" He made his way to the kitchen.

"Like a certain doctor that just came to town," she called after him.

Isaac returned and poured himself a large glass of bourbon before plopping back down on the couch. "Do we have to?"

"Yes, we do. My house, my rules." Reggie held her glass of wine with both hands as she waited for Isaac to start talking; she was dying to grill him about Theo. Isaac had gone on a few dates over the years, but Reggie was never aware of him being serious about any of them. She always thought he viewed dating as a social obligation. The only thing he really cared about was his studies, and until now, no one could compete with that. It was clear to her that Isaac and Theo had feelings for each other, and she was dying to know all the details.

Isaac sighed. "What do you want to know?"

"Everything," Reggie said with a wicked grin.

"Can't we go back to talking about how you're the family disappointment?"

"Nope. That's old news. Start spilling or I'll be forced to get the details from Theo instead."

Isaac took off his glasses and brushed a strand of brown hair off his forehead. "We met when we were undergrads."

"Wait." Reggie set her glass down on the table and leaned forward. "You've known him all this time and you never mentioned him."

"It was always casual. We were friends that occasionally hooked up. We were both focused on our studies, and agreed it was better to keep things that way until after we graduated."

"You both graduated a long time ago." Reggie picked up her glass and took a sip. This was too good not to savor.

Isaac sighed. "The timing never seemed right. He was busy seeing patients and doing research, and I was focused on developing the technology that would make this place possible." Isaac gestured around him in an exaggerated fashion. Reggie was amazed that he didn't spill his drink.

"You always were too focused on work. I blame Mom and Dad. They never taught us to find balance in life. You can have a successful career and a love life, you know."

"You'll have to teach me how that works one of these days."

"The first thing you're going to have to do is take a risk and open up. I like Theo, and if there's any chance you two can have what Charlie and I did, you need to give it a shot. Even if you can't predict how it's going to turn out."

"I'm not sure he's even interested in being more than friends."

Reggie laughed. "Are you kidding? He absolutely is. You know, for someone who is supposed to be a genius, you can be pretty dense sometimes."

"How can you be sure?" Isaac poured himself

another glass.

"I've seen the way he looks at you." Reggie took a sip of wine as Isaac rolled his eyes at her. "And he told me on the train."

She had timed it perfectly, causing Isaac to choke on his drink. He sat up and coughed while she laughed. They might have been adults, but they were still siblings.

"He just came out and said it?" Isaac croaked between coughs.

"He said he had a friend here that he was hoping would become more than friends. He didn't mention your name, and at the time, he had no idea that we were related." Reggie couldn't keep the smile off her face as she watched Isaac process what she was saying.

"I don't know what to do with this information." Isaac had a faraway look in his eye, as if he had uncovered a new data point that would change the entire course of an experiment. She guessed in a way he had.

"You could start with telling him how you feel," Reggie said with a smirk.

"Just, like, come out and say it?"

"Yeah." Reggie could see the discomfort on his face. He might have been the brilliant mind behind the Sanctuary Cities, but when it came to matters of the heart, he was clearly out of his depth. "Or you could lower your walls a little bit and let things with Theo play out naturally. Knowing that both of you want the same thing, and that all the obstacles you guys have created are gone, I don't think it will take long before you start a real relationship."

Isaac nodded slightly without looking in her direction.

"Sorry, there's no preset list of steps to follow when it comes to love. You just have to figure out what works for you and hope the other person wants the same things. But I can tell you, when it happens, it's so worth it."

Reggie thought back to her first official date with Charlie. He asked her out a few weeks after they met. He had offered to help her and Jesse with some grant applications for Homes, Hearts, and Hammers, which at that was run out of her small, one-room efficiency apartment. Charlie had hung back after Jesse left and asked her to have dinner with him. At first Reggie had turned him down, claiming she needed to focus on getting the company off the ground, but that wasn't the real reason. She was scared to let anyone in. She had finally gotten to a place where she liked her life, where she felt good about herself, and she didn't want to do anything that might jeopardize that. Jesse had been the one to encourage her to call Charlie and accept his offer. She fell in love with him during that first date, though she wouldn't admit it to herself until months later. What she wouldn't have given to get those first months back and let herself love him fully from the start. They had wasted so much time when they both knew what they wanted from the beginning.

Reggie wiped a few tears from her cheeks and took a sip of wine, hoping Isaac wouldn't notice that she was no longer focused on his love life.

"This is getting a little heavy for this late at night,"

Isaac finally said. He picked up the TV remote from the coffee table. "Let's watch something to lighten the mood." He turned on the TV and put on an old comedy they had watched over and over as kids.

"Good idea." Reggie leaned back into the chair and propped her feet up on the edge of the table. Watching movies with Isaac was one of the few good childhood memories she had. It felt right to be doing it again, even if she was too drained to really pay much attention to what was on the screen.

She wondered if this was what her life would be like now: small moments of peace amid the chaos and stress that came with living near her parents. She hoped it would be enough.

Chapter 11

Reggie hummed along with the music playing softly in the kitchen as she made breakfast. The boys were still asleep, but she knew they would be up soon. If she was lucky, the events of yesterday might buy her an extra half-hour of peace. She wanted to use that time to ensure they would start their first full day here on the right foot, and that meant a good breakfast. Especially after the junk she had let them eat last night. She knew the sooner they got into a solid routine, the easier everything would be.

There was a schedule for their first week hanging on the fridge. Reggie pulled it off to read through it while she waited for the bacon pan to heat up. Today, they were supposed to tour the town, go to a meet-and-greet at the school, and have their first round of chelation treatments. At some point, she would also need to figure out where to get some groceries. The house was stocked with some basics, but she wanted to round out what they had with a few more items the boys were familiar with. Did they even have dried pasta and jarred sauce here?

A groan came from the couch. Isaac was awake. They had stayed up later than they should have, watching the movie. Reggie had polished off the whole bottle of wine while Isaac had finished half of the fifth of bourbon. He'd been snoring quietly on the couch when the movie had ended around 2 a.m., and she stumbled up to her bed. She didn't remember much of the middle of the movie, and assumed she had fallen asleep at some point.

"How are you awake already?" Isaac mumbled as he sat up.

Reggie stepped out of the kitchen so she could see him. He was a mess—his hair was matted to the side of head, his clothes were wrinkled, and there were huge bags under his eyes. "I'm a mom. I don't get to sleep in. Not even when my big brother comes over to get me drunk."

Isaac stumbled into the kitchen. "Did you shower already?" He grabbed a glass from the cabinet and filled it with water, all without giving it a second thought. She wondered how long it would take not to have to question the water coming from her tap.

"Yeah, and I started to cook breakfast."

"How are you not hungover?"

"Who says I'm not? I just don't have the luxury to indulge in it." Reggie found an electric skill in the back of the pantry and brought it out. Pancakes would go perfectly with the bacon she was frying up. "Are you staying for breakfast?"

"Sure. Do you have coffee?"

"I haven't looked." Reggie poured small circles of batter onto the hot griddle, careful not to make them too big for Miles. He wouldn't eat them if they weren't the right size, claiming they tasted different. It drove Charlie crazy, but she always tried to accommodate his preferences. She knew it was better than fighting with him for half an hour. She prayed he would grow out of it at some point, and she wasn't causing some kind of long-lasting habit by indulging him.

"How is that not the first thing you do when you wake up?" Isaac started to look through the closets until he found a tin of coffee.

"Good morning, Mommy." Miles appeared in the kitchen, still rubbing the sleep out of his eyes.

Reggie turned away from the counter and gave Miles a huge smile, despite the slight throbbing behind her temples. "Good morning, baby. How did you sleep?"

Miles shuffled over to her and leaned his head against her leg. She warped one arm around him while flipping the pancakes with the other hand. "Okay," Miles said through a yawn. "It's too quiet here."

"It is weird having this whole house to ourselves, isn't it?" Reggie said with a smile. "We'll get used to it, though." A soft thud sound from upstairs caused both of them to glance at the ceiling. Jace was awake. "And we always have your brother to make noise if we need it." She winked at Miles. "Go sit down. Breakfast is almost ready."

Reggie listened to Isaac and Miles whisper at the table while she finished cooking. She wondered if Isaac was whispering because they didn't want her to hear or if it was due to the hangover. Either way she was glad to have someone to entertain Miles while she cooked.

By the time she finished putting the pancakes and bacon onto a platter Jace had emerged from his bedroom. She set the food out and sat down across from Isaac. She couldn't keep the smile off her lips. This was nice. This was what their family dinner last night should have been like: everyone relaxed and comfortable, simply enjoying one another's company. Reggie sat back in her chair and sipped the coffee Isaac had poured for her and soaked in the serenity.

It was short-lived, though, as someone knocked on the front door. They let themselves in before Reggie even had a chance to get to her feet. Did people here not believe in privacy? She glanced at the door to see her parents coming in. The calm she had been feeling was instantly replaced with a growing sense of dread. She should have known better than to believe this was actually her home. She was back to living under her parents' unrelenting scrutiny, even if they were in separate houses.

"Good morning," Lena said as she made her way over to them. "Isaac, I didn't realize you'd be here."

"You don't look good. Are you feeling alright?" Oscar came over and took a closer look at Isaac. Did they not realize he was a thirty-nine-year-old man who could take care of himself?

"I'm fine," Isaac grumbled. "Just came over for some

breakfast." He loaded his plate with pancakes.

Reggie smirked and nodded to the empty bottles by the sink.

"Honestly, Regina," Oscar said once he saw the bottles. "You've been here one day and you're already a bad influence on your brother," he said as if she had forced Isaac to polish off half a fifth of bourbon in one night. Reggie opened her mouth as if to say something, but she was at a loss for words. It was like they were teenagers again and she was being blamed for everything, whether it was her fault or not. She shot Isaac a look, but he kept his eyes fixed on his breakfast, the traces of smirk visible on the corners of his lips.

"Don't you have any fruit? This doesn't look like a very healthy breakfast," Lena said as she looked over the table. "Let's get rid of this and I'll make you some oatmeal." She reached for Jace's plate.

Reggie jumped to her feet and blocked Lena's hand. "What are you doing here, Mom? Other than trying to ruin what was a very nice breakfast until you barged in here."

"Am I allowed to eat this?" Jace asked quietly while looking at his plate.

"Yes." Reggie handed Jace the maple syrup. She stared at her mother, daring Lena to challenge her.

After a few seconds, Lena relented and answered Reggie's original question. "You and the boys have a full agenda today before you start work and school on Monday."

"I know. I was going to take care of it," Reggie said

"We're here to help you get through it all," Oscar

said as if Reggie hadn't spoken at all.

"That's really not necessary." Reggie's words flew out of her mouth. There was no way she would be able to get through everything if she was having to deal with her parents on top of the boys.

"Nonsense. This is exactly why we match new residents with established families. We'll show you where everything is, and how things work," Lena said. "Now finish up so we can get started. No use wasting time."

"I should probably head to Theo's and see if he needs anything this morning." Isaac downed the rest of his coffee. Reggie noticed that his plate had been cleaned; he was too busy eating to help her deal with their parents.

"You might want to shower before you head over there." Reggie watched Isaac rush out of the house. She hoped he remembered some of what they had talked about last night.

~

They had only been at the grocery store for ten minutes, and already, Reggie was over it. Her parents seemed to know everyone they passed and insisted on introducing her and the boys to each and every one of them. It felt like they were showing off their newest pet project. At this rate, they would never get through the list of things she needed to get done today.

Reggie pushed her cart forward while her mom continued to chat with someone whose name Reggie had already forgotten. Her dad had taken the boys to the bakery to get a treat. If Reggie was fast, she might be able to finish her shopping before anyone caught up with her. She focused on finding foods that Jace and Miles would actually eat.

Reggie was in the middle of deciding what kind of cereal to get when she heard someone coming up behind her. She hung her head as she prepared to argue with her mom about the nutritional properties of whatever cereal she chose. It made Reggie want to pick the most full-of-sugar-and-dye box of cereal on the shelf, even though the boys wouldn't eat it.

"Fancy running into you here."

Reggie turned to see Theo standing behind her with a shopping cart of his own. "Hey, Theo. Is Isaac with you?"

Theo reached past for a box of corn flakes. "No. I sent his hungover ass back to bed."

"That was completely his doing." She held her hands up in surrender, expecting to be blamed for Isaac's condition again.

"Oh, I know." Theo laughed. "You seemed to have managed much better."

"I'm a mom. I don't have a choice."

Theo leaned casually on his shopping cart. She noticed dark stubble on his face. He hadn't bothered to shave. It only highlighted the amused smile he always seemed to be wearing. "Speaking of the boys, where are they?"

"They're around here somewhere with my dad."

"So things must have cooled down since last night."

Reggie shot him a look and started to push her cart

again. "Just another thing I didn't have a choice about."

"I see." Theo fell into step beside her. "I'm sure they're just trying to be helpful."

"Grocery shopping is something I definitely don't need help with." She reached over and grabbed a box of granola bars. "I can't even remember the last time I saw my mom in a grocery store."

They reached the end of the aisle. Reggie glanced behind her. Lena was still nowhere in sight.

"It is weird that even in this utopic society, we still have to do our own shopping," Theo said.

"I guess it's the whole 'preserving normal' thing they were going for." Reggie looked past him. She was sure her mother would appear at any moment. She really needed to get back to her shopping.

"Well, I can see you're in a bit of a rush," Theo said with a smirk. "I'll let you get back to it before your shadow catches up with you."

"It was good seeing you, Theo."

"You too, Reggie." Theo winked at her and pushed his cart away. Reggie turned in the opposite direction and started down the next aisle.

"You're very focused this morning," Lena said once she finally caught up with Reggie in the frozen food section.

"We have a lot of things to get through today, and the boys' patience is only going to last so long." Hers was already nearly gone, but she kept that to herself. Reggie grabbed some frozen carrots and peas and tossed them in the carts.

"You don't need those." Lena removed the items

from the cart. "We have plenty of fresh produce you can choose from."

"That's great," Reggie took the bags of frozen vegetables from her mother and put them back in the cart, "but Miles won't eat them." It was taking everything in her to keep her cool. She really wanted to have it out with her mother right there but knew it would do no good, even if it would make her feel immensely better. Charlie was always the calm one in high-stress situations. She wished she had listened more when he told her how he'd managed it.

"He's going to have to get used to them, then," Lena said, reaching for the frozen vegetables once again.

Reggie maneuvered the cart out of Lena's reach. "First of all, they are my kids, not yours. You don't get a say in what they eat or how I choose to raise them. I do not want or need your opinions on the validity of pancakes for breakfast, or the benefits of fresh produce over frozen. You have not been a part of our lives for the last five years—you don't get to step in now and pretend like we're all one big happy family. You don't know me or my kids. You never have. Secondly," Reggie said before Lena could say anything, "the boys have been through enough change in the last year. If crinkle-cut frozen carrots is going to give Miles some sense of normalcy, then frozen crinkle cut carrots is what I'm going to give him." She was proud that she managed to keep her voice even. Charlie would be proud.

Lena stared at her in shock, which Reggie simply shrugged off. Her mother needed to know she wasn't the scared, depressed teenager she'd been the last time the two of them had shared a roof. She had changed a lot in the nineteen years she had been on her own. Reggie quickly finished her shopping while Lena followed silently in her wake. She was determined to get through their errands with as little help from her parents as possible.

Reggie made her way to the front of the store to check out, but there wasn't a register in sight. Lena stood next to her with a smug look. Reggie might have won the frozen carrot battle, but she wasn't going to win this one.

She looked over the walls trying to find a sign with directions for how to complete her purchase, but she couldn't see anything that would be helpful. She decided to change her tactics and see if she could find a worker to walk her through the process, unfortunately there were none to be found. Reggie weighed her options, trying to calculate how much time she could realistically waste before throwing off their whole day. She knew the answer wasn't much. With a resigned sigh, she turned to Lena. "So, how does this work?"

A satisfied smile formed on Lena's lips. "It's good to see you aren't *as* stubborn as you were as a child. Follow me." Lena's self-righteous stroll made Reggie's skin crawl, but she followed her mother over to a large metal arch near the exit. "Even though there's no money here, we still ask that everything be scanned so we can monitor the inventory. All you have to do is walk the cart through the arch and it will record everything you have."

Begrudgingly, Reggie did as she was told. After a series of pleasant beeps, they were on their way to the new car Reggie had picked up after getting a tour of the school that morning. They still had a few hours before their appointments at the hospital—it would be more than enough time to get the groceries put away and relax for a bit. She was sure the boys needed it, and she was looking forward to any excuse to get a break from her parents. Across the parking lot, she saw Jace and Miles walking out of the store with her father. All three of them had ice cream cones in their hand. A smile formed on her lips before she realized what was happening. It was good for the boys to have an adult male role model in their lives again, though she would have preferred Isaac to her father.

"Why doesn't your father take the boys home and they can put the groceries away for you?" Lena asked.

"That's not necessary," Reggie said quickly.

"Of course, it is. I want to take you over to the nursery. You don't want the groceries to spoil in the car do you?" Lena took the key from Reggie's hand and handed it to Oscar, who had just arrived at the car.

They both nodded. This had been planned.

"Maybe finish your ice cream first." Reggie knelt down, grabbed a napkin sticking out of Miles's pants pocket, and used it to wipe his face. She looked up at her father, who was watching her carefully. She had forgotten how uncomfortable that look made her. It reminded her of the looks he would give her while reading over the extra research papers he had assigned her when she'd been growing up. It never seemed to live up to his expectations. She had gotten used to seeing the disappointment in his face whenever he looked at her, but she had no idea what could be causing it now. She wondered if she really should be sending Jace and Miles home with him. What was he going to try to force on them the moment she was gone?

Reggie caught Jace's eye and motioned for him to come over. She grabbed both of their hands. "Listen to me," she said, glancing back at Oscar. "I want you both to be respectful and help your grandfather put the groceries away. Once that's done, you can have some time for yourself. I don't care if you want to play, or read, or watch TV. If your grandfather wants you to do any kind of school stuff, you can politely say no. Okay?"

Both boys nodded, but Reggie wasn't really concerned about their responses. It was her father's eyeroll that held her attention. She fixed her gaze on him to let him know that she was serious before releasing the boy's hands. "Okay. Be good." She kissed the tops of their heads and helped Miles get into the car.

"Was that really necessary?" Lena asked once the car had pulled out of the parking lot.

"Yes, it really was." Reggie turned and got into the front seat of her mother's car. If they were going to have a relationship with her kids, it was going to be on her terms, not theirs.

~

Reggie and Lean drove to the nursery near the outer limits of the town in silence. As the tension grew between them, Reggie tried to come up with something to talk about, but the two of them had nothing in common. She had learned long ago it wasn't worth the effort to try to engage her mother in a topic that she did not have an interest in. So, the silence grew between them until the only noise was the soft hum of the electric car.

As they pulled into the parking lot, Reggie could almost see the gears turning in Lena's head. Her mother was a botanist. Her focus had been on sustainable farming practices, which Reggie assumed Lena had continued here. She would spend hours tenderly maintaining the plants in the greenhouse they had in the backyard when Reggie was growing up. To this day, Reggie found herself getting irrationally jealous of plants—they saw a side of her mother Reggie never did. She was dreading walking into the massive greenhouses in front of her. That was her mother's world and it had never felt like there was a place for Reggie in it.

Lena started for the rows of greenhouses the moment she stepped out of the car, completely bypassing the main office. "This is where the majority of our food comes from," Lena said, completely unaware that Reggie was not behind her.

Reggie shut her car door and looked longingly at the main building. She figured most people would be able to head there and have a neutral party help them. What she wouldn't have given to be one of those people. Reggie wondered if the requirement that everyone maintain a garden was really her mother's way of forcing her interest upon the rest of the city. She wouldn't have been surprised if there were mandatory lectures on soil nutrients and proper planting techniques for all residents. Her parents had always loved preaching to a captive audience.

"Keep up, Regina," Lena called over her shoulder.

With one last look at the main building, Reggie followed Lena to the first greenhouse. Her mother was already inside by the time Reggie caught up with her.

"Oh, here she is," Lena said to the woman she was chatting with. "This is my daughter, Regina Torres."

"It's Reggie Stone, actually." Reggie shook the woman's outstretched hand while trying to keep the anger simmering below the surface from erupting.

"Miranda." The woman looked to be about her mom's age. "I run the day-to-day operations here at the greenhouses." Reggie was sure this woman had been hand-selected by her mother for the job. She was entering enemy waters and had no idea how long she would be able to stay afloat before her frustration dragged her under.

"*Regina,*" Lena said, stressing her proper name, "needs to get some plants to start a vegetable garden at her house."

Miranda turned to Reggie. "Was there anything in particular you were looking for?"

Reggie shrugged. She hadn't managed a garden since her mother had forced her to help with theirs while growing up. "Umm, something easy and kid-friendly."

"I'm thinking zucchini, green beans, maybe some melons," Lena said without asking for Reggie's input. "We need to get the boys exposed to more fresh produce."

Reggie rolled her eyes. "Do you want me to just wait

in the car?" She pointed over her shoulder.

"Don't be rude, Regina." Lena started off through the greenhouse, with Miranda following behind with a cart.

Reggie wondered if they would notice if she was there or not, but figured it wasn't worth the risk, so she fell in behind them, the caboose on her mother's plant train. It quickly became clear that even though this was supposed to be her garden, it actually belonged to her mother. She stopped listening all together at that point.

Instead she found herself surveying the overhead piping for the sprinkler system as they moved from greenhouse to greenhouse. In the third one, she noticed an excess of water on the ground compared to the other two. Along the far wall, she spotted a valve that was leaking pretty heavily. The sight of all that clean, drinkable water being wasted made her sick. Reggie couldn't help herself. She cut through the row of plants as she made her way to the valve. There was a toolbox sitting open on the table next to it. She glanced around, looking for the owner, but Lena and Miranda appeared to be the only other people in there.

She didn't want to step on anyone's toes, but she couldn't just walk away when she knew she could fix the problem. She was part of the maintenance team, after all. She rolled up her sleeves, picked up a wrench, and got to work. It didn't take her long to isolate the valve and realize the leak had been caused by a bad O-ring. She smirked at the simplicity of it. She found a replacement in the toolbox and quickly swapped it out.

"Regina!" Lena's voice ran out behind her. "What are you doing?"

"I'm fixing the sprinkler system." She didn't turn around to look at her mother, focusing instead on tightening the valve.

"Someone from the maintenance team came out to look at that a few days ago but got called away before they could fix it," Miranda said.

Reggie glanced over her shoulder. "Let me guess, they haven't been back since?"

Miranda nodded.

Reggie turned the water back on and watched the valve to make sure the seal held. After seeing no water seeping through she turned around. "Well, it's fixed now." She put the wrench back in the toolbox. "Are we done here?" she asked Lena.

"Yes," Lena said through gritted teeth.

"Good." Reggie plastered a huge smile across her face. "It was nice to meet you, Miranda." Reggie held her hand out to the woman. "If you need help with anything else, let me know." Reggie turned and left the greenhouse, forcing her mother to follow her for a change.

Chapter 12

Mile's fingers dug into Reggie's arm. For a six-year-old, he had a surprisingly strong grip. "I don't want to do it," he whined as he tugged on her arm.

They were at the hospital for the first round of chelation treatment. Reggie really hoped it would be the only round the boys would need. She pried Mile's fingers from her arm and knelt down to eye-level. "I know, baby, but we have to. The doctors need to get all the metal from your blood so you don't get sick."

"Is it going to hurt?" Tears streamed down Mile's face.

"It only hurts for a second." Jace was already sitting in the chair with the IV in his arm.

"I'll be here the whole time," Reggie said. She took Miles's hand and nodded to the nurse. "Just focus on me." Miles scrunched up his face as the nurse inserted the IV. She was impressed that he didn't yell or cry, though he did manage to cut off circulation to her fingers.

"This will take about an hour," the nurse said. "Regina, I can take you to get your treatment started."

Reggie turned to look at the nurse. "It's Reggie. And can't I do it here, with them?"

"No, I'm sorry. We're only set up for pediatric treatment here."

"Mommy, don't go," Miles whined.

Reggie turned back to him. "Don't worry. I'm not going anywhere."

"Reggie, your parents requested that you have a private room for your treatment. If we don't take you now, we won't be able to accommodate that request," the nurse said.

Reggie rolled her eyes and let out a small sigh. The last thing she wanted was special treatment. "I can't leave my kids. I really don't need a private room. I have no idea why my parents would request that. Is there any way we can reschedule?"

"I'll see what I can do." The nurse left.

"Mommy, can you tell us a story?" Miles asked.

"Sure, buddy." Reggie grabbed the rolling stool from the other side of the room and brought it over so she could sit next to Miles. "What kind of story do you want?"

"Can you tell one about Dad?"

"Sure." Out of the corner of her eye, she saw Jace setting down his book. "Let's see." Reggie moved her chair so she was between Jace and Miles. "Oh, I know a good one. Miles, you were three, and Jace was six."

"That's how old I am now," Miles interjected.

"Yes, it is," she said with a smile. "We were driving home from somewhere, I don't exactly remember where, but it was late, and your dad and I thought you both were fast-asleep in the back of the car. We hadn't heard a sound from either of you for a while—that is, until we drove by this carnival. Jace yelled the moment he saw the lights. Scared your dad so much he almost drove the car up onto the sidewalk." Reggie turned to smile at Jace, who had put the book away to listen to her. She couldn't remember the last time that happened. "For days after that, you kept begging us to take you there. We thought eventually you'd forget about it, but a week went by, and you were still asking. The carnival had moved on by then. You guys were so disappointed, it broke your dad's heart."

She left out the part about how she and Charlie had fought over taking the boys. The fight lasted almost as long as the begging did. Reggie really wanted to take them—she remembered seeing carnivals like that growing up, and her parents refusing to take them. They weren't allowed frivolous time-wastes like that, not when there were books to read and research to do. Reggie had wanted to cut back on their drinking water budget to cover the entry fee. She figured at that point a few extra days of contaminated water for herself and Charlie wouldn't make that big of a difference. She tried to argue that the memories would more than make up for it, but he wouldn't budge.

"I had no idea that your dad had come up with a plan to make it up to you. It was a Friday, and we were running late as usual," Reggie said. Miles giggled. "I was so annoyed with your dad that morning. I was trying to get Jace ready for school and feed you breakfast at the same time. He flew through the apartment saying he had some big meeting and couldn't stay and help."

"But that wasn't true, was it?" Jace asked.

Reggie shook her head. "I still don't know how he did it, but he got everyone in the building to help him turn the courtyard into our own private carnival."

"I remember that," Jace said with a hint of childlike excitement that had been missing for a long time. "We got home from school and there were tables set up with games, lights hanging off all the railings, people cooking everywhere. It was the best smell in the world."

"They even managed to turn one of the stairwells into a huge slide."

"Mrs. Elmenheimer made funnel cakes for everyone, didn't she?" Jace's eyes were closed.

"Yes, she did. I can't believe you remember that."

"They were the best thing I've ever eaten."

"Is that where I got Scruffles from?" Miles asked.

"It is." Reggie had almost forgotten about that. "You won it in a duck pond game." Scruffles was a stuffed dog that someone in the building had donated to the cause. It was gently used when Miles won it, but that didn't matter to him. After that, only Scruffles would do whenever Miles was sad or scared. She probably should have remembered to bring him today.

Motion at the door caught Reggie's attention. She

turned to see Isaac leaning against the doorframe with a smile on his face. She returned it before turning back to the boys. "The whole building came out that night and it turned into a huge party. Everyone contributed what they could. There were a few people who got out their instruments and played. Everyone took turns singing."

"Didn't you and dad sing a song together?" Jace asked.

"We did. Not well, though," Reggie said with a laugh. Charlie had dragged her up to sing. He loved being the center of attention. Normally she would have hated it, but that night she went with it. The alcohol didn't help the situation, either. Charlie handed her a mic, wrapped an arm around her, and together they belted out a terrible rendition of "Don't Stop Believing" that echoed around the apartment courtyard like a war cry. "It was an incredible night. Your dad had this way of bringing people together. I'd never seen anything like it until I met him."

"I miss him," Miles said softly.

Reggie rolled her chair closer so that she could reach Miles's hand. "I know, buddy. Me too."

"Me three," Jace said, his eyes downcast.

Reggie reached over so she could hold his hand as well. "He's always with us, though. He's in your smile, Miles, and your love of reading, Jace. He lives in our memories and our hearts. As long as we have that, he'll never really be gone."

Miles scrunched up his eyes. "Then I'm going to make sure I remember him every day so that he never leaves me."

"That's a good idea." Reggie stood up.

The nurse was back to remove the boy's IV. Reggie stepped over to the door to give her room to work. "What are you doing here?" she asked Isaac, who was still leaning in the doorway. Reggie didn't take her eyes off the boys in case they needed her.

"I brought Theo up for his first treatment and found out that you pushed yours back so you could stay with the boys. I figured I could take them back to your house, so they aren't bored out of their minds waiting for you to finish up."

"Thanks," Reggie said. "I had no idea how I was going to keep them entertained while I got my treatment."

"It seemed like you were doing a pretty good job keeping them entertained."

Reggie shrugged as she watched Jace and Miles.

"Was all of that true?" Isaac asked.

"Every word."

"Charlie was a pretty incredible person."

"He was. A better man never lived." Reggie quickly wiped a tear from her eye. She didn't want the boys to see her cry.

"I'm sorry," Isaac said. "I shouldn't have said anything."

"No, it's fine. I'm glad you did. It was hard at first to talk about Charlie, but every day, it gets a little easier. Besides, it's important for the boys to hear stories about their dad. It will help keep him alive."

"Mrs. Stone," the nurse said as she walked over to Reggie and Isaac. "You guys are all set. They both did great. We'll check their blood again in a week to see where their levels are, but given how low they were to start, I'd be shocked if they needed another round of treatment."

"Thank you," Reggie said to the nurse who slipped past them and out the door. "Alright, boys, Uncle Isaac is going to take you home so you don't have to sit here while I get my treatment."

"I mean, we might swing by the ice cream shop on the way home," Isaac said casually.

"Dad already got them ice cream today," Reggie said.

"I'm not sure if you're aware of this, but there's no law here stating you can only have ice cream once a day."

"Yay! Ice cream," Miles said as he jumped out of the door.

"Thanks, Uncle Isaac." Jace followed Miles out in the hallway.

"You're going to spoil them," Reggie said as she watched the boys with a smile.

"I sure hope so. That is my plan, after all." Isaac winked at her and took off after the boys.

~

No one came to get her after the boys were done, so Reggie was left to try to find her way to the treatment room for her appointment on her own. The only thing she knew for sure was that she needed to get out of the children's wing of the hospital.

She walked back towards the main entrance, hoping she would come across someone who could point her in the right direction. She didn't want to be late, especially after insisting they reschedule at the last second.

At the end of the hall, a man in a white lab coat stood looking at a chart. She hated to bother him, but he was the only person she had seen since leaving pediatrics. "Excuse me," Reggie said as she approached him.

The man lowered the clipboard and looked at her. "What can I do for you?"

"I'm scheduled for a chelation treatment, but I'm not really sure where I'm going."

The doctor put the clipboard back on the wall. "I'm heading in that direction. I'd be happy to take you there." He held his arm out to usher her down the correct hallway. "I'm Dr. Aaron Standforth."

"Reggie Stone," she said as she fell into step next to him. Out of the corner of her eye, she saw his lips twitch into a smirk. "What is it?"

"It's just that I've heard a lot about you, that's all." He paused for a moment. "From your mother."

Reggie groaned and rolled her eyes. Of all the people in the hospital, she had to stop the doctor her mother was trying to set her up with. "Look." She stopped and looked at him. She needed to make sure he understood what she was going to say. "I don't know what my mother told you, but—"

Aaron held up his hand to stop her. "Don't worry about it. Isaac filled me in before you arrived."

Reggie let out a sigh of relief. "So, you aren't disappointed?"

Aaron chuckled. "I don't know if I'd say that, either. You're a very beautiful woman, Reggie. The picture Lena showed me didn't do you justice, though I'm pretty sure you were a teenager in the photo, which was a little weird."

"That's probably the most recent picture she has," Reggie muttered before she could stop herself.

"And as much as I'd like the chance to get to know you better, I get it. It took me a really long time to even think about dating after my wife died."

"I'm really sorry," Reggie said.

Aaron shrugged. "We had only been married for a few years when they discovered the cancer. By that time, it had already spread from her lungs to the rest of her body. At least she went quickly."

Reggie nodded. There was nothing she could say to make him feel better and she knew from personal experience that anything she tried would only feel like pity. Cancer rates across the country had been steadily gone down before the roll back of the EPA regulations that allowed industries to emit chemicals into the air and water without any kind of treatment. Cancer numbers skyrocketed after that. By the time the government tried to change things back, it was too late. The damage was done.

"How long has it been for you?" Aaron asked.

"Just over a year. He was a lawyer, did mostly legal aid work. He was at a clean water rally trying to get more people signed up for relief programs when things turned violent and he..." Even after all this time, it was still difficult to talk about that day.

"If you ever need someone to talk to, I'm here." Aaron pointed to a door just ahead. "That's where you want to go. I'll see you around, Reggie." He gave her a smile and headed to the nurse's station.

Reggie glanced over her shoulder as she slowly made her way to the treatment room. That was not at all how she'd expected that conversation to go.

The nurse was already in the room hooking up another patient when Reggie arrived. She knocked on the open door before entering. It was bad enough that she had already pushed her appointment back so she could stay with the boys; she didn't want to come across as entitled or rude.

The nurse looked up. "Mrs. Stone, please come in and take a seat. I'll be with you in a minute."

Reggie slowly made her way into the room, trying to give the other patient some semblance of privacy as the nurse worked on them.

"It's good to see you again, Reggie," Theo said from behind the nurse.

"You too, Theo." Reggie sat down in the chair next to him. Why hadn't she realized when Isaac showed up that it was Theo's appointment slot she was now sharing? "Sorry about hijacking your appointment." The nurse finished with Theo, then turned to start working on Reggie. She put on a brave face as she rolled up her sleeve. She hated needles just as much as Miles did. She was glad the boys weren't here to see how big of a baby she was.

"I don't mind at all. Having someone to talk to will make the time go by faster."

"You sure you didn't get enough of me last night?" Reggie flinched as the nurse ran the cold antiseptic wipe across her arm.

Theo suppressed a laugh. "That was the most entertaining dinner I've been to in a long time."

"I'm sure it was." Reggie closed her eyes and turned her head away from the nurse as the IV was inserted into her arm. The nurse finished and left.

"How are you doing?" Theo asked.

Reggie let out a breath as she got used to the feeling of the needle in her arm. "I'll be fine in a second." She peeked at the IV out of the corner of her eye, convinced the pain would increase if she looked directly at it.

"I meant, how are you doing after everything that happened last night?" he asked gently.

Reggie looked at him. She wasn't sure if he really wanted to know, or if he was just trying to make small talk. "I'm great," she managed to say.

Theo shot her a look. "I don't believe that for a second."

"Fine." Reggie sighed. "I'm nowhere near great. I've been through the whole array of emotions in the last twenty-four hours, and if I'm being honest, I'm exhausted and a little embarrassed."

"What do you have to be embarrassed about?"

"I shouldn't have let what my parents said get to me as much as it did."

"I think your response was completely justified," Theo said.

"I don't know," Reggie said with a shrug. "Isaac said that our parents had changed, that they were different now. I didn't really believe him until we stepped off the train and they were all warm and welcoming. It was so unlike them. I started to let myself believe that they really had changed. So, when dinner rolled around and they showed they were the same self-centered people I remembered growing up with, I couldn't handle it. There's a reason I left and never looked back. Until now, that is."

"Old habits are hard to break sometimes. Maybe they're trying to be better people, but that doesn't mean they're going to be perfect all the time."

"After the day I spent with them, I don't believe it for a second. Isaac's always had a better relationship with them than I have. It makes sense that he would think they're better here—he never had to deal with their unrelenting disapproval the way I did. It's been so long, he probably forgot how hard it actually was for me. I'm sure I'll get used to it again. I'm just out of practice. Yesterday was the first time I've seen them in over five years."

"Well, if you ever want to talk about it in a professional capacity, I'm here. There's a lot to unpack there. You could probably keep me busy for years." Theo winked at her.

"That sounds dangerous," Reggie said with a smirk. "All that family drama might scare you away for good, and Isaac would never forgive me for that. How are things going between the two of you? Was it the reunion you were hoping for?" Theo wasn't the only one that could read a situation.

A slight blush crossed Theo's cheeks. "How did you

know?"

It was Reggie's turn to smirk. "It was pretty obvious from the moment I saw the two of you together, *Teddy*."

"We talked about that," Theo said with a chuckle.

Reggie held her hands up. "Just trying to prove my point."

Theo shook his head, but he was smiling, so Reggie didn't think she had pushed her luck too much. "Isaac and I have been doing the friends with benefits thing for so long, I honestly thought that was all we'd ever be to one another." He took a deep breath. "I had made my peace with that. Not everyone gets a happy ending, and I was determined to be grateful with whatever I could get."

Reggie nodded; it was a feeling she knew all-too-well. She knew she was lucky to have lived her fairytale life with Charlie for as long as she had. Of course, she wished she could have had him longer, but she wouldn't have traded their time together for anything.

"I don't know what I expected when we first arrived, but he was the same as he always was. But then today, he was different. More open about his feelings than I've ever seen him."

The smile on Reggie's face grew. Isaac must have taken her advice and told Theo how he felt. After the amount of bourbon he drank last night, Reggie was a little surprised he even remembered their conversation.

Theo watched her closing. "I'm guessing I have you to thank for that."

"I might have told him to stop wasting time and be honest with you about how he felt," Reggie said with a shrug.

Theo chuckled. "I thought I was the shrink here."

"I'm not trying to take your job, believe me. This just happens to be one area where I have more experience than my brother."

"Well, I owe you."

"Just don't hurt him, or you'll have to deal with me, and I have a whole lot of suppressed anger that's always looking for an outlet." Reggie leaned forward and gave Theo her best evil stare.

"Believe me, Reggie, I never want to hurt anyone." Theo adjusted in his seat so he was sitting up straight with his legs crossed. "Now, about that suppressed anger."

"Oh, no," Reggie said with a laugh. "I think our hour is nearly up, Doc."

Chapter 13

Reggie knocked over a glass of milk as she reached across the counter for her coffee. "Shit," she muttered as she quickly wiped it up. They did not have time for this. "Boys, let's go! We can't be late for your first day of school." The boys had gone upstairs ten minutes ago to brush their teeth and grab the new school supplies that had been waiting for them in their rooms when they'd moved in. She quickly finished packing their lunches and made her way to the front door. "Let's move," she called again. They weren't the only ones who were going to be late.

Today was Reggie's first day at her new job as well. Isaac had told her that she would be working on the maintenance team and given her the name of the department head, but he hadn't given her any information on what she would be doing. She figured he probably didn't have any idea what the maintenance team actually did. He'd always assumed she was a simple handyman. She had given up trying to correct him years ago—it wasn't worth the effort.

She knew she had to make a good first impression. Teams like this generally didn't open up easily to outsiders, especially ones whose parents ran the town. She knew they all probably thought she was looking for an easy position while she'd coasted on her parent's name. Her only goal for the day was to destroy those misconceptions. If she couldn't find her place among the maintenance team, she wasn't sure she'd ever find a way to fit in here.

Jace and Miles appeared on the stairs. Miles was trying to get ahead of Jace, who was refusing to move to the side. "Can't you two get along just this once?" Reggie said with her hand on her head. "We don't push on the stairs, Miles." At least they were both dressed and had their bags. "Get your shoes on and let's go." She glanced at the clock on the stove as she watched them put their shoes on, which she had made a point of staging right next to the front door so they wouldn't lose time trying to find them. As long as they left in the next three minutes, everyone should make it where they needed to be on time.

She ushered them out of the door and to the car. It seemed silly to be driving when they could see the school from the back of the house, but she wouldn't have time to get back to the house and make it to her job on time. So for, today they were driving the four hundred yards around the corner to the front of the school.

There was a steady stream of people heading into the school when they pulled up. At least the boys were going to be on time. They got out of the car and made their way to the front entrance. Miles was clinging to Reggie's hand. They had been able to check out the school and meet their teachers, but she knew that that didn't alleviate all the stress of the first day.

It was times like this that she missed Charlie the most. He always knew exactly what to do to make them feel better, no matter what the situation was. He knew how to motivate them—like when she had to give the keynote speech at a community improvement convention. Reggie had been so terrified, she'd nearly thrown up before going onstage, but Charlie was there to remind her of everything she had accomplished with Homes, Hearts, and Hammers. He'd made her feel valued and respected. Or how he had strategized with Jace on how best to present his science fair project. And on Miles's first day of kindergarten, he had been full of jokes to distract Miles from his nerves. Reggie wished she had some jokes to tell now, but she wasn't good at this sort of thing.

A woman started to make her way towards them as soon as they got out of the car. "Mrs. Stone, I'm Ana Flynn, the principal here. I'm sorry I wasn't able to meet you during the tour the other day."

Reggie shook Ana's outstretched hand. "It's nice to meet you. This is Miles," Reggie said, carefully prying her hand free from his, "and this is Jace."

"It's wonderful to have you both here," Ana said.

"Let's go inside and get you settled into your classes."

Reggie bent down in front of the boys. "You're going to have a great day. I'll see you after school." She quickly gave each of them a hug. Jace didn't hug her back, but at least he hadn't pulled away.

"Don't worry, they'll be fine," Ana said.

"Thank you." Reggie watched as Ana ushered the boys inside. Part of her wished she could stand there all day in case they needed her, but she had her own first day to get to.

~

The front desk in the lobby of the maintenance office was empty. Given the layer of dust covering it, she suspected it always was. A handful of people walked past her while she waited, most of them didn't even bother to glance in her direction. She watched them closely. Most of them looked like they were still waiting for their morning coffee to kick in, but their faces lit up when they greeted each other.

Reggie felt herself relax. These were her people. She knew it would take awhile before they accepted her completely, but this was where she belonged. It had the same energy as Homes, Hearts and Hammers.

"Regina Stone." A tired-looking man walked out into the lobby. His face was buried in a tablet, offering her only a brief glance.

"I go by Reggie, actually." She got to her feet and made her way over to him. She offered him her hand. He didn't take it.

He looked her up and down. She was sure he was taking in her small size and making a snap judgment about her skills. She was used to people thinking she couldn't do this kind of work, and she lived for the moment when she would prove them wrong. "Follow me." He held open the door leading into the heart of the building just long enough for her to grab it before it closed.

Reggie followed him through an open office with large tables covered in blueprints and discarded lunch items. The far wall was lined with toolboxes and workbenches. There was a sitting area in the back corner outside of the locker rooms, where most people had congregated to finish their coffee while they chatted. The man she was following led her away from all of that to one of the glass offices. He closed the door once she was inside, all without saying a word.

The man sat down behind his desk and set his tablet down. "Sit down, Stone."

Reggie took a seat. She knew better than to start talking. She had worked under managers like this before. She wouldn't win any points if she came in acting like she owned the place.

"I'm Mason Crawford. I'm the maintenance manager for the whole town. I have no intention of stepping down from that position anytime soon." The look he gave put her on high alert. There was something else going on here, and while she suspected she knew what it was, she prayed she was wrong.

"Okay," Reggie said slowly. She didn't want to do anything that might escalate the situation. While she hadn't expected to be accepted out of the gate, this was a huge departure from anything she had experienced before.

"I know who you are. I know who you're related to," Mason started, and Reggie slumped down in her chair. "I don't take kindly to being told how to run my department."

"Mr. Crawford, I'm not sure I really understand what you're trying to say." She had her suspicions, of course, but a part of her was holding out hope that it was something else, anything else.

"That kiss-ass routine isn't going to work on me, Stone." Mason leaned across the table. "I received a note from your parents last night requesting that you only be assigned work they deemed appropriate for a future leader of the city."

Reggie groaned and rubbed her forehead. Her parents had no idea how her world worked and they were going to end up isolating her from the only people here who were likely to understand her. "I assure you that this is the first I'm hearing about this and I apologize."

"Do you really expect me to believe that, after getting this clearly exaggerated resume from them? There's no way this can be real." He picked up a printed copy of her credentials and dropped them back to the desk.

It was Reggie's turn to lean forward. She would tolerate a lot of things, but not that. "I worked my ass off to earn each and every one of those credentials all on my own. Everything I've gotten in my life, I've gotten on my own, and I don't appreciate you insinuating otherwise."

"Really? You're forgetting, I know your parents. I've seen how they treat your brother. I'm sure they cleared the way for you just like they did for him."

"Not that it's any of your business, but I've had very little contact with my parents since I was eighteen years old." Reggie hated talking about her past, but right now it might be the only chance she had at being accepted here. "They've never approved of what I do, and they certainly don't deserve any credit for my success. I have no intention of coming in here and trying to take over. If my goal had been to take on a leadership role in the city, why would I have waited five years to come here. I could have been running this department since the beginning if I'd really wanted to. I'm only here now to keep my kids healthy. Believe me, if there were any way for me to accomplish that out in the real world, that's where I would be," Reggie stressed to make sure she was getting her point across. "I'm sorry my parents are trying to interfere with how you run your team. It's the last thing I wanted to happen. I suggest that you ignore their request. I've been doing it most of my life, and it's worked out pretty good so far."

Mason let out a small chuckle and leaned back in his chair. She was slowly winning him over. "So, tell me—if you had your choice, what job would you want?"

"I don't care what job you give me. I want to be useful. Give me the jobs no one else wants to do. You've seen my credentials. Let me prove myself."

"I think I'll do that." Mason got to his feet. "Let's introduce you to the rest of the team and then we'll see if you're really as good as you claim to be." He walked out of the office. Reggie jumped to her feet and followed. She had no idea if she had convinced him that she wasn't interested in his job. She just wanted to keep her head down and do what she enjoyed.

Chapter 14

By the time Reggie and Mason left his office, the rest of the team had all changed into their uniforms and were sitting around waiting for the day's work assignments.

Reggie noticed right away that there was a clear divide among the team. To one side was a rowdy group whose uniforms were peppered with small rips and grease-stains. They looked like they worked hard and played harder. The other group was much more subdued. She noticed most of them appeared to be older, like they had been doing this kind of work for years and lost some of the thrill of doing it. Their uniforms were pristine, as if today were the first time they were putting them on. Reggie knew right away which group she wanted to be a part of.

"Alright, everyone, gather up," Mason called. The talking slowed down, but it didn't cease altogether. "I want to introduce you to our newest team member, Reggie Stone."

"Hi," Reggie said as she raised her hand in acknowledgement. She wasn't sure where she stood with Mason yet, but she was grateful he hadn't introduced her as Regina.

A man about ten years older than her stepped out from the subdued pack. "I told you already, Mason, my team's full." He didn't look at Reggie as he spoke.

"Calm down, Dale," Mason said with an eyeroll. "I'm going to have Reggie work with Sasha and Cam on the wall." Mason pointed to one of the women from the rowdy group—she was standing slightly apart from the rest of them with a young man next to her. "Make sure she goes through all the training protocols and get her outfitted before you head out. Alright, everyone, get to work." Mason waved them away and went back to his office.

"Looks like we dodged a bullet there," one of the pristine-looking team members said as he filed past Reggie.

"I told Mason we were too important to take on a charity case. We're the only thing keeping this town running," Dale said. He sneered at Reggie as he led the rest of his team past her.

Reggie took a deep breath as she watched them go, knowing that was the team her parents would have preferred her to be on. Thank god Mason had listened to her over them.

"Don't let them get to you," Cam said as he came over to her. "Dale leads the interior maintenance team. They take care of all the building maintenance inside the town. They think it makes them better than the rest of us."

"And he's a huge asshole in general," Sasha said. "I'm Sasha. I lead the perimeter maintenance team. Welcome to the club."

"What's perimeter maintenance?" Reggie asked as she looked over her new team.

"Only the single most important job in the entire city," one of them said as they moved past her.

"And the most dangerous," another said, patting her shoulder before heading out the back door.

"We keep the wall up," Cam said in response to Reggie's looks of confusion.

"The smart grid surrounding the town," Sasha clarified.

Reggie chuckled. "When I told Mason to give me the job no one wanted, I assumed I'd be unclogging toilets or something. Seems like working on the wall would be the job everyone aspires to get." Reggie made sure to use their terminology—it was the fastest way to show that she was one of them.

"It's complicated," Sasha said as she finished handing out job assignments to the rest of the perimeter team. "It's easily the most important job here. If the wall goes down everyone in the town is at risk, but working on the wall is dangerous. The lasers are unstable and go down all the time, and in order to fix them, we have to take sections of the wall down exposing the team to the pollutant we came here to get away from."

"And what's waiting outside of the wall," Cam chimed in. He had to be at least ten years younger than Reggie, and was easily the youngest member of the team, based on the quick survey she had done before everyone had left for their jobs.

Reggie cocked an eyebrow. "What's outside the wall?" She couldn't think of a single thing that would make the area outside the city dangerous. From what she had seen on the train, the city was hidden in the middle of a densely wooded area; there wasn't another structure around for miles. As for the pollutants in the air, Reggie was used to them—the dangers they carried took years to take hold. There had to be something she was missing.

"It's better if we show you. You have to watch the safety video anyway before you can take you out there." Sasha waved her over to a desk with a computer on it. She clicked a few things, then stepped back for Reggie to take a seat.

She started the video assuming it would be like every other training video she had watched during her career. She even had one made for Homes, Hearts, and Hammers to streamline their training process. There were the normal reminders to wear the correct personal protective equipment, the importance of 'lock out, tag out,' and how to properly wear fall protection. Reggie was about to question if this was the right video when things took a turn.

Apparently, the area outside of the city wasn't just remote, it was radioactive. They were located in the outer band of contamination from a nuclear power plant failure. That's why there was no one in the area. The smart grid filtered out more than the standard pollutants they found in the air and water, and it also kept out the radiation and the mutated animals that lived in the woods around the city. Doing work on the grid meant being exposed to all of it. And if the grid couldn't be repaired fast enough, the rest of the city would be exposed as well.

She couldn't understand why Isaac and her parents had chosen this location for their first Sanctuary City. The environmental hazards around the city were sure to keep trespassers at bay, but it was risky to build a town here. All it would take was one failure to expose everyone in town to dangerous levels of radiation.

"Is all of that really true?" Reggie asked once the video had ended. Maybe this was some kind of initiation prank they pulled on new arrivals.

Sasha nodded. "It's in line with the readings we get every time we have to go out there. Thankfully, I've never seen any mutated animals, but we've all heard the stories of people getting dragged off never to be seen again."

"They certainly don't include that in the brochure," Reggie said, still trying to wrap her head around it. Was this really better than lead poisoning? At least that took time before you really started to see the effects.

"We should get going," Cam said. "There's some safety suits in here. You should be able to find one that fits." He opened a door to a storage room. One full wall was covered in hanging hazmat suits. She had done a lot of strange and dangerous jobs over the course of her career, but this one certainly claimed the top spot.

~

It took another hour to get Reggie outfitted in the proper gear before they could head out to the wall. Despite all the warnings in the training video, she was excited to get a closer look at the smart grid Isaac had developed. Even though her passion had always lain outside the scientific world, she admired what Isaac had been able to accomplish. She remembered him studying lasers when they were kids. He'd loved to take them apart and try to boost their power. At one point, he nearly burned the house down with a modified laser pointer. Their parents had converted the guest room to a lab for him to work in safely after that, while Reggie had been forced to sleep on the couch while her room was being repaired. He had come a long way since then.

"So, how long have you guys been here?" Reggie asked as they drove out to their job site.

"It's been four years for me," Sasha said as she turned the truck onto a service road behind the greenhouses. "My husband's the chief of medicine at the hospital."

"My mom is the original city planner for the project. She moved my family out here a year before construction began. We lived in a compound about an hour away from here with the rest of the build team," Cam said.

"You had to just be a kid when you moved here."

"I was twelve. They weren't the most exciting

teenage years, but I wouldn't have changed it. This is all I know. I've been training under Sasha for the last two years."

Was she looking at Jace's and Miles' future? How many opportunities were here for them once they became adults? Her only thought had been to keep them safe now—she hadn't really thought about what they would do long-term. Would they be allowed to leave to go to college? What if they wanted to pursue a career that wasn't of value to the city—would they be asked to leave? Had she really saved her kids or condemned them to a life of isolation with limited opportunities?

They rounded a corner, and the wall came into view. Reggie craned her neck to try to take in the full height of the laser grid. It was at least a hundred feet tall before it arched inward, forming an incomplete dome over the city.

"So, what exactly are we doing out here?" Reggie asked as they drove parallel to the wall.

Cam turned around in the passenger seat to look at her. "For all the good the wall does keeping pollution and unwanted species out of the town, it's crazy-temperamental. We have to change fuses and replace fried wiring almost daily. If by some miracle nothing faults out overnight, we do inspections and try to get ahead on the preventive maintenance."

"Which has never actually happened," Sasha added.

Reggie knew the grid was difficult to maintain, but she was surprised to hear that there were daily problems. Isaac had been testing this technology for years; she would have thought someone would have figured out how to increase stability by now. Serenity, being the first of the Sanctuary Cities, had taken three years to get ready for the first residents, plus the five years it had been open to residents. That was a lot of time to let the grid go without making improvements.

"Have you tried wiring it differently so it doesn't overload as frequently?"

Sasha slammed on the brakes. Reggie had to grab the back of Cam's seat to keep herself from face planting into it. "We aren't allowed to make modifications to the design," Sasha said through clenched teeth. She turned the truck off and got out, slamming the door behind her.

"It's a touchy subject," Cam added before getting out.

Reggie could understand Sasha's frustration. She would have to ask Isaac about the policy. It didn't make any sense. Why wouldn't he want the people working on it every day to improve it if they could? He might be the mastermind behind the technology, but he wasn't an electrical engineer. He needed to get over his ego and let them fix it correctly, for the sake of the whole city.

"So what issues are we going to be dealing with today?" Reggie stood back and looked over one of the wall's support beams. She had to crane her neck to see the top of it.

"Section 145 experienced some unusual surges last night and has been operating in low power mode since. We need to get it back up to full strength before it goes out completely."

The damaged section didn't look any different from those surrounding it, but Reggie knew better than to take it at face value. The real problems always seemed to reside deep inside where it was difficult to reach. "Do we know what caused the power surge?"

"Could be anything, really," Cam said as he came to stand next to her.

"The grid is able to sense anything moving within ten feet of the wall, whether it's pollutants in the air, insects, larger animals, or manmade equipment. It then determines if it can let it pass through, keep it out, or destroy it. Based on that determination, power is sent to that section of the grid. So, a large gust of wind carrying a lot of pollutants with it will take more energy to destroy the pollutants before the purified air can pass through and enter the town. Small insects and animals can pass through with no interference while larger animals are kept out." Sasha opened the tailgate of the truck and pulled over the duffel bag with their PPE in it.

"Won't we be exposing the town while we work on this section of the wall?" Reggie studied the beam that housed the mechanics of the smart grid from afar. They would need to take the grid offline in order to get inside and check the circuits.

"That's why we have these." Cam grabbed a black box from the back of the truck and opened it. Inside were several small disks. "These will create a temporary grid while we work on this section. It's not strong enough to filter anything, but it keeps anything from entering the city."

"Cam, why don't you take Reggie and show her how to set up the temporary grid?" Sasha said while tossing them the bags with their suits.

They quickly put on their gear and made their way over to the wall. Cam handed her the toolbox he was carrying. "The only safe way to set up the temporary barrier without compromising the safety of the rest of the town is from the outside." His voice was muffled by the hazmat hood covering his head.

Reggie sensed a hint of fear in his voice when he said *outside* that she didn't understand. Cam was young, probably early-twenties, so he would have been a teenager when the city's first residents had arrived. He had to have some idea what it was like outside of the smart grid. There were dangers, sure, but there were ways to protect yourself from most of them. It wasn't like there was a mob on the other side waiting to trample them. In fact, all Reggie could see through the red glow was rocks and trees.

"How do we get to the other side?" It wasn't like there was a door nearby.

Cam showed her the computer on his wrist. "I'll set the barrier to allow humans to pass through. We'll have ten seconds before it reverts back to the normal setting." Cam moved closer to the grid and waved for her to stand next to him. "Are you ready?"

Reggie doublechecked that her suit was properly sealed. "Sure am."

Cam's gloved hand hovered over the wrist computer. "Lowering the grid's defenses now." He gently grabbed Reggie's forearm and stepped through the grid.

Reggie wasn't sure what to expect when they stepped through—maybe a tingling sensation or a flash of bright red light—but there was nothing. One second, she was inside the city, and the next, she wasn't. She wondered what would happen if they hadn't made it through during the ten-second window. She considered asking Cam, but he seemed on-edge now that they were on the outside of the wall.

Reggie waited for Cam to tell her what to do next, but he wasn't paying attention. His gaze was fixed on the treeline. She could see that his body was tense, even with the bulky hazmat suit covering him.

She walked over to him and gently put her hand on his shoulder. He flinched at her touch. "What's next?" she asked gently.

Cam took a deep breath, causing a light fog to form on the plastic window inside his hood. "We need to set up the temporary grid." He pointed to the toolbox she was carrying. Reggie knelt down and opened it. Cam knelt down and pulled out one of the disks. "These pucks will connect to the main grid system. We need to place them every three feet around the section we need to take down. When we activate them, they'll connect seamlessly with the rest of the grid."

"Seems simple enough." Reggie took a few of the pucks, and with Cam's guidance, set up an arch around the support beam they needed to work on. Cam was more at-ease now that they were focused on their work, but Reggie couldn't stop herself from keeping an extra-close eye on him. Some mothering instincts she couldn't turn off. It didn't take them long to get the temporary wall set up.

"I almost forgot," Cam said as he pulled something out of the toolbox. "Can you take a radiation reading while I finish the verification on the grid? The scientists ask that we take one every time we go out, so they can track the radiation levels around the city."

"Sure." Reggie took the Geiger counter from him. She had never used one before, but how hard could it be?

She turned the device on. It spiked instantly. She watched it for a few seconds to see if it would fluctuate before recording the reading on her wrist computer.

"All set?" Cam asked as he closed the toolbox.

"I think so. Is the reading always this high?" Reggie turned the Geiger counter around to show him the reading.

Cam glanced at it. "Yeah, which is why I'd really like to get back inside."

They moved so they were standing inside of the temporary grid and powered it up. They waited a few seconds to make sure it would hold before powering down the damaged section of the grid. Cam took his hood off and made his way back to the truck.

Reggie followed. She glanced down at the Geiger counter still in her hand and realized she had forgotten to turn it off. She expected to see the needle move now that they were back inside the city, but it hadn't changed. "That's weird," she muttered and went to the back of the truck where Sasha was gathering the tools they would need to repair the grid. Reggie set the Geiger counter down on the tailgate next to her and started to remove her hazmat suit. "When was the last time that thing was calibrated?"

Sasha looked down at the device. "It gets a full

calibration test on the first of every month, and daily bump tests."

"Then why is it showing high radiation levels inside the wall?" Reggie asked, nodding towards the device sitting on the back of the truck.

"I'm not sure." Sasha pulled out another Geiger counter. It didn't look as robust as the one she had used. There was no protective case on the device, and it didn't appear to give as detailed a reading as the other one. Reggie wasn't sure if it would be able to handle the radiation levels outside of the wall. Sasha turned it on. "That one must be faulty. I'll have someone look at it when we get back."

Sasha showed Reggie the other device, which showed no signs of radiation. "It happens sometimes. With all the funding this place gets, you'd think they'd give us higher-quality equipment. Think you can talk to someone about that?" she asked with a smirk.

"I'll see what I can do." She knew Sasha had meant it as a joke, but it was just another reminder that her life was no longer her own. How long would it be until the maintenance team realized she had exactly zero influence over her parents and brother? Reggie grabbed her toolbox and made her way over to the support beam. She needed to focus on work before she let her insecurities take hold.

~

Reggie was helping Cam take down the temporary barrier when another truck pulled up next to theirs. It had taken the better part of three hours to get the wall back to operating at full capacity. Reggie had seen several simple ways she could improve the stability of the wall and had to be reminded a few times that they weren't allowed to change the configuration of the wiring. It was incredibly frustrating to know that she couldn't fix the wall properly, and that they would likely be back here doing the same thing in a few days. She didn't want to use her family connections to get ahead, but she might have to talk to Isaac about it, if only to save her own sanity.

"Hey, Cam," Reggie called and nodded towards the truck that had just pulled up.

Cam glanced up. "That's Mason's truck. I wonder what he's doing out here."

"We should probably go find out." Reggie picked up the last of the pucks and joined Cam by the wall.

Cam looked at Reggie and nodded. "Lowering the wall's defenses in three, two, one."

They stepped through the wall together. She noticed Cam's posture relaxed the moment they were back inside. They made their way over the truck.

"Stability looks good," Sasha said once they were within earshot. "We're done out here for the day."

"Stone," Mason called and waved her over. She knew exactly why he was here now. It was time for the first day check in. She had done the same thing a few times to her new guys. She should be grateful he wasn't doing it in front of the whole team like her first supervisor had.

Reggie shot Cam a look before making her way over

to Mason and Sasha. "What can I do for you?"

Mason turned to Sasha. "So, how'd she do?"

Sasha looked Reggie up and down. "She's good."

"That's all you got for me? You're the best on the team, Sasha. You got to give me more. Can she handle this?"

Reggie thought about asking if they wanted her to leave, but she knew that wouldn't win her any points. She needed to stand there and take it while they discussed her skills.

Sasha laughed. "Yeah, she can more than handle it. This was a simple repair, but she picked it up immediately. She even had some great suggestions for how to increase the overall stability of the wall if you would grow a pair and confront Isaac about letting us make improvements."

Mason crossed his arms. "Is that really what you're doing here, Stone? Taking notes to report back to your brother? Looking for new ways to cut our funding?"

"I'm not a spy. If anything, I want to tell Isaac to let the experts handle the maintenance of the wall and keep to what he's good at. He'll never understand that what works in the lab isn't always going to translate to the real world. If he wants this to work, he needs to let go of his ego and let us help. Not that he'd listen to me. I hate to tell you, but I'm the black sheep of the Torres family."

Mason didn't say anything as he continued to look her over. She had no idea what he was looking for. Part of her wanted to do a spin so he could see her from all angles, but she didn't think that would be a good idea. It was too soon to push it.

"Good job today, Cam, Sasha, Stone." Mason nodded and got back in the truck.

"Well, that was interesting," Reggie said as she watched Mason drive away.

"Don't mind him," Sasha said as she loaded their gear into the back of the truck. "He thinks this intimidation tactic makes him look tough, but he's really a big softy once you get to know him. He does it with all the newcomers and tries to see how easily they'll fold under pressure. You did good. Don't stress about it."

"Is that why I'm the only one he calls by their last name?"

Cam laughed. "That's Mason's big power move. He'll use your last name until he feels like you've proven yourself."

"How am I supposed to do that when he's convinced I'm here to steal his job?" Reggie carefully packed her hazmat suit in its bag and loaded it on the truck.

"Just keep doing what you did today. Let your work speak for itself—that's the only way to win him over. From what I've seen today, it shouldn't take long." Sasha closed the tailgate and got back in the driver seat. "Congrats on surviving your first day, Reggie."

Chapter 15

The fog made the red glow of the wall feel all-the-more imposing as they drove to the worksite. Reggie had been working with Sasha and Cam on the wall all week. The work was tedious and frustrating, but Reggie was starting to feel like she was part of the team. Mason was still calling her by her last name, but Sasha assured her that it was normal. It usually took people months to prove themselves to the point that he would use their first names.

"I hate coming out here when the weather's like this." Cam got out of the truck and looked in the direction of the wall. Reggie knew they were about a hundred yards away, but they couldn't see the support beams through the fog.

"Afraid something's going to jump out and get you,"

Sasha said with a laugh.

"It's not outside the realm of possibility," Cam said, his gaze locked on the wall of fog ahead of them.

"I heard bigfoot prefers colder climates this time of year," Reggie said, soliciting a laugh from Sasha.

"Make fun all you want," Cam said. "You know the stories. There are *things* in the woods. Why would they mention it in the safety video if it wasn't true?"

"All I know is, I've never seen any signs of monsters in the four years I've been coming out here," Sasha said. "It's just like everything else in that video. It's only in the training to clear their liability in case some freak accident happens."

"I can set up the temporary wall myself if you're too scared," Reggie said. She had gotten used to the sibling style of joking from the team. It almost felt like she was back at Homes, Hearts, and Hammers.

"And give the team more of an excuse to treat me like a kid? I don't think so. I'm perimeter maintenance— I'm not afraid of going outside the wall." It seemed like Cam was trying to convince himself more than them.

"Here you go, hotshot." Sasha tossed him the box with the pucks in it.

Reggie went with him and together they were able to quickly set up the temporary. She did have to admit that being outside the wall in the fog added a level of creepiness to the operation that hadn't been there before. She could almost believe that there were radioactive, mutated animals lurking in the treeline, waiting to jump out and attack them. She quickly recorded the radiation level off of the Geiger counter and went to join Cam, who was anxiously waiting for her at the wall. They entered the city together, and Cam instantly relaxed.

"So, what are we fixing today?" Reggie dumped her gear in the back of the truck. She wouldn't need it again until they went out to take the temporary wall down.

"There was a small fire in the top portion of the wiring in section 204 last night," Sasha said. "The internal fire-suppression system put it out pretty quickly, but the whole thing is going to be a disaster. We need to clean out all the spent foam, strip out all the damaged equipment and replace it."

"Sounds like fun," Reggie said.

"I'm glad you think so." Sasha tossed her a harness. "You've trained for working at heights, right?"

Reggie caught the harness. "I have."

"Good. You're going to make the repair while Cam and I spot from the ground. There's not enough room up there for all three of us."

Half an hour later, Reggie was suspended thirty feet in the air, removing the top access panel in the support beam. The inside was a mess, with a white dust from the fire suppressant covering everything. She got to work wiping everything down and stripping the wires.

"How's it going up here," Cam's voice asked in the headset she was wearing.

"Slowly," Reggie said as she continued to work. "I'm going to send down the cleanup material. Can you send up the new wiring?" Reggie pulled a rope to lower a bucket she had filled with burned wiring and dirty rags.

"Sure thing." Cam emptied the bucket and reloaded it with the material Reggie would need to start rewiring the lasers. "So, what's it like out there?" Cam asked. Reggie glanced down to see him looking towards the wall. The fog had started to lift, increasing the visibility, but it still hung heavy between the trees outside the City.

"Out where?" Reggie started to pull up the bucket.

"Outside the City."

"It's just normal. You have to remember some of it, right?"

"Not really. I was a kid when construction started, and I haven't left since."

Reggie started to work on the wiring. "It's kind of like here, I guess. People got to work, go to school, things like that, except there isn't the betterment of the community aspect you have here."

"Then why do people work if it's not to help their community."

Reggie laughed. "For a paycheck. Money is the main thing that matters to most people. You want a nice place to live, clean water, good food, clothing, entertainment, all of it, you need to pay for it. Nothing's free. The more money you have, the better your life is."

"How much would a job like this make?"

"It depends on who you work for. There's some skilled trade jobs that make good money." Reggie looked over the schematics for the section she needed to rewire. There were so many flaws in the design, she'd have been back up here within a week to fix it again. She couldn't do it. She shoved the schematic back into the bucket and started to wire the system the way she'd wanted to. It wasn't like anyone would know until they inspected this section, and by then, she was sure she'd be able to show that her design was stabler. Isaac would have to deal with it at that point.

"Did you make good money?"

"God, no," Reggie said before she could stop herself. "If I did, I could afford clean water for my kids and wouldn't be here."

"You had to pay for clean water?"

"Yeah. You guys don't know how good you have it in here." Reggie wasn't sure what to make of Cam's questions. They all seemed like things he should know. He had lived outside of Serenity at one point, even if he'd been a child. He should remember at least a few things about what life was like out there. It made Reggie wonder what Jace and Miles would remember of the real world in ten years. Miles was still so young, he might remember a few details, but would he know where he came from? Would he remember why she had decided to move them here? Would they forget what their life was like before they came here? Would they remember Charlie?

~

They had almost made it through their first week at Serenity. Miles was thriving at the new school. There had been kids at their back door almost every night looking for him to come out and play. Reggie had never seen him this happy. Even Jace was starting to open up. He still wasn't talking much, but at least he wasn't constantly attacking her anymore. The nicest surprise had been how little they had seen of her parents. They seemed far too wrapped up in their own lives to spare much time for them, which worked out great for Reggie.

Unfortunately, that was about to change as they had been told they were to go to her parents' house for a family dinner that night. She knew family dinners were going to be an ongoing part of the arrangement. She was just hoping they would be spaced further apart. At least they still had some time before they needed to arrive.

The boys were occupied by the television, so Reggie headed up to her room where she could call Amber without being overheard. She tucked her legs under her and sat down in the desk chair. Her computer was already on, and she quickly pulled up her video messenger and called Amber. It rang twice before disconnecting.

"That's odd," Reggie muttered as she tried to place the call again. This time, it took a good thirty seconds to even connect, and then failed after one ring.

Reggie checked the connection strength. It looked good. There was no reason why the call shouldn't have gone through. She tried again. Finally, after eight rings and a solid two minutes, it connected.

A highly pixelated image of Amber appeared on Reggie's screen. "Amber, are you there?"

"I'm here." Amber's voice was barely comprehensible over the static filling the speakers. "I can't really see you, though."

"Same. Turn off your camera, maybe it'll help." Reggie clicked a button on her screen to turn off the camera. She knew the smart grid interfered with the outgoing single at times. As much as she wanted to see

Amber, as long as they could hear each other, it would be good enough.

"Is that any better?" Amber asked.

"A little," Reggie said. "How are you? How are things in the real world?"

Even through the static, Reggie could hear the frustration in Amber's sigh. "You know that bill I've been fighting to get through the Senate for the last year?" Amber started.

"The one that would reinstate the municipal drinking water treatment requirements?" Increasing access to affordable clean water had been one of Amber's major platforms when she'd first run for Senate last year. It was a big promise to make, but Amber was determined to make it happen. Even Reggie had told her to start smaller, but she never listened, and very rarely had Reggie seen her fail.

"Yeah. It was up for a vote today and it failed."

"Oh, Amber, I'm so sorry."

"I really thought I had the numbers this time, but Senator Bailey rallied his side at the last minute and turned enough people his way."

Reggie had never had any interest in politics, but once Amber had decided to run for office, she'd tried to keep up so she could understand Amber's world a little better. It had been easier when Amber was at the state level, but things got way more complicated once she hit the national stage. "Isn't he the one that leads the Committee for National Growth?"

"That's the one, but I'm pretty sure the only thing he has an interest in growing is the privatized water supply." The sound of the static intensified. "I will never understand people who are opposed to such a fundamental human right. It makes me sick." Reggie wasn't sure if Amber was yelling because of her frustration, or to be heard over the static.

"Isn't that the same committee that has oversight over the Sanctuary Cities?" Maybe it was worth knowing a little bit more about how this place operated. Especially if she wanted the chance to upgrade the wall so that it functioned properly.

"It is, but I think oversight might be too strong of a word," Amber said.

"What do you mean?" Reggie glanced at the clock— they would need to be heading over to her parents' house soon.

"They authorize funding for the cities, but they don't have any control over how they are run. They don't even inspect them the way they are supposed to. It's all a joke."

"Are you serious?" Reggie wasn't sure why she was surprised. The government had been cutting programs for years in favor of private business. The Sanctuary Cities were no different. She had no doubt that her parents had had a hand in getting several people on that committee elected through the promise of a batter life once the technology that kept the Sanctuary Cities protected was thoroughly tested. And until that point, her parents had had free reign to run the cities however they'd seen fit.

"Hell, I might be further with my bill if I can get your parents to tell Bailey to push it through." Static overtook the line as Amber's voice faded into the background.

"Amber, are you there?" Reggie yelled. She didn't get any response. "Amber." The call ended suddenly. "Damn it." Reggie slammed the lid of her laptop closed.

~

For the first time Reggie could remember, the boys were ready to go before she was. Granted, she had been dragging her feet, but it was still impressive. After triple-checking that her shoes were tied, they started the short walk over to her parents' house. Reggie's legs grew heavier with every step she took until she stood frozen at the steps leading up to their porch.

"Mom, are you alright?" Jace asked. Miles had already jumped up the steps and rang the doorbell.

"Yeah," Reggie said, giving her head a slight shake. "Of course." She climbed the steps.

The front door opened the moment Reggie stepped on the porch. "Hi, boys," Oscar said as he stepped aside to let them in. "Regina."

"Dad." She gave him a curt nod before entering. She tried to think about what Amber would have told her if their call hadn't been cut short. She would have reminded Reggie that she was an adult, and she didn't have to bite her tongue and let her parents dissect her every flaw. She was allowed to defend herself and her kids, and there was nothing her parents could do to stop her. She held her head high as she looked around. "Where's mom and Isaac?" If Isaac had bailed on dinner, she didn't know what she would do. There was no way she was ready to go through this without a buffer.

"They're out back. Your mom thought we should take advantage of the nice weather and eat outside." Oscar waved them forward as he made his way towards the back porch.

Reggie racked her brain for a time when they had eaten dinner outside. She remembered picnics along the riverfront with Charlie while they were dating, and big cookouts with the entire apartment building, but she couldn't recall a single time she had eaten outside with her parents. Dinner growing up was a time for reporting on their research projects, not for casually enjoying the weather while eating a hamburger. That was something less serious people did, not the Torres family.

"Mom, can I go play?" Miles asked the moment they were outside. They were still within sight of the school park where Miles had been playing with a group of kids before she called him in for dinner.

"Don't you want to stay and spend time with your grandparents?" Reggie asked slowly. She glanced up at her mother.

"Let him go," Lena said from the grill. Reggie had to do a doubletake to make sure she was in the right backyard.

"Okay, go have fun," she said to Miles without taking her eyes off her mother. She turned to Jace. "Do you want to go too?"

Jace shrugged. "Don't you need me here?" His voice was low, so no one heard him except her.

She hated that Jace already felt like he had to mediate between her and her parents. "I promise, I'll be okay. You don't have to worry about me." She smiled at him.

"Are you sure?" Jace's gaze shifted to Lena's back.

"I'm positive. Now go while you still have the chance to escape," she said with a wicked grin.

Jace returned her smile. "Thanks, Mom." He slowly made his way over to the playground. She didn't know what he was going to do over there, but she was pretty sure the new e-reader Isaac had gotten for him was tucked in the bag he had insisted on bringing with him.

"Figured you could use this." Isaac handed her a glass of white wine.

"Thanks." Reggie watched the kids playing, their joyous shrieks and laughs a soft melody in the wind. "No Theo tonight?"

"No," Isaac said with a slight sigh. "He had to take care of a few things in the lab."

Reggie nudged him with her shoulder. "How are things going between the two of you?"

"Good. Really good, I think. We're having our first official date tomorrow night."

"That's great," Reggie said. "I think you guys will be good for one another."

"It looks like the boys are adjusting well to life here," Lena said. She had finished what she was doing at the grill and was gesturing for Reggie and Isaac to join them at the patio table.

Reggie took a seat. "Yeah, they're doing good." It was surprising how quickly they had adjusted to their new life. They were getting the fresh start she'd so desperately dreamed of having herself.

"And how are you?" Oscar asked. "Are you settling in okay? I know Mason can be tough."

"He's been great. I haven't had any issues."

"Most of the maintenance team is a little rough around the edges," Lena said. "I don't understand why they can't take a little more pride in their work."

Reggie suppressed a scoff. "They take a lot of pride in their work."

"Dale isn't so bad," Oscar said, ignoring Reggie's comment. "He at least knows how to behave, unlike the rest of them."

"Seriously?" Reggie rolled her eyes. "If Dale's so good, why is his team constantly having to go back and fix problems they created?" She hadn't spent a lot of time with the interior maintenance team, but the few conversations she'd had with them had been enlightening. They all thought they were special since they didn't have to work on the wall. She had overheard them brainstorming fixes for an ongoing lightning issue at the greenhouses and offered a quick and easy solution for how to fix it. She even offered to show them how to do it, but they laughed her off. Reggie had checked in with Miranda, and the lights in greenhouse seven still weren't functioning properly.

"I think what Mom and Dad are trying to say is that the maintenance team tends to attract a different kind of person," Isaac said, trying to ease the tension building around the table just as he had done when they were growing up. He was usually much better at it. This time it felt more like he was doubling down on what their parents had said instead of defending her.

Reggie turned in her seat and shot Isaac a look. "What exactly do you mean by that?"

Isaac slumped down in his seat and mumbled something under his breath that Reggie couldn't understand.

"Don't take it personally, Regina. We value everyone's contributions to the town, even the unskilled laborers," Oscar said.

"Unskilled? I'd like to see any of you do what the maintenance team does. I know all three of you look down on my team. It's the reason why we're allowed to make improvements to the wall, right?"

"I hate that they call it that, as if the smart grid isn't the most sophisticated piece of technology on the planet," Lena said, completely ignoring the rest of what Reggie said.

Isaac jumped to his feet. "Does anyone need another drink?"

"Answer the question, Isaac. I've been working on the wall all week, and the design of the power distribution system is terrible. It can't handle the surges of energy that are required when large plums of pollution come into contact."

"You weren't supposed to be working on the smart grid," Oscar said. "I told Mason to give you a job that would better-suit your status in this city."

"And I told Mason to ignore any and all requests he gets from you," Reggie countered. "I do not have any status in the city, nor do I want any."

"But working out there isn't safe," Lena said. "We're only doing our jobs as your parents by keeping you out of danger."

"I'm not afraid of the wall, or the ghost stories about what's waiting in the woods. Maybe if Isaac could let go of his ego for once and listen to someone who actually knows what they're doing, he would have been able to improve his tech in the last five years. But that's not the case, is it? You're stuck and too damn full of yourself to accept help. Maybe then the wall wouldn't be failing on a daily basis." Reggie was sick of everyone brushing over what she thought was a legitimate concern. It was time they started to take her seriously.

"My shitty system is what made this place a possibility," Isaac said. He had done a decent job keeping his cool, but her last comment had clearly hit a nerve. "It's what keeps you and your kids safe—something you couldn't do on your own. So forgive me for not wanting some idiot with a hammer from fucking it all up because they think they know better than I do."

Reggie let out a laugh. "It's good to finally know what you think of me." She got to her feet. "I'm sure you've wanted to say it for years."

Isaac sighed. "That's not what I meant, Reggie, and you know it."

"I think it was. Those are my people you're talking about. People with the same training I have. I know I didn't get it at some fancy Ivy League school, but I'm damn good at what I do, even if none of you can see the value in it." She turned back to the table where her parents were still sitting. "Thanks for another stellar family dinner, but I think it will be best for everyone if I go."

Reggie held her head high as she left. She wouldn't let them walk all over her anymore. She was done being the family doormat. Without Charlie here to stand up for her, she would find the strength to do it herself. She would use this victory to give her the courage to fight the next one and the one after that until her family finally learned to respect her or they cut her out completely.

Either option was fine with her.

Chapter 16

Reggie tapped the steering wheel as she waited for her turn to pull out of the parking lot at the maintenance office. She hadn't even managed to make it a week without being late to pick up the boys from school. The damage to the section of the wall they had been assigned that day was the most extensive Reggie had seen yet. One of the support beams had buckled, its integrity compromised from several small fires that had occurred over the years. The entire beam needed to be replaced, which was a massive undertaking. Sasha had been forced to put the entire perimeter maintenance team on the job and they'd still had to work two hours of overtime in order to get it repaired.

At least there was very little traffic as she made her way across the town towards the school. A voice in the back of her head kept saying she should have called her parents to pick up the boys the moment she'd realized the job would go over, but she pushed it down. With the way their family dinner had ended last night, there was no way she could ask them for help. She'd rather get lectured by the principal than deal with her family.

She was surprised to see a good number of kids on the playground behind the school when she pulled up, even though school had ended forty-five minutes ago. She pulled into the parking lot and got out. She saw Miles at the top of the slide. He was yelling down to a group of kids at the bottom with a huge smile on his face. She couldn't hear what he was saying, but it was clear he didn't care that she was late. In fact, she couldn't remember the last time she had seen him that happy. The kid was in his element.

Reggie noticed Mrs. Flynn standing on the edge of the playground watching the kids and made her way over to her. "Mrs. Flynn, I'm so sorry I'm late," Reggie said before she reached the woman. She knew from past experience that it was best to get the apology out of the way first, though it never did much to stem the lecture.

Mrs. Flynn turned and smiled at her. "Please call me, Anna. And it's not a problem at all."

"Really?" This was not what Reggie had been preparing for, and she wasn't sure how she was supposed to react now.

"Of course. Mason called and left a message saying there were some repairs being done on the wall that would take a while, and his team wouldn't be done in time for pick up," the woman standing next to Anna said. "We haven't officially met yet. I'm Charlotte Crawford, Miles's teacher."

"So, you stay after and watch the kids?" Reggie's defenses were still up. There had to be something she was missing. Where were the threats, the insinuations that she was a terrible mother, the accusation that she wasn't prioritizing her children?

"Of course. Most of the kids like to stay after and play with their friends anyway. Besides, if the smart grid isn't working properly, we're all at risk. We're just doing our part for the betterment of Serenity," Charlotte said as if reciting from one of the promotional pamphlets.

"You're actually the first parent from the maintenance team to show up," Anna said with a small laugh.

"Huh," Reggie said, finally allowing herself to relax. "Alright, then." She scanned the playground for Jace. She saw him sitting under a tree off to the side. She was surprised to see a girl sitting next to him. Even more shocking was the fact that he looked like he was engaged in a deep conversation with her. "Who's that girl sitting with Jace?"

"That's my daughter, Sam," Charlotte said.

"The two of them have really hit it off. I've seen them having lunch together the last few days," Anna added.

"Really? Jace has had a hard time connecting with anyone since we lost his dad last year. He normally keeps to himself. He pushed all his friends away at his old school." Reggie's heart ached as she remembered watching him retreat further and further into himself—nothing she tried seemed to make any difference. It had gotten to the point where the only thing he cared about was his books. She was having a hard time wrapping her head around the sudden change. Maybe it would be worth talking to Theo about setting up some sessions for Jace.

"The poor kid," Anna said. "Coming here should help him. I know life outside of the Sanctuary Cities is stressful, especially for kids. It doesn't take them long to get comfortable here."

"We usually see it happen faster in the kids than the adults," Charlotte said.

"His teacher only has good things to say about him. He's quiet but very smart," Anna reassured her.

"He gets that from his dad." Reggie looked away from Jace, who was currently showing Sam something in his book. She gave Anna and Charlotte her full attention. "Have you always been teachers?" It was best not to focus on Charlie for too long.

"For as long as I can remember," Anna said.

"It was a second career for me," Charlotte said. "I stayed home when the kids were little and worked my way through the teaching courses online. We were fortunate that Mason always made enough to support the household while I was in school."

"Where was your first teaching job?" Reggie asked.

"Oh, it was..." Charlotte's voice trailed off. After a moment she let out a small laugh. "You know, I can't for the life of me remember the name of the school. It was the same school our kids went to. Isn't that crazy? I should know this."

"Well, it's been a crazy week getting all the new

students settled in," Anna offered with a smile. She turned to Reggie. "How are you liking it here?"

"It's different," Reggie said carefully, "but it's been good." It wasn't really a lie. She had enjoyed all the time she'd spent here that hadn't included her parents.

"It's got to be nice being around family again," Charlotte said.

"Sure." Reggie wasn't sure how to answer. She had no idea if Charlotte and Anna were close with her parents; it was better not to share too much in case it found its way back to her parents. "It's been great having Isaac around. The boys love him."

"Who doesn't?" Anna said with a laugh. "He really is the heart of this place."

"Right," Reggie said with a forced smile. She needed to end this conversation before they asked something more personal. "Well, I should get the boys home and start cooking dinner."

Charlotte and Anna exchanged a look and nodded. Reggie had no idea what to make of it. She was about to walk away when Anna turned back to her. "Do you have any plans for tonight?"

"No," Reggie said cautiously.

"You should come to book club tonight," Charlotte said.

Reggie put her hands up. "Oh, um, I'm not really much of a reader."

"That doesn't matter."

"I don't have anyone to watch the boys." Reggie really wasn't in the mood to spend her Friday night listening to a group of people she didn't know discuss a book she hadn't read. It would be better to stay in and try to call Amber again. There was so much Reggie hadn't been able to tell her before their call had gotten cut short yesterday.

"Bring them to my house. The dads watch all the kids together while we're out. They won't mind a few more," Charlotte said. "We live right over there." She pointed to a house around the corner from the school.

"Okay, sure, why not," Reggie said, unable to come up with a good excuse to get out of it. Besides, it wouldn't hurt to get to know a few more people in the town. There were bound to be a few that didn't worship her parents.

"Good. We'll see you at seven," Charlotte said.

Reggie gave them a weak smile before going to collect Jace and Miles. At least the evening couldn't end up as bad as the previous had. Unless her mother was part of this book club. Reggie really needed to start vetting things better before she caved to peer pressure.

~

By some miracle, Reggie managed to get them all fed and out the door with enough time to walk around the block to the Crawfords' house. It hadn't been easy. Jace made his feelings known to anyone within earshot the moment Reggie told them the plan for the evening. His anger subsided a little when she mentioned that Sam would be there, but it hadn't dissipated completely. As long as he kept it in check while she was gone, she would be happy.

Reggie hadn't given it any thought when she'd accepted the invitation, but it was now dawning on her that since the dads would be watching the kids, it meant her boss would be looking after her kids—her boss that still refused to call her by her first name. She wasn't sure how she felt about it, but it was too late to back out. She could only hope that the boys would be on their best behavior. She didn't need to give Mason another reason to question her motives.

She wiped her palms on her pants as they approached the door. She could hear the noise inside before the door opened. It sounded like there were at least twenty kids running wild on the other side. Miles looked excited, but Jace shot her dirty looks from the corner of his eyes. She knew this was not his idea of a fun Friday night. "Don't worry," she said. "I'm sure you'll have fun."

"Why can't I just stay home?" Jace shifted the backpack he had insisted on bringing to the other shoulder.

"Because you aren't old enough," Reggie said for the tenth time that night.

"Then why can't I go stay with Uncle Isaac or your parents until you're done partying?"

"Excuse me," Reggie said as she stared down at him. "It's been a long week. Jace and I do not appreciate your attitude right now. Believe me, I'm doing you a favor by not sending you to your grandparents' house. It's good for you to spend time with kids your own age." It was also good for her to get out of the house, but she kept that part to herself. She hadn't gone out since Charlie had passed. Not that she was turning down invitations left and right. She just didn't have time in her life to think about friends or nights out on the town. As much as she would have liked to stay home too, she knew she needed this. They had no shot at finding happiness here if they couldn't find people to connect with.

"I do enough of that at school. What's wrong with wanting to be at home?" The whine in his voice sliced through her.

Reggie rubbed her hand over her face. She could see where Jace was coming from; it had been a long week full of big changes. There was nothing wrong with wanting some down time after that. She knew he needed it to recharge, but she also knew that if he was left up to his own devices, he would never talk to anyone. She needed to teach him to find balance. "We all need to make friends here, so how about we make a deal? You go in there and try to have a good time and then tomorrow you don't have to do anything. Okay?"

"Fine," Jace said in a huff.

Miles pulled on her hand. "I'm excited, Mommy."

"I'm glad, baby." Reggie smiled down at him before turning back to Jace. "It's only for a few hours. You'll be fine." She stepped up onto the porch and knocked.

Mason answered the door with a glittery pink paper crown on his head. It did not diminish his authority as he looked her up and down. "Stone," he said with a curt nod.

"Mason." She tried her best to keep a straight face, though she was sure a smile broke through. This was not the tough, no-nonsense manager she'd been dealing with all week.

"And this must be Jace and Miles." He offered Jace his hand and ruffled Miles's hair. Reggie's respect for the man grew. "Come on in. There's a bunch of kids doing crafts in the kitchen, and Sam is reading on the back porch if you want to join her."

Jace looked up at Reggie, who nodded. He took off towards the back of the house without another word. Reggie stepped inside and shooed Miles towards the kitchen where shrieks and laughter filled the air. "Thanks for watching them tonight."

"It's not a problem. Honestly, I think the dads have come to enjoy book club night almost as much as the moms."

"Yeah, I'm not sure book club is going to be for me." Reggie looked down the hall for Charlotte but didn't see her. She wondered how long she'd have to keep up the small talk. She had no issues talking with him at work but was struggling to keep her nerves in check now that they were outside the safety of the maintenance office.

"Don't judge it too quickly," Mason said with a smirk. "You've done good this week. You deserve a night off."

"I can't remember the last time I had a night off," Reggie said with a sigh.

Mason gave her a gentle smile and nodded. "Go enjoy yourself. The boys will be fine, I promise. Go relax and have a good time."

"Thank you," Reggie said, thrown off-guard by the sudden sincerity.

Charlotte emerged from the kitchen. "Reggie, you're

here," she said as she made her way over to her. "We should get going. Everyone else is probably there by now." She gave Mason a quick kiss, then waved Reggie back towards the front door. Reggie's heart tightened as she watched them. God, she missed Charlie. She could see him here with a paper crown and glitter on his face, spending the evening doing crafts with the other dads. Or maybe he'd be on the back porch with Jace and Sam engaged in a heated debate about the best genre of book. If only they had been able to get past their moral objections of the Sanctuary Cities and come here sooner.

If only they had come here before Charlie was killed.

Chapter 17

"I'm excited you agreed to come out with us tonight. Mason has been going on and on about you all week." Charlotte hadn't told Reggie where they were going, so she fell in step next to her on the sidewalk. She figured book club would be at someone's house nearby. Though now that she thought about it, the purse Charlotte had on her shoulder was much too small to hold a book.

"Nothing too terrible, I hope," Reggie said jokingly, though the concern she felt was real. If she couldn't win Mason over, she would never truly feel like part of the team. She'd spend the rest of her time at Serenity on the fringes, never fully accepted. It was how she had spent her childhood, and she didn't have any desire to go back there. Charlotte just laughed and brushed off the comment.

"How long have you guys been married?" It was the only thing Reggie could think to ask to keep the conversation going. She had so little time to socialize that she had forgotten how to do this. Even when Charlie was alive, they rarely went out. She regretted the question the moment it left her mouth, fearing Charlotte would ask her the same thing in return and she'd have to talk about Charlie. She never knew how sharing memories of him would affect her. She didn't want to show up to book club as a tear-streaked mess.

"Eighteen years. We got married shortly after high school."

She gave Charlotte a smile. She had always been a sucker for a good love story. "Were you guys high school sweethearts?"

"We were. We met at some sporting event. I think he was one of the players. It was so long ago, the details are a little fuzzy." Charlotte laughed. "It's just up here," she said before Reggie could ask any follow-up questions.

Reggie was too busy trying to get her head around the fact that Charlotte didn't remember how she met Mason to realize that they had left the residential section and were now walking down Main Street. "Where are we going?"

"You'll see." Charlotte opened a door to the local bar causing the noise inside to spill out into the street. There must be a backroom or something they used. It would be hard to have a casual conversation in there, let alone a deep discussion about the inner workings of whatever book they had been reading.

A cheer erupted from the back table as soon as they

walked in. Charlotte walked over to it with Reggie trailing in her wake. There was not a single book to be seen—not that there would be room for them with the number of glasses on the table.

"So, this is book club?" She laughed as she sat down in one of the empty chairs.

"To be fair, it did start as an actual book club," Anna said. "But after a few months, no one was reading the books anymore, and eventually we dropped the pretense all together. Is beer okay?"

"It's great." Reggie took the glass Anna offered her. She took a small tip, letting it dance over her tongue before swallowing. It had been years since she'd had a beer.

"Reggie, you know Sasha, right?" Charlotte asked.

"I do. She's been stuck training me all week." Reggie raised her glass towards her.

"And this is Ronda. She works in the labs," Charlotte gestured towards the woman sitting next to Reggie.

"I'm a chemist," Ronda added before taking a long sip of beer.

"Where are you from?"

Ronda waved her question away. "Somewhere on the west coast, but that's not important. We're all residents of Serenity now." She raised her glass and all the ladies at the table did the same. They must have gotten started without them.

Reggie was confused by Ronda's response, but rather than dwell on it, she decided to switch gears. "So do you do this often?"

"Once a month, the dads all get together with the

kids, and we get to go out. Next week, we'll swap. I'm not sure if you've noticed yet, but there's not a ton of nightlife here," Sasha said. "So, we've been forced to find a way to make our own fun."

"Evening, ladies," a familiar voice behind her said. Reggie turned to see Isaac standing behind her with a pitcher of beer. His eyes locked onto Reggie, and she could see the conflict in his eyes, even if his smile never faltered. She knew he took it hard anytime they fought. "Book club night?"

They all raised their glasses to him. "Cheers."

Isaac set the pitcher down and pulled over a chair. "I didn't expect to see you here, Reg. Book club is the most coveted invitation in town, and you got in on your first week."

Reggie could tell that Isaac was trying to keep things casual. She was sure he had an image to preserve here, and she didn't want to ruin that for him, even if she was still pissed at him for not taking her side last night. "It's only because they don't know me that well yet," she said in what she hoped was a casual tone. "Are you here alone?" She gave him a look that she was sure everyone at the table would understand. It was only fair.

Isaac's cheeks pinkened slightly. "I am not."

Reggie leaned back in her chair. It was time for Isaac to get a taste of the unwanted spotlight that was so often shined on her. "And where is the good doctor?" Around the table, she saw the other woman scanning to try to spot who she was talking about. She wondered if Isaac had ever shown any romantic interest in anyone before.

"He's in the bathroom. We had dinner and then

decided to come out for a few drinks."

"I didn't know you did that," Reggie said.

"Drink? I thought I proved that on your first night here," Isaac said with a smirk.

"No, I meant, take a night off. I figured you lived in your lab."

"Normally, he does," Ronda offered. "I believe there's a cot in your office, isn't there, Isaac?"

"Be careful, or I'll have you running samples from the greenhouse for the next month." Isaac pointed at Ronda with his glass of beer still in his hand. Reggie had never seen Isaac like this before. She realized she knew very little about her brother's life. Who were his friends? Was he a normal participant in book club, or maybe he was just here often enough to know about it? Did people like him as a leader, or did they tolerate him because of the benefits that came with living in Serenity? Everything she knew about Isaac was from their childhood. She had changed so much since then, the same must have been true for Issac.

The awkward, caring, nerdy boy that was frozen in her mind was long-gone. It was time to get to know her brother as an adult.

"You wouldn't dare," Ronda shot back, failing to hide the amused smirk on her face.

"Ladies," Theo said as he approached the table. He walked up behind Isaac and put his hands on his shoulders. "Can I steal this one from you?"

"Get him out of here. This is an invite only party, anyway." Anna shooed Isaac away with a smile. Reggie noticed that her glass was empty. These ladies knew how to have a good time.

"You and your brother seem to be pretty close," Sasha said.

"I guess," Reggie said with a shrug. "We were close as kids, but I moved out the moment I could, and he stayed. It was harder after that. Then he created this place, and I barely got to talk to him anymore." Reggie glanced over at the bar where Isaac and Theo were sitting. They were leaning towards each other and laughing as if they were the only people in the bar. "Do any of you have any extended family here?"

Ronda shook her head. "Unless you count my son and his wife, who are about to have their first baby, but they met inside Serenity."

"That has to be tough." Reggie picked up her glass and took a sip.

Sasha shrugged. "It's really not as hard as I thought it would be when we moved here. I mean, I miss my friends and family from before, but everyone here is so close that this becomes your family. It's clique, I know, but that's the way it is. You'll see soon enough."

"Or maybe you've just had too much to drink already," Charlotte joked, sending a wave of laughter around the table.

"Hey, I had a long week. I had a newbie to train," Sasha said.

"I didn't need that much training," Reggie said with mock-offense.

"Fair. You're more competent than most of the men on the team." She raised her glass to Reggie, who reciprocated.

"So, do you like living here?" Reggie said to Sasha as several side-conversations took place.

"It's better than any place I remember living," Sasha said.

"Even with the whole 'being part of a social experiment' thing?" It was something that had been gnawing at the back of her mind since they'd arrived. This place was one big experiment, though she had yet to see anything to suggest they were being evaluated or tested. Was she part of the control or variable group? How was data being collected and analyzed? How would they know if the experiment was a success? The welcome packet Isaac had sent was annoyingly vague when it came to the details of the experiment.

Sasha shrugged. "Most of the time, you forget you're even part of an experiment. At the end of the day, we're all just trying to live our lives."

Reggie leaned forward and lowered her voice. "So, they aren't watching us all the time?" She made sure to smile so Sasha wouldn't think she was a paranoid lunatic.

"No," Sasha said with a laugh that echoed throughout the bar. "There're security cameras in the public areas, but that's mainly for safety purposes. It's not like anyone is monitoring us all the time. We still have the right to privacy. In fact, I think there's a clause that any surveillance equipment discovered in residents' homes would be enough cause to terminate the experiment altogether."

"Has anyone actually checked?" Reggie made a mental note to do a quick sweep of her house when she got home.

"The government had to clear everything before we moved in." Sasha cocked an eyebrow. "Where are all these questions coming from? Do you think your family is spying on us?"

"No," Reggie said quickly. "Of course not." Even if that was her biggest fear.

"That's not real convincing," Sasha said.

Reggie rolled her eyes. "I'm just trying to figure out how the experiment side of things works. My parents have to be collecting data on the residents, somehow. Personally, I'd like to know what that data is."

"They're collecting data," Ronda said, joining their conversation. "But it's not what you think. We monitor crime rates, work performance, spending habits, things like that."

"Don't forget the survey," Sasha pointed at Ronda, nearly knocking over her half-filled glass.

"Survey?"

It was Ronda's turn to roll her eyes. "The annual resident happiness and feedback survey. Some of our residents take it more seriously than others." She gave Sasha a pointed look.

"I knew those surveys weren't anonymous," Sasha said, fighting back her laughter.

"Who else would have requested rocket packs for their team?"

Sasha burst out laughing. "It would make repairing the wall a lot more fun."

The conversation turned to what sounded like a long list of ridiculous requests made by the maintenance team. Reggie couldn't help but smile as she imagined filling out the survey with them next year. Even if the idea of living inside one of her parents' experiments made her uneasy.

After an hour, Reggie found herself zoning out of the conversation as the topic turned to town gossip. It was hard to care about the scandalous goings-on of people she had never met. Instead, she tried to come to terms with the fact that this was her life now. After a year of only having the energy to be Boss and Mom, it felt weird just being Reggie again. Part of her was afraid she had forgotten how to enjoy herself, especially when the spikes of guilt about leaving the boys with people they barely knew hit.

Reggie noticed that the pool table in the backroom was open. The book club moms were now complaining about their partners. Reggie couldn't blame them; she knew she had complained to Amber about Charlie more times than she could remember, but she had a hard time joining in now. Rather than bring the mood down, she excused herself and made her way over to the bar, where Theo and Isaac were still deep in conversation. She figured they'd had enough time alone that it wouldn't be too rude of her to cut in.

"You two are looking awfully cozy over here," she said as she stood beside them.

"We are," Isaac said. "Is there something you need, Regina?"

Reggie smirked. Isaac only used her full name when he was annoyed with her. For a second, she considered making up an excuse and leaving, but she noticed Theo trying to stifle a laugh. He must not have minded the interruption. "I was wondering if you were up for a little geometry challenge," she said with a wicked grin.

Theo turned in his seat to look at her. "Did you say geometry challenge?"

"I did." She nodded towards the empty pool table.

The confusion on Isaac's face melted away as soon as he saw it. "Do you mind?" he asked Theo.

"Not at all." Theo grabbed his drink and stood up. "In fact, I think I'd enjoy watching your sister kick your ass in a game of pool." He looped his arm through Reggie's. "You're good, right?"

She winked at him. "I am."

"I seem to remember beating you more often than not when we played as kids." Isaac grabbed his drink and made his way over to the pool table.

"That was a long time ago. I'm a different person than I was back then." Before the kids were born, she would spend most Friday nights at a bar similar to this one with Jesse, Charlie, and a few friends. For a long time, Reggie and Charlie were the pair to beat.

Isaac turned back towards her. "That doesn't mean you're better than me."

"Oh, we'll see about that." Reggie smirked. She grabbed a stick and examined it carefully. She regretted donating hers before coming here, but it had never occurred to her that she would need it.

Isaac stood next to her, grabbing a pool cue without giving it much thought. "Before we start," he said softly, "I wanted to apologize for yesterday. I didn't mean to imply–"

"Don't worry about it," Reggie said, cutting him off. "I know you didn't mean it. I criticized your work first."

"Still, I crossed the line and I'm sorry," Isaac said.

"It's okay, really. It's nothing I haven't heard before, believe me. Even if I never understood where the stereotype came from. It might not be glamorous, but it takes a lot of skill to do what I do."

"I know that," Isaac said.

"Good. Then let's play some pool." She was ready to show her brother just how much she'd grown up since leaving home.

Chapter 18

Reggie sat at her kitchen table with her robe wrapped tightly around her while she sipped a cup of coffee. It felt like a luxury, and she wanted to savor it. She wondered how long it would take before the thrill of being able to drink clean water from the tap would wear off.

Jace and Miles were sitting across from her slowly eating their breakfast. They both looked half-asleep. "Did you guys have fun last night?" The boys had been exhausted when she picked them up. Miles only made it two houses before she had to pick him up. He was getting too big for her to carry, but she figured she would take advantage of it while she could. Jace looked like he was sleepwalking, dragging his feet along the sidewalk as he went. She was afraid to see how badly his shoes were scuffed. Neither had spoken a word as she tucked them into bed.

To her surprise, Jace spoke up first. "Yeah. They had games and crafts for the little kids. Sam brought out some comics and we spent a long time reading those. Then we had a movie night with all kinds of snacks."

"No wonder you were so tired when I picked you up," Reggie said with a smile. "How about you, Miles?"

"It was fun. All the dads played with the kids, but why wasn't our dad there?" Miles looked up from his bowl of cereal.

Reggie didn't know how to answer. Her mind went blank as she tried to process what Miles had asked. Did he really not know why Charlie wasn't there? Was it normal for a kid his age to forget that his dad was dead? Or was this something else? He had never asked where Charlie had been before coming here. Maybe something about this place was affecting his memory—the same something that seemed to make the book club moms forget about their lives before coming to Serenity, and had Cam asking her basic questions about life outside of a Sanctuary City.

Maybe she'd just misheard him. Jace didn't seem to notice that Miles said anything unusual. "What do you mean?" she asked, trying to keep the rising panic out of her voice.

Miles shrugged and went back to eating his cereal. "I thought it was weird how every other kid's dad was there and mine wasn't. Was he stuck at work?"

Reggie reached across the table and put her hand on

top of his. "Miles, honey, your dad died last year."

"He did?" Miles looked at her. She could see the tears starting to form at the corners of his eyes. Reggie had no idea how to help. This shouldn't have been new information for him. They talked about Charlie all the time. Reggie had never tried to hide the truth of what had happened from Jace and Miles, though she'd left out the more gruesome details.

"Yeah, he did. It was before we came here. Do you remember? We had a funeral and lots of people came and shared stories about Dad." It was a struggle to keep her voice calm.

Miles scrunched up his eyes, as if trying hard to picture the funeral in his mind. "I think so. It was really sad, wasn't it?"

"Yes, it was."

"Remember when Mom got into a fight with Uncle Scott?" Jace said. It wasn't exactly what she wanted the boys to remember about the funeral, but at least Jace remembered something and for now she'd take it.

"Oh, yeah," Miles said with a small smile. "Can I be done?"

And just like that, conversation was over. "Of course. Take your stuff to the sink," Reggie said without thinking. Her mind was still reeling over the fact that Miles didn't remember that Charlie had died. Was Miles forgetting Charlie or was this normal kid stuff?

"Don't worry, Mom," Jace said. Reggie looked at him. This open communication from Jace was just as concerning as Miles forgetting Charlie was dead. It had only been a week, and she was already seeing drastic changes in the boys. She just wasn't sure if they were for the better or worse. "Miles remembers Dad. He's just little. He didn't mean anything by it."

"Thanks, buddy. That makes me feel better," she said, even though it wasn't true. "Do you have any big plans for today?" She needed to change the subject before she broke down.

Jace shrugged. "Not really. Sam lent me some of her comics, so I'll probably read them, then I don't know."

"You and Sam seem to be getting close." If Jace was talking Reggie figured she might as well take advantage of it. Who knew when he would be willing to talk to her like this again?

"She's cool. We both like a lot of the same things."

"That's really great. I'm glad you found someone to hang out with."

"Yeah, I wasn't sure, since there aren't that many people here." Jace got to his feet and picked up his empty cereal bowl. "I can wash the dishes this morning, if you want."

Reggie nearly choked on her coffee. Jace had never volunteered to do any chores before. "Who are you? Did body-snatchers show up last night and switch you out with a different kid? Have you been possessed by a ghost with a passion for housework?"

Jace rolled his eyes and made his way over to the sink. "Sam and I were talking about how life works here, since there's no money. She said that she only knows what money is because of TV and books. Isn't that weird?"

"Yeah, that is weird," Reggie said, filing that detail

away with the rest of the odd comments she'd heard from the residents of Serenity in the last week.

"Anyway, she said it only works if everyone pitches in and does their fair share. I figured going to school would be enough, but I guess all the kids help out around the house too, since their parents have to work. I figured I'd give it a shot. I don't want to get us kicked out."

Reggie got up and went over to him. She turned him away from the sink and pulled him close. To her surprise, he didn't resist the hug—instead, he wrapped his arms around her waist and squeezed. He hadn't hugged her like that in over a year. "We aren't going to get kicked out. I don't want you to worry about that," she said while trying to fight back the tears forming in her eyes.

Jace leaned back to look at her. "So, I don't have to do the dishes then?"

Reggie laughed. "I didn't say that. I think it's a great idea to have you and your brother help out more around the house. You do the dishes this morning, and later, we can sit down and come up with a few things that will be your job moving forward. How does that sound?"

Jace nodded against her chest before pulling away. Reggie watched him as he started to work on the sink full of dishes. She hadn't had a chance to do them before going out the night before. The sudden change in Jace's attitude was concerning, but she didn't have any idea how to address it. She liked this Jace that talked to her and offered to help around the house, but she didn't want Jace to be something he wasn't just to fit in, either.

If only she knew what had caused the switch, then maybe she would know if it was something to be worried about or not.

Instead, she grabbed her phone off the counter and headed to the front porch to call Amber. She hadn't had time to call Amber in the last few days, and Reggie knew she would be starting to worry. She had no idea what time it was for Amber—she didn't really know what time zone they were in—but it didn't matter. Even if Amber didn't answer, Reggie could leave a message so she knew they were alright.

Reggie clicked on Amber's name and held the phone to her ear while it tried to connect. She heard it ring twice before silence filled the line. "Hello? Amber?" Reggie pulled the phone away from her ear and looked at the screen. The call had failed.

The phone started to ring again before Reggie had a chance to try again. She saw Amber's name and quickly answered. "Hello?"

"Hey!" Amber's voice filled the line. "Reggie are you there?"

"I'm here, though the connection sucks," Reggie said over the static that was starting to fill the line.

"You should really fix that," Amber said.

"I'll get right on it," Reggie said with a laugh. "That is, if I can convince Isaac to actually let me make modifications to anything. It seems the maintenance protocol here is replace like for like. We aren't allowed to make any changes to actually fix things the right way."

"That's annoying." Amber had raised her voice, though Reggie was still having a hard time hearing her over the growing static on the line. "How are things there? Are you guys doing okay?"

"We're good. The boys seem to be thriving. Jace and I had a real conversation this morning, and he was the one that started it."

"That's huge, Reg."

"I know. I was shocked. Something weird happened with Miles, though." A high-pitched beep blared from the phone's speaker. Reggie had to pull it away from her ear until it stopped. She looked at the screen. They were still connected, though Reggie wasn't sure how much longer it would last. "Amber," she said tentatively once the beeping had stopped.

"Reggie?" Amber's voice was barely a whisper on the other end of the line.

"I'm here."

"What happened with Miles?"

"He didn't re—" The static on the line increased until Reggie was sure Amber wouldn't be able to hear her. "Amber, if you can hear me, I just wanted to tell you we're good and I'll try calling later," Reggie yelled over the static. She had no idea if Amber heard what she said, but a moment later, the line went dead.

~

The sound of the packing tape pulled off the roll was music to Reggie's ears. She had spent most of the morning boxing up all the science equipment her parents had set up in the back room of her house. She couldn't get the smile off her face as she imagined their reaction when they found out. She knew they would be pissed, but she didn't care. She would not subject the boys to the same pressure she'd had to deal with growing up, no matter how much her parents protested. This act of defiance gave her the boost she needed after her failed call with Amber.

It had taken her a few days to decide what she wanted to do with the room. Part of her wanted to board-up the door and pretend it didn't exist, but that felt like a waste. The best thing to do was to reclaim the area for herself.

She decided to convert it to a workshop. It would have been nice to have a place to work that wasn't the kitchen table. She couldn't count how many times she'd had to stop a project halfway-through so they could have dinner. More than once, she had discovered that parts were missing, only to find them later in one of the boys' rooms. Miles, especially, had a tendency to walk away with anything that looked like it could be used in a superhero battle.

Reggie brought the box she had just finished packing out to the porch. She had no idea how her parents had managed to get so much equipment into the small room. It would take her most of the day just to get it all packed up. She wiped her brow on the back of her arm as she watched Miles playing in the large, grassy area behind the house with a group of other kids. He had been out there since leaving the breakfast table. He was living his best life, with newfound independence that she would never have been able to give him out in the real world.

She grabbed another empty box from the pile on the

porch and headed back in. The sooner she was done, the better she would feel.

"Regina!" Oscar's voice boomed through the open door.

Reggie hung her head and took a deep breath. She knew this was going to happen at some point, though she had hoped to finish before they realized what she was doing. She had to be strong. She was an adult and this was her house. Her parents had no say on what she did with it.

She gathered all her strength and waited for her father to appear in the doorway. She would not back down, and she refused to yell like she had when she was teenager. Reggie focused all her energy on packing the box in front of her, carefully wrapping each beaker in bubble wrap so it wouldn't break during the short drive over to the school.

"What is the meaning of this, Regina?" Oscar was silhouetted in the doorway.

Reggie glanced up at him and went back to her work. "I'm packing up this room," she said, making sure to keep her building frustration from escaping in her voice.

Oscar crossed his arms and glared like he had when she hadn't completed her extra assignments to his satisfaction. "And why would you be doing that?"

Reggie fought the urge to shrink away. "Because we aren't going to use it," she said with as much confidence as she could. Why was this so hard? She hadn't lived with her father since she was eighteen. She didn't need his approval then and she didn't want it now.

Oscar flexed his fingers, a clear sign of his building

frustrations. "This isn't about you, Regina. This is about the boys and their future."

She stopped packing and looked him in the eye. "They're the reason I'm doing this."

Oscar made his way over to her so there was only the lab table between them. "I won't let you destroy their future like you destroyed yours so you can fulfill your need to rebel against us."

"Let me make one thing crystal-clear to you, Dad," she said through clenched teeth. She had to keep her cool. She needed to prove to herself that she was a better parent than Oscar had ever been, and she couldn't do that if she let her anger get the better of her. "You do not get a say in how I raise my kids. There will be no extra science lesson on the weekends, or assignments for them to earn your love."

"This has nothing to do with love," Oscar said.

"Oh, believe me, I know that all-too-well."

Oscar rolled his eyes. "Your mother and I wanted to ensure that you and Isaac had the best possible chance of success in life. Frankly, I think it's irresponsible of you to deprive the boys of the same opportunities that you had when you were young. What's wrong with that?"

"When you only have one idea of what success looks like and it doesn't account for things like passion, happiness, or love, then there's something very wrong with it. You never accepted that I wasn't going to fit into your idea of success, no matter how many times I tried to tell you. You just kept pushing me in the direction you wanted me to go. You made me hate myself. For years, I thought there was something wrong with me because nothing I did was ever good enough for you and Mom. I won't do that to my kids." Reggie picked up the tap and closed the box she had been packing to drive her point home.

"You were always so dramatic. This temper tantrum of yours is over. Now I expect you to put everything back the way it was and get Jace and Miles ready for their first lesson."

Reggie set the packing tape back down gently. She closed her eyes and took a deep breath. When she opened them, she looked her father straight in the eye. "No."

Oscar took a small step back as if she had tried to strike him. "No?"

"That's what I said." Reggie nodded slightly to reassure herself. "This is my house and my kids. You can't tell me what to do anymore."

Oscar stomped his foot. "Enough, Regina. I am your father, and you will respect my wishes."

Reggie let out a small laugh and shook her head. He really thought she was going to cave to his demands. "You lost the last shreds of my respect when I was thirteen. Now get out of my house and don't come back unless you're invited." She picked up the box and walked past Oscar without looking at him.

She made a point of staring into the trunk of her car as Oscar walked past. She had nothing left to say to him. She didn't move until the sound of his footsteps had faded away.

"Mom?"

Reggie turned to see Jace standing behind her.

"Yeah, bud?" She took a few deep breaths. It was in moments like this that she missed Charlie the most—the moments when she wasn't sure who she was and started to question everything. She needed Charlie to remind her that the strong capable woman he fell in love with was the real her.

"Are you okay? I saw Grandpa leaving and he looked mad."

"Yeah, of course." Reggie tried to smile but she couldn't hold it. Tears formed in the corners of her eyes. "We just had a little disagreement about what the back room should be used for."

Jace nodded and wrapped his arms around Reggie's waist without saying a word. He pressed his head to her chest as he hugged her. Reggie felt her whole body sag as she wrapped her arms around her son. She couldn't hold back the tears anymore. She wasn't sure how long they stood there, but Jace made no move to free himself. As she felt her tears start to slow, she kissed the top of his head and released him. "Why don't you help me get the rest of the boxes loaded up, okay?"

"Sure, Mom."

Reggie watched him go. She couldn't deny that Jace's new attitude was a massive improvement over the moody, sullen preteen she had been dealing with for the last year. She just wished she had an explanation for the sudden switch, and what it was costing him to make it happen.

Chapter 19

Reggie felt lighter as she dropped the kids off at school Monday morning. Despite the argument with her father, the weekend had been the most relaxing one she'd had since Charlie had died. Jace's happy and helpful attitude had stuck around, and Miles loved all the family time they were able to have. She was starting to think that maybe she could find happiness living here, as long as she was able to limit the amount of contact she had with her parents.

She was starting to find her flow at work too. While most of the maintenance team regarded working on the wall as the worst assignment, Reggie honestly didn't mind it. She was fascinated by the mechanics of the laser grid. She saw so many opportunities to improve it—she just had to convince Isaac to let her try out a few of them.

The changes she had made while repairing section 204 were still holding. Once she was sure it wouldn't short out again, she would tell someone what she had done and use that to convince Isaac that letting them make changes was what was best for the city. Until then, she would do what she could to make improvements without making the drastic changes the system required to be stable.

"I'm shocked to see you had the guts to come back for a second week," Dale said the moment Reggie walked into the lobby of the maintenance building. He was leaning against the deserted front desk with two members of his team. "I figured you'd have begged Mommy and Daddy to have you reassigned by now."

Reggie rolled her eyes and tried to walk past them, but someone moved to block her path. Reggie hadn't bothered to learn his name. "Too scared to fight back?" he said.

"You're not worth the effort," Reggie said. Weren't they too old for this high school bullying behavior?

"Or you know you don't stand a chance."

"You're full of shit, Joe," Sasha said. "Reggie has forgotten more about fixing things than you've ever known and you know it, which is probably why you're so scared of her."

Joe took a step forward. "I'm not scared of anything."

"Oh, really? Then I'll talk to Mason about having you transferred to the perimeter team."

"I don't—that's not what I meant. You don't have that kind of power. Dale?" Joe stumbled over his words, looking frantically from Sasha to Dale.

"Like I said, you're full of shit. Now get the hell out of our way." Sasha patted Reggie on the shoulder and led the way into the building.

Reggie glanced back at Joe as she left. All the color had drained from his face and a faint sheen of sweat was visible on his forehead. She didn't understand the fear so many people had about what lay beyond the laser grid. She knew there were dangers outside of the City, but they had precautions in place to protect against them. Honestly, it was far more likely that they would get hurt by an electrical arc or working at heights than by an attack from a radioactive mutated animal or someone trying to break into the city.

She was busy putting her things away in her locker when Mason walked over to her. "Stone, drop your gear. You won't be working on the wall today."

Reggie turned to look at him. "Why not?" Had she done something wrong? She had checked the board on her way to her locker and saw that there were several hot items that needed to be addressed. At least three sections of the wall had shorted out overnight.

"I have a different assignment for you. Follow me." He didn't wait for a response, just turned and walked away.

Reggie quickly closed her locker and followed him. She racked her mind for a reason why she was being pulled from the wall. She wondered if her parents had somehow pressured him to give her a different job as punishment for taking out the lab at her house. She didn't think Mason would cave that easily, but she knew how unrelenting her parents could be.

Mason didn't say anything as he brought her to the back room. He flicked the lights on. The room was a disaster. Broken items littered the half dozen rows of shelves along the back wall. The tables were covered with overflowing boxes of equipment. There was a desk in the corner covered in paper and one workbench with a layer of dust covering it. "What is this?" Reggie asked as her eyes scanned the room.

"This is our workshop. We're supposed to repair anything that's broken before getting rid of it. Technically, there should be a few people working back here all the time, but I can rarely spare the manpower, so things tend to accumulate here."

"I can see that."

"Since you have to leave early for your treatments on Mondays, you'll be working one day a week here until you're done with your chelation treatments."

Reggie let out a small laugh of disbelief. It would take ages to sort through all this stuff. "Any suggestions on where I should start?"

"There should be a work order list on the desk." Mason pointed to the desk that was barely visible under the boxes and papers piled on top. "But I honestly couldn't tell you when it was last updated."

"That's helpful."

"Just do whatever you can." Mason patted her on the back. "I got to head over to City Hall for a meeting. I'll be back in a few hours."

Reggie put a hand on her forehead and sighed. She knew her office back at Homes, Hearts, and Hammers was disorganized, but this took things to a whole new level. There wasn't even a flat surface to work on.

She made her way over to the desk, careful not to knock over any of the boxes. The papers on top were nine months old, and covered in grease-stained fingerprints. She picked up a small stack and looked them over. There was no way to tell if the jobs had been completed or not. She tossed them back on the desk in frustration—there had to be a better way to do this.

She noticed a laptop under the stack of papers. She pulled it out, sending the papers flying to the ground. Looking over the computer, she had no way to know if it was there for them to use or if it needed to be fixed as well. Taking a chance, she turned it on. "Now we're getting somewhere," she muttered as the screen came alive, showing her a list of work orders. She scanned over the list, noticing that several of the items were marked 'urgent.' That seemed as good a place to start as any. She quickly picked up the fallen papers and tossed them in the trash. If they hadn't been touched in over nine months, she doubted they were worth saving.

The first urgent work order was from the school. It looked like it had first been put in over a year ago and escalated several times. There were ten desks that needed to be repaired. Reggie looked around and saw them piled in the back corner of the room. It took her an hour to fix them all, and she called the school to let them know they were done. The place would look better once they were gone.

Reggie lost track of time as she alternated between the work orders and trying to clean the place enough to have a place to work. While wiping off the last coat of stain on a large wooden map of the city she had found while organizing the desk, she noticed a note attached that said the three-foot-by-three-foot map was to be displayed in the entrance of city hall. It was dated three years ago. It wasn't on the work order list, but it had been beautifully carved, and she hated to see it collecting dust.

"Stone, what are you still doing here?"

She hadn't heard Mason enter. She glanced up to see him standing in front of the workbench. "I just wanted to finish this up."

"How much more do you have? If you don't leave soon, you'll be late for your appointment."

"Just a few more spots." Reggie applied more stain to the edges of the map.

"You know I made that." Mason was standing on the other side of the workbench looking down at the map.

"Oh, I'm sorry," Reggie said quickly. "Should I not have finished it?"

"No, it's fine. I had forgotten all about it. It's probably been years since I last saw it. I never thought I'd see it finished."

"I still need to put the sealant on, but that can wait for another day." Reggie carefully wiped the last of the stain off the map. "The craftsmanship is beautiful," she said, admiring Mason's work. "The first apprenticeship I had was as a carpenter. I've always loved working with wood."

"There is something special about it," Mason said.

"Are you a trained carpenter?"

He shook his head. "No, it was only ever a hobby."

Reggie started to clean up the workbench. "What was your first job?"

"It was with some construction company. I don't remember what they were called."

Reggie froze. "What did you do with them?" Her words were carefully measured to hide the panic rising inside her. Was this another instance of memory loss? They were adding up quickly. How many more could she explain away before she stopped denying there was something odd going on here?

"You know the usual," Mason said with a shrug. "Anyway, you should get going before you're late. Good job today, Reggie."

A smile formed on her lips, momentarily replacing the concern growing in her mind. "Thanks, Mason." She had finally won him over.

~

Reggie was shocked that she remembered the way to the treatment room at the hospital, though she found herself searching the halls for Aaron as she went. She wasn't interested in anything romantic, but she had enjoyed their short conversation while he showed her where to go last week. He was one of the only people she had met that really understood what she was going through. Jesse had taken her to a support group for widows shortly after Charlie had died. She hadn't made it through the whole meeting; she hadn't wanted to sit around in a circle and talk about her feelings. They were still too raw and too painful to think about for more than a few minutes. She had talked to Amber about it, of course, but she couldn't really understand how Reggie felt. Maybe it was time to find someone who knew what losing a spouse felt like. Unfortunately, she made it to the treatment room without crossing paths with the good doctor.

Theo was already hooked up to the IV when Reggie arrived. She checked her watch to make sure she wasn't late, but for once, she was actually a few minutes early. "Hi, Theo," she said as she made her way over to the chair next to him.

"It's good to see you again, Reggie," Theo said, as the nurse started to work on her.

Reggie squeezed her eyes shut and turned her head away as the needle was inserted into her arm. "How was the rest of your date with Isaac?" she asked through gritted teeth. She didn't release the tension in her face until the nurse had finished and left the room. "I hope Isaac wasn't too much of a downer the rest of the night. I know how much he hates to lose."

Theo chuckled. "It took a little extra effort, but I was able to get the evening back on track."

Reggie saw the smirk on his face and the faraway look in his eyes. She did not ask any follow-up questions. There were some things she didn't want to know about her brother. "I'm glad."

"How was book club?"

Reggie chuckled. "It wasn't what I was expecting. I had a surprisingly good time. I've never really been invited to a moms' night out."

"Why is that?"

"Oh, because all the moms at the boys' old school despised me."

"I have a hard time believing that," Theo said.

"Believe it or not, they did. We were different, and therefore easy targets. I'm pretty sure the PTO sent out a letter warning people not to talk to me or the poor could rub off on them."

"You don't think very highly of yourself, do you? We'll have to work on that."

"Let's save that for another day," Reggie said, fighting the urge to roll her eyes. "I think you should share all your deep dark secrets. I've already told you all of mine—how about a little reciprocation?" Reggie cocked an eyebrow at him.

Theo shifted in his chair. "What do you want to know?" There was a hint of hesitation in his voice.

"How about why you got into psychology?" Reggie leaned back into the vinyl cushions on her chair, grateful to be out of the spotlight for a change.

Theo took a deep breath. "Self-preservation."

It was the last answer Reggie had expected. She turned to look at him. "What do you mean?"

"My family has a long and complicated relationship with Alzheimer's. I figured if it was going to be my fate, I wasn't going to just wait around for it to take me. It was on me to try to stop it. To save myself. And if I could help a few people along the way, then even better." Theo shrugged and shifted his gaze to the other side of the room.

"That's really noble," Reggie said.

"Or selfish."

"No. Shellfish is when your main motivator for success is prestige and fame," she said with a pointed look. They both knew exactly who she was referring to.

"I see your point," Theo said with a small smile.

"Was that why you had to delay coming here? Did your mom have it?"

Theo nodded. "It was really hard at the end. She didn't have any idea who I was most of the time. At least it was peaceful when she finally went."

"I'm sorry." Reggie knew Theo was still grieving— she could see all the signs on his face. He had the same pained expression she remembered seeing in the mirror for months after Charlie's passing. "Were you an only child?"

"Yeah. I'm the lone survivor of the Nicholls clan."

"Maybe we need to start our own clan, then. One for all the loners, outcasts, and misfits," Reggie said.

Theo smiled. "I would be honored to be a part of her clan, Reggie."

Chapter 20

Reggie felt anxious as she wheeled a cart with Mason's wooden map of Serenity through the lobby of City Hall. It had been a long time since she'd felt self-conscious about her job, and something about this building was bringing all that self-doubt to the surface again. Her eyes darted towards every sound, expecting to see someone storming over to her demanding to know what she was doing in the building. This wasn't an assigned job, and even if it was, this wasn't her department. Dale would lose his mind if he found out she had done work at City Hall without permission.

She wanted to get the map installed as a way to say thank you to Mason, especially with how much time Jace was spending at his house. He was actually having dinner over there tonight so that he and Sam could work on a project for school together. Sam had been over to their house a few times, but Miles never left them alone, so Reggie could understand why they preferred to hang out at the Crawfords'.

Reggie stood in the center of the empty lobby and scanned the walls trying to find the perfect spot to install the map. Mason had mentioned it was always meant to end up here, but he hadn't said exactly where. Reggie's eyes came to rest on a blank stretch of wall to the left of the front desk. There was a small seating area right in front of it. It was perfect. She wheeled her cart over and got to work prepping the wall.

She quickly got lost in the work. Occasionally she'd hear someone pass through the lobby but no one stopped to speak to her. She wondered if any of them even noticed that she was there. It had been a long time since she last worked in an office setting. It always amazed her how completely overlooked maintenance workers tended to be in this environment. She might as well have been another decorative planter box. She didn't mind, though—it wasn't like she really wanted to talk to these people. She wanted to do her work and move on.

"I got another message from Senator Bailey's office today. They are insisting we set up a meeting."

Reggie paused at the mention of Senator Bailey. Amber had been complaining about him for months. The way she spoke made it seem like the Sanctuary Cities had his unwavering loyalty, but given the stress in the speaker's voice, that might not have been the case.

"Keep trying to push him off," Isaac responded.

Reggie froze, her hammer raised in the air.

"So, you still haven't fixed the issue with the smart grid?"

"No," Isaac said. Reggie didn't need to see his face to feel his frustration. It was so intense, it seemed to fill the entire lobby. What issue were they talking about? Reggie could think of any number of things that needed to be improved on the smart grid, starting with the stability issues, but she didn't think that was it. All the issues they came across while repairing the wall every day could be fixed if Isaac just got the right people involved. No, it had to be something else—something bigger for the government to get concerned. Reggie's mind jumped back to breakfast after book club. Could issues with the smart grid have been the reason Miles had forgotten about Charlie passing?

"What will happen if we can't figure it out?"

"They're threatening to take over control of the cities, which would only make things worse. The government's scientists can't hold a candle to the people we have here."

"They have to know that."

Isaac sighed. "I don't think they really care. The government has been looking for an excuse to take over control of the cities since we started. I won't let this be the thing that finally tips the scales in their favor. I'll figure out how to fix it. I just need more time."

"Do you think it's time to bring Oscar and Lena in?"

"No," Isaac said a little too quickly. Reggie was shocked to learn that Isaac was keeping things from their parents. She had always been under the impression that they were ultimately the ones in charge, but maybe that wasn't the case.

"I don't want to worry them unnecessarily. But let's sit down tomorrow and review where we are with the isolation protocols, just in case."

Reggie had no idea what the isolation protocols were. They could be something completely innocent, like isolating a section of the wall to give it a massive overhaul. Maybe the reason there were so many stability issues with the wall wasn't because Isaac hadn't figured out how to fix it. Maybe he just didn't want to take it offline to complete the necessary upgrades. Though that didn't explain why her stomach twisted into knots at the mention of it.

"Now go home," Isaac said with a forced lightness in his voice. "Isn't it your wife's birthday?"

Reggie quickly shifted her focus back to her work while Isaac and the other man exchanged goodbyes. She breathed a small sigh of relief when she heard the front door close. If she was fast, Isaac would never know she had been there.

"Reggie?"

So much for slipping out without being noticed. She rolled her eyes as she finished securing the last bracket to the wall. When she was done, she plastered a smile on her face and turned around. "Hey Isaac, funny running into you here," she said casually as the guilt over her eavesdropping started to build.

Isaac leaned on the back of one of the lobby chairs. "What are you doing here?"

She could feel his gaze on her as he waited for her to

respond. "I'm trying to get this installed." Reggie wheeled the cart holding the wooden map between them.

"Did you make this?" Isaac stood up to get a better look.

"No. Mason did. I just finished it off. I thought I'd surprise him by getting it hung up."

"It's beautiful."

"Would you mind giving me a hand?" She gestured to the map.

"Sure." Isaac grabbed one side of the map while Reggie took the other. "So, how much of that did you hear?"

Reggie cocked her head so she could see between the map and the wall as they lined it up with the brackets. "I wasn't trying to spy on you," she said as the map went into place. "Is everything alright?"

Isaac turned away and ran his hands through his hair. "We've been under a lot of scrutiny from the government lately. It's nothing new—it seems to happen every election cycle."

"Are they threatening to shut the cities down?" Reggie had seen the political ads over the years. The Sanctuary Cities were often used as a pawn to gain supporters. Reggie always brushed them off. She didn't think any of it would amount to anything, but she hadn't considered the effects it could have on the people here.

"No. They just want to take over control." Isaac plopped down in one of the black armchairs and put his face in his hands.

Reggie sat on the table in front of him. "Would that

really be so bad?"

Isaac shot her a look through his fingers. "When have you ever heard of government interference making things better?"

"Fair point." Reggie leaned back. "Is there anything I can do to help?" It really didn't matter to her who was in control of the cities. In fact, it might have been easier for her if the government pushed her parents out, but she hated seeing Isaac like this. If she could help, she would.

Isaac sat up. "No," he said with a smile that didn't reach his eyes. It looked like a smile he practiced often. "Don't worry. I got everything under control." He got to his feet. "You just enjoy your life here and let me worry about how we keep it going." He shot her one more smile that did nothing to ease the concern growing inside of her.

~

Reggie sat at the bar nursing a glass of whiskey. Her mind raced as she replayed the conversation she overheard in City Hall a thousand times. Despite Isaac's reassurances, it was clear that there was something seriously wrong with Serenity, and Isaac was worried. So worried he had brought up the Isolation Protocol. As much as she tried to convince herself that it was innocent, she knew in her gut what it really meant. If Isaac decided to move forward with them, how quickly could they turn paradise into a prison?

If only she knew exactly what the issue was, she might be able to help. Reggie took a sip of her drink as she thought over the last week. If the problem was big enough that the government was threatening to get involved, there had to be some signs of what was wrong. Unless the threat was external. Could public opinion of the Sanctuary City program be changing? Reggie doubted it. Most people she knew idolized the cities. Pulling government support wouldn't win the politicians any votes. No, it had to be something happening inside of the city. The logical answer would be the wall, but she didn't think the mechanical issues there would be enough to cause the level of concern she had seen in Isaac. Sure, the wall was flawed, but it still did what it was supposed to do, even if it was in desperate need of an upgrade.

Maybe it wasn't the wall itself but a side-effect of the wall. She was sure they would have tested the technology to make sure it was safe prior to moving people into the city, but it wasn't uncommon for things to get missed. Especially if it took a long time for the side-effects to present themselves.

She thought back to see if anything unusual jumped out at her. The realization hit her like a freight train. Could this have something to do with the weird memory gaps people seemed to have here? Did Isaac even realize it was happening? If they were caused by the wall, it would be affecting him too. Was that what had caused Miles to forget that Charlie had died?

Reggie threw back the rest of her drink, hoping the burn of the whiskey would calm the panic rising in her chest. She had moved them here because it was supposed to be safer than the rest of the world. She thought she'd be able to protect Jace and Miles here. But how was she supposed to protect them from this?

She needed to keep their memories intact. She couldn't let them lose Charlie again.

She stared across the room as she worked to get her emotions in check. Her gaze fell on Theo, sitting alone in the corner. She looked around the bar for Isaac, but there wasn't any sign of him.

Reggie got up and made her way across the bay. "Are you alone?"

Theo looked up from the book he had been reading. A half-eaten burger sat discarded off to the side. "Isaac was supposed to join me for dinner, but he had to cancel at the last minute."

Normally, Reggie wouldn't have batted an eye at Isaac putting work before his social life, but given what she had overheard, she knew there was more to it than that. She pulled out a chair and sat down. "How is he doing?"

Theo closed his book. "What do you mean?"

"Does he seem more stressed than normal?" She chose her words carefully. The last thing she wanted was to be overheard and spread rumors throughout the city.

"Not that I've noticed." Theo was watching her closely. Maybe she shouldn't have come over here, but there was no one else in the city that knew Isaac as well as Theo did, and she needed to make sure he was alright.

"Good." If Theo hadn't noticed anything, maybe she was overreacting. She didn't want to worry him unnecessarily. Reggie averted her eyes. Across the bar, two people had just started a game of darts. Maybe she could use that as a distraction. "Do you play darts?"

Theo didn't take the bait. "You know something."

"No," Reggie said a little too quickly. "I'm just worried about him."

"It's more than that. You weren't worried about him the last time I saw you. Something happened, didn't it?"

Reggie looked around the bar as she tried to figure out what to do. She didn't really know anything yet, but she had her suspicions. Was it worth telling Theo when she had nothing to back it up? Would she be causing him unnecessary stress? Could this damage the relationship between him and Isaac?

Or maybe he could help her. They were the two people that cared about Isaac the most. Theo wouldn't have wanted to see Isaac's life's work destroyed either. If she was going to have any hope of figuring out what was happening to the people of Serenity, she would need help, and Theo seemed like her best bet.

"It's getting kind of late." There were too many people around to tell him in the bar. "Would you walk me home?"

"Sure," Theo said slowly. He gave her an odd look and gathered his things. Once they were outside, he turned to her. "So, are you going to tell me what's going on?"

Reggie took a deep breath and looked around. They were alone. It was now or never. "I was working in City Hall, and I overheard Isaac talking to someone. Something's wrong with Serenity. Isaac knows, and from what I heard, so does the government. They're threatening to shut the Sanctuary Cities down."

"Do you know what's wrong with the cities?" Theo nodded his head in the direction of her house, and they slowly started to walk.

Reggie shook her head. "Isaac didn't say. From the sound of it, I'm not sure he even knows exactly what's going on." Reggie paused. "I have a theory, though."

Theo stopped walking and looked at her. "What's your theory?"

"I've started to notice that people here have these weird gaps in their memories—things they should know but can't recall. And none of them seemed to be concerned about it. My theory is that the laser grid is putting out some kind of interference or something that's affecting people's memories. Like some crazy unknown side-effect. I'm guessing the longer a person is inside the city, the worse the effects are. We've only been here a week, so it's probably not bad for us yet, but for everyone else, the gaps are bigger." The words flew out of Reggie's mouth.

Theo put his hands up. "Slow down one second."

"You think I'm crazy, don't you?" Reggie turned and walked towards her house. She wouldn't stand by and be laughed at.

"Reggie, wait," Theo said as he jogged to catch up with her. "It's a lot to take in. You've got to give me a second to process it."

"I'm sorry." She pushed away the defensiveness that had taken over.

"Tell me about the memory gaps."

"For example, I was talking with the book club ladies the other night. They couldn't remember very basic things from their past. Things that people would normally have no trouble remembering."

They were standing under a streetlight, and Reggie could just make out the concern on his face as shadows danced across his eyes. Maybe he had noticed something and hadn't wanted to admit it. "Things like what, exactly?"

"Like the name of the school they used to teach at, where they used to live, how money works."

Theo crossed his arms over his chest. "Wait, seriously? Someone forgot how money works?"

"Okay, well, that one was Cam, who came here as a kid when construction first started," Reggie relented.

"Those are all relatively small things," Theo said gently. "Details fade with time. It's normal."

They seemed like pretty important details to Reggie, but she didn't say that. She had to get him to see that whatever was happening wasn't normal. "How about the fact that Charlotte couldn't tell me how she met Mason? That's not a small detail that fades with time. You remember how you met the person you fell in love with? Those details are important—believe me, I know. I can tell you the color shirt Charlie was wearing when we first met, and what we ate on our first date."

"I agree that is a little odd, but that could just be Charlotte. How well do you really know her?"

Reggie sighed. "I just met her."

"Then how can you be sure she's not simply a forgetful person?"

Reggie turned away and stared off into the darkness. She knew she was onto something. She just had to make him see it. She would have to tell him about Miles, even though thinking about it broke her heart.

"I'm not trying to be discouraging," Theo said quickly. "Really, I'm not. It's just that what you're suggesting could have serious implications for the town and the people here. We can't go jumping to conclusions when there really is no evidence to suggest that something is affecting people's memories. The last thing we want is to cause panic. That won't help Isaac, and it could be what gets the city shut down. We need to be careful."

"Miles didn't remember that his dad was dead." There was a robotic quality to Reggie's voice. She didn't look at Theo as she spoke. She knew if she did, she would never be able to say the words.

"What?" The single word was weighed down with concern. "You mean he didn't remember *how* his father died?"

Reggie shook her head. "No. He didn't remember that Charlie had died at all." She turned to look at Theo. "It was the morning after book club. The dads had watched all the kids while we were at the bar, and Miles wanted to know why his dad wasn't there. When I told him that his dad was dead, it was like he was hearing the news for the first time, except he didn't have any kind of emotional response. He shrugged it off like it was no big deal then went out to play."

Theo rubbed his chin. "That's a little more concerning, but it could still be an isolated thing. Kids process grief differently."

"I know Miles, and that wasn't like him. I saw him

grieving for Charlie, and while there were times where he'd play like nothing was wrong, he always knew what had happened to his father."

"I don't know, Reggie. I still think it's a pretty big jump to go from a handful of people forgetting a few minor details of their life to something about this place affecting people's memories."

Reggie crossed her arms. "Tell me, where were you from before you came here?" Maybe if she could get Theo to realize his memory was being affected too, he would believe her.

Theo cocked an eyebrow at her. Did he know what she was trying to do? "I lived in Bloomington, Indiana."

"You had your own practice there, right?" She wouldn't give up that easily.

He smirked, he definitely knew what she was doing. "I did."

"What street was it on?"

"Really? Next you'll ask me what color the walls were."

"You didn't answer my question."

Theo sighed. "It was downtown on..."

A satisfied smile formed on Reggie's lips. She was right. Theo's memory was being affected too. "What was the name of the street?"

Theo closed his eyes as if concentrating. "I should know this. I had an office in that building for seven years. It has to be the beer I had with dinner."

Reggie rolled her eyes and started to walk again. They were almost at her house. "What was the building called?"

"The something medical center," he said slowly.

"That's a pretty unusual name for a medical facility. Do you need me to ask you about the color of the walls or have I proved my point?" They had reached the path to her front door. They were out of time.

She watched Theo who looked like he was still trying to come up with the answers. She had seen the look on Isaac's face before when their father had given them a particularly challenging math problem to solve. Reggie would normally try to get through it as fast as she could, not caring if she got it right or not, but not Isaac. He had to figure it out, no matter how long it took him. The pained expression on Theo's face suggested it was taking the same amount of brain power to recall these simple details about his life.

"If what you're saying is true and the wall is putting out some kind of interference that's affecting people's memories, then it stands to reason that you should also be having memory issues, but it doesn't seem to be affecting you," Theo finally said.

"We don't know that for sure. Maybe I just haven't realized it yet. I mean, how can you remember something that you've already forgotten?"

"Fair point," Theo said with a sigh. "We'll need proof before we can approach Isaac. Like you said, right now it's just a theory. We could be way off. This might not even be what Isaac was talking about."

"But you believe me," Reggie said slowly.

"I don't know what I believe, but I think it's worth looking into."

Reggie would take it. "So, what do we do?"

Theo was quiet for a moment. "We need to increase the sample size. As far as we know, it's only a handful of people that seem to be affected."

"Then we talk to more people and see if the pattern continues."

Theo nodded. "But we can't come right out and say it, or it could raise concerns. We don't want people to panic. Why don't you bring the boys in for a session this week? That way, I can see if their behavioral changes are a normal part of the grieving process, or if there's something else going on."

"Okay," Reggie said. She knew that between the two of them, they would get to the bottom of what was happening in Serenity, and hopefully save Isaac's life's work in the process.

Chapter 21

"Do we really have to do this?" Jace dragged his feet across the driveway pavement as they made their way to the car.

"Yes," Reggie said as she followed behind him. She wanted to say something about his attitude, but she kept quiet. This was the Jace that she had been used to dealing with for the last year-and-a-half. As much as she liked the pleasant, helpful Jace, this current attitude was less concerning. At least he was being himself.

"I don't want to talk about my feelings," Miles mumbled next to her.

"Well, you need to. We all do. Losing Dad has been hard on all of us, and talking it through with Dr. Nicholls will help us move forward in a healthy way." It wasn't really a lie—a little therapy would be good for them. She tried to get them to see someone soon after Charlie died, but she was never able to find anyone she could afford.

Miles tugged on Reggie's arm. "Does this doctor give shots?"

She knelt down and took his hands in hers. "He's not that kind of doctor. Dr. Nicholls is Uncle Isaac's friend. Remember? You met him at dinner our first night here." Reggie held her breath as she waited for Miles to respond. She had been asking them small questions like that to test their memories. It seemed they had no issues recalling events that had happened in the two weeks since they arrived here, but they sometimes struggled to recall details from their lives outside of the city.

Miles finally nodded, and Reggie let out her breath.

"He takes care of people's minds. He just wants to talk to you about how you're adjusting to moving here, and Dad dying." She knew Miles was only protesting because Jace was.

"That doesn't sound too bad," Miles said. "As long as there's no shots."

"No shots, I promise," she said with a smile. She bopped him on the nose, then helped him into the car.

They drove to the far side of town. Reggie hadn't been over here yet. She expected Theo's office to be in the hospital, but the directions he had given her took them to a large, industrial-looking building. There was a sign out front with the words **Serenity Research and Development Laboratory**.

Reggie pulled into the parking lot and double-checked the address. They were in the right place.

"Are we here?" Jace asked when Reggie didn't make a move to get out of the car.

The longer she looked at the building, the more anxious she got. This was where her parents and Isaac worked. This was the life they'd tried to force her to have while growing up. An irrational part of her felt like they would demand that she work there now if they knew she was in the building. She did not have the words to express just how much she did not want to go inside. "Yeah," she finally said, "this is it."

They got out of the car and made their way to the lobby. Unlike the unoccupied reception desk at the maintenance building, there was a man in a security uniform sitting behind the lobby desk. "Hi," Reggie said as they approached the front desk. "We have an appointment with Dr. Nicholls."

The man behind the desk looked up at her. "You're the Stones, right?"

Reggie nodded.

"Do you know where you're going?"

"Not a clue."

The man stood up and pointed at the facility layout that was on the desk. "His lab is on the third floor. Go down this hallway here and you'll find an elevator. Then take the second hall to the left. You can't miss it."

Reggie wasn't listening anymore. Her eyes were scanning over the layout. The last thing she wanted to do was run into her parents. Unfortunately, the labs weren't labeled on the layout, so she had no idea if they were likely to cross paths. It felt like she was walking into a cave with no idea if there was a bear inside.

Jace led the way to Theo's lab. Reggie's eyes never stopped scanning the hallways as they went. They were just exiting the elevator on the third floor when she heard her mother's voice. Reggie didn't look in the direction it was coming from, hoping that it was her mind playing tricks on her. From what Reggie could make out, it didn't sound like Lena had spotted them yet. Theo's office was around the corner. If they were fast, she was sure they could make it without being seen.

She started to usher the boys away from the elevator when Miles looked behind him and said, "Grandma?"

Reggie let out a sigh and lowered her head. Maybe she should have told the boys before they entered the building to ignore their grandparents if they ran into them.

"Miles? Jace? Regina?" Lena's voice got louder with every name until Reggie had no choice but to turn to face her.

"Hi, Mom."

"What are you guys doing here?"

"The boys have a session with Dr. Nicholls," Reggie said. She made a show of looking at her watch. "In fact, we're running late, so we probably should go. Don't want to waste his time." She put her hand on Miles's shoulder and tried to gently steer him away from Lena.

"I have a few minutes. I'll walk you there," Lena said with a smile as she held out her hand for Miles to take. Reggie couldn't remember a time her mother had offered her that kind of affection.

"That would be great," she said as she forced a smile on her face.

"It's good seeing you here, Regina. I always pictured you running your own lab, leading a team of researchers."

"Don't start," Reggie said. "That was your dream, not mine."

"I know, I know," Lena said in an offhanded way. As if it hadn't been one of the biggest pain points in their relationship. "So, what kind of session are you having with Dr. Nicholls?"

Reggie wasn't sure how to respond. The last thing she wanted to tell her mom was that she had concerns that the smart grid protecting this town was actually affecting people's memories, and Theo was trying to help her prove it. She also didn't want to embarrass the boys, especially Jace, who seemed apprehensive about the appointment. "Oh, you know, I figured after everything we've been through in the last year, it might be helpful to talk to someone."

Lena nodded. "Moving here can be an adjustment. I'm so glad we have a psychologist here now to help people with the transition. Tranquility City was the first to have a mental health staff for residents, and it's done wonders for the quality-of-life scores there."

Reggie stopped and turned to Lena. "That's not what I was referring to."

"What else could they have to worry about?"

"You're not serious, are you?" This couldn't be happening again. Was Lena intentionally leaving Charlie out, or was this the same thing that had been affecting other people's memories? Reggie honestly didn't know. Given how little interest her mother had shown in her life, it felt completely plausible that Lena simply didn't care enough to remember that Reggie's husband had been killed last year.

"I think Mom wants us to talk about Dad," Jace said. "Is this it?" He pointed to a nameplate on the door that read Dr. Nicholls, Psychologist.

"Well, I should get back to my lab. I want to have a family dinner this week. I'll check with Isaac on his schedule then let you know what day." Lena walked away before Reggie could respond. She noticed how her mother didn't ask what her schedule was. Reggie would have to deal with that later. She didn't want to keep Theo waiting. Jace must have already knocked, because the door opened the moment Reggie turned her attention to it.

"Hi, guys," Theo said with a warm smile. "I'm glad you found the place alright." He stepped aside to let them into his lab. "Sorry we have to meet here today. I'm running some tests that I have to babysit."

Reggie hadn't moved. She kept glancing down the hallway at her mother's retreating back. Theo stepped into the hall and followed her line of sight.

"What happened?" He kept his voice low so the boys wouldn't overhear.

"We ran into my mother." Reggie finally turned her attention to Theo.

Theo sighed. "I should have warned you that my lab was in the same wing as hers. I wasn't thinking. I'm sorry."

"It's fine. I have to get used to running into her. It's just, she forgot about Charlie again." Reggie's mind was running a million miles an hour as she tried to make sense out of the interaction with Lena.

Theo tilted his head and glanced down the hall. "Maybe you are onto something with your memory-loss theory."

"I don't know. I don't want to be. I want you to prove me wrong, but my gut is telling me that I'm right and that terrifies me."

"We're going to get the answers Reggie. I promise," Theo said.

"And what if we don't like what we find?"

"We'll deal with that then." Theo looked into the lab where the boys were waiting for him. "Is it okay if I talk to the boys alone first?"

Reggie nodded. "Yeah, of course."

"There's a cafe one level down if you want to hang out there. I'll send you a message when we're done."

"Sure." Reggie gave Theo a weak smile, waved goodbye to the boys, and made her way back to the elevator. This was good. They were going to figure out what was going on. The boys wouldn't forget Charlie. She wouldn't forget Charlie.

~

Reggie wandered through the halls of the building in search of the cafe. She needed to find something to occupy her mind while she waited for the boys, otherwise she would end up obsessing over the run-in with her mother and Reggie knew that wouldn't be good for her.

She'd always hated buildings like this, with their stark halls filled with people looking down on her. She couldn't count how many holidays her parents had forced her to spend in places like this. Instead of an egg hunt, she got to count microbes in soil samples for Easter. Places like this had stolen so many childhood moments from her.

Most of the doors she passed were closed, and the few that were open held mundane things like the copy room or an empty office. She wondered how many more scientists her parents would try to recruit to come here. The building looked like it was capable of supporting a lot more. Reggie shuddered at the idea of living in a town primarily populated by scientists. There would be no escaping her inadequacies then.

Out of the corner of her eye, Reggie saw a Dr. Torres' nameplate on the door ahead of her. She froze. She'd already had a run-in with her mother—she didn't want one with her father too. For a second, she thought about going back to Theo's lab and waiting there, but she wanted to give the boys their privacy. Besides, she didn't want to let her parents control her. She took a deep breath and started forward.

The door to the office was cracked open. Careful not to make a sound, she peeked through the opening. A smile formed on her lips when she saw the metal pencil holder on the desk. She had made it in shop class her freshman year and given it to Isaac as a Christmas gift. This had to be his office. She couldn't believe that he'd kept it all this time. She looked at the nameplate next to the door again. Logically she knew Isaac had his doctorate, but it always threw her whenever he was referred to as Dr. Torres.

Reggie knocked on the door. "Isaac?" She gently pushed it open. Isaac wasn't there, but given the half-full cup of coffee on the desk and the music softly playing in the background, she knew he couldn't have gone far. She let herself inside. This seemed like a safe place to wait for the boys to finish.

She moved around the lab slowly. Almost every surface was covered in paper. Isaac's organizational skills hadn't improved since they were kids. It was comforting. She had spent countless hours hiding in his room when they were growing up. Her parents were convinced that she was helping him with his research—it was the only surefire way she had found to keep them off her back. As Isaac's assistant, she had value.

A large digital board took up one full wall. Reggie went over to see what Isaac had been working on. Displayed were several calculations that Reggie didn't understand and a schematic for a section of the wall. Could this have been the answer she was looking for? Maybe Isaac did know about the memory side-effect and was already at work on a solution. It made sense. No one knew the system better than him. He probably hadn't made it public knowledge so that people didn't panic while he worked on a solution. She felt her anxiety start to ease for the first time in days. She knew Isaac would figure everything out, and they would be fine. Isaac would make sure she didn't forget Charlie.

She studied the drawings. Maybe there was something she could do to help. He might be a supergenius, but he didn't have the practical knowledge that she did. It was different from anything she had seen out there, but she couldn't see how it would affect the frequencies coming from the lasers. If anything, it looked like he was working to solve the stability issues that kept them constantly repairing the wall. It was an issue that desperately needed to be solved, even if she didn't understand how it could solve the memory issues. She followed the wiring on the schematic with her eyes.

"That will never work," she muttered.

She searched the table behind her and grabbed a notepad and pen. She started to sketch out a new design for the electrical—one that wouldn't fail every time the grid required a surge of energy to do its job. She knew better than to change Isaac's work directly. Once, when she was ten, she'd noticed an error in one of the formulas on the whiteboard in Isaac's room. She had fixed it as a way to impress him. Instead, he'd blown up and refused to speak to her for a week. It was one of the worst weeks of her life.

"Reggie? What are you doing here?" Isaac was back.

Reggie whipped around, hiding the notepad behind her back. She couldn't explain it, but she didn't want Isaac to know that she had been correcting his work. "Same thing I used to do as a kid: hiding from mom and dad."

"Coming to the lab probably wasn't the best idea if you wanted to avoid them," Isaac said with a laugh.

Reggie shrugged. "The boys are having a session with Theo. Mom already cornered me while we were walking in, and that was enough for me for one day."

"Oh," Isaac said. "That's good. Hopefully, Theo can help them process their feelings about Charlie."

"That's my hope," Reggie said. "What is all this?" She pointed at the screen. She didn't want to talk about Charlie or why the boys were really talking to Theo. She couldn't let Isaac know that his invention was affecting people's memories until she had proof, especially since she was starting to believe he didn't realize it was happening. If he didn't, she doubted he would be working on the stability issues. It was better for him to live in his ignorance until they knew more.

Isaac went over and stood next to her. "It's a new idea I had to fix the stability of the smart grid. I haven't been able to figure out how to stop it from shorting out whenever there's a sudden surge of energy."

Reggie fiddled with the notepad behind her back. She had the answer he was looking for there, but she had no idea if he would be open to hearing it. "Have you thought about increasing the amps the breakers can handle?"

Isaac turned to look at her. "I've run all the calculations myself three times. If we increase the breakers, then the system might not shut down in the event that it becomes overloaded, and the entire system could run to failure."

"Not if you run the circuits in parallel," Reggie said. "Most of the time, when we have reset the breakers, it's because of a minor power surge that the system is more than capable of handling without tripping the breakers. We waste so much time fixing issues that could easily be prevented if the system were sized correctly."

Isaac crossed his arms. "I think it would be best if you left the science to the professionals and stick to what you're good at."

"This is what I'm good at." Reggie's frustration was building. She expected this from her parents, but not from Isaac. "I repaired a section of the wall last week using this design." She waved the notepad she had been hiding at him. "It hasn't gone down since. It's more stable than anything you designed."

"You modified my work?"

"I did, and it worked."

Isaac ran his hands through his hair. "Why would you do that?"

"I was trying to help. The maintenance team is so busy fixing preventable issues with the wall that the rest of the work we should be doing gets neglected. The design is flawed and you know it." Reggie pointed to the board. "It's not my fault that your ego is too fragile to accept my help."

Isaac pointed towards the door. "Get out of my office." There was a coldness in his voice she hadn't heard in a long time. If he got this upset over some wiring improvements, how would he feel if he found out what she was really doing? Would his ego even allow him to hear it, or would he dismiss her again? How many memories would be at risk if he didn't listen to her then?

"Sure." Reggie threw that notepad at him. Isaac fumbled to catch it before it hit him in the face. "That will fix all your issues." She stormed out of the room, her own ego getting the better of her. At least she'd acknowledged that she didn't have all the answers and was willing to accept help. The boys should have almost been done with Theo by now anyway. She would go see if they had found anything she could throw in Isaac's face.

~

Reggie managed to make it back to Theo's lab without running into anyone. She was glad she hadn't told Isaac why they were really at the lab. If he didn't believe her on how to fix the electrical issues with the wall, there was no way he would believe her theory about it affecting people's memories.

She glanced at her watch once she reached the door to Theo's lab. The boys had been in there for an hour. She figured they had to be about done, though this wasn't a typical therapy session. She didn't want to interrupt if Theo was close to figuring out the truth. Tentatively, she knocked on the door.

A second later Theo answered. "We were just getting ready to come find you."

"How did it go?" Reggie wasn't sure she really wanted to know but knew it was what she was supposed to say.

"Let's talk inside," Theo said as he glanced up and down the hallway.

"Sure." Reggie's voice was laced with apprehension. Theo must have noticed something off with the boys. Reggie stepped inside, her eyes searching for her kids. Jace and Miles were in the small office in the back corner of the lab watching something on Theo's computer. She couldn't hear them through the glass walls, but she could tell they were laughing. They were alright. She willed her heartrate to return to a normal rhythm.

"You have some really great kids there," Theo said following her line of sight. "From what I could tell, they both have strong memories of their father."

It was like Theo was in her head. Reggie breathed a sigh of relief. "Good."

"They both seem to be handling their grief appropriately for their ages."

Reggie nodded. "What about their memories? Did you notice anything odd?"

Theo picked up a notebook from a nearby table flipped through it. "There were a few simple questions I asked that they struggled to answer. Jace, especially."

Reggie felt like all the air had been sucked from her lungs. "So, we were right."

"Not necessarily. It could have been nerves or maybe he just didn't want to answer. It happens a lot with kids his age."

"So, his memory is fine, then?"

"I didn't say that, either."

Reggie put her hands on her hips. She was quickly getting annoyed. She wanted a straight answer. "So, what are you saying?"

"I'm saying we still don't have enough evidence one way or the other to draw any kind of conclusions."

"Great, so this was all a big waste of time." She turned away from Theo, not bothering to hide her frustration.

Theo put a hand on her shoulder. "This wasn't a waste of time. This was only the first step. I think we need to keep digging. Between the two of us, we've seen too many instances of people forgetting details of their lives for it to be a coincidence."

"So, you still think there's something affecting people's memories?"

"I think it's a possibility," Theo said with a nod.

"Okay, then what do we do now?"

"I want to run some tests on your blood and the boys. See if I can find anything there to give us some answers. We should probably do some brain scans as well."

"I don't know if I can get the boys to give you a blood sample." Reggie remembered the promise she'd made Miles: no needles. She would hate to go back on it.

"We don't have to. The hospital should have some samples stored from when they had their treatment. I just need you to sign this so they will release them to me." Theo handed her a tablet with a release form already filled out.

Reggie read through it quickly, trying not to think too hard about the fact that the hospital had samples of their blood in storage to be used for research purposes. She had to remember that they were living inside a giant experiment. Of course they would be collecting all kinds of data about the residents—this was what they had agreed to when they'd moved here. A certain amount of privacy had to be sacrificed for the good of the experiment. She signed the release form and handed the tablet back to him.

Theo smiled. "Thank you. Maybe now I can get you the answers you're looking for."

Chapter 22

Every muscle in Reggie's body ached. There was no easy way to access the section of the wall they'd been assigned, so they had to lug their equipment in and out on foot. Things didn't get any better once Reggie accessed the grid system controls. There were patches on top of patches, making it impossible to find the circuit that had failed. They needed to strip out most of the wiring and replace it all. It was hard work, but it left Reggie with a sense of accomplishment that would keep her going for days.

Reggie had already changed into her street clothes and was heading out to go pick up the boys when Dale blocked her path. She had no idea why, but he had been trying to get under her skin for the last few days and she was tired of it. "Is there something I can do for you?" she asked with a heavy sigh.

"Yeah," Dale said casually, putting Reggie instantly on-edge. "I was wondering if you could clear some things up for us." A few members of Dale's team were still hanging around and they gathered behind Dale. She knew this was going to be bad.

"What?" The single word dripped with annoyance. She did not have the patience for this today.

"My team and I hear things while we're working in the labs and city hall."

"I'm happy for you." Reggie tried to move past him but Dale continued to block her path.

"Recently, there's been a lot of talk surrounding you and the fact that you could have been one of the first residents here, and how odd it is that you've only come now."

Reggie crossed her arms. "What's your point?" This wasn't new information, so why bring it up now?

"People are curious as to why, and so far, the general consensus is that your family didn't want you here. That they took pity on you once your husband died and let you in."

"Are you done?" Reggie said, folding her arms over her chest. He would really need to try harder if he wanted a reaction from her.

"So, you're not denying it."

"You can believe whatever you want. I really don't give a shit what you think. Now get out of my way."

"I'd watch my language if I were you," Dale said with a laugh. "I'm a supervisor, after all."

"Yeah, but you aren't her supervisor," Sasha said as

she worked her way through the crowd until she stood next to Reggie. "Are you alright?"

"Of course," Reggie said with a smile. She turned back to Dale. "Your childish bullying tactics don't scare me. I have my reasons for not coming here sooner, and they are just that: mine. You can believe I'm this terrible person if it makes you feel better. Hell, it will probably even win you favor with my parents, which I'm sure is your ultimate goal here, but let me clear some things up for you first. My parents don't respect you, or anyone in this department. They feel that working with your hands is beneath them, and that people who aren't worth associating with. They tolerate you because you do what you're told without raising a fuss. They would replace you with a robot in a heartbeat if they could."

"That's not true," Dale said through gritted teeth. Reggie had clearly hit a nerve.

"Sure, it is," Reggie said with a smile. "It's about time you come to terms with it. I have. My parents don't respect anyone that doesn't have an advanced degree hanging on their wall. It's just a fact of life. Now, if you'll excuse me, I need to go get my kids." Reggie patted Dale on the shoulder as she pushed her way past him to the front door.

She collapsed against her car the moment she reached it and let out a breath. She'd known something like that was bound to happen at some point, she just didn't think it would be from someone in her department, or that they would bring Charlie into it.

"Reggie, wait!" Sasha called from the other side of the parking lot. Cam was with her. "Are you alright?"

she asked once they reached her.

"It's nothing I haven't heard before." Reggie leaned on the trunk of her car and looked at the maintenance building. She didn't tell them that even though she had heard it all before, it still stung.

"Don't let Dale get to you. He always picks on the newcomers," Sasha said.

"That's Sasha's way of saying he's an asshole," Cam said.

Sasha rolled her eyes. "Sorry if I still feel a little bad for the guy. A couple of years back, he had an accident. It was bad—it almost cost him his spot on the team. He was never the same after that. He used to be a decent-enough guy, but now he constantly feels like he has to prove himself to his guys or they won't follow him."

"That's a great quality to have in a leader," Reggie said.

"He's in there right now, trying to convince his team that what you said isn't true," Cam said.

Reggie scoffed. "Everything I said was true. He might think that my parents respect him, but they don't. It's all an act."

"But they seem so nice, usually." Cam looked at Reggie as if he was pleading with her to confirm what he was saying. She hated that she would have to disappoint him.

"I'm sure they do. They're really good at pretending when they have to, but I wouldn't worry about it. It's not like you're their kid."

"Were they really that terrible as parents?" Sasha asked, taking Reggie by surprise. She suspected that there really were rumors spreading throughout the city about her. She was sure most of them cast her in a bad light, given that most people here considered her parents to be their saviors. Normally she would let it go, but she didn't want anything to get back to the boys. She decided she would trust Cam and Sasha; it couldn't hurt for a few more people to know the truth.

Reggie took a deep breath. "I've had very little contact with my parents since I turned eighteen. I was told if I didn't go to college and pursue a science degree, I would no longer be welcome in their house. So, I left," Reggie said with a shrug.

"Really?" Cam said.

Reggie nodded. "Growing up, I always had to prove my worth to them through scientific achievement, which I managed to do for a while. I was eleven when I saw my friend's dad working in his garage—he was a carpenter—and everything changed for me. I knew that was what I wanted to do with my life. I knew my parents wouldn't approve, so I kept it hidden for years. The moment I told them was the moment I stopped being their daughter. They kept trying to push the sciences on me, and I kept resisting. They made it very clear on a daily basis how much of a disappointment I was, especially when compared to Isaac."

"That's terrible," Sasha said.

Reggie shrugged. "I didn't know anything different until I started working and made friends outside of the scientific community. Suddenly, I had joy in my life. I could just be me, and it turned out I was pretty good at fixing things. I started my own non-profit construction company, met Charlie, we fell in love, got married, had the boys, life was great. My parents wanted us to move here when the City first opened, but Charlie was against it. He claimed it was wrong due to a whole list of moral reasons, but I think a large part of it was him knowing what living this close to my parents would do to me. He didn't want me to have to deal with that again."

"What changed? Why did you decide to come now?" Cam leaned on the car next to her.

"Things changed. Charlie was killed, the price of clean drinking water skyrocketed, and I couldn't keep up with it all on my own. It got to the point where I had to put the boys' needs above my own."

"Well, we're glad you're here," Sasha said.

"Thanks."

"And don't worry about Dale. I'll talk to Mason about it. Now don't you have to go get your kids?"

"Shit," Reggie said. She scrambled to get in the car and started the short drive to the school, where she knew she'd find Miles and Jace happily playing on the playground, completely oblivious to the fact that she was late picking them up.

~

Reggie was busy cleaning up dinner when Theo called. Her palms sweated as she fumbled to answer. It had only been a few days since he saw the boys. She wondered if he had found anything—maybe something in their blood that would prove that their memory was being affected. Not that she had any idea what that would even look like.

"Hi, Theo," she said the moment she answered the phone.

"Hi, Reggie. I hope I'm not interrupting." His voice was calm, giving nothing away.

"No, not at all," she said, keeping up the niceties of social norms. She glanced into the living room where Miles was watching TV. She made her way to the back door, then stepped outside and quietly closed the back door. She knew if Miles heard her going outside, he would want to come out and play. "Have you found anything?"

"Not yet. I've done what I can with the blood samples, and so far, everything looks normal. I couldn't find any contaminants that might explain the memory-lapses."

Reggie tilted her head back and took a deep breath. She knew she wasn't crazy. There had to be a way to prove that something about this place was affecting people's memories. "So what do we do next?"

"The equipment I have here is limited, I want to send the results to an old colleague outside of the city and see if they can find anything I might have missed," Theo said. He wasn't giving up on her.

"You have a way to communicate with people outside of the City?" Reggie asked, ignoring the memory investigation for a moment. After all the issues she'd been having getting in touch with Amber, this information was almost more important to her than discovering what was happening to people's memories.

"Only at the lab. It's necessary to have access for

research purposes, but it's all highly monitored," Theo said.

A swarm of new questions filled Reggie's head. She thought an unfortunate side-effect of the wall was that it blocked out all communication with the outside world, but it seemed that that wasn't the case. If there were a workaround that allowed residents to contact the outside world, why weren't they more widely implemented? She couldn't be the only person here that missed people outside of the city. There was no reason to hinder open communication unless someone was hiding something. And why were the lab's communications heavily monitored? Were they trying to keep track of the work being done there? Maybe it was a security measure to make sure no one was giving away the location of the city or other classified information about the Sanctuary Cities?

"I wanted to get your thoughts before I send the sample data out," Theo said.

"What? Why would you need my opinions?" Reggie had stopped listening to Theo, her mind racing in different directions. She felt like she was trying to put together a puzzle, but she had no idea what the picture was supposed to be, and half the pieces were missing.

"Because." Theo's annoyance breaking through. Clearly, he had already told her this when she hadn't been listening. "If they find something that proves the smart grid is affecting people's ability to recall memories and it gets out before we have a plan in place to correct it, Isaac will be the one to take the blame."

"Oh." The last thing she wanted to do was get Isaac

in trouble. She knew he'd never intended to hurt anyone. He had developed the smart grid because he wanted to keep people safe. It was going to be hard enough to tell him that his tech was hurting people's minds. It would be so much worse if he found out from someone other than them.

"Yeah. Big oh," Theo said.

Reggie sat on the back step, looking out at the grassy area behind her house. Isaac had created all of this. There was so much beauty in this town. She knew that had to be his influence. Their parents had never cared about aesthetics. Her gaze settled on a magnolia tree. She hadn't noticed it before. It was still too early for the pink flowers to bloom, but Reggie could imagine what it would look like in a few weeks. There had been a magnolia tree in the park near their house growing up. Reggie would often find solace in its shade when things at home got too much for her.

She was sure Isaac had planted it for her. Her own private refuge in paradise.

"How is Isaac?"

Theo sighed. "He's stressed, for sure. I haven't seen him like this since we were in school. He brushes it off every time I ask. If he knows anything about what's happening, he's not telling."

Reggie wasn't surprised. Getting information out of Isaac had never been an easy task.

"How well do you know the person you want to send the data to?"

"Pretty well. We were in the same doctorate program together."

"Do you trust them?"

"I do, but it's still a risk. I'm always surprised what people are capable of doing."

That answer did not give Reggie the warm fuzzy feeling she was looking for. "I think it's worth the risk to get answers. If we're right, this is going to suck for Isaac no matter what. I'd rather know the truth and deal with the fall out after."

"I know you're right, but it makes me nervous," Theo said.

"Me too." Reggie squeezed the bridge of her nose in an attempt to stop the headache developing behind her eyes.

"Then I'll send the data in the morning, and hopefully we can start getting some answers."

"Thanks, Theo. I really mean it."

"Have a good night, Reggie." Theo hung up the phone.

Reggie set her phone down on the step. She wanted to pick it up and call Amber, but she didn't think she could handle the disappointment of another failed call. Instead, she looked at the magnolia tree and hoped she had made the right decision.

Chapter 23

A soft light cast over the front porch. Reggie was wrapped in a blanket on one of the white wicker chairs. She hadn't been a fan of them when she'd first seen them—they reminded her too much of her childhood home—but she found herself heading there more and more often. Especially when she didn't want the boys to see her upset. Which was exactly why she had retreated out here tonight.

A tear ran down her cheek as she looked at her phone. She really needed to talk to Amber, but she hadn't been able to get a call to go through all week. More than once, she'd thought about sneaking into the lab and using one of the computers in there to call, but she didn't like the idea of her calls being monitored.

All the stress and fear she had been struggling to

keep at bay all week was taking hold. She needed to talk to someone she trusted. She needed someone who had her best interests at heart to tell her what to do, before her mind pulled her down a dark path she couldn't come back from. There was only one living person on the planet that fit that description, and the technology meant to keep them safe was keeping Reggie from talking to her.

"Hey, what are you doing out here in the cold?" Isaac was making his way up to her front porch.

Reggie quickly wiped the tears from her eyes and tried to smile. She had no idea why Isaac was here. "Just thinking."

"That's dangerous," he said with a smile Reggie didn't return.

Isaac climbed the three steps up to the house, knocking over the signal booster she had set up on the top step. "Sorry." He picked up the device and looked it over. "What is this thing?"

Reggie waved it off. "It might as well be a paperweight, for all the good it's doing."

Isaac sat down next to her. "Seriously, what is it?"

"A signal-booster. Charlie got it years ago when he had the bright idea to take us all camping."

Isaac laughed. "You went camping?"

"I did, under protest. Worst weekend of my life, and that includes all those weekends I was forced to spend cleaning lab equipment for Mom and Dad."

"I find that hard to believe."

"It rained the whole time, the tent leaked, Miles ended up getting sick, and Charlie needed five stitches in his hand after an accident with a hunting knife. We never did need the signal-booster, which is probably for the best, because the damn thing doesn't work." Reggie took the booster from Isaac. "I don't even remember packing it, but I found it mixed in with my tools and figured I'd give it a shot." She set the booster down on the table between them.

"Who were you trying to contact?"

"Amber," Reggie said with a sheepish shrug. She could feel her emotions starting to rise when she said Amber's name. Reggie didn't have words to describe how much she missed her.

"I'm sorry," Isaac said. "Are you guys ready to go?"

"Go where?" Reggie ran through their calendar in her mind to try and figure out what she had forgotten. Was this the first sign that her memory was starting to be affected?

"To Mom and Dad's for family dinner," Isaac said slowly.

Reggie shook her head as she thought back over the week. Lena had said she wanted to have a family dinner, but she had never given Reggie a date or time. Any other night, she would have sucked it up and gone to avoid a fight, but not tonight. Her parents were the last people she wanted to see. "I don't know anything about it." She did feel a moment of relief over the fact that she hadn't forgotten anything. This was just her parents being their usual thoughtless selves.

"Mom said she told you."

"Well, she didn't."

"I'm a little early. Go get the boys and we can head

over together."

"I'm not going, Isaac." Her tears were threatening to make a return. "Tell them I'm not feeling well or something."

Isaac twisted in his seat so he could look at her. "What's going on, Reggie?"

"Today is my and Charlie's anniversary." Reggie choked back a sob and took a deep breath. "I almost forgot about it, actually. With the boys starting therapy sessions with Theo and everyone still getting settled into a routine here, it was a crazy week." The tears flowed freely down her cheeks now, but she didn't brush them away. This was a pain that deserved to be felt. "Even this morning, we were in such a rush to get out the door that I didn't even realize what the date was until an hour ago." She picked up the signal booster again, hoping it would help her feel closer to Charlie. It didn't. "How could I forget one of the most important days in my life? How could I forget about Charlie today of all days?"

"I'm sorry," Isaac said again with such sincerity that Reggie stopped crying to look at him closer.

"It's not like it's your fault." Reggie brushed the remaining tears off her cheek.

Isaac took one of her hands in his. "What can I do to make this better for you?"

"What can I do to make this better for you?"

"Fix the smart grid to allow cell singles to go through so I can call Amber," she said with a sad smirk.

Isaac chuckled. "That might take some time."

"Then don't make me go to dinner. I can't handle their comments tonight. It might destroy me if they don't remember Charlie again."

"I'll tell you what." Isaac let go of her hand and pulled his keys out of his pocket. "How about I take the boys to dinner while you go to my apartment. There's a phone there that's connected to a signal booster outside the wall. It's supposed to only be for City use, but I think we can make an exception. Go call Amber."

"Are you serious?"

Isaac nodded. "Of course, I am. If talking to Amber is going to help you feel better, then I'll do whatever I can to make that happen for you. I know I wasn't around much the last few years, but I'm here now. You're my baby sister. I'll try to take care of you. I love you, Reggie."

"I love you too. Thanks, Isaac." She took the keys from him and went to get the boys. She felt a little bad about sending them to her parents without her, but she knew Isaac would look out for them like he had done for her when they were kids. Like how he was still looking out for her now.

~

Reggie had never been to Isaac's house. Even before he moved to Serenity, he had always visited her wherever she was living. Technically, Isaac was still living at home when she moved out, though at that point he was spending most of his time at his college dorm. She was pretty sure he had his own apartment at some point, but by then, Reggie had moved away from their hometown. The more distance she could put between her and her parents, the better.

She felt like she was intruding as she opened the door to let herself in. She remembered Isaac's room growing up being cluttered with books and notepads covering every flat surface. He was always too wrapped up in whatever he was working on to worry about decorating. Over the years, it had become a hodgepodge of colors and material as he'd used whatever was close at hand to decorate his room. The only spot that was put-together was his awards shelf—or shelves, to put it more accurately. There were plaques and trophies from all the science fairs and robotic competitions he had won, except for the big nationwide competitions. Those were kept in their parents' display case for anyone who came to the house to admire.

She'd expected his apartment to be similar, but she was wrong. The living room was carefully decorated with splashes of green and gold mixed in with the white walls and black leather furniture. She couldn't see a book or stack of papers laying on any of the surfaces, though one whole wall was covered in carefully arranged bookshelves Jace would envy. She scanned the room looking for the phone but couldn't find anything. Maybe Isaac had an office?

She moved farther into the apartment, passing a sparkling-clean bathroom and a bedroom that looked more like a room at a luxury resort than the bedroom of a lifelong bachelor. There was one final door at the end of the hallway. Reggie prayed that it was his office—she didn't want to have to call him during dinner to ask where the phone was. She breathed a sigh of relief as she opened the door and saw a messy office on the other side. This was the Isaac she remembered.

Her heart swelled the moment she spotted the phone half-buried under a pile of papers on the desk. She crossed the room in three steps. She was going to get to talk to Amber. And not a broken conversations yelled over static filled lines—a real conversation.

Reggie's emotions threatened to overtake her as she dialed Amber's number and waited. With every ring, she prayed Amber would answer. Reggie knew Amber didn't usually pick up unknown callers, and she had no idea how this number would appear on Amber's phone.

After the fourth ring, she picked up. "Hello?" It wasn't Amber's normal confident voice, but it made the tears Reggie had been holding back start to flow.

"Amber, it's me," she said as she choked back sobs.

"Reggie?"

She nodded even though Amber couldn't see her. "Yeah."

Amber let out a breath. "Thank god. I've been trying to get through to you all day. How are you holding up?"

"I've been better." She leaned back in Isaac's desk chair and looked at the ceiling.

"How did you manage to get a call to go through? I thought the laser grid blocked out all cell service?"

"I'm using a special phone Isaac has hooked up to an antenna outside of the grid."

"Why don't all the houses have phones like that?"

"That's really a great question. One I wish I had an answer to," Reggie said without thinking. For a brief moment, she wondered if Isaac's line was monitored like the outside connection at the lab, though she had no idea who would be monitoring Isaac's calls. "I can't tell you how much I need to talk to you."

"I've got nowhere else to be, so tell me everything. What's been going on? How are the boys?"

"They're good. Really good, actually. Jace met a girl. Too soon to tell if there's anything more than friendship there, but they're spending all their free time together. And I'm pretty sure Miles is the most popular kid in his class."

"That's really great, Reg. I'm glad that things are improving for them. But what about you? How have things really been for you?"

Reggie let out a small sob as a new wave of tears started to flow. Amber always knew exactly what she needed. "It's been hard. My parents are the same as they've always been, but so far, I've been able to hold my own against them. Which hasn't been easy, between the lab waiting for the boys at the house and my mom trying to fix me up with a doctor. I feel like I'm waiting for another bomb to go off every time I see them."

"I'm sorry you're having to deal with all of that again," Amber said.

"I haven't even gotten to the bad stuff yet." Reggie wasn't sure how much she should tell her. She didn't have any proof to back up her theory. She knew Amber would freak out if Reggie told her that Miles had forgotten that Charlie was dead. Theo might have been able to explain it away, but Amber knew Miles better than he did. Would she push to have the Sanctuary City program shut down completely? Reggie doubted she'd get real far with Senator Bailey blocking her every move. No, Reggie would wait until she had more to go on. "I almost forgot today was my and Charlie's anniversary." The moment the words left her lips, Reggie started to break down.

"Oh, Reggie," Amber said. "I know it probably feels like a huge betrayal, but I promise you, it doesn't mean anything."

"I promised myself that I wouldn't forget him when we came here, and two weeks in, I'm starting to do just that," Reggie said between sobs.

"That's a little dramatic, don't you think?"

Reggie shook her head and wiped her nose on her sleeve. "It's the truth."

"No, it's not," Amber said gently. "You've been through a major life-change. It's completely understandable. Hell, people forget their anniversaries all the time with less going on than you're dealing with. It's normal."

"Charlie never would have forgotten," Reggie mumbled in response.

Amber laughed. "Reggie, he forgot about so many important dates the entire time you were married."

"No, he didn't. He always had something planned."

"Don't hate me for this, but that was because of me."

Reggie sat up straight in the chair. "What do you mean?"

"I think it started around your fourth anniversary. Jace was a baby, and you were both so sleep-deprived. I stopped by to check in on everyone. You were sleeping and Charlie was struggling to get Jace down for a nap.

Once I took Jace and got him to calm down, I asked Charlie if you guys had plans for your anniversary since it was that weekend. I'll never forget the look of pure panic on his face."

"No, that can't be true. I remember that year. He had Mrs. Elmenheimer babysit while we had a picnic on the roof. The whole place was decorated with lights, blankets, and pillows. He wanted to stargaze but there was so much smog that we could barely see the moon. Instead, we counted airplanes that flew overhead. It had to of taken him forever to put it together."

"I hate to burst your bubble, but he threw all that together the day before," Amber said with a laugh.

Reggie rolled her eyes. "He was good at that kind of thing."

"After that, I would send him a message before any big dates to make sure he remembered. I had to make sure he was treating you the way you deserved."

"You're lying," she said with a smile. She wasn't surprised that Amber had been looking out for her all those years. They had been doing it all their lives.

"What are friends for?" Amber said offhandedly. "The important thing is that not remembering your anniversary right away isn't a big deal. In fact, I think it's a sign that things are getting back to normal for you."

"What if I don't want to know what normal looks like without Charlie?"

"Oh, honey, you don't have much of a choice," Amber said gently. "Besides, Charlie wouldn't want you wasting your life because of him. Remember him, honor him, but also find a way to live your life, because that's what he would have wanted for you guys."

"What if I don't want to?"

"Then do it for Jace and Miles. They deserve to have a mom that's happy."

Reggie sighed. "I know you're right."

"I always am. When are you going to learn that?"

"Don't get your hopes up. It's the rest of my family that are geniuses, not me." She let out a small, self-deprecating laugh.

"Genius is overrated, if you ask me."

"I love you, Amber."

"I love you too. And talk to your brother about getting you a phone with a decent connection to the real world. We can't go this long without talking again."

Reggie thought back to the backlog of service requests at the maintenance office. "It might be easier if I figure out how to hook it up for myself."

"Do that, then. I'll talk to you soon, Reggie." It sounded more like a threat than a friendly goodbye.

"Bye, Amber." Reggie hung up the phone and spun around slowly in Isaac's desk chair. She felt better after talking to Amber, but the sadness deep within her heart was still there.

~

Reggie sat alone at the bar nursing a glass of whiskey. She didn't want to go back to her house after her call with Amber for fear that her family would try to pull her into the end of their dinner. She didn't have the energy to deal with her parents' disapproval tonight. She had her own concerns to obsess over without their input.

She knew Amber was trying to make her feel better, but Charlie forgetting their anniversary when they'd been sleep-deprived new parents was completely different than what she was going through. But how could she explain that to Amber? It wasn't like there was a guidebook to telling your best friend that you think your new home is stealing your memories. She decided she would tackle that problem another night.

Tonight, all she wanted to do was remember Charlie. She wanted to remember the way his voice sounded when he told her that he loved her. She wanted to remember the overwhelming peace she felt when he'd wrapped his arms around her and pulled her close to him. She wanted to remember how he had loved her unconditionally right from the start. He was the first person outside of Amber she hadn't felt like she had to prove her worth to. She wanted to cement all of these things in her mind—to protect them if she could from whatever was stealing moments like this from the rest of the people in Serenity.

Across the bar, Reggie saw Aaron sitting at a table with a couple of guys she hadn't met. She wondered if they also worked at the hospital. He caught her gaze and smiled at her. Reggie tried to smile back, though her heart wasn't in it, before averting her gaze.

Reggie tried not to stare as he got up and walked over to her with his drink in hand. "Hey, Reggie. Mind if I take a seat?" He gestured to the empty bar stool next to her.

"Help yourself," she said in a voice she hoped

sounded normal. Her emotions were so raw at the moment she had no idea what would spill out.

Aaron pulled out the barstool and sat down. "So, what brings you here?"

Reggie took a sip of her drink. "It's my and Charlie's anniversary." She didn't look at Aaron when she spoke, instead fixing her eyes on the row of opened liquor bottles behind the bar.

Aaron nodded, wrapping both his hands around his drink. "Is this the first one since he passed?"

Reggie shook her head. "The second, but the first one was only a few months after and everything felt so fresh then, I couldn't even acknowledge it."

"I'd tell you it gets easier with time, but I'd bet that's the last thing you want to hear right now."

Reggie turned to look at him. "You would be correct," she said with a small smirk. "I'll be alright. I didn't mean to interrupt your evening."

Aaron glanced back at the table he had come from. "Believe me, you didn't interrupt anything. Those guys talk about the same things every time they're together. They won't miss me, and I'd much rather talk to you."

"I'm not sure I'll be good company."

"It's okay, Reggie. I get it, more than anyone else, and I know it'll be worse if you're alone."

Reggie turned on her stool so she was facing him. "Do you remember your wedding?" It was a normal-enough question, given the topic of conversation, but asking it terrified her. She didn't know how she would react if he couldn't remember.

"Of course," Aaron said with a small chuckle. "I was

still in medical school and we were both broke, but we didn't care. We had a nice ceremony at the courthouse on a Wednesday night with a handful of friends and family. It was the only day I had off. Twenty-four hours later, I was back at the hospital, while she worked a part-time job to make enough to cover the rent. It was the best day of my life."

"It sounds amazing." Reggie couldn't describe the relief she felt at hearing Aaron talk about his wedding day. If he still remembered after being inside the smart grid for years, maybe there was hope for her.

"It really was."

"It sounds like the wedding I had wanted." Reggie watched the ice move in her glass as she gently swirled it.

"You didn't enjoy your wedding?"

"It's not that. We never planned on having a big wedding. We both thought all we could afford was a courthouse wedding with a few friends, but once people found out that was all we were doing, things started to get out of control." Reggie chuckled to herself as she remembered how the calls had started to flood in only hours after telling Amber their wedding plans.

"Your parents must have wanted to go all-out."

Reggie shook her head. "Not my parents. They weren't involved. Honestly, I was shocked that they actually showed up. It was people that Charlie and I had done work for over the years. They'd started to call and offer us things for free. We'd tried to turn them down, of course, but no one would take no for an answer."

"That's incredible," Aaron said.

"It was. We ended up getting married at this beautiful old summer camp that my company had helped renovate. The owner was a chef, and his wife was an event planner, so they turned it into the hottest event location in the area. Everyone that worked there was struggling—a lot were on parole or had spent time in and out of jail. Charlie was working legal aid, and was able to direct a lot of his cases there where they would learn life skills they would need to turn their lives around. A few of the kids actually ended up coming to work for me after helping with the renovations. They hosted our wedding as a thank-you, I guess. It was so much more than we would have been able to do on our own."

"It sounds like you and Charlie helped a lot of people."

Reggie shrugged. "We tried."

"People don't do things like that for just anyone. You and Charlie are amazing people."

"Thanks," Reggie said halfheartedly.

Aaron picked up his glass and held it up to her. "To Charlie."

Reggie smiled and picked up her glass as well. "To Charlie." She went to tap her glass on his, but he pulled it away.

"The luckiest man that ever lived. And to the amazing woman he got to spend his life with." Aaron clinked his glass on her.

Reggie didn't say anything. She knew if she tried, the only thing that would come out would be tears. So she just nodded and sipped her drink.

Chapter 24

It was the second week Reggie had been sent to the workshop for her Monday shift. She spent the day bouncing between tasks while trying to organize the workshop. By the end of the day, she had managed to complete a dozen work requests, cleaned off two workbenches, and organized half of one of the six racks that were currently overloaded with boxes and broken items. It was easily her most productive day since she'd arrived at Serenity. She was feeling pretty good about herself, something she hadn't felt in awhile.

"Damn, what happened in here?" Sasha scanned the room as she slowly made her way over to the workbench where Reggie was cleaning up.

"Just a little organizing." Reggie put the last of her

tools back in her toolbox and closed it.

"I guess no one told you that you're not supposed to work this hard when you have workshop duty. It'll make the rest of us look bad."

Reggie shrugged. "Sorry, I've never been good at taking it easy."

"You better be careful or Mason will assign you here permanently, and I can't have that. No one else on the team can fix the wall as well as you." Sasha tossed a sack of parts down on the workbench.

Reggie opened the bag and looked inside. "What's all this?"

"Blown fuses, broken laser tips, even a couple of pucks that went out when we were working today. Someone needs to verify they can't be fixed before I can trash them." Sasha leaned on the stool next to Reggie and lowered her voice. "You should have seen Dale freak out when the pucks failed."

Reggie pulled one of the pucks out of the sack. "How long was it down for?"

"Ten seconds, tops." Sasha rolled her eyes. "Long enough for Dale to drop his tools and run screaming for the truck. He left Cam suspended twenty feet in the air. I could have killed him."

Reggie laughed. "I would have loved to have seen it." She didn't normally like to relish others' misfortunes, but after the way Dale had been treating her, she felt no guilt imagining him running from the wall like a terrified child. She could tell from the smirk on Sasha's lips that part of her had enjoyed it as well, even if he had abandoned Cam, who Reggie assumed was fine. The kid probably didn't even realize what had happened until it was over. As the interior maintenance supervisor, it was unusual for Dale to be working on the wall at all. He thought working on the wall was beneath him, and those that did weren't worth his time. Reggie wondered what he had done to piss Mason off enough to have him covering for her on the wall.

"Yeah, because you weren't the one that had to clean up his mess." Sasha turned to Reggie. "How many more weeks of treatment do you have left?"

"I'll try to find out today," Reggie said with a laugh. "Was this Dale's first time on the wall?"

Sasha shook her head. "No, but it's been a few years since he's been out there. He was part of the first group of residents to move in. He was working on the wall when I came with the second group. He was always an arrogant prick, but he did decent work."

"What changed? Why did he stop working on the wall?"

"Something happened with his partner Steve when they were working out there. They were attacked or something. No one knows exactly what happened. The security cameras were shit back then. Dale swears that something dragged them into the woods. It took us hours to find them. They were both in rough shape when we did. Dale was never the same. He refused to work on the wall, and he got away with it for years. Mason only makes him fill in when there's no other option. Honestly, I would have preferred to be shorthanded. He's too much of a liability."

"What happened to the other guy? Steve?" Reggie

was still getting to know the maintenance team, but she was pretty sure she hadn't met anyone named Steve.

"He left a few months after the attack," Sasha said with a shrug.

"Like, left the team?"

"No, like, he left Serenity all together. It was weird. He didn't say anything to anyone. He just packed up his stuff and left. He didn't have any family here, so I guess there was nothing keeping him here."

"I didn't know people did that." With all the attention the Sanctuary Cities get in the news, she felt certain she would have heard if anyone had left. They would likely be flooded with interview requests. People were desperate to know what the cities were actually like, and any tricks to securing a spot at one, but Reggie had never seen anything from a former resident.

"It's been years since anyone left, but a handful of people did the first year. I think they adjusted the criteria to get in after that. People only see the upside when they apply for a spot in one of the cities. They don't think about what they have to give up to live here. Not everyone can handle being isolated from the rest of the world."

"Do you know what happened to Steve after he left?"

Sasha shook her head. "No idea. We never heard from him again, which I guess is a little weird. Then again, we know how hard it is to communicate with someone outside the wall. I imagine he wanted to put this chapter of his life behind him and move on."

"Yeah," Reggie said, though she wasn't really listening anymore. There were too many questions swirling around in her head. Was there a reason no one had wanted to leave in the last four years? Was this connected to what was affecting people's memories? Had they eventually forgotten that there was a whole world out there? She looked down at the sack of broken parts in front of her. Maybe she could find some answers there. "Is it alright if I take some of this home?" She nodded at the sack. "I need something to keep me busy after the boys are in bed. I have some ideas on how to keep the wall from blowing fuses all the time that I'd like to test out."

"Go for it. Mason won't care, especially if you find a way to free up some of our time to work on other things. Just make sure you enter what you're taking in the log."

Reggie put the parts she had taken out back in the bag. "Who keeps track of the log?"

Sasha laughed. "No one. It's just paperwork in case something goes wrong. Shouldn't you be heading over to the hospital?"

"Shit," Reggie said as she grabbed the bag. "I'll see you tomorrow, Sasha." She quickly made a note that she was taking some broken parts home to repair, though she left the descriptions vague just in case. She ran out of the building with the bag of parts tucked safely under her arm.

~

As expected, Theo was already in the treatment room when Reggie arrived. They exchanged pleasantries while the nurses hooked them up. Reggie was dying to ask him if he had any news, but knew they shouldn't talk in front of anyone. If word got out that their memories were being taken against their will, there was likely to be mass panic in the city, which would be bad for everyone.

The moment the door shut behind the nurses, Reggie turned to Theo. "Have you heard anything from your friend outside of the city?"

Theo's smile faltered. "Nothing yet, but it's only been a few days. These things take time, especially when I couldn't tell him exactly what to look for."

"Why not?" It shouldn't have been this hard to get some answers. Reggie needed to figure out what was going on before it was too late.

"Because all communication coming or going to the lab is monitored. I didn't know what would tip people off, so I figured it was best to keep things vague. Don't worry, though—he knows what we need him to do. We just have to give him time."

Reggie threw her hands up, causing the IV tube to rattle gently against the metal pole. "And what do we do in the meantime? Sit around and wait for our memories to disappear?"

"We don't know for sure that anyone's memories are being erased." Theo took off his glasses and gently massaged the bridge of his nose.

"Something is happening to them." She didn't want to take this out on Theo, but her frustration was getting the best of her.

"Maybe. I did have an idea of something else we can try, if you're up for it," Theo said.

"What is it?"

"I wanted to ask you some questions and see how your memory is holding up. Since you're aware that there might be something affecting your memory, you should be more aware of the effects."

"Yeah, sure, let's do it," Reggie said, even though she absolutely hated the idea of sitting here for an hour answering questions about her life, but she would do almost anything to get answers.

"Great." Theo picked up a tablet from the tray next to his chair. Of course, he would want to take notes. "Let's start with some basic stuff. Where did you live before coming here?"

"Oakwood Apartment complex, building 3, apartment 4D," Reggie said without hesitation, making sure to give as much detail as she could.

"Great." Theo scribbled something on his tablet. "What can you tell me about your company?"

"It was called Homes, Hearts, and Hammers. We did free construction work for low-income areas."

"And how did you get started in that?"

"I was working at a manufacturing plant at the time with my friend Jesse. We'd started to pick up odd jobs afterhours, and that's when we realized how many people needed help making their properties livable but couldn't afford to pay for it. Things like schools, community centers, low-income housing. We had to find a way to help. So, we started Homes, Hearts and Hammers. When we started, it was just Jesse and me working out of our truck. Eventually, with Charlie's help, we were able to secure government funding, and expanded."

"It seems like that all came pretty easily to you," Theo said. "Was there any struggle to recall any of the details?"

Reggie shook her head. The whole community had come out to help with the repairs, and she could remember everything—from the first official job they'd gotten fixing a community playground that had been condemned years ago, to the names of every person working for her when she turned the company over to Jesse before coming here. "I remember it all."

"Okay, let's get a little more personal. Tell me something about Charlie. Something only you would know."

Reggie's palms started to sweat. She was hoping they would ease into this, but it seemed like Theo wanted to jump in headfirst. Reggie took a deep breath, her fears fighting to get to the surface. She pushed them back down. "He was silly, was constantly playing make-believe with the boys. I like to listen to music while I'm cooking. He would always sneak up behind me and start dancing. We burned a few dinners that way." A small laugh escaped her lips. "He always put his cream in before his coffee. He hated pickles. He had to sleep on his right side. He was starting to get some gray hairs around his ears. He needed reading glasses but hated wearing them. I can't tell you how many times he intentionally left them at home. It would drive me crazy."

"Is that where Isaac learned it?" Theo said with a chuckle. He scanned over the notes he had made on the tablet. "Well, it doesn't seem like you've forgotten any of the details, but what about the emotions? How did Charlie make you feel?"

"He made me feel..." Reggie's voice trailed off.

"Did you forget?" Theo asked.

"No. I don't know how to put it into words. Charlie was the only person who made me believe that I was enough, just as I was. I didn't need to prove anything to him, I didn't have to earn his love. He gave it willingly with no strings attached. We were married for fifteen years, and I still got butterflies every time he kissed me. I felt like I was the luckiest person alive because he loved me. He made me whole."

"Well, there you have it," Theo said, putting the tablet back down. "If there's something about this place that is affecting people's memories, I think it's safe to say that it hasn't affected you the same way."

"But why?" Reggie said as she quickly wiped away the tears that had started to form in her eyes.

"I have no idea. Believe me, I wish I did," Theo said with unexpected seriousness. Up until that point, Reggie hadn't been sure if he was really trying to help, or simply humoring her.

"But it doesn't make any sense." The door to the room opened. Reggie whipped her head around to see the nurse coming in. They were out of time.

"I'll figure it out Reggie. Don't worry," Theo said softly before the nurse reached them.

Reggie nodded and bit her lower lip as the nurse removed the IV from her arm.

Chapter 25

Reggie tried to be patient as she waited for Theo to hear back from his contact outside the city. Over a week had passed since he had sent them the data, and they were still waiting. Reggie was starting to think maybe he was keeping the information from her, but she knew that was her paranoia taking over. Her birthday always put her on-edge, and being around her parents for it for the first time in years had sent her anxiety through the roof.

She had gone years without acknowledging it, but that had stopped once Charlie had come into the picture. He'd insisted they celebrate her, and made sure that she was treated like royalty. A stark contrast to how her birthdays had been treated while she was growing up. Now that Charlie was gone and she was back with her parents, she had no idea what to expect from the day.

Reggie slowly dragged herself out of bed and started to get ready. She wanted to prolong starting the day as long as she could, but she needed to get the kids ready for school and get to work. At least it was Monday, so she'd be spending the day alone in the workshop, where she wouldn't have to pretend like she wasn't a complete mess.

Halfway down the stairs, Reggie froze. There were noises coming from the kitchen. She glanced back up the stairs and saw that the doors to Jace and Mile's bedrooms were still closed. Normally, she had to drag them out of bed on Monday mornings. A loud bang echoed through the house. There was definitely someone downstairs.

"Miles, be careful. You'll wake up mom," Jace's voice reached her ears.

"Sorry," Miles said. "Can I crack the eggs?"

"How about you make the toast?"

A small smile formed on Reggie's lips. What were they doing? She quickly snuck downstairs and peered into the kitchen, careful not to let the boys see her. Jace was at the stove cooking scrambled eggs. Miles was pushing a chair over to the counter near the toaster, with the bread wedged under his arm. Looks like she'd be eating misshapen sandwiches for lunch this week.

She watched in amusement as Jace and Miles attempted to cook breakfast. Neither of them had ever shown any interest in cooking and watching them try to figure it out on their own was amusing. That was until Miles went to use a fork to dig the toast from the toaster.

"No!" Reggie said as she rushed into the kitchen.

"Miles, stop." She managed to reach him before he stuck the fork in and electrocuted himself. "Let me help." She unplugged the toaster and safely removed the stuck toast.

"But we're supposed to be making you breakfast," Miles said as she handed him the toast.

"And you're doing a wonderful job," Reggie said as she gave him a squeeze.

"Here, Mom, sit down." Jace pulled out a chair at the table for her.

"Okay," Reggie said with a laugh. "What did I do to deserve all this?"

"It's your birthday," Jace said as he pushed in her chair. "We wanted to make you a birthday breakfast like Dad used to do."

Tears formed in Reggie's eyes, and she made no move to stop them. She couldn't believe the boys even remembered her birthday, let alone did all of this. "Thank you," she managed to say as she pulled Jace into a side hug.

Never in a million years would she have thought the boys would do something like this. The amount of forethought and planning that went into it was impressive. Jace was right—it was exactly what Charlie would have done. He always went out of his way to make her feel special on her birthday. The first year they were together, Reggie hadn't even mentioned it, and the day passed completely unnoticed, which annoyed Charlie. His family always made a big deal out of birthdays, and he'd had a hard time coming to terms with the fact that Reggie had stopped celebrating hers when she was thirteen. The following year, he surprised her with an elaborate breakfast before taking her shopping at the hardware store, followed by a picnic lunch at their favorite park. The evening had ended with a small party with their closest friends. It was the first time Reggie had understood what birthdays were supposed to be. She had given up the idea of that ever happening again once he'd passed.

Miles set a plate with two pieces of buttered toast down in front of her. Large holes had been ripped in the toast from the cold butter he had attempted to spread on it. Jace returned a moment later with a plate of scrambled eggs that appeared to be burnt and undercooked at the same time. The boys took their seats at the table with bowls of cereal and looked at her in anticipation. Reggie took a small amount of the eggs and put it on the toast. "This looks amazing," she said before taking a bite. "It's so good," she managed to say after forcing herself to swallow.

"Happy birthday, Mommy," Miles said.

"Happy birthday, Mom," Jace echoed.

"Thank you. This means so much to me. Now eat up. You two still have to get ready for school." Reggie picked at her food as the boys quickly ate their cereal. She would have to make sure to hide the rest of it in the bottom of the trash can once they left the room. She loved the thought and effort they put into it, but that didn't mean she wanted to risk food poisoning

~

After an uneventful day in the workshop, Reggie managed to make it to the hospital for her treatment a few minutes early. She thought there was a chance she would beat Theo, but he was already there. Reggie plopped down in the chair next to him and waited for the nurse to finish with Theo.

Reggie bit the inside of her cheeks as the nurse inserted the IV into her. She would have thought it would have been easier to handle by now, but it still put her on-edge every time. "How many more weeks will I have to do this?"

The nurse secured the IV before she turned to look at the computer. "Looking at your numbers from last week, we should only need a few more rounds to get you back into a normal range. And happy birthday."

"Thanks," Reggie said softly. She wondered what the odds were that Theo hadn't heard that. The breakfast from the boys was all she needed. She didn't think she could handle everyone else wishing her happy birthday while her parents ignored it completely. The nurse gave Reggie a warm smile and left.

"So, today's your birthday," Theo said the moment the nurse was gone.

Reggie sighed and leaned back in her chair. "Yeah."

"Well, happy birthday. Are you planning on doing anything special?"

"The boys surprised me with breakfast this morning," Reggie offered.

"That's really sweet," Theo said.

"Yeah, it was something their dad always did."

"Anything else?"

Reggie shook her head. "Honestly, my plan was to ignore it. I've never been big on celebrating my birthday, and with Charlie gone, it seemed easier to treat it like any other day."

"Come on, you have to celebrate. Aren't your parents doing something to acknowledge it?"

A laugh escaped Reggie's lips before she could stop it. She wasn't sure if she had heard anything so ridiculous in her whole life.

"What's so funny?" Theo asked.

Reggie took a few deep breaths to get her laughter under control. "Isaac didn't tell you much about how we were raised, did he?"

"He told me that your parents pushed you both towards the sciences," Theo said. Reggie could see the confusion on his face. He had no idea what her parents were really like.

"They didn't just push us towards the sciences, they forced it down our throats. The last time my parents acknowledged my birthday was when I turned thirteen." She normally didn't like to share details from her childhood because people would end up feeling sorry for her, which was the last thing she wanted. But if Theo was going to date Isaac, he should know the kind of baggage came with that.

"You have to be exaggerating," Theo said.

"I'm not. My parents believed that we had to earn our birthday celebrations." She rolled her eyes. She remembered the first time she had celebrated Amber's birthday with her family, and the betrayal she had felt when she realized that normal people didn't have to do anything to earn their birthday celebrations.

"Earn it how?" There was a cautiousness in his voice that made Reggie suspect he was afraid to hear the answer.

"So, you know how Isaac and I are named after scientists?"

Theo chuckled. "I always thought he was joking when he told me that."

"Nope, he's actually named after Isaac Newton." Reggie shook her head and sighed. It was one thing to name your kid after a famous figure, but it was another thing altogether to expect that kid to follow in their namesake's footsteps. The pressure she felt as a kid to live up to it was huge. It was one of the main reasons she had started going by Reggie in the first place.

"Okay, so who are you named after?"

"Regina Fleszarowa. She was a geographer and geologist. The first Polish woman to receive a PhD in natural science from the Sorbonne."

"I'll have to take your word on that," Theo said.

"Every year for our birthdays, we had to do a report of some kind related to our namesake. We had free reign over the exact topic and format—my parents wanted it to be fun, since it was our birthday project, after all." Reggie rolled her eyes as she thought back to all the reports she had done on Regina Fleszarowa. "A month before our birthdays, we would present our projects to our parents, along with a birthday request form detailing the kind of celebration we would like to have, who we wanted to be included, and what gifts we would like. My parents would grade our projects and plan a celebration based on how well they thought we did. The higher the score on the project, the more elaborate the party and gifts would be."

"This started when you were older, right? Surely you didn't have to jump through all these hoops when you were a child?"

Reggie shot him a look. He still wasn't getting it. "I had to do it for every birthday I can remember. I was shocked when I got to elementary school and found out no one else even knew what a birthday project was."

"That explains so much," Theo muttered to himself. "What happened when you turned thirteen?"

"It really started the year before. I was at my friend Amber's house and saw her dad fixing one of the kitchen chairs in the garage. I was fascinated. More so than I had ever been about anything my parents had tried to get me interested in. He was a carpenter, and he started to teach me how to fix things. I would go over and work with him every chance I got. I even changed my schedule at school so I could take shop class without my parents finding out. I got away with it until report cards came out at the end of the semester."

"How did they take it?" Theo asked. This was starting to feel a lot more like a therapy session than two friends chatting.

"Surprisingly well, actually. They agreed to let me keep taking the class as long as it didn't affect my grades, and I kept up with the extra science work they gave me. I was naive enough to think this meant they approved of me learning how to work with tools. I started working on my birthday project three months before my birthday that year. I thought if I did enough, my parents would get me the toolset I asked for. It wasn't anything over-the-top—just some basic things to get me started. I spent every spare moment I had working on that report. I even tried to replicate some of her work myself and wrote fifteen pages on her contributions to women's rights."

"I take it they didn't grade it well," Theo said.

"Actually, it was the highest score I had ever gotten. My mom made all my favorite foods in an extravagant meal. It was the only time they'd ever gotten out the good dishes for me. My parents spent all dinner telling me how proud they were of the work I had done, and that I had shown them how much potential I had. It was the happiest I had ever been up to that point in my life. After dinner, they brought me to the study where there was a huge pile of gifts waiting for me. Way more than I had asked for. I assumed they had been so impressed with what I had turned in that they expanded on my gift request. The first box was a set of laboratory grade beakers, then a rock tumbler, then a centrifuge. I stopped opening the boxes after that."

"They didn't get you anything that you asked for?"

Reggie shook her head. "They told me they had allowed me to indulge in my new hobby long enough, and since I liked to work with my hands, they wanted me to focus on more of the practical sciences to see which field I preferred. I was devastated."

"What did you do?"

"I left," Reggie said with a shrug. "I went to Amber's house. I was a blubbering mess when I got there, but her dad had a gift waiting for me. It was one of his old toolboxes filled with tools. Most of them were used—he had told some of his buddies about me, and they all pitched in what they could. It was the best gift anyone has ever given me. I still have it in my workshop back home. The next year, I didn't bother to do my birthday project. I mean, what was the point? My parents let my birthday pass without a word. Eventually, Isaac stopped turning in projects too, though I think he still did them." Reggie smiled as she imagined Isaac hiding the reports on Newton he had done so she wouldn't feel bad. "Birthdays were never mentioned in our house after that."

"The more I hear about your childhood, the more impressed I am that you and Isaac aren't more messed-up," Theo said with a chuckle.

"Just give it time. I'm sure it'll come out at some point," Reggie responded. The nurse was back to remove their IVs. Another treatment session was done, and they didn't even get to talk about any updates with their investigation.

"How about we go get a drink?" Theo stood up and started to put on his jacket. "Your birthday deserves to be acknowledged."

"I have to go get the boys."

"They're with Isaac, right?"

Reggie nodded as she put on her jacket.

"I'll send him a message. I'm sure he won't mind. He loves getting to spend so much time with them."

"You're not going to take no for an answer, are you?"

"Nope." Theo put his arm around her shoulders and

guided her out of the room. "Reggie Stone, it's time to celebrate the amazing person you are."

Chapter 26

The parking lot behind the bar looked pretty full for a Monday afternoon. She wondered if there was any way she could back out. How mad would Theo be if she texted him with some excuse? She pulled into the parking lot.

Theo was waiting next to the back door of the bar. His eyes locked on hers the moment she pulled in. There was no backing out now. She took a deep breath, plastered a smile across her face, and got out of the car.

"It's just a drink, Reggie," Theo said with a laugh. "You don't have to look so miserable."

"This is my happy face." She let the muscles in her face relax, hoping it would make her smile look more natural.

"That's better." Theo winked at her then opened the door.

The moment she was through the door, the entire bar erupted with a round of "Happy Birthday!"

Reggie whipped around to look at Theo in shock. "What is all this?" She knew she should have stayed in the car.

Theo held his hands up in surrender. "It was all Isaac's idea. My only job was to get you here."

She turned back to the bar to see Isaac standing there with a huge smile on his face, his hands resting on Jace and Miles's shoulders. Her parents were standing next to them. Reggie blinked a few times to make sure what she was seeing was real. The book club moms were at their normal table while the maintenance team huddled around the pool table in the back. It looked like everyone she knew in Serenity was there ready to celebrate with her. Tears started to roll down her cheeks. The last time someone had done something like this was the surprise party Charlie and Amber had put together for her thirtieth.

Miles ran over and wrapped his arms around her waist. "Mommy, are you crying?"

Reggie bent down and picked him up. "Happy tears, baby, I promise."

Miles gently wiped the tears from her cheek and kissed her. Reggie held him tight as more tears fell. How did she get so lucky to get to be his mother?

"Happy birthday, Mom," Jace said as he hugged her.

"This is too much," Reggie said as her family gathered around her. She had no idea how to process what was happening. Her family didn't do things like this, especially for her.

"You deserve it." Isaac kissed her cheek and whispered, "Happy birthday, Reg."

"I think Reggie could use a drink," Theo said. He hadn't left her side since they entered.

Isaac nodded, took Miles from Reggie, and led them all over to the bar. "Thank you," Reggie said to Theo. "Though don't think that will be enough for me to forgive you for springing this on me." She tried to sound threatening, but she couldn't seem to get the smile to leave her face.

"I'm so glad you're here and we can finally celebrate your birthday as a family again," Oscar said as he handed Lena and Reggie a glass of wine.

"Thanks, Dad," Reggie said in confusion while shooting Isaac a look. They'd had so many opportunities to celebrate her birthday as a family and had chosen over and over not to acknowledge the day. Her paranoia kicked into overdrive, but she honestly couldn't tell if her dad didn't remember how they used to treat birthdays, or if he was trying to save face with the other people in the bar.

Lena gave Reggie a quick one-arm hug. "Happy birthday, darling."

Reggie was pretty sure she was sleeping. This had to be a dream. It was the only thing that made any sense. "Are you two feeling alright?"

"Of course." Lena gave her an odd look that put Reggie at ease. She was used to her mother looking at her like she was talking nonsense. It was a look she was accustomed to. "Oh, Oscar, you said you wanted to talk to the Crawfords. Would you excuse us?" They didn't wait for Reggie to answer before they left.

Reggie looked for Isaac who was busy showing Jace and Miles one of the arcade games in the corner. She turned instead to Theo, who was leaning on the bar next to her waiting for his drink. "Do you think whatever is affecting people's memories could also be making my parents nicer people?" She was only half-joking. There had to be a reason why her parents' behavior had changed so drastically.

"First, we haven't proven that there is anything affecting people's memories," Theo said with a smirk. "But if there is, I suppose it's possible that it could change people's behaviors as well."

Reggie cocked an eyebrow. "Enough to make them forget what a massive disappointment I am?"

"I'm sure they don't think you're a disappointment."

Reggie tipped glass at him. "See, that's where you're wrong. They absolutely do. They've told me several times over the years."

Theo turned around so his back was now to the bar. "The way I see it, you have two options."

"And what are they?"

"You can sit here with me all night and we can dig deeper into your childhood, see if we can start to mend some of that childhood trauma," Theo said.

"What's the second option?" Reggie asked with a groan.

"You can stop stressing over your parents' behavior, be grateful for the fact that they've acknowledged your birthday for the first time in years, and go enjoy this fabulous party your brother put together for you."

"I think I'll do that one." Reggie took a sip of her drink. "Thanks, Theo." She walked across the bar to where the maintenance team was hanging out. They let out a round of cheers as she approached.

~

Reggie moved around the bar, thanking everyone for coming. She was surprised how many people she recognized, given the short amount of time they had been there. Isaac and the boys looked like they were having the time of their lives. He was currently teaching them how to play darts, which Reggie thought was risky, but decided not to say anything. Between her dad and Theo, they were doing a good job at keeping anyone from getting hit with a stray dart.

Reggie headed to the bar for another drink. The bartender came over to get her order. "Can I get sparkling water with lime?" The bartender nodded then went to get her drink.

"Smart choice. People here know how to drink," Aaron said. He sat two seats away from where she was standing. She wondered how she hadn't noticed him there before.

Reggie smiled and sat down, leaving an empty barstool between them. The bartender set her drink down before going to help someone else. She picked up her drink and toasted him. "A trick I picked up from Charlie. I didn't expect to see you here tonight."

"Lena insisted I come. I'm sorry, I didn't want to intrude."

"It's fine. I'm glad you're here," she said awkwardly. She hadn't spoken to him since her anniversary, but had found herself thinking about him from time to time. "I never got to thank you for listening to me the other night."

Aaron turned to face her. "You never have to thank me for that. How are you holding up?"

Reggie shrugged. "I'm alright, but I'd be lying if I said it hasn't been rough. There's always a lot of extra reminders this time of year that Charlie is really gone." She looked at the door, imagining what it would feel like to see Charlie walk through. He would have loved this place. He was always the life of the party wherever he went—he would have had the whole bar convinced he was their best friend by the end of the night. They couldn't afford to go out often, but when they did, Charlie was in his element. Reggie would often find herself alone at the bar, taking in the atmosphere while she watched him. She would give anything for one more night like that.

"Holidays, birthdays, anniversaries are still tough for me too, but it's a duller ache than it used to be," Aaron said.

"I'm dreading that," Reggie said without thinking.

"Why's that?"

Reggie looked down at her drink cradled in her hands. "The pain reminds me that what Charlie and I shared was real. It hurts so much because we loved each other that much. I wouldn't trade that for anything."

"Hey, Reggie, you're up," Cam called from across the bar. He was standing next to the pool table chalking the tip of his pool cue.

"Go enjoy your party," Aaron said with a nod. "We can catch up another time."

"I'll hold you to that." Reggie got up and walked across the bar.

She took her time selecting her cue, not that she really had a preference. She just wanted Cam to think she took this more seriously than she actually did. "Are you sure you're ready for this?" she asked with a wicked grin.

"I've been holding the table all night. I'm not scared of you."

"You should be," Sasha chimed in from the table where most of the maintenance team was drinking. Their table was filled with empty glasses and pitchers. "I've seen her play. She's good."

"Sasha, this is the one place where I do not trust your judgment. You don't know anything about pool," Cam said, causing the table to erupt in laughter.

Sasha looked unfazed. "She beat Isaac." That caused Cam to pause. Isaac must have spent a fair amount of time here to have that kind of reputation.

"Are we going to talk all night, or are we going to play?" Reggie racked the balls and looked at Cam.

"It's your birthday. Why don't you break? Age before beauty." Cam smirked and bowed towards her.

"I'm going to make you regret that comment." She took her shot, sinking two solid balls as she did. Reggie sank two more before she missed a shot.

"Finally, a challenge." Cam slowly circled the table before he took his shot. He managed to get two before missing.

The spectators from the table went back to drinking, leaving Cam and Reggie to focus on the game. Reggie looked around the bar as she waited for Cam to finish his turn. She spotted Dale by the dartboards. "Hey, Cam, how much do you know about Dale?" She stepped forward to take her turn.

"You mean other than the fact that he's a colossal asshole?"

Reggie laughed. "Yes, besides that."

Cam shrugged. "Not much. He doesn't venture outside of his team much, but then again, all the guys on the interior team think they're better than us."

"Sasha mentioned that he had an incident out at the wall once and his friend ended up leaving the city all together because of it," Reggie said, making sure to keep her tone casual.

Cam took a shot and missed. "That was before my time. It was a big deal when his buddy left, though. I remember people talking about what would happen if he shared information about our tech or location with the outside world. As part of the maintenance team, we know a lot about what keeps this place running. There was an uptick in security for a while after he left, and a handful of upgrades were made to the wall too. That was about the time we stopped being able to get a signal to the outside world."

Reggie wondered if there was some kind of connection there. Did they not want people in the city to contact Steve once he left? Maybe the reason Steve left had nothing to do with the incident at the wall. Was it possible the cell service was being intentionally blocked and only being passed off as a side-effect of the wall? Could what happened to Steve somehow have been connected to what was happening with people's memories? If the cell service was being intentionally blocked, was it possible that residents' memories were being altered intentionally? All these questions swirled through Reggie's mind as she called her final shot.

A round of cheers erupted from the table the maintenance team was sitting at as the black ball fell into the pocket she had called. Reggie hadn't realized they were still watching. "Looks like we have a new champion," Sasha said as she handed Reggie a beer.

"I took it easy on you because it's your birthday," Cam said.

"You keep telling yourself that." Over Cam's shoulder she saw Jace wandering around the bar looking for someone. "Excuse me for a second." She weaved her way through the people as she made her way over to him. She saw Miles sitting at a table with her parents, Isaac, and Theo. He looked half-asleep. She glanced at her watch. It was later than she'd realized. Jace was probably looking for her to take them home.

"Hey, buddy," Reggie said as she approached him.

Jace turned to look at her. "There you are. Grandma wanted me to tell you that she was going to take us home. Miles is bored."

"We can all go. It's getting late and you guys have school tomorrow." She put her hand on his shoulder to turn him towards the table. A song started to play over the jukebox. It was Charlie's favorite song. He would sing it to the boys when he was trying to get them to sleep as babies. It had been their wedding song, and he would often sneak up behind her in the kitchen while she was cooking and start to dance with her while he sang it. They'd even played it at his funeral. For the first time since arriving at Serenity, it felt like Charlie was there with them. "Did you put this on?"

Jace pursed his lips and shook his head as he listened. "I don't think I've ever heard it before."

"Of course you have. Your dad used to play it all the time."

"I don't recognize it," he said with a shrug. "Should I get Miles?"

"Yeah," she managed to say as she fought to regain her breath. Reggie was frozen to the spot. There was no possible way that Jace would forget this song. There had to be another explanation, and she was determined to find it one way or another. She would not let the boys forget Charlie.

Chapter 27

Reggie groaned as she rolled over in bed and blindly felt for her phone on the nightstand. She almost never had the ringer on, since being woken up by a ringtone grated her nerves. This was her first weekend on-call. Mason and Sasha had assured her that they rarely got emergency calls but everyone on the team still took turns covering on the weekends. It figured that she would get a call on her first turn.

"This is Reggie," she mumbled into the phone while lying in bed. She glanced at the clock, six in the morning on a Sunday. This used to be her day to sleep in. She and Charlie would take turns getting up with the boys on the weekends so they each had one morning where they could relax in bed. It had been a long time since she'd had a relaxing morning in bed.

"Hey, this is Glen from security. We need you to get over to the lab. There's been some kind of incident and they're requesting a safety check."

"What kind of incident?" Reggie tossed the blanket aside and sat up. "Was anyone hurt?"

"I don't know, exactly. They didn't request medical support when they called it in, so I doubt anyone was injured."

"Okay, thanks. I'll be there as soon as I can." Reggie ended the call and rubbed the sleep out of her eyes.

She'd need to get someone to watch the boys. Reggie tried to come up with a better option while she got dressed, but she knew there was only one person she could ask. How much harm could he really do while the boys were sleeping?

With a resigned sigh she picked up her phone and hit call. "Hi, Dad," she said.

"Regina? Why are you calling so early? Are the boys alright?"

"Yeah, everyone is fine," Reggie said, taken aback by the concern in his voice.

"Then why are you calling? You know I like to work in the morning with no interruptions," Oscar said. There was the annoyance Reggie had been expecting.

"I know. I'm sorry," she said out of habit. "I'm calling because I need someone to come sit here while the boys sleep."

"Why can't you do it?" The frustration in his voice had Reggie second guessing if she should drag the boys along with her. If she had a little more information about what happened at the lab, she'd have known if it was safe to bring them or not.

Reggie took a deep breath. It was too early for this. "I'm on-call and was just informed that I'm needed at the lab. So can you come over or not?"

"What happened at the lab?"

"That would be a really great thing for you to look into once you get here. Unless getting the lab back up and running isn't your top priority."

"I'll be right there," Oscar said.

Reggie hung up without responding. He always had to make things difficult. She quickly finished getting dressed. Her toolbox was sitting next to the front door. She grabbed it and headed out. She was putting the toolbox in the trunk of her car when Oscar walked up. "They boys should sleep for a while. I'll be back as soon as I can." She didn't wait for him to answer before getting in her car.

It only took her a few minutes to get to the lab. She was surprised how many cars were in the parking lot, given the early hour. Didn't these people believe in weekends?

There was a security guard waiting for her in the lobby. He didn't say much as he led her through the building. Reggie tried to figure out what could have happened as they went. There were no odd smells in the air, so she doubted it was a chemical lead. The power seemed to be functioning properly and she couldn't see any signs of damage. It took her a minute to realize the path they were taking was familiar.

"Whose lab had the incident?" Reggie asked as they stepped out of the elevator. Her mother's lab was on this floor. And so was Theo's.

"Dr. Nicholls," the guard said.

Reggie's blood turned to ice. She pushed past the guard and ran to Theo's lab. What she found shocked her. The glass window in the door had been shattered, and the frame had been partially ripped from the wall. Reggie hadn't been aware that Serenity had a police force, but an officer was waiting for her in the hallway.

"Are you from the maintenance team?"

"Yeah." Reggie tore her gaze away from the damaged door. "I'm Reggie." She held out her hand to the officer.

"There's a good amount of damage," the officer said while briefly shaking her hand, "but it all seems pretty superficial. They want you to check the gas lines and make sure nothing is leaking." The officer ushered her into the lab.

Her shoes crunched on the broken glass as she stepped inside. The entire lab was trashed. Tables and chairs were on their sides, papers littered the floor, and a large red X was spraypainted across the floor. Every shelf in the room had been swept clean, the contents scattered on the floor. "What happened?"

"We think it was just bored teenagers," the officer said with a shrug.

Reggie hadn't realized there was anyone else in the room. A man with a sheriff's badge made his way over to her. "We haven't met yet. I'm Wes Skelton, Sheriff of Serenity."

"You really think this was bored teenagers?" She gestured around the room.

"It's happened before. There's not a lot of ways to have a rebellious teenage phase in this place. We have a pretty good idea who did it. I'll question them once we wrap up here. Usually, they just need a little scare to get them back in line."

Reggie wasn't buying it. If this was kids acting out, they wouldn't have picked a lab on the third floor to vandalize. This was targeted, and Reggie had a sinking suspicion she knew why.

"Someone from the maintenance team should be here soon," Isaac said as he walked into the lab.

"They're already here," Wes said.

Reggie smiled and waved at Isaac.

"Reggie?"

"I'm on-call this weekend," she said.

"You two know each other?" Wes pointed from Reggie to Isaac.

"Yeah, she's my sister," Isaac said.

Reggie turned back to the sheriff. "Is it alright if I get started?" She didn't want to get into the whole family connection. Getting this place put back together was going to take some time and Reggie didn't want to leave the boys with her dad any longer than necessary.

"Be my guest," Wes said.

Reggie steadied a lab table that was leaning against a bookshelf, set down her toolbox, and pulled out a meter to start looking for gas leaks. She didn't really expect to find any, but she needed to do something to keep the growing panic at bay. She wasn't sure how, but she knew this had to be connected to the memory-loss somehow. Though she couldn't understand why anyone would want to stop them from getting answers.

She noticed that Isaac kept his voice down while speaking to the sheriff. She wondered if he was doing it on purpose, knowing she was in the room. Did he think this was tied to something bigger. Maybe someone was trying to send Isaac a message by going after Theo. Everyone in the city knew they were together at this point. Though if that was the case why wouldn't they go after Isaac's lab directly?

After a few minutes she heard someone leaving. Reggie glanced over her shoulder to see Isaac with a broom in his hand. The sheriff was nowhere to be seen.

"Are you buying this 'teenage vandals' story?" Reggie made sure to keep her voice casual. She didn't want Isaac to know that she was worried.

"Who else could it have been?"

Reggie shrugged and finished securing a shelf to the wall that had come loose. "It's a lot of damage for bored kids to cause."

"I'll check with Wes after he's had a chance to talk to the kids. This is a lot more destructive than we've seen from them in the past. If it's who we think it is, their parents work here, so it wouldn't have been that hard for them to get access. There are some issues at home. They probably meant to trash their parents' lab and ended up in the wrong place." He kept sweeping as he talked, never once making eye-contact with her.

Isaac's story seemed plausible enough, but Reggie wasn't sure she bought it. "Does Theo know what happened yet?" She turned to face Isaac. If his expression was going to give anything away, she didn't want to miss it.

"Yeah." Isaac leaned the broom against a table and sat down. "He was expecting some results this morning, so he came in early. The lab was like this when he got here."

"Where is he now?"

"He was really shaken-up, so I sent him back to my place." Isaac leaned forward and put his head in his hands. "I keep thinking about what could have happened if they'd still been here when he showed up. I don't think they would have hurt him, but you never know." His shoulders started to shake. Isaac was crying. She couldn't recall another time she had seen her brother cry. If he believed the story he had told, there was no way he'd been this upset. There was more to this than he was letting on.

"Hey," Reggie said as she pulled him into a hug. "Everything's okay. Theo's fine. The damage isn't even that bad. Like the sheriff said, it was just some dumb kids blowing off steam." She held him close, rubbing his back until the tears started to subside.

Isaac pulled away slowly. "I know you're right," he said, wiping away the last of his tears. He got up and picked up the broom again.

Reggie gently took it from him. "Let me do that. It's my job," she said with a weak smile.

"Thanks."

"Why don't you go check on Theo? I can finish up here."

"Okay," Isaac said with a nod. There was no emotion in his voice. He looked around the trashed lab. "Be careful, Reggie. I don't want to see anything bad happen to you."

~

Reggie couldn't get what happened to Theo's lab out of her mind. By mid-afternoon, it was driving her crazy. She needed to talk to Theo. She couldn't be sure, but she suspected he had gone into the lab to get the results from their bloodwork, which made the timing of the attack extremely suspicious. Had someone figured out what they were doing and had trashed the lab as a way to keep them from seeing the results? It was the only thing that made sense, but the implications scared her. A coverup suggested that whatever was happening to Serenity wasn't a side-effect of the wall like she'd first suspected.

She needed to see what Theo made of the whole situation. With the boys at friends' houses until dinner, now was as good a time as any. She grabbed her keys off the kitchen counter and headed for the door.

She pulled her phone out and texted Theo, **Can we talk?** Reggie tapped the steering wheel while she waited for a response. Why wasn't he answering? He had never taken this long to respond to a text. After a few minutes with no response, she texted again. **Are you alright?** She hoped nothing had happened to him. Was it possible that the people who had destroyed his lab had come after him directly? Based on the concern Isaac had shown, she figured it was a possibility. It was taking every ounce of self-control to keep her thoughts from going down that dark path.

After another minute with no response, she said, "Screw it," put the car in reverse, and backed out of her driveway.

She took a chance and drove to Isaac's apartment, since she knew Theo was there earlier in the day. Knowing that Theo was likely at Isaac's was the only thing keeping her panic at bay. She breathed a sigh of relief when she pulled up and saw his car parked out front. She was able to keep a normal pace as she walked to the building and knocked on Isaac's door.

"How's Theo?" Reggie asked as soon as Isaac opened the door.

"See for yourself." Isaac stepped aside to let Reggie in.

It didn't take long to spot Theo slumped in the corner of the couch. He was staring at the wall, completely oblivious of her arrival. She had come here ready to get to work, but seeing Theo like this deflated her.

"How long has he been like this?" Reggie whispered to Isaac.

Isaac ran his hand through his hair. "Since he got back from the lab. I don't know how to snap him out of it."

"Let me talk to him." Reggie gently squeezed Isaac's arm as she moved past him. She sat down in the armchair next to Theo. "Hey. How are you holding up?"

Theo shifted his gaze to meet her eye. She waited for him to say something, but he just shrugged before averting his gaze again. This wasn't like him. Theo always had something to say, a way to make sense of any situation. It almost felt like he was playing the part of someone else; his actions were so far removed from his normal demeanor.

"I fixed all the damage in your lab. It'll be good as new when you're ready to go back."

"Thanks," he said softly.

This was getting her nowhere. She needed to snap Theo out of it. She noticed Isaac gesturing for her to join him. He was standing next to the front door with his phone out. Reggie got up and walked over to him.

"I need to go to City Hall and take care of something. Do you think you can stay with Theo? I don't want to leave him alone right now," Isaac said while putting on his jacket.

"Of course," Reggie said. This was exactly what she needed. They could talk openly without Isaac there.

"Thanks. I shouldn't be long." Reggie waited for Isaac to leave before returning to Theo.

"Isaac had to go," she said as she retook her place in the armchair. "Tell me what really happened at the lab this morning. Were you attacked?"

"No," Theo shook his head slightly. "The lab was trashed when I got there this morning. Whoever did it was long gone."

"Why did you go to the lab so early on a Sunday morning?"

Theo shot her a look.

"So, you were working on the memory issues." Reggie leaned back in her chair. "Do you think it's connected?"

"It would be a pretty big coincidence if it wasn't. I

think it might be time for us to let this go. We haven't found any proof, and looking for it is starting to get dangerous."

"That's exactly why we have to keep looking. Don't you see? Whatever is affecting people's memories isn't some unknown side-effect of the smart grid. It's being done on purpose."

"That's a bit of a stretch, don't you think?" Theo said, shifting in his seat.

"I don't think so." Reggie's determination was starting to build again. This was the first real lead they'd had. "If someone destroyed your lab to stop you from seeing those results, we must be getting close to uncovering what's really going on here. We have to push forward. But I think we need to change our approach. I think we need to start looking for people who have some kind of vendetta against the city or my family. Someone who might have a motive to sabotage Serenity." It was like Reggie was seeing things clearly for the first time.

"If what you're saying is true, it might be time for us to step aside and let someone with more experience handle this," Theo said.

Reggie crossed her arms. "Like who?"

"Like the police."

"And what makes you think you can trust them?" she scoffed. "The sheriff had no issue blaming some teens for the break-in. How do we know he's not the one who really did it?"

Theo got to his feet and started to pace. "Do you hear yourself, Reggie? This is getting out of hand. You're becoming paranoid."

"Who wouldn't be when their memories are being stolen from them?"

"We don't have proof that is even happening," Theo said. Reggie rolled her eyes. "I'm sorry, but we don't. We have a theory with no concrete data to back it up. And now things are starting to get dangerous. What do you think would have happened if the people that trashed my lab were still there when I showed up?"

"We don't know that they would have done anything to you."

"Are you willing to take that risk? Because I'm not."

"But don't you want to know the truth?" Reggie's voice dripped with desperation.

"Of course I do, but not if it costs me my life. Or yours. I get that you're trying to protect your kids, and I respect that, but what do you think will happen to Jace and Miles if something happens to you?"

Reggie looked away so she wouldn't have to answer.

"Maybe we should cool it for a while. Let things settle so we don't attract any more unwanted attention," Theo said gently.

Reggie crossed her arms over her chest. "And in the meantime, hope we don't forget who we are?" She tried to understand where Theo was coming from, but she couldn't. This was too important. They couldn't wait.

"I'm sorry, Reggie."

Chapter 28

Reggie was distracted when she got to work the next morning. She couldn't get her conversation with Theo out of her mind. At least she didn't think the boys noticed. She was still shocked by how willing Theo was to give up at the first hiccup, especially now that they finally had something to go on. Granted, the idea that someone was messing with people's memories intentionally was a lot more terrifying than it being a side-effect of the smart grid, but that was all the more reason not to give up. If they could figure out who was behind it, they could stop it. They could save Isaac's life's work. They could save everyone in Serenity. There was no backing down now.

"Alright, people," Mason said. "We're switching

some things up today, so listen up."

The hair on Reggie's arms stood on end. She didn't know why, but she was certain this was because of her. Mason ran through the job assignments for the day. So far, everything was normal. Reggie's stomach twisted into tighter knots with every job. "Sasha, sections two and three of the wall need some work. The power output was all over the place last night. Cam and Quinn are with you today."

Reggie could feel everyone's eyes on her. "Dale, you take Reggie today. There's some plumbing issues going on at City Hall that she should be able to handle. Alright, everyone, be safe out there today."

Reggie jumped to her feet and followed after Mason. Dale beat her to him. "What the hell, Mason? You can't just pull Quinn from my team like that," Dale said.

"Pretty sure I can, since you know I'm in charge of this department."

"Quinn hasn't worked on the wall in years. He's not the best person to send out there," Dale said.

Mason crossed his arms. "I can send you out instead." His voice was calm, but the threat was clear. Dale took a small step back.

"I have no problem going to work on the wall. In fact, I enjoy it," Reggie interjected. She wondered where this sudden change was coming from. Was Mason trying to keep her away from the wall? Was there a reason he wanted her at City Hall instead? Could this have something to do with Theo's lab?

Mason's posture sagged. "Sorry, Reggie. This wasn't my idea. The change came right from the top."

She shouldn't have been surprised. Her parents had never wanted her to work on the wall. Was this them finally getting their way, or was something else going on?

Mason moved to head back to his office, but Reggie stepped in front of him with her hands on her hips. "I thought we agreed to ignore the requests of my family."

"This wasn't a request. I was told in no uncertain terms that if I don't pull you from the wall, I'd lose my job. And if that happens, then I won't be contributing to the city and they could throw my whole family out."

Reggie didn't know what to say. She wanted to tell him that her parents wouldn't let that happen, but she knew from experience it wasn't true. They had done it to her when she hadn't done what she was told.

"There has to be something you can do," Dale said. "My guys shouldn't be punished because of her family drama."

Reggie rolled her eyes, but she knew Dale was right. This was her fault. "I'll talk to them," she promised Dale. "Believe me, this is the last thing I want."

Mason sighed. "Until I hear otherwise, the assignments stand. Let's just get through today okay." He stepped around them and headed to his office, shutting the door behind him.

"I promise, I'll handle this," she said to Dale.

"You better, because if one of my guys gets hurt doing your job, I'll hold you personally accountable. Now, get down to city hall. The bathrooms on the third floor have been acting up all week. All of my guys have taken a crack at it, and they're still getting clogged regularly. Let's see if you're as good as you say you are." Dale walked away, leaving Reggie alone in the maintenance office.

~

Doing work in City Hall was a pain in the ass. Everyone there looked at her like she was in the way. It was clear that they all thought they were better than her—something she was used to dealing with in her line of work. She'd have liked to see any of them try to fix the plumbing. She couldn't imagine why anyone would have wanted this assignment over the wall.

It took her an hour to figure out what had already been done to fix the third-floor bathroom. It looked like they had replaced the float, fill valve, chain and all the seals around the toilet, none of which would have actually prevented the clogs they were seeing. Reggie took one look and could tell the issue was with the piping. There had to be a block somewhere in the line. Honestly, Dale should have been ashamed of his team. She never would have tolerated these half-assed repairs from her team at Homes, Hearts, and Hammers. At least she was used to fixing crappy work like this.

She spent a few hours scoping the lines to try to find the blockage. It looked like there was a bent pipe right before it connected to the main sewer line. It would need to be replaced. She wondered if anyone had even bothered to check the lines. She cleaned up her gear in the bathroom and set out to find the basement.

She moved through City Hall with her head held

high, despite the looks she could feel on her back. She passed a conference room and stopped in her tracks. Through the opened door, she could hear her parents and Isaac discussing the management of the city. Now seemed like as good a time as any to set some boundaries. Maybe it would be easier with them all together.

She took a deep breath and turned back to the room. She didn't knock before she entered. Thankfully, it was only the three of them in there. They didn't notice her entering. With more force than was necessary, she set her toolbox down on the table. "Which one of you was it?"

"Regina? What are you doing here?" Oscar asked as they all turned to look at her.

Reggie rolled her eyes. "Like you don't know."

"We don't." Lena turned to Oscar then Isaac who Reggie noticed was avoiding looking in her direction. She had found the culprit.

"Why did you do it, Isaac?" She walked over to him, making it impossible for him to ignore her.

"Do what? For goodness's sake Regina, tell us what you're so upset about," Oscar said, making no attempt to hide his annoyance.

"One of you," she said looking pointedly at Isaac, "called Mason and threatened to have his family thrown out of the city if he didn't pull me from working on the wall."

"Isaac," Lena said in shock. "Tell me you didn't threaten Mason's family."

"I didn't threaten him, exactly," Isaac said.

Reggie glared at him. "He thinks you did."

"What did you say to him?" Oscar crossed his arms and Reggie was instantly transported back to the lab in her childhood home. Though this might be the first time his disappointment was directed at Isaac instead of her.

Isaac ran his hand through his hair. "I told him I didn't want you working on the wall. That it was causing you too much stress. Besides you're a Torres, and really should have a more respectable position."

Reggie folded her arms and glared at him. "Tell me how working on the most important piece of equipment here isn't respectable? Your little experiment would have failed a long time ago if it hadn't for the maintenance team. I think it's about time you show them the respect they deserve." With everything she was doing to protect his work, he still thought of her as a defenseless child that needed protecting. She was tempted to tell him everything right there but knew it would only cause more problems, so she kept it to herself. Though she did plan on making him eat his words once she had uncovered the truth and saved Serenity for him.

Isaac came over to her. "I only did it because I was worried about you," he said softly. "Theo mentioned that you're having a hard time adjusting to life here."

She was under the impression that they were waiting to tell Isaac their suspicions until they had proof to back them up. The way Theo had spoken on Sunday, she thought he wanted to pretend like nothing was happening. Now he's telling Isaac about it without even giving her a heads-up? Something wasn't adding up. "What exactly did Theo tell you?"

Isaac held up his hands. "Just that he's worried about you. I swear."

"I'm fine," Reggie snapped.

Isaac's posture sagged. "I don't think you are, and that's okay. Isn't that why you decided to come here? I'm just trying to make things easier for you. I know how dangerous and stressful working on the wall can be. I thought if I could get you a different assignment, you'd be able to relax a bit. Maybe you'd finally be able to process Charlie's death and start moving on. I want you to be happy, Reggie, that's all."

Reggie could see the pain in Isaac's eyes. He really thought he was doing what was best and she tried to take that into consideration. It did little to alleviate her anger though.

"Your brother was only trying to help," Lena said gently. She came over and put her hand on Reggie's shoulder.

She jerked her shoulder away. Lena had never bothered to comfort her before. Reggie wasn't about to let her start now. "I don't need his help. I don't need any of your help. I've been taking care of myself since I was eighteen. None of you cared about my work back then. You have no right to interfere now."

"We're family. We want what's best for you," Oscar said.

Reggie smirked. "You have no idea what's best for me. You don't actually care about what I want. You never have. None of you understand what it is that I do. I love my work and I'm damn good at it. Now if you'll excuse me, I have to go fix your plumbing." Reggie snatched her toolbox off the table. She stopped in front of Isaac on her way out the door. "You're going to call Mason, apologize, and tell him he can run his team without your input from now on. Do you understand me?"

"Fine," Isaac relented.

Reggie glared at him for a moment to drive home her point before leaving the room. Her anger didn't start to subside until she was down in the basement. She focused all her energy on tracking the piping to locate the damaged section. She knew it had to be down here somewhere. She hoped she wouldn't have to bust a wall open to find it, though that might be a nice way to work out some anger.

The line went into a locked maintenance closet. She guessed Dale had the key somewhere, but she wasn't about to call him. She bent down to look at the lock. It was just a basic knob lock. It didn't take her long to pick it and open the door.

The room was filled with pipes. She spotted the bent pipe immediately—it wouldn't be hard to replace. She looked over the pipe to see if there was an easy way to isolate this section, but there wasn't. They'd have to shut off water to a large portion of the building. She wouldn't be able to fix this today. She wondered why the door had been locked in the first place. There was nothing critical to the building operation in here. She was about to leave when she noticed a blinking light behind a cluster of pipes.

Reggie went to investigate. Electrical equipment wasn't usually staged right next to the water main. The area behind the pipe was tight, but she was able to squeeze behind it. What she found didn't make any sense. It looked like some kind of high-powered antenna. She slid down the wall to try to get a better look.

She was wrong. It wasn't an antenna. It was sending out a signal of its own. Maybe it was a booster of some kind—a high-tech version of what Charlie had purchased for their ill-fated camping trip. But then why was it tucked away in the corner of the basement? Surely it would be more effective if it were positioned somewhere with less interference. It would make sense for City Hall to need access to the outside world.

Unless that wasn't its purpose. Maybe it was tucked behind the piping so no one would find it. Was this some kind of illegal connection to the real world, or was this the reason no one inside Serenity could get a call to go through? Could this be blocking out the signals instead of boosting them?

Reggie contorted her body to try to get a better look at the device. If it had any specs written on it, she couldn't see it. Whatever this was, she doubted it was supposed to be there. She tried to dismiss the thought, but her gut was screaming at her. Maybe the wall wasn't affecting the cell reception after all. Maybe someone was intentionally trying to keep residents from contacting people outside the city. The same someone who had trashed Theo's lab.

Someone who could come after her next if they found out what she was doing.

Reggie knew she wouldn't be able to figure this out on her own. She needed help. She thought about going to Theo, but banished the idea from her mind. She needed someone she could trust completely, and she wasn't sure that applied to Theo anymore. There was only one person on the planet she knew she could trust with anything. She needed Amber.

~

The raised garden beds behind her house should have been filled with weeds. Reggie hadn't touched them since moving into the house. She needed to do something that would keep her hands busy while she tried to work through everything that had happened, and pulling weeds seemed as good of a choice as any.

She headed outside once she and Miles had finished dinner. Jace was having dinner at Sam's house. The two of them were inseparable these days. Miles followed her outside and ran off to play with the other kids that seemed to gather every evening in the large, grassy area that separated the houses from the school.

Normally, Reggie would find something to work on in her workshop while Miles played, but it felt stifling tonight, and it wasn't just because the evenings were starting to get warmer as spring started to give way to summer. For once, she didn't want to work with tools. Tools couldn't fix what was bothering her this time. She was still angry after her run-in with her family, and the workshop reminded her of all the ways her family looked down on her.

The grass cushioned her knees as she knelt down next to one of the garden beds, expecting to see it filled with weeds, but there were very few. She suspected her mother had been sneaking over when she hadn't been home to take care of the gardens. Reggie should have been annoyed, but she didn't have the energy to care tonight. She focused on what was there, hoping it would be enough to relieve some of the pent-up stress she had been carrying. Isaac had been right about one thing, she needed to find a way to relax a little or her growing anxiety would destroy her.

A new wave of panic washed over her every time she thought about the device she found in the basement of City Hall. The more she thought about it, the more she convinced herself it was some kind of signal-blocker. If only she could have gone online and researched it. Instead, she'd spent hours trying to come up with a reasonable explanation for it. Unfortunately, every idea she came up with was more terrifying than the last. She didn't want to think that they were prisoners, but the more she thought about it, that was exactly what it felt like. Everyone was convinced the area outside the wall was filled with radiation and violent mutated animals. They couldn't contact their loved ones outside of the city, or even get news of what was happening in the real world. To make matters worse, whatever was affecting people's memories made it so that the residents didn't even realize what was happening to them. And yet everyone thought this place was paradise. She wished she had been stronger and never come here. She had sacrificed all of her principles to give her boys a better life, but this wasn't the life she'd had in mind for them.

"Would you like some help?"

Reggie looked up to see Lena standing on the other side of the garden. "Sure," Reggie mumbled as she tugged at a weed that had taken root next to a tomato plant. She didn't really want her mother there, but she was scared, and she didn't want to be alone with her thoughts.

Lena knelt down across from Reggie. "Things got a little heated today."

"I don't need a lecture, Mom," Reggie mumbled as she looked at the soil in front of her.

"I know we were hard on you when you were growing up, but it was always because we loved you. Maybe we should have said it more, but I assumed that you knew," Lena said as she worked.

Reggie stopped working and looked at Lena. "How was I supposed to know that when the only time you talked to me was to tell me how much of a disappointment I was?"

"We only wanted the best for you and your brother. We knew how much potential you had, how smart you were. It was our job to help you realize that potential. You were made to do amazing things, Regina. We had your IQ tested a few times when you were growing up—yours was always so high. Higher than Isaac's, even."

"What's your point?" She didn't know what her mother was trying to do. What did her IQ have to do with anything? Clearly it wasn't enough to get her parents' approval.

"My point is, we love you. We always knew you would grow up to do amazing things. While not the life we wanted for you, I know you helped a lot of people with your construction company. I am proud of you, Regina."

Reggie sat back on her heels in shock. "You've never said that to me before." She had to be dreaming. She had longed to hear her mother say those words for years. Now she couldn't help but feel like they came with a catch.

"Of course I have. When you went away to college. You went out to conquer the world and never looked back. That was the proudest day of my life."

She stared at her mother. What was happening? Was Lena trying to mess with her? "That's not what happened," she said slowly as she watched the confusion wash over Lena's face.

"It might not be exactly what happened," Lena said, "But the sentiment was real."

The anger Reggie had managed to set aside was back with vengeance. Her mother had twisted everything so she didn't have to deal with the fact that she was a terrible parent. "What reality are you living in?" A twisted laugh escaped Reggie's lips. "I didn't go to college. The day I told you and dad that I was going to turn down my acceptance to Princton, you kicked me out of the house. I was eighteen years old and had nowhere to go. Amber's family took me in. You never even tried to find out where I was. I could have been living on the streets for you all you knew. I lived with Amber's family until high school graduation, which you didn't attend, and I started working the next day. You didn't care then, so don't act like you care now."

The look of pure confusion on Lena's face shook

Reggie to her core. Her mother really believed her version of events was real. She couldn't face the truth, or she couldn't remember it. That had to be the answer. Whatever was affecting people's memories was affecting her mother. She was kinder because she didn't remember how horrible she had been to Reggie as a child. She doubted Lena even realized what was happening to her. There was no way her parents could be behind it and still be affected. They wouldn't have done anything that would alter their minds.

Reggie was at a loss for what to do next. Anyone in the city could have been behind the memory loss, and that terrified her. No matter what it costs, she would find a way to save Miles and Jace. She would not let them be turned into brainwashed versions of themselves. She would find a way to get them out.

Chapter 29

Reggie had been trying to get Dale on his own all week. She was done waiting patiently for answers that never seemed to come. It was time for her to find them herself. She wasn't sure how, but she knew that what had happened to Steve was somehow connected. Since she couldn't talk to Steve, Dale was her next best option.

Unfortunately, he always seemed to be surrounded by people. It was getting to the point where she was thinking about asking to switch assignments so she could spend the day on his team. She had asked a few people about Steve, and most only had a vague memory of the attack and his departure. No one could tell her what happened to him after he left.

It wasn't until Thursday afternoon that she managed to corner Dale. She had been out with Sasha and Cam working on the wall when Sasha had sent her back to the shop to get some extra fuses. The damage from the latest power surge had been worse than they'd initially realized.

She was pulling the items they needed when Dale walked in. She knew she needed to get back to the job site, but when was she going to have a better chance to talk to him alone. "Hey, Dale," she said casually as she looked over the parts on the shelf in front of her.

"Reggie," he said with a curt nod.

"How's the piping repairs at City Hall going?" She had no idea how to bring it up. It wasn't like she could come right out and say *hey I think something is wrong with the city and I think it's somehow connected to your friend Steve and the attack.*

"We have it handled," Dale said.

"Right." This wasn't going well. "Did you see the signal-booster hidden behind all those piping? It might be a good time to relocate it somewhere with less interference." She wasn't sure why she was bringing up the device she found in the basement. Maybe she was hoping he would confirm what it actually was. Either way, it seemed like the best option to get the conversation going before she could ask what she really wanted.

"What are you talking about? There's no signal-booster down there," Dale said.

"Then what's that antenna-looking thing wedged behind the pipes?"

"I don't have any idea what you're talking about." Dale grabbed something off the shelf and shoved it into his toolbox.

"There's no way you could have missed it. It was right by the damaged section." Was Dale screwing with her or did he really not know what she was talking about? Was he covering something up or had the device she'd found been moved before the maintenance team had started their repairs?

"What are we doing here, Reggie?" The annoyance was clear in his voice.

Reggie held up her hands. "I was just trying to be friendly."

"We're not friends."

"Sorry. I'll let you get back to whatever you were doing." It looked like she wouldn't be getting any answers from Dale. She grabbed the fuses she had been sent to get and turned to leave the storage room.

She made it to the door when she heard him say, "I know you've been asking about me."

Reggie turned back to him. She wasn't sure what to say, it wasn't like he was wrong. "I'm sorry," she said again, though she wasn't entirely sure what she was sorry for.

"I know what people think of me, you know. They think I'm weak, scared of my own shadow, but none of them were there. They don't know what happened." Dale hesitated for a moment. "Or why it happened."

Reggie walked over to him. "What *did* happen?"

Dale crossed his arms. "Why the hell should I tell you?"

"Why bring it up if you didn't want to tell me?" Reggie countered. Dale rolled his eyes and turned away.

"I think something odd is going on here and I have a feeling that what happened to you and your friend Steve is somehow connected." She knew telling him her suspicions was a risk, but it was the best chance she had at finding out the truth.

Dale took off his hat and rubbed his head. "You aren't the first person to think that. Steve did too. He was on the team that originally installed the wall. One of the few that actually secured a spot inside the city. At first, everything seemed to be fine, but after the first year, he started to notice people forgetting things, especially with the new residents coming in. They would have these moments where they would space out, and when they snapped out of it, they had no idea where they were."

Reggie's heart was beating so fast she was sure Dale could hear it. This was it. This had to be connected to what she had been seeing. "What did he do?"

"He brought his concerns up to your dad. They had been working together for years and developed a good relationship, or so he thought. Steve was sure Oscar could help figure out what was going on, but Oscar blew it off. He said Steve was overreacting and should stick to what he was good at."

Reggie rolled her eyes. "That sounds like my dad."

"He can be a real asshole sometimes," Dale said.

"Try all the time."

"Anyway, Steve was stubborn. He kept digging, trying to find some kind of proof that something weird was going on," Dale said.

Excitement started to build inside Reggie. "Did he ever find any?"

Dale shrugged. "If he did, he never told me. A few weeks after he talked to Oscar, the two of us were out working on the wall when the temporary barrier failed. The next thing I know, I'm in the hospital with three broken ribs and a concussion."

"What happened to Steve?"

"He was in a coma for a few days. He wasn't the same after that. As soon as he was healed, he left the city."

"What happened to him after he left?"

"I don't know," Dale said.

"You never tried to reach out to him or anything? He was your friend, wasn't he? You never thought to check on him, see how he was doing?"

"Sure, I tried to get in touch with him after he left, but he never responded to any of my messages. Then we lost the ability to contact anyone outside the city."

"Don't you think that's a little odd? I mean, the timing alone is suspicious," Reggie said.

"Look, I don't know if it's connected or not, and honestly, I don't really care. I remember how bad it is out in the real world. I have no interest in returning to it. So, I keep my head down, do my job, and try to enjoy the rest of my life as best as I can. I suggest you do the same. Nothing good comes from digging around in things that aren't your business."

"Wait," Reggie said, her mind spinning with all the information Dale had given her. "Are you suggesting that my dad planned the attack to stop Steve from digging further into what was really happening in Serenity?"

"I'm not suggesting anything, but you're welcome to infer whatever you'd like."

"I can't imagine he'd do that," Reggie said, though her words lacked conviction.

"Hey, it's your family that runs this place, so if you say they wouldn't hurt someone to protect what they've built here, then I guess it's true." Dale took a small step closer to her and lowered her voice. "Though I suspect you wouldn't be asking questions if you really believed that." Dale grabbed his bag from the table next to him. "I need to get back to work, and you really should too."

"Thank you, Dale."

"Whatever you decide to do, be careful. I don't like you, but I don't want to see you or your kids get hurt."

Reggie leaned back against the table as she watched Dale leave. Could he be right? Could her father have orchestrated the attack to keep Steve from finding out the truth? If he found out what she was doing would she suffer a similar fate? She didn't want to believe it, but people did crazy things to protect their life's work. If it came down to her or their work, Reggie had no doubt where she'd fall.

~

Reggie couldn't get what Dale told her out of her mind. She was distracted through the rest of her shift on Thursday, and Friday hadn't been any better. Reggie was having a hard time focusing on anything. The idea that someone was sabotaging the city consumed her thoughts. She refused to believe that her family was involved, but that didn't mean that the people around them couldn't have done it. Maybe they thought they could take over control of the city if they proved her parents weren't capable of keeping the residents safe. Maybe the government had sent someone in undercover to seize control. Maybe it was revenge for someone's loved one getting denied. She knew people would do just about anything to get into a Sanctuary City.

Not feeling up to a family dinner, Reggie made a pizza and let the boys eat it in front of the television, something Charlie would never have let them do. He thought there was nothing more important than having dinner together. Normally she agreed with him, but not today. She knew she wouldn't have the patience to get through it. Today she needed a little space while the kids thought they were getting a special treat.

Reggie still couldn't get her mind settled after the boys went to sleep. She thought about trying to go up to bed herself, but knew that she would lie there awake for hours until she was more frustrated than she currently was. She eventually found herself out in the workshop. If fixing something couldn't calm her mind, then nothing would. She paced around the room, trying to find something to work on when her eyes fell on the sack of broken parts she had taken from work weeks ago.

She dumped the sack out on the workbench to see what was inside. There were a few pucks, a handful of burned-out fuses, some wiring, and a Geiger counter. Reggie pulled out the fuses and dumped them in the trash. There was no use trying to fix them. She set the Geiger count aside and picked up the three pucks.

They were starting to see the pucks fail with a greater frequency, and Reggie wanted to know why. She doubted anyone was tampering with them, but it didn't hurt to check.

She pulled out the toolbox Amber's dad had given her all those years ago and got to work. She carefully disassembled one of the pucks, laying each piece out carefully on the workbench. She made sure to look for any signs that the puck had been manipulated in some way, but she didn't see anything unusual.

What she did find was frayed wires, loose connections, and misaligned beams. The pucks weren't failing because someone had tampered with them; they were failing because they were reaching the end of their lives. She wondered how often they were checked for damage. All of this seemed simple enough to fix. In fact, Reggie had most of what she needed on-hand.

The inner workings of the pucks were extremely intricate. It took all of Reggie's concentration to replace the damaged components and put them back together. She made a few small tweaks to the original design that would make the pucks stabler and increase their lifespan. It took her over an hour to repair just one of them. It was no wonder they were usually scrapped when they failed.

She picked up the next one and took off the backing. The damage to this one was less extensive than the first. She carefully removed the damaged components, hoping to save herself a little time by not taking it apart completely.

She had no idea what time it was when she finished,

but her eyes were starting to burn. Focusing on the tiny components was giving her a headache. She set the three repaired pucks on the table in front of her. She set them to the 'testing' setting and turned them on. They fired up and formed a small laser grid in front of her. She monitored the pucks' readouts on her tablet. They seemed to be holding with more stability than they normally had. She wished she could test them at full strength, but she wasn't sure what setting off a sixty-foot laser grid in her workshop would do to the house.

She was about to power them down when she saw the Geiger counter sitting on the end of the table. They had stopped taking readings out by the wall. Sasha had reported the issues with the Geiger counter to the lab and they decided it was best to hold off on getting readings until the equipment could be checked for accuracy. It sounded like the scientists weren't even using the data the maintenance team had been collecting for them, anyway.

Her curiosity got the better of her and she reached for the Geiger counter. She hesitated before turning it on. She wasn't sure why, but she was nervous, as if the device were going to start talking and tell her the truth about what was going on in Serenity City. She took a deep breath and switched it on. The needle went crazy, reading high levels of radiation in the room. The reading was so high that she was pretty sure she'd have been dead if it was accurate.

She set the Geiger counter down on the table and switched off the pucks. If the radiation was coming from the laser grid, the needle would drop down once they were off. She watched it closely, waiting for the readout to change. She had no idea how long radiation would hang around once the pucks were off. She waited fifteen minutes, but the needle didn't move.

She picked up the device and looked it over. There had to be a reason it was reading so high. It could be that the machine was miscalibrated, causing the readout to be wrong, but in her gut, she knew that it was something else. Maybe if it had only happened on one, but this wasn't the same device she had used when she'd noticed the issue her first day out at the wall.

There was a thick protective cover around the device. She knew they had to take the cover off to do the daily calibration tests before heading out. Reggie had never done one herself, but she hadn't ever heard anyone mention issues with the bump tests. She took the cover off and set it down on the table. The moment she did, the needle on the counter dropped to zero.

"What the hell," she muttered to herself as she turned the counter over in her hand, as if that would tell her what had happened. She didn't trust herself to take the Geiger counter apart, so she set it aside and picked up the case.

She didn't see anything off with the thick yellow covering. It was mildly flexible, with reinforced corners. She moved the case so it was close to the Geiger counter and watched as the needle spiked again. The case was causing the high readings—something that should not have happened. She examined the outside of the case. Maybe something stuck in the silicone was setting the counter off. Aside from the normal nicks of everyday use, the outside of the case looked to be in perfect condition.

She turned her attention to the inside of the case. She noticed a tiny slit in the top of the case, right where the gauge was. She folded the top of the case back so she could get a better look. There was something lodged inside the silicone.

Reggie worked at the slit, being careful not to damage the case. The cut was deep and perfectly clean. This wasn't something that happened by accident. She finally removed a small vial with silver material inside. Without taking her eyes off the vial, she picked up the Geiger counter and held it next to the vial. The needle spiked. She moved her hand with the vial away and the needle dropped back to zero.

Someone had rigged the Geiger counter to give a false-positive reading. Reggie tested the vial a few more times as her mind tried to catch up with what she was seeing. She couldn't understand why someone would want to make it look like the area outside of the city was radioactive when it wasn't. Unless they were trying to keep people away from the colony. High levels of radiation were a decent deterrent, but it wouldn't stop everyone.

Unless it wasn't meant to keep people outside the city from trying to get in. Maybe it was meant to keep the residents from trying to get out.

Chapter 30

Reggie was a bundle of nerves when she went to work on Monday morning. She hadn't told anyone about the Geiger counter, though it was the only thing she had been able to think about since she'd discovered the radioactive vial hidden in its case.

Normally, she would go to Isaac with something like this, but something was holding her back. Steve had voiced his concerns to her father and ended up being attacked. She didn't want to believe that the two were connected, but she couldn't shake the feeling that they were. She couldn't risk her parents finding out that she had the same concerns Steve had had. She didn't think being their daughter would be enough to keep her safe if they really were behind it.

She barely spoke to anyone as they got ready for the

day, counting down the minutes until she could escape to the relative peace of the workshop.

"Hey, Reggie, you doing okay?" Sasha asked quietly as she leaned next to Reggie's locker.

"Yeah, of course," Reggie said without looking at her. She didn't want to bring Sasha into this. The less people who knew, the better.

All through Mason's morning meeting, Reggie found her gaze shifting to Dale. At first, he didn't notice but by the time Mason was done handing out the day's assignments he was making a concerted effort not to look in her direction. For a second in the storage room, she had thought he might be willing to help her, but it seemed passing along information was as far as he was willing to go. Not that she could blame him. Reggie was very aware of how crazy she must have looked.

The moment the meeting was over, she headed to the workshop. She was determined to prove that what she found hadn't been a fluke. She just needed to get her hands on another Geiger counter. While the rest of the team headed to the storage room to gather the tools they would need for the day, Reggie started to search through the boxes in the workshop for another Geiger counter. She had only organized half of the stuff in there, so there was a chance that one could be tucked away in the overflowing boxes scattered throughout the room.

She searched for over an hour and came up empty. The building was empty now, everyone else having gone to their jobsites for the day. She knew there were four Geiger counters in the storage room waiting for the teams sent to work on the wall. She had no idea if they had started to take readings for the lab again or not. If they had, then all the devices would be gone. She really should have tried to pay more attention during the morning meeting. She prayed there would be at least one there. One was really all she needed to prove her theory. If she found a vial in any of the other cases, then she'd know it had been put there on purpose.

She peeked out of the workshop door. She felt like a kid trying to ditch class, even though she was absolutely allowed to leave the workshop. She was starting to wonder who on her team could be trusted. If that material had been planted in the case on purpose, like she suspected it was, then someone on the maintenance team had to know it was there, right?

There was no one in sight. The storage room was only a few doors away. She walked as casually as she could. It was completely normal for her to be going to the storage room, even on a day when she was assigned to the workshop. How was she supposed to repair things without supplies?

"Hey, Reggie," Mason said behind her.

Reggie froze. Did Mason know what she was doing? Was it possible that he knew what she had found inside the case? She turned to face him. It would have been weird not to. "Hi, Mason. What's going on?" she said as normally as she could, though she was pretty sure her voice was an octave or two higher than usual.

"I was in the workshop the other day," Mason started. Reggie was positive that he was about to tell her off for taking those parts home. He had to know that the Geiger counter had been tampered with. Maybe he was trying to see if she had figured it out. He was one of the few people on the maintenance team that her parents would talk to. Didn't her mother say Oscar had wanted to talk to Mason at her party? Had they been talking about her? "You've really done a good job in there," he finally finished.

"Oh." Reggie let out a breath. "Thanks."

"I mean it. The whole place is transformed. For the first time during our monthly check-in with the city managers, I've been able to tell them we are making progress on the backlog. I guess your credentials weren't exaggerated."

Reggie smirked. "They were not, but you aren't the first to think that."

"I'll let you get back to it. I'll be around if you need anything." Mason turned and left.

Reggie didn't move as she watched him walk back to his office. She felt even worse about her suspicions now. These were good people, and she didn't want any of them to get hurt. Maybe it would be better to let it go. The people here seemed genuinely happy, even if they were missing pieces of their memories. Reggie longed to be one of them, but she wasn't willing to pay the same price. She needed to figure out the truth before she went crazy. When she was sure Mason wasn't coming back, she quickly finished her trek to the storage room.

Her eyes locked on the charger for the Geiger counters the moment she was inside. There were two still sitting on the chargers. Reggie smiled. This was it—she was finally going to get the proof she needed to validate her concerns. She grabbed them both and ran back to the workshop before anyone else could interrupt her.

She set them on the workbench and gave herself a moment to catch her breath. Once her heart rate returned to a normal rhythm, she looked them over. They were identical to the one she had stashed away in her workshop at home.

Slowly, Reggie reached for one as if it would jump up and bite her hand. A loud laugh outside of the room froze her. Her gaze shot to the door. She was sure someone was going to come in and catch her, but the door remained closed. With trembling hands, she picked up one of the devices. She almost dropped it twice as she removed the cover. Every few seconds, her eyes would go to the door, but she couldn't hear anyone outside anymore.

She set the Geiger counter down on the workbench and wiped her sweaty hands on her parts before giving the case her full attention. Part of her didn't want to find anything inside—she really wanted her suspicions to be wrong. It was bad enough to think that the memory loss was an unfortunate, unknown side-effect of the smart grid, but if this case had also been tampered with, they were dealing with something much bigger. Something intentional. Something much harder, and more dangerous, to put an end to.

She ran her finger along the inside of the case, closing her eyes the moment they found the slit in the silicone in the exact same place as the other one. She didn't open her eyes as she worked her fingers into the slit and pulled out the tiny vial. If she didn't see it, then she could pretend it wasn't real. She stayed like that for a few seconds before she finally worked up the courage to open her eyes. The vial pinched between her thumb and index finger looked to contain the same material as the one she had found the other night.

She set it down and reached for the second Geiger counter. This time, she didn't hesitate and was able to remove the cover within seconds. There was a cut in the silicone identical to the other two. It took her thirty seconds to dig out the third vial. She looked at it and cursed to herself.

Two could have been a coincidence. Two could have been explained away. But not three. Three was intentional. Like it or not, Reggie had her proof now. Someone was tampering with the city. Now she had to figure out who and why. Questions she was terrified would lead her back to her family.

~

For the first time, Reggie was early for her treatment. She was dying to tell Theo what she had found. He was the only one she could trust with the information. She hoped he had gotten over the shock of the break-in at the lab and was ready to get back to work. She didn't want to be insensitive, but they couldn't wait—they needed to find the people responsible before they realized what Reggie and Theo were doing.

The treatment room was empty when she arrived. She doublechecked her watch—she was early, but not by much. She'd expected Theo to be there by now. Could something have happened to him? Did someone find out about the samples he had sent outside of the city? He had said his computer was monitored.

"Hi, Reggie," the nurse said as she walked into the room. "I hope I didn't keep you waiting."

"No, I just got here." She didn't take her eyes off the empty chair that should be occupied by Theo. Why wasn't he here?

"Let's get started." The nurse ushered her over to her normal chair.

"Is Theo coming in today?" Reggie had to fight to keep her growing panic from her voice. Maybe someone had seen her take the Geiger counters after all, and knew she was going to tell Theo what she'd found.

The nurse shook her head as she looked at the computer next to Reggie's chair. "Last week was his last treatment."

"Oh," was all Reggie could say as the relief washed over her. Theo was fine. She wondered why he hadn't mentioned finishing his treatment.

"And good news: Based on your numbers from last week, today should be your last treatment."

"That's great," Reggie said, though there was no emotion in her voice. She didn't even flinch as the nurse inserted the needle into her arm. Her mind was racing. She needed to talk to Theo without letting Isaac know. She didn't want to drag him into this until she absolutely had to.

She waited until the nurse was gone before she pulled out her phone. She opened the messaging app that worked inside the smart grid and clicked on Theo's name. **Can you meet me at my house in an hour? Alone. I have something I need to show you.**

Reggie turned her phone over in her lap and tapped her foot while she waited for Theo to respond. She wasn't sure what she was going to do if he didn't. Isaac was picking the boys up from school today so Reggie knew there would be a very small window for her to talk to Theo alone before Isaac brought the boys home. Probably after feeding them an obscene amount of sugar right before dinner.

The phone buzzed in her lap, causing Reggie to jump. She fumbled to flip it over. There was a message from Theo. She clicked on it. **I'll be there**.

Reggie leaned back into the chair. Good. She would tell Theo what she found and together they could figure out what to do next. Now all she had to do was wait. She glanced at the IV bag and wondered if there was a way to make it go faster.

~

Theo was sitting on her front porch when she pulled into the driveway an hour later. She hoped he hadn't been there long. She didn't want people to see him sitting there and wonder what they were doing. Even though it was unlikely anyone would know exactly why he was there. Besides, they were friends; he was dating her brother. There were any number of innocent reasons why Theo could be at her house. She was letting her paranoia get the best of her.

Theo got to his feet as she got out of the car. "What's

going on, Reggie?"

"I'll show you. Follow me." She led him around the house to her workshop. She didn't say anything as she moved boxes out of the way to get to the old tool chest where she had hidden the Geiger counter and pucks. "I found proof that someone has been tampering with the city," she said as she stood up to face him.

"Really?" He moved closer to the workbench where she set down the Geiger counter.

She nodded. "We use these to measure radiation levels outside of the wall when we have to go out to do repairs."

"Okay," Theo said slowly. She could tell he was trying his best not to look at her like she was crazy.

"Someone has tampered with them."

Theo moved closer. "What do you mean 'tampered with'?"

Reggie picked it up and started to remove the cover. "Someone has planted this in the case so that it gives a false positive reading." She removed the vial from the case and held it up to show him. "I checked two more at the maintenance office today. They had a vial like this implanted into the case too."

Theo took the vial from her and held it up to look at it. "How do you know this isn't part of the sensor? Especially if it was exactly the same in every one you checked? It kind of sounds like they were designed and built that way. It's not like you're that familiar with this type of highly sensitive scientific equipment, are you?"

Reggie rolled her eyes. She knew people underestimated her intelligence because of her chosen profession, but she thought Theo was better than that. "Because how often have you seen a sensor like this that's dependent on something hidden in the protective case to function properly? We have to remove the case to do the daily calibration." Reggie picked up the Geiger counter and turned it on. "So, when we're inside the city and turn them on, they read zero radiation. The procedure clearly states to turn it off then put the case back on. We don't turn them on again until we're outside the wall, with the case on." She moved the Geiger counter so it was close to the vial in Theo's hand. The needle started to go crazy. "Someone put that in the cases so we would think the area outside of the city has a high level of radiation. I would bet good money that there's no radiation out there at all."

"It's an interesting theory," Theo said as he set the vial back on the table. "But what would be the purpose of falsifying the radiation levels?"

"To make people think it's not safe to leave, or maybe to deter people from trying to sneak into the city. I don't know, but we need to figure it out."

"Why?"

Reggie looked at him in shock. "Because whoever did this is probably the same person that trashed your lab and is responsible for the memory loss. It all has to be connected."

Theo sighed. "There's nothing affecting people's memories."

"Of course there is. It's happening to you too." This couldn't be happening. Was Theo turning on her?

"No, Reggie, there's not. If there were, I would have

found something by now, but every test I run comes back normal. I've tested my blood, the boys', yours, and any other sample I could get, and there's nothing there."

"What about your contact outside of the city?"

Theo shook his head. "They haven't been able to find anything either. I think it's time we accept the fact that there isn't anything to find."

Reggie was sure she had heard him wrong. He was supposed to be on her side. Tears formed in her eyes. There had to be something else they could try—she wasn't willing to accept the fact that they would all slowly forget Charlie. "There has to be something else we can try."

Theo gave her a sympathetic look. "There's nothing else to try. I think it's time for you to move on."

"How can you say that? This is proof that something isn't right here." She picked up the Geiger counter and case and thrust them at him.

"I understand how badly you want that to be true," he said gently.

"So, you're pulling the shrink card now, are you?" She grabbed the sack and put the Geiger counter back inside. "You think I'm crazy."

"I don't think you're crazy, Reggie. I think you're still grieving the loss of Charlie. I think you feel guilty about coming here. I think you're looking for any plausible explanation so don't have to deal with the fact that you and the boys are moving on with your lives. You've manifested this theory so you don't have to deal with your guilt. But you don't have to feel guilty. It's a good thing that you guys are starting to go back to normal. You don't need to find someone to blame. It's part of the grieving process."

Reggie shook her head as tears started to flow down her cheeks. "You're wrong. I know something isn't right about this place."

"You need to stop villainizing the Sanctuary Cities. It won't bring Charlie back."

Reggie took a step back. "You never believed me at all, did you? Was this some twisted form of amusement for you?"

"Of course not. I did believe you—why else would I spend all that time running tests? But the fact is, we didn't find anything. Doesn't it make more sense that this might have more to do with what you're going through?" Theo's voice was gentle and kind, but Reggie couldn't help but feel like he was patronizing her.

"Hey! Anybody home?" Isaac's voice sounded muffled from inside the workshop.

"We're back here," Reggie called as she quickly wiped away the tears on her cheeks. She didn't want the boys to see her like this.

"I want to help you, Reggie," Theo said softly. Reggie held up her hand to stop him. She couldn't do this now.

Isaac appeared in the doorway. "Hey, Reggie. Theo, I didn't expect to see you here."

"We were just talking," Theo said with a smile. "Now that I'm done with my chelation treatments, we don't get much time to chat anymore."

"Anything I should be worried about?" Isaac asked with a smirk.

"Of course not." Reggie tried to sound casual but

failed miserably as the tears reformed. She felt like the whole world had turned against her. She had never felt so alone in her entire life.

Isaac's smile faltered. "What's wrong?" He slipped his arm around her shoulders and pulled her close. He looked over at Theo. "Did you slip into therapy mode again?"

Theo shrugged. "Maybe a little. Sorry."

Isaac rolled his eyes. "Don't pay attention to him. He can't help himself sometimes. Now come inside—the boys and I are going to cook you dinner."

Reggie let out a small laugh. "That sounds like a terrible idea." She let Isaac lead her into the house.

She shot a look at Theo as she passed him. This might have been over for him, but it wasn't for her. She knew she wasn't making this up. This wasn't a manifestation of her grief or whatever psychobabble he had said. This was real. Something was wrong with Serenity City, and she would find out what it was before it could take anything else from them.

She would not let Jace and Miles forget their father. She would not let herself forget Charlie.

Chapter 31

Reggie spent the rest of the week trying to come up with a plan. She knew she needed help, and that help had to come from outside of Serenity. The problem was figuring out how to get a message out without the wrong person figuring out what she was doing. Things would be easier if she knew for sure who the wrong person was. She considered trying to use Isaac's phone again, but wondered if that would be too suspicious. She hadn't tried to call Amber since her anniversary. How would it look if she brought it up now?

She had to find a way to get outside of the wall and send her message without anyone knowing—something she suspected would be almost impossible to do. They never went out to work on the wall alone, and she wouldn't drag Sasha or Cam into this, even though she was sure they would have her back. The wall itself was monitored around the clock with cameras covering every inch of it and real-time monitoring of all its functions. If she used one the remotes to allow humans to safely pass through the smart grid they would know instantly. She had to figure out a way to get out of the city long enough to get a message out and get back in before anyone realized she was gone.

The following Monday she was back in the workshop even though she had finished her chelation treatments. Mason had decided to keep her working there one day a week. She was pretty sure he liked getting to report her progress at the city management meetings. Reggie didn't mind, especially if she could help get the team the credit they deserved.

It was still early when the emergency phone in Mason's office rang. Mason was at a budget meeting or something. Reggie stopped what she was working on and went to answer it since she was the only one in the building. They rarely got a call on the emergency line, so whatever it was had to be important.

"Maintenance, this is Reggie," she said once she picked up the phone.

"Yeah, this is security. I just got an alarm that section eighty-six is offline."

This was perfect. Someone would need to go out and get the wall back online and she was the only one in the office. She knew Sasha's team was working on a section of the wall on the other side of the city. If she was fast, no one would even realize she was out there. She could get outside of the city and send a message to Amber. "I'll take care of it," she said into the phone. She hung up before the person on the other side could respond.

She ran to her locker and grabbed the backpack she had stashed in there. She had been carrying it with her all week. Inside was her old laptop, the Geiger counter with the vial of radioactive material removed, and Charlie's signal-booster. She wanted to be ready in case the opportunity to get a message out presented itself, and now it had been served up to her on a silver platter. She slung the backpack over her shoulders and headed to the storage room to get the rest of the equipment she would need to get the wall back online.

Her nerves frayed exponentially as she drove out to the wall. She kept checking her rearview mirror to make sure she wasn't being followed, which was ridiculous. No one knew what she was going to do. As far as anyone was concerned, she was simply responding to an emergency call, which was part of her job. She had no reason to be nervous.

She pulled up to the section of the wall that was offline. The red grid flickered off and on at random—this wasn't going to be an easy fix. She quickly dressed in the radiation suit, even though she was pretty sure she didn't need it. It did hide her backpack from the cameras, so it wasn't a complete waste of time. She powered down the wall before it could hurt anyone and set up a line of pucks to close the gap in the wall.

She made sure she was outside of the city when she turned the power back on. The pucks formed a temporary wall in front of her. The city was safe for the moment. With one last look at the grid, she turned to the woods surrounding the city and started walking. She needed to make sure she was out of sight before she could send her message.

Reggie stopped once she was out of sight of the wall and pulled out the Geiger counter. She turned it on and watched the needle. It barely moved. "I knew it," she said to herself. There was no radiation outside of the city. She took off the suit. It made it difficult to walk through the woods, and it wasn't like she needed it.

Up ahead she saw an outcropping of rocks. She headed for it. This seemed like a good place to record her message. She needed to be fast. The longer she was out there, the greater the chance that someone would realize she was missing.

She brushed a pile of leaves off one of the rocks so she could use it as a table. She quickly set up the laptop and booster, and held her breath as she waited for it to find a signal. She wasn't sure what she would do if it didn't.

It took a solid minute, but it finally connected. It was weak, but hopefully it was good enough to get her message through.

She opened the program for the computer's camera. She hadn't recorded anything ahead of time on the off-chance that someone would find it, though she had rehearsed what she wanted to say a thousand times in her head. Reggie took a deep breath and hit record.

"Amber, I need your help. Something isn't right in the Sanctuary Cities. Someone is tampering with the city and its residents. I don't know who, but whatever they're doing, it's affecting people's memories. They have no idea what's happening to them. I know how crazy this sounds, but you have to believe me. The boys are starting to forget Charlie. I don't know who I can trust here. People have gotten hurt when they ask about it. I know this is a lot to put on you, but I don't know what else to do."

A twig snapped behind her. Reggie whipped her head around to see if she could see what had made the noise. She hoped to see a squirrel or rabbit moving nearby, but there was nothing. She heard another twig break and the rustling of dead leaves. It sounded much too big to be a harmless woodland creature.

She turned back to the camera. "I think someone's coming. I have to go. Whatever happens to me, I need you to promise you won't let the boys forget Charlie." She ended the recording, quickly attached it to an email and hit send. She knew it would take a few minutes for the message to go through with how weak the signal was. She needed to make sure no one found the computer before then.

She picked up her backpack and started to run. She didn't try to keep quiet. Her goal was to keep whoever was out there from finding the computer. It wasn't long before she heard something behind her. Reggie tried to pick up the pace as the fear in her started to build.

Her breathing was ragged. She hadn't realized how out-of-shape she was. The noises behind her were getting closer. There was no question that something was chasing her. She turned her head to see what was behind her and tripped on a raised tree root. She tried to catch herself, but her hands slipped on the wet mud. Her head smashed into a tree trunk.

Reggie scrambled to her feet, ignoring the throbbing in her head and the trail of blood she could feel running down her cheek. She had caught a glimpse of what was chasing her. It looked like a person, but she couldn't tell who it was. She didn't wait to find out. She started to run again with a limp that wasn't there before.

The red glow of the smart grid was visible through the trees. She was close. She pushed herself to run faster. She needed to make sure she reached the wall with enough time to get through and close the grid behind her—the last thing she wanted to do was let someone into Serenity. The footsteps behind her were louder than before. She wasn't going to make it. She would need to fight. Reggie looked around and found a decent-sized stick. She held it up like a baseball bat and waited.

The woods around her fell silent. Reggie slowly spun in a circle with the stick ready, looking for whoever was chasing her. She didn't hear anything. She doubted she had lost them. They must have been waiting to see what she would do, but the only thing she could think of was to wait for the attack she knew was coming.

A twig snapped to her left. She whipped around to face that direction. She still didn't see anyone. She took a small step back while she studied the trees. A rustle of leaves caught her ear. They were moving towards her slowly, careful to stay out of sight. Reggie stepped backward slowly to keep the space between her and her attacker.

She was so focused on the noises hidden in the trees that she didn't realize there was someone standing behind her until she backed up into them. Reggie screamed as the person slipped a cloth sack over her head. She swung the branch wildly, hoping to connect with something. The person grabbed her free arm to keep her from getting away as they pulled the sack cords at the bottom of the sack tight around her neck.

She finally made contact with the stick and felt her attacker's grip loosen. Reggie pushed them away, scrambling to loosen the bottom of the sack, but she couldn't find the strings in her panic. She needed to get away, to fight back, but she couldn't do anything blind. She felt something hard hit her calf and she tumbled to the ground. She started to crawl, reaching in front of her to make sure she didn't run into anything. She felt something hit her back. The force forced her flat against the ground. Her head bounced off a rock as she fell, building on the headache she already had from her first fall.

"Try not to hurt her too badly," a voice said. Reggie froze. The voice was familiar, but she was having a hard time placing it through the pounding in her skull.

"Then get over here and hold her still. I didn't think she'd fight this much," a second voice said.

She was outnumbered. She tried to get back up on her hands and knees, but the moment she had one knee under her, she was pushed back to the ground. She was trapped. Someone grabbed her arms and pulled them behind her back.

"Do it quickly. We have to get her back inside before anyone realizes," the first voice said again.

She was certain she knew that voice. It sounded like

Isaac, but that didn't make any sense. Her brother would never attack her like this. She opened her mouth to say something, but a stinging sensation in her shoulder kept the words from coming. Her veins were on fire. They had injected her with something. She wanted to scream, but her body was no longer responding to commands.

"Let's go, she won't be out for long."

The last thing Reggie felt before she passed out was two sets of hands lifting her off the ground.

~

Reggie had no idea where she was or how she'd gotten there. Her head was throbbing and the whole right side of her body ached. She tried to open her eyes, but her eyelids were too heavy. She took a few slow breaths as she tried to remember what had happened. She remembered going outside the wall to send a message to Amber. God, she hoped the message went through. Amber would be able to use her connections in the Senate to help. She would get Jace and Miles out of here before they forgot Charlie all together. Reggie focused on that instead of the fear that she would never see her kids again.

"This is incredible," she heard someone say. "Come take a look at this."

She felt a presence next to her move. Her brain felt like it was processing information in slow-motion. Was this because of whatever they had injected her with, or maybe the repeated head injuries she'd suffered while trying to get away?

"What is it?" That was Isaac's voice. She was sure of it now, though she was still having a hard time processing that he was here. Had he found her and saved her, or was he one of her attackers?

"Her brain activity is off the charts. That's why the memory suppressant hasn't worked on her yet. Looking at this—she might even be smarter than you." Reggie knew that voice too, though she couldn't put a name to it yet. Maybe she was safe. She focused on her breathing as she willed her fear to subside.

"But she's a plumber," Isaac said in disbelief.

"A master plumber, actually," Reggie groaned. She took a deep breath and forced her eyes open. "And a master electrician, carpenter, pipefitter," her voice faded as her eyes fluttered shut again. It took every ounce of energy she had to open them again.

"Welcome back, Regina." Theo stepped into her line of sight.

Theo. The one person she had trusted to help her. What was he doing here? Was he behind what had been happening in the city the whole time? No, he couldn't have been. He arrived on the same train she had, and she knew the memory issues predated him. This had to be something else. She had to be in the hospital; it was the only thing that made any sense.

"What's going on?" Reggie tried to sit up. It was only then that she realized she was tied to the table. She couldn't move her arms or legs. Thick straps pressed against her chest and stomach as she fought to pull herself free. Panic overwhelmed her as she pulled fruitlessly at her binds.

"Hey, just relax. I don't want you to hurt yourself any more than you already have." Isaac was by her side now, gently stroking her hair. He was looking at her like she was a scared child.

Reggie jerked her head away from his hand. An action she regretted instantly as the throbbing in her head spiked. "I'll relax once you tell me what the fuck is going on."

"We're trying to figure out why the memory suppressant hasn't worked on you," Theo said simply.

"Wait," Reggie said. "You're part of this? But you were helping me." She felt like a child again, three lessons behind Isaac and trying desperately to catch up.

"It was the best way for us to know if you were a threat to the city or not. I am sorry I deceived you Reggie, I really am, but this is bigger than any one person. The whole of the human race is at risk if the cities fail."

Reggie's head was spinning. She barely had time to comprehend a piece of information before they told her something else that threw everything into chaos again. "What are you talking about?"

"You know what the world is like," Isaac said. "Eventually, humans will destroy themselves. The Sanctuary Cities are a way to ensure the continuation of the human race. That's why we have to do whatever it takes to protect it. To protect you and the boys."

"But your lab was destroyed." She had to understand how everything fit together. She had to make sense of it so she could tell Amber when she got here.

Amber. God, Reggie hoped Amber saw her message.

"You were getting too close to figuring everything out. We had to do something to get you to stop looking into the memory gaps," Isaac said.

"If only you had listened to me and let it go, we wouldn't be in this mess," Theo said. "You could be home with your kids right now." The warmth Reggie was used to hearing in his voice was gone. The coldness that replaced it felt clinical. This was a side of Theo she hadn't seen before. This was Theo the scientist.

"What the hell did you do to my kids?" Reggie started to pull at her binds again. She didn't think Isaac would hurt Jace and Miles, but it was clear he wasn't the person she thought he was.

"I can't believe you think I'd hurt the boys." The pained expression on Isaac's face made her pause. "I love them, Reggie, and I love you."

"Then let me go," she snarled at him.

"I can't do that. Not yet. You'll understand one day. You have to. Everything I'm doing is to keep you and boys safe." It was like Isaac was trying to reassure himself instead of her. It made her stomach churn.

Reggie turned her gaze to Theo. "Why even bother with the whole charade?"

"This was my first chance to study the effects of my memory suppressant firsthand," Theo said matter-of-factly. "It took us a long time to perfect the formula. Some of the early versions did more than suppress the desired memories—they changed the individuals' personalities too much. I'm sure you've noticed some of the side-effects in your parents."

Reggie turned back to Isaac as a new wave of disgust

renewed her anger. "You experimented on Mom and Dad?"

"It seemed only fair, after everything they put us through," Isaac said softly. "I told you they were different now."

"This can't be happening." Her emotions were all over the place. She had no idea if fear, anger, or heartbreak would take hold next. Why had she ever agreed to come here? "No. This is just a bad dream. This isn't real." Tears streamed down her face. She stared at the ceiling tiles, wishing she could hide her pain from them.

"Reggie," Isaac said softly. "I need you to focus, okay?" He gently put his hand on her cheek and guided her gaze back to him. "This is important. I need to know what you were doing outside of the wall."

"I was," Reggie started and stopped. She couldn't tell them that she was trying to get a message out. She hadn't told Theo that part of her plan. He didn't know she had found the signal blocker. She had to come up with an explanation they would believe. If only her mind wasn't so fuzzy. Her gaze fell on her backpack sitting on the floor in the corner. "I wanted to test my theory that the Geiger counters had been tampered with. I needed to know if there was radiation outside of the city."

Isaac sighed and leaned back in his chair. "Alright, we can deal with that. Did you tell anyone besides Theo what you found?" He was all business again. Any guilt he was feeling had been banished. She was just another problem for him to solve.

Reggie shook her head as the tears continued to roll

down her face. "Why are you doing this? It's not right. You can't just take people's memories away from them."

"It's not that simple," Isaac said.

She couldn't see Theo anymore. She focused all her attention on Isaac. "Explain it to me, please. Help me to understand," she pleaded. Even in her current situation, she wanted to believe that Isaac was good. That there was an explanation for his actions, and once he explained it to her, she would understand too. She needed to believe Isaac was the good, caring person she always thought he was.

"I guess it won't matter anyway," he mumbled to himself. "The Sanctuary Cities only work if the people chosen to live here stay inside the wall. Things were great in the beginning. People understood what they were agreeing to when they came here, but after a few months, some people started to realize they weren't cut out for this kind of isolation. They forgot how bad things really were in the real world. They started to romanticize the memories of their lives in the outside world. We knew the city would be at risk if people started to leave. We feared what would happen if people found us and tried to break in. I needed to find a way to keep the people here safe. To make sure the experiment was successful. That was about the time Theo was starting trials of his memory suppressant."

Theo stepped back into her line of sight pushing a metal tray. Reggie couldn't see what was on it, but she didn't think any of it would be good for her. "I had developed it to help patients get over trauma. The formula can be adjusted to target memories based on the feelings associated with them. Grief, for example, or fear, longing, pain, nostalgia. We worked out a formula that would target people's memories from before they came to the city. Memories that evoked strong feelings of longing. Memories that would make people think life outside the Serenity was better than it was."

"We started to introduce small amounts into the water supply. After a few weeks, people didn't want to leave anymore," Isaac said.

Reggie couldn't believe what she was hearing. This wasn't the Isaac she knew from her childhood. "That's because you took away their memories without their consent."

"They gave their consent when they signed the paperwork to move here. It was written right in there that the parameters of the experiment could be changed at any time," Isaac said.

Reggie rolled her eyes. "Does that help you sleep better at night?"

"Besides, the memories aren't gone," Theo said. "They're just harder to access." He picked up an alcohol wipe off the tray and rubbed it against Reggie's arm.

"That doesn't make it any better." Reggie strained her head to try to see what Theo was doing to her.

"It was necessary, and more importantly, it worked. The people here are happy and productive. We've created a society with no crime. Where everyone works together for the betterment of the community."

"Because they don't remember any other way," Reggie said. Out of the corner of her eye she saw Theo filling a syringe. What were they planning on doing to her? Surely Isaac wouldn't let Theo kill her. "You took away their ability to choose, to feel life fully. Longing, pain, grief—that's all part of being human. You're stealing all of that from people."

"We aren't stealing anything," Theo said with a hint of frustration in his voice. "All of your memories are still there, even if you can't access them anymore. You still went through it, you just aren't going to feel it as intensely as before. It won't change who you are," Theo said.

"How do you know? It doesn't seem like either one of you have taken the memory suppressant. You're forcing people to do something you aren't willing to do yourselves." Reggie looked from Isaac to Theo. She had to make them understand.

"We're doing what has to be done to keep the residents safe. I know it might be hard to accept right now, but give it time and you'll see how great things can be here," Isaac said. He looked up and nodded to Theo.

Reggie turned her head to see Theo bringing a syringe to her arm. "What's that?" She was sure they could both hear the fear in her voice.

"Because of your higher-than-average brain activity, we need to jumpstart the memory suppressant. The small amount in the city water supply will take too long to work on you," Theo said.

Reggie started to fight against her bonds again. She couldn't let them inject her with the memory suppressant. "Please, Isaac don't do this to me," she pleaded between sobs. "I can't lose Charlie again. Please."

Isaac gently stroked her hair to try to calm her. "You aren't going to lose him, but this will help you move on." He looked up at Theo. "You're sure this is going to work?"

He nodded. "It will. She'll likely lose the last twenty-four to thirty-six hours completely, but otherwise it should be the same for her as everyone else."

"Good," Isaac said. He turned to look at her again.

Reggie was still pulling at her binds, muttering pleas in between sobs. She couldn't believe Isaac was doing this to her. He was the one person she thought she could trust, no matter what. He was supposed to have her back. He swore things would be better for her here, and now he was the one causing her harm. "Please don't do this. I don't want to forget Charlie. Please, Isaac. I can't."

"It's going to be okay, Reggie. I'm not going to let anything bad happen to you. I promise." He stopped stroking her hair and stood up. "Are you ready?"

"Yes," Theo said as he brought the needle to her arm.

Reggie jerked away. "Theo, please, I thought we were friends. I'll let it go like you said. I'll go along with whatever you want. I won't tell anyone what's going on. Please don't take away my memories."

"Can you hold her still?"

Isaac nodded and grabbed her shoulders. He used just enough pressure to keep her from moving. Reggie continued to plead with them as tears poured out of her eyes. This had to be some kind of nightmare. Any moment she would wake up at home. The needle burned as it entered her arm.

"We're only trying to help you, Reggie. You'll see

when you wake up. Things will be better," Theo said.

Reggie's mind grew foggy as the memory suppressant worked its way through her veins. Her eyes closed and her muscles relaxed. She felt the pressure ease from her shoulders and her binds loosen. Her mind was telling her to make a run for it, but she couldn't get her body to listen.

"We need to get her back out by the wall before we call in the search party," Isaac said, though it sounded like he was talking underwater. She felt him lift her from the bed before the memory suppressant took hold and she lost consciousness completely.

Chapter 32

Reggie knew she was in the hospital before she opened her eyes. She had spent enough time here over the last few weeks to recognize the sounds and smells. What she didn't know was why she was there. She tried to take inventory of her body—everything ached, though the throbbing in her head was by far the worst. She raised her hand to feel for a bump, groaning from the effort it took.

"Mommy," a scared little voice reached her ears. Miles.

Reggie opened her eyes slowly. "Hi, baby." Miles knelt on a chair next to her bed. She could tell from the puffiness around his eyes that he had been crying. She reached up slowly and brushed her fingers across his cheek.

"Mom." She turned her head to see Jace leaning on the wall on the other side of her bed. He rushed forward and grabbed her hand. "You're okay?"

"Yeah, I think so," she said, though she had no idea if it was true or not. She scanned the room slowly. She was in a private room surrounded by machines. The familiar IV was inserted into her arm. Her parents were near the door, whispering with Isaac and Theo. They hadn't realized that she was awake yet. "What happened?"

At the sounds of her voice, Lena spun around and rushed over to the bed. "Thank god you're waking up."

"How long have I been here?" Reggie tried to sit up, but it was a struggle.

"Let me help," Theo said with a huge smile. He pressed a button on the side of the bed to raise her head. He adjusted her pillows for her until she found a relatively comfortable position.

"Thanks." Out of the corner of her eye, she saw Miles trying to climb onto the bed, but her dad was trying to stop him. She reached out her hand to pull him close to her. She didn't know if it was allowed, but she knew Miles needed to be close to her right now, and that was all she cared about. Once she had him tucked under one of her arms, she said, "Can someone please tell me what is going on? Why am I here? What happened?"

Isaac came and sat on the bottom corner of her bed. "We're still trying to piece it all together. Mason confirmed that you were working alone in the maintenance office when an emergency call came in. A section of the grid was failing. You went out to fix it. We pulled the security footage and can see you setting up the temporary barrier. From the video it looks like you might have heard or seen something out in the woods while you were working and went to investigate. You were out of range of the cameras after that."

"Do you have any idea what made you go into the woods?" Oscar said.

Reggie looked at her father and shook her head slightly. "I don't even remember going to work this morning." She brought her free hand to her temple hoping it would ease some of the pain building there.

"It's Wednesday morning," Theo said gently. "You were unconscious for over twenty-four hours."

"I was?"

"We think something in the woods attacked you, though we aren't sure what. You weren't conscious when we found you. Your radiation suit was ripped to shreds," Isaac said.

"I don't remember anything," Reggie said as she tried to process the information.

"That's to be expected. Between the concussion and the trauma of the attack, you might not ever remember exactly what happened," Theo said.

"I have a concussion?"

Lena nodded. "And some pretty bad bruising along your right torso. Thankfully, there are no signs of radiation poisoning. It could have been much worse."

"You're going to be sore for a while, but you should make a full recovery," Theo said. He winked at Miles, who squeezed Reggie tighter, causing her flinch.

"Boys, now that we know your mom is going to be fine, why don't you let grandma and grandpa take you home so you can get some rest?" Isaac said as he extracted Miles from Reggie's arm gently.

Reggie caught his eye and mouthed thank you. She was sure the boys had been here the whole time, waiting for her to wake up. She hated that she had put them through that. After losing their dad, she didn't want them to think she was dying too. A brief flash of her and the boys standing next to a casket entered her mind, but it was gone before she could really remember whose funeral they were at.

"Your dad and I will stay with the boys at your house until you're released," Lena said. "They'll feel more comfortable there."

"Thanks, Mom," Reggie said as she leaned back into the pillows. She felt incredibly tired after only being awake for a few minutes. "Remember, Miles is allergic to strawberries."

"We remember," Oscar said. "Now rest up." He squeezed her hand. Miles and Jace both gave her a quick kiss on her forehead before following Oscar out of the room.

"Are you going to come with us?" Lena asked Isaac.

"No, I think I'm going to stay here for a while. Make sure Reggie has everything she needs."

"Alright. Call us if you need anything." Lena leaned down and kissed Reggie's cheek. "You rest up. We'll be back up to check on you in a little bit."

"Thanks." Reggie was uncomfortable with all the attention she was getting. It didn't help that she couldn't remember anything that had happened. It was like the last few days had been wiped from her mind completely.

She supposed it was possible she had gone out to repair the wall on her own, but why hadn't she told anyone she was going out there? There was a reason they always went out as a team, and while she liked to push the limits from time to time, she didn't disregard safety protocol. She was sure Mason was pissed at her—she knew she would have been, if she was in his shoes. The whole situation made no sense. There had to be something they weren't telling her.

"So, now that the boys are gone, how do you really feel?" Isaac watched her closely as he waited for her response.

"Embarrassed, mainly," Reggie said.

"You have nothing to be embarrassed about," Isaac said. "We all know the area outside of the smart grid can be dangerous. You were trying to keep the city safe. Imagine if what attacked you got into the city because the smart grid was malfunctioning."

Isaac did have a point. There was a reason they had to drop everything to respond to emergencies at the wall. She had done what she needed to do to keep the city safe. To keep her kids safe. "I wish I could remember why I went out into the woods."

"Give it time. Maybe it will come back to you," Isaac said, but he wasn't looking at her. His gaze had shifted to Theo. Reggie had no idea what to make of it.

"What is the last thing you remember?" Theo asked.

Reggie closed her eyes and thought. She tried not to let the gaps in her memory bother her. She had suffered a traumatic head injury; it made sense that her memory might be affected. There was nothing more to it.

Or was there? She had the feeling she had been concerned about memory loss before she was attacked, but she couldn't remember why. "Doing homework with the boys. It must have been Sunday evening."

"That's good, Reggie," Theo said with a small smile. "You could have lost so much more. We're only starting to understand how memory works. Your mind is probably trying to protect you from having to relive the attack. I know it can feel scary to be missing chunks of time, but look at it as a gift instead of something being wrong with you."

Reggie laughed. "Are you being serious right now?"

"A little over-the-top?"

"More than a little," Isaac said with a laugh.

She might not know what happened to her, but this right here felt right. She knew nothing truly bad could happen to her while Isaac was there. He had been looking out for her for as long as she could remember. Reggie knew she had been nervous to move the boys here, but Isaac was right. They would have a good life in Serenity.

~

Amber let out a sigh the moment she walked through the door of her D.C. condo. It had been an extremely long and tedious day. She had been pushing a bill to get the public water treatment systems back up and running for the last three months and had made very little headway. The bottled water lobbyists were blocking everything she tried. She had spent all day in committee meetings discussing the financial impact of her bill, and the conversation had not gone in her favor. She needed a glass of wine and a quiet evening at home to relax. And she needed to talk to Reggie.

It had been weeks since Amber had heard from her last, and she was starting to worry. She knew the smart grid that protected the Sanctuary Cities made communication between the residents and the outside world tough, but this was getting ridiculous. They had never gone this long without talking. If she didn't hear from Reggie soon, she might have to pull some strings to get a call through. She knew Bailey had a way to communicate with the Cities, though it might have been easier to apply for residency than to convince him to help her.

Amber's girlfriend, Trina, was sitting at the island in the kitchen with a computer in front of her. Amber gave her a quick kiss on the cheek. "Is that my computer?"

"Yeah, I hope you don't mind that I borrowed it. Mine finally crapped out on me and I had meetings with clients I couldn't miss this afternoon."

"Just don't let me find it covered in glitter." Trina was one of the best party-planners on the east coast, and occasionally Amber would find traces of those parties on her floors, in their furniture, and one time in her bathtub as the remnants of an ice sculpture with gemstones embedded in it safely melted away.

Trina batted her away playfully. "Don't worry. My meetings didn't involve samples."

"That's something, at least." Amber went over to the fridge and grabbed a bottle of water. She really wanted something stronger, but she hadn't eaten since breakfast, and figured she should probably make dinner first.

"I saw a message from Reggie come through while I was on my last call, though," Trina said.

"Really?" Amber set down her water and came over to the computer. "What did she want?"

"I didn't look at it," Trina said with a small laugh. "I don't tend to go through your emails." Trina got up and offered Amber her seat in front of the laptop.

Amber was nervous as she opened up her emails. This wasn't their normal form of communication. She saw the message from Reggie at the top of her inbox. The subject line was blank and there was nothing written in the body of the email, but there was a video file attached. She hesitated. This looked a lot more like some kind of phishing email than an actual message from Reggie. Her mouse hovered over the attachment, bringing up a small preview window. That certainly looked like Reggie in the tiny thumbnail that popped up. Amber decided she would risk it.

The video loaded and sure enough there was Reggie's face in the middle of the screen. "Is she in the woods?" Trina asked as she looked over Amber's shoulder.

"It looks that way." Amber knew in her gut that whatever was on this message wasn't going to be good news. She could tell from the lines around Reggie's eyes that she was stressed. Something must have happened, and Amber was afraid to find out what. She took a deep breath and pressed play.

"Amber, I need your help. Something isn't right at

the Sanctuary Cities," Reggie said in the video. Her words were rushed and her eyes kept darting away from the camera as if she was afraid someone was watching her. "Someone is tampering with the city and its residents. Whatever they're doing, it's affecting people's memories. They have no idea what's happening to them. I know how crazy this sounds, but you have to believe me. The boys are starting to forget Charlie." Amber's hand slowly moved to cover her mouth. What Reggie was saying didn't make any sense—they had never gotten any reports of unethical behavior from any of the Sanctuary Cities. But that didn't matter. Amber trusted Reggie, so if she said there was something wrong, then Amber believed her. "I don't know who I can trust here. People have gotten hurt when they've asked about it before. I know this is a lot to put on you, but I don't know what else to do."

On the screen Reggie turned away from the camera. She was looking for something out in the woods behind her. She must have heard something. The hairs on Amber's arms stood on end as she watched. "I think someone's coming. I have to go. Whatever happens to me I need you to promise you won't let the boys forget Charlie."

The video ended, but Amber didn't move. She sat there staring at the black screen in front of her while she processed Reggie's message. It didn't make sense, but one thing that was completely clear: Reggie was in trouble.

"Do you think this is real?" Trina asked softly. Amber had almost forgotten she was there.

"I do," she said with a nod, her eyes still fixed on the black screen.

"What are you going to do?"

Amber turned in her seat to look at Trina. "I'm going to find a way to get into Serenity City."

Also by Holly Ash

The Journey Missions Series
Crystal and Flint
Family Binds
Thicker Than Blood
Shattered Refuge
Divided They Fall

The Cleansing Rain Duology
Cleansing Rain
Crashing Tide

The Sanctuary City Trilogy
Sacrificing Serenity
Escaping Serenity - 2026

www.ingramcontent.com/pod-product-compliance
Lightning Source LLC
Chambersburg PA
CBHW030544260626
47157CB00006B/2178